THE HEARTLESS AND THE WICKED

BOOK THREE

THE DAUGHTER OF THE SCARRED ELF

MAHAM FATEMI

Paperback ISBN: 978-1-961171-04-6

Cover Design: Covers by Combs

Developmental & Line Editor: Dana Boyer

Copy Editor: Lawrence Editing

https://mahamfatemi.com

http://instagram.com/authormahamfatemi/

For my family. Thank you for always believing in me.

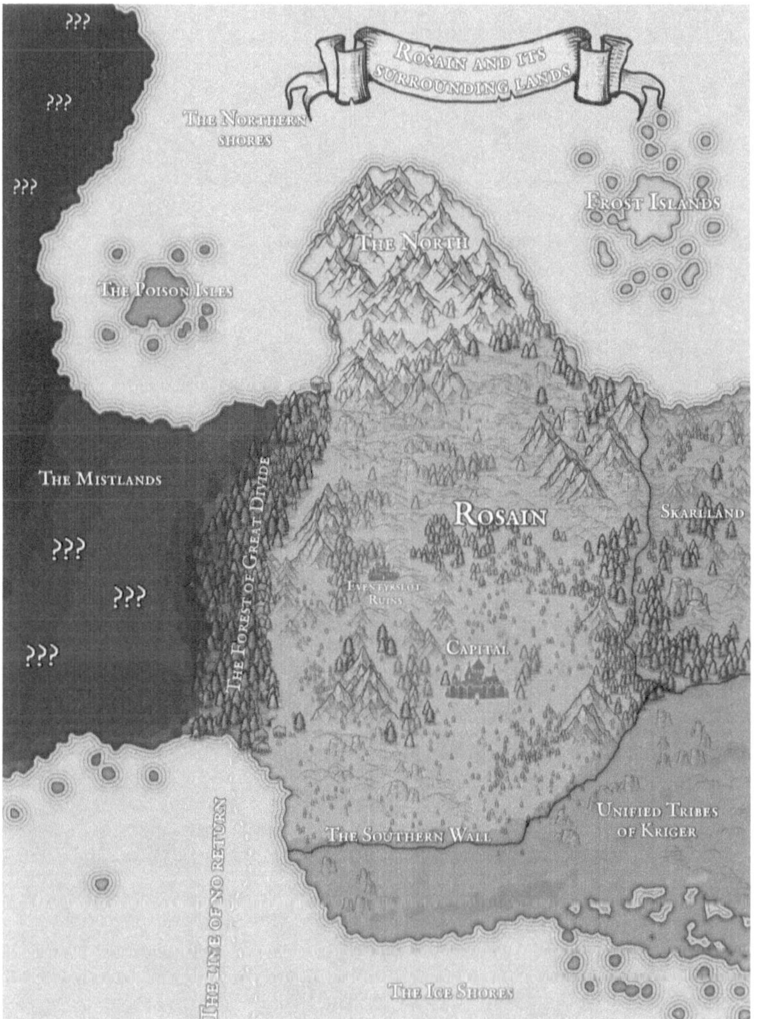

ROSAIN AND ITS SURROUNDING LANDS
???
???
???
THE NORTHERN SHORES
FROST ISLANDS
THE NORTH
THE POISON ISLES
THE MISTLANDS
???
???
???
THE FOREST OF GREAT DIVIDE
ROSAIN
SKARLLAND
EVENTYRSLOT RUINS
CAPITAL
THE LINE OF NO RETURN
THE SOUTHERN WALL
UNIFIED TRIBES OF KRIGER
THE ICE SHORES

NEWSLETTER

Join Maham Fatemi's newsletter to find out about new releases, sales, bonus content, and more! You can also find signed copies of her books on her website.
https://mahamfatemi.com

1

———

IF THERE WAS ONE THING KOLFINNA WAS SURE ABOUT as she stood outside the throne room, it was that she had made a deal with a demon. She hated that the Royal Guards, Hilda, and every other person who wanted her imprisoned or dead—which was probably the majority of the country—had driven her into a corner. And although she didn't particularly *like* Sijur Bernsten— the man she had traded *fifteen years* of her life in exchange for his help—she sure as hell hoped he kept his end of the bargain.

But was it even worth it?

Kolfinna shot down that small, niggling thought in the back of her mind. She didn't have the luxury to think about anything other than her potential doom. She couldn't think about what it meant to be Sijur's soldier, or what it meant to be rune-marked with their deal stamped in gold on her wrist.

Just thinking about it made Kolfinna absentmindedly touch her wrist where Joran, the fae male she had met yesterday, had placed the rune. She had been awed to find the glowing rune still there when she awoke that morning, albeit slightly dulled from the night before and softly shimmering.

One of the guards to her left shifted on his feet. She recognized him. Just two weeks ago they had fought Ragnarök in the

1

throne room. And now he wouldn't even meet her eyes. He probably thought she was guilty. That, or maybe he had witnessed her attacking the Royal Guards promptly after defeating the majority of the attackers that day. Or maybe he thought she was just another heartless fae ready to kill whenever she felt like it. It was hard to tell.

Save for Kolfinna and the two guards, the hallway was empty. She couldn't even hear what was going on beyond the gilded doors. Were the nobles and the king discussing how to end her?

She slipped her hand in the pocket of her pants and grazed the crumpled paper she had read, reread, folded, and unfolded a hundred times since she had gotten it that morning. Without thinking better, she snatched the paper from her pocket and stared at the elegant, hurried strokes.

> *I'm sorry I can't be there for your trial today, but I know you will be fine. Stay strong.*
>
> *Blár Vilulf*

HE HAD SENT ANOTHER NOTE AT THE BEGINNING OF her house arrest, which had simply stated that he couldn't visit her but that he would try to help. Neither note reassured her because how was it reassuring that her most influential and powerful ally wasn't going to be by her side while she faced the king, the hunters, Hilda, and everyone else who wanted to condemn her as a criminal?

The painful sting of disappointment and betrayal burned her chest. She had thought that she and Blár had shared precious moments together. Like when they ran across that frozen lake a few weeks ago, and they had laughed and laughed on the icy surface, their breaths misting out in front of them. Or when they danced at the ball, their bodies flush together, their gazes trapped on each other. Or even after the battle two weeks ago at the palace, where he had held her weakened body. When he had wiped her tears. When she had shown that vulnerable side to him, and he had shown such tender care.

But apparently, none of that mattered because he couldn't even be bothered to be here for her today, when she truly needed him. When she truly needed *allies*.

It hurt that she wasn't important enough for him to stand by her side when she needed him the most.

Kolfinna's fingers inadvertently traced the smooth lines of his name. Whenever she ran her fingers over the dried ink, her buzzing nerves seemed to calm a tad. It was pathetic how despite the cutting pain in her heart, he had that effect on her.

Kolfinna folded the paper and tucked it back in her pocket. She could think about the betrayal later. She could ask him about his feelings about her—if she was the only one who felt this connection and attraction. She could face him and ask him why he hadn't been here with her, but she first needed to make it out of this trial.

She really, *really* needed Sijur to keep his end of the bargain.

Right as she was thinking that, the gold-embossed door to the throne room creaked open and a blond guard waved her forward. "They're ready for you," the woman said with a frown at Kolfinna's Royal Guards uniform, with its scarlet cape, silver-accented white pants, and silver-buttoned shirt.

Kolfinna could practically hear the woman say, "*You won't be wearing that uniform for much longer.*"

She rubbed her clammy hands over her thighs. *It will be fine*, she told herself. Sijur would help her like he promised, and then she'd be free.

As she made her way through the doors, every step shot her heart rate up until she was almost dizzy. Light bathed the room, making the throne seem even more golden and regal. King Leiknir sat upon it, drumming his jeweled hand against the armrest, his dark gaze set on her. In front of him was a small box-shaped stand with wooden railings, and in front of that was a court-styled seating arrangement with at least two dozen people.

The dents she had remembered were on the crumbled walls had been hastily covered with white sheets. The broken pillars were partially repaired, but there were clear cracks and missing chunks here and there. The most damaged tiles had been replaced, but the new tiles didn't match the older remaining ones that had been charred by fire and lightning. Even though the tiles had likely been scrubbed for hours, they weren't restored to the old ones' original luster. And, as much as the king liked to pretend the battle two weeks ago hadn't ruined the room, the evidence was clear to see.

He probably didn't want to show that Ragnarök had damaged the royal palace to the extent it had.

Kolfinna instantly found Hilda Helgadottir within the crowd of nobles sitting in their cushioned, velvet seats. Her graying blond hair was pulled back into a tight bun, further accentuating her harsh features, and those hawkish eyes were pinned on Kolfinna as if they had found their prey.

It was suddenly hard to breathe. She wasn't in the throne room anymore—she was in a windowless cabin with an array of sharp and serrated weapons lying on a table in front of her. And Hilda was there, running her wrinkled fingers over the leather ends of a whip.

Kolfinna blinked the memory away and swallowed down the nausea clawing up her throat. She forced herself to ignore the sudden rush of emotions flooding her—the anxiety, the fear, the need to flee.

Breathe.

In and out.

In and out.

Somehow, she didn't crumble under the weight of those oppressive eyes or those harsh memories.

One leg forward, then the other, repeat.

So long as she could ignore what had happened those long days in that cabin with that monstrous woman, she would be fine.

Another step. Then another.

Kolfinna's gaze skirted over the crowd, searching for familiar, kind faces, but the only other familiar face she found was Fenris's. He sat in the front row, his red hair brushed neatly and his white and gold uniform standing out regally. She scanned the crowd again. Her heart sank as she realized Blár really wasn't there—and she chided herself for that, for *hoping*. And then it sank even further when she realized Sijur wasn't there either.

She was on her own.

Kolfinna bent in a rigid bow in front of the throne. "Greetings, Your Highness."

King Leiknir only peered down at her with dark, disapproving eyes.

One of the Royal Guards beside him motioned her toward the raised, boxed dais, and she complied. Her fingers rested over the smooth wooden railing to keep herself upright, to keep herself rooted in the room, and to not tarry on any memories. Particularly memories linked with the woman sitting two rows away from her.

"Kolfinna the fae," King Leiknir drawled after a moment of stilled silence. Kolfinna felt everyone watching her, impatiently waiting to rip her to shreds and prod at what remained. "We are here to discuss your actions two weeks ago during the attack on the palace."

Kolfinna clasped her sweaty hands together in front of her to keep them from shaking. She didn't know where to look, so she stared down at the gold-veined marble floors.

"Frode Nyborg." King Leiknir waved forward the Lieutenant Captain of the first unit of the Royal Guards, who were in charge of protecting the royal palace. The aging guard came forward and dropped to one knee.

"Your Highness."

"Nyborg, what is your report on this matter? You've had two weeks to investigate and interview all the parties involved." The king drummed his fingers on the armrest again, his rings catching the light.

The last time Kolfinna had spoken to Nyborg, he had told her that she would likely be fine, and that he too felt a strange, ominous presence from the black sword that had controlled her. Kolfinna clung to the tiny sliver of hope that he would side with her.

Nyborg straightened and Kolfinna held her breath as the older man turned to face the crowd. He pointedly didn't look at her and instead addressed everyone else. "Kolfinna the fae made statements that she was being 'possessed' by the royal sword and that her actions were not her own. She attacked several Royal Guards with the intent to kill them. I suspect she might have had motives to steal the sword."

Murmurs filled the room and Kolfinna's mouth almost dropped to the floor. She could feel the heat crawling up her neck as more people stared and pointed fingers.

This can't be happening.

"That's not true—" Kolfinna started, her voice barely above a whisper.

"Silence." The king's voice boomed across the throne room and she flinched. He narrowed his eyes at her. "Do not interrupt, *fae.*"

He spat the word like it was poison and she knew she had no allies here.

Her face tingled with humiliation and she tightly gripped the banister of the trial box until her knuckles turned white with exertion. Almost as white as the immaculate uniform Nyborg wore and the immaculate white gloves all Royal Guards wore. The uniform that was supposed to symbolize the purity of *justice.*

"Kolfinna the fae attacked several of my men." Nyborg motioned to the crowd and three guards stood up on cue and marched to the front of the throne. They bowed to the king while

Nyborg spoke. "Audun Jacobsen, Garth Austr, and Haskell Westergaard were the primary victims."

Kolfinna recognized the three men. She remembered begging them to run away and not fight her, for fear that she would cut them down like she had killed the Ragnarök members. She had cried to them while they had fought her. They had only stopped attacking her because of Blár.

The blond of the trio spoke first. "Two weeks ago, we were fighting alongside her against the other fae, but then she suddenly turned on us. She tried to kill us."

Another murmur ran through the room.

"I told you they were heartless," someone whispered. "They're monsters. All of them."

Nyborg nodded at his guard and raised his voice. "She only stopped because she knew she couldn't fight Blár Vilulf and win. I believe her goal was to steal the royal sword."

Lies. Lies. Lies.

She wanted to open her mouth to shout at him. She wanted to tell everyone the truth, but the way everyone was gobbling up his words left her deflated and scrambling to think properly. She should've expected him and the Royal Guards to turn on her. She should've—

"I have a question." Fenris raised his white-silk, gloved hand in the air, his velvety voice halting the hushed whispers in the room. His steely eyes fell on Nyborg, and the older man straightened. "Nyborg, your guard, Auden Jacobsen, just mentioned that Kolfinna was fighting alongside the guards against Ragnarök and that she then turned on the guards. If it's true that she was planning on stealing the sword, why bother to fight Ragnarök in the first place and defeat the majority of its members before turning on her own team? Wouldn't it have made sense for her to *pretend* to be on the Royal Guards' side, let both sides whittle their numbers down, and once the battle was over, for her to then make an excuse and flee? I hardly see how facing the other guards would benefit her. Especially since she was clearly outnumbered." He waved to the three guards beside Nyborg with a dismissive hand. "You three have at least ten years of experience as a Royal Guard. Are you telling me that you three couldn't defeat Kolfinna if she truly was against you all? She's barely been in the Royal Guards for five months. She would've known how experienced you three are."

Silence filled the room while the guards in front of the room slowly reddened. Kolfinna's chest stopped painfully squeezing and she could breathe for a few seconds. Maybe she wasn't alone after all.

"W-Well," the blond guard, Audun, stammered, "she's a strong fae and it doesn't change that she fought against us—"

"It almost appears like Ragnarök made this entire commotion in order to steal the royal sword," Fenris said, "and they fought Kolfinna in order to take it from her. That sword is known to have belonged to the last fae queen and her empire, in which King Harald took it as a war trophy when he won against the fae. It isn't too far-fetched to believe that they wanted to steal it back. And who are we to know the full properties of a fae artifact?"

King Leiknir frowned while Nyborg pursed his lips together. "Captain Asulf," the king said, "do you believe Kolfinna is speaking the truth that she was *possessed* by the royal sword?"

"I do." He turned his silver gaze to her and she wanted to cry right then and there—he was on her side. "She has been under my watch for five months. I would've known if she had shown a single sign of disloyalty. She has been nothing but obedient, loyal, and faithful to this country. She has put her life on the line several times—"

"She still tried to attack my men, Captain," Nyborg said. "She—"

"*My* men." Fenris's voice cracked like a whip and his eyes flashed. "Do not forget that all Royal Guards are under me, Frode."

Nyborg flinched and lowered his gaze.

"She has put her life on the line several times," Fenris

repeated, his smooth voice growing louder for everyone to hear. "She is an asset to the Royal Guards and I don't think we should dismiss her claim about the royal sword."

Hilda raised her aged hand before Kolfinna could breathe a sigh of relief. "Captain Asulf, I believe you're being biased and overlooking the fact that she *did* attack the men and that she was wielding a sword that is meant only for the royal family. That in itself is treason."

"That sword is evil," Kolfinna said, forcing herself to stare at anyone but Hilda. She tried to look for someone in the crowd who might believe her, but they all looked at her as though she were a monster. "Ragnarök—"

"Silence." The king's voice boomed across the cratered, scorched walls of the expansive room, which felt like it was shrinking the longer the trial went on.

Kolfinna swallowed down the bile rising up her throat. Her frustration grew and the anxiety gnawing at her core intensified. How was she going to tell her side of the story if no one would let her speak?

King Leiknir motioned to Nyborg. "Continue."

Nyborg glanced between the king's encouraging nod and Fenris's steel-cut gaze. He cleared his throat. "Err, I also spoke to a few guards from the city and they said they spotted Kolfinna running to the royal palace rather than remaining on the streets of the city to help with the attacks and the evacuations. This tells us that she wanted to fight in the palace rather than fulfill her guard duties. I can only imagine it's because she wanted to steal the sword."

Kolfinna cringed. That was right after Yrsa had fought her. She had suspected Yrsa was a member of Ragnarök and had rushed to the palace to confirm that the dreki ambush was just a distraction for something more sinister. She had never thought it would come back and bite her like this.

The gossipy murmurs began again, and the crowd's suspicion seemed to refuel Nyborg because he stood straighter. "Kolfinna's commanding officer, Edwin Karlsson, also confirmed that she doesn't work hard and that she always seems to have some sort of ulterior motive." He waved to the crowd and a white-blond man stood up. Edwin had been sitting beside his aunt, Hilda, but Kolfinna hadn't even noticed him until now.

"Furthermore," Nyborg continued while Edwin sat back down. "Kolfinna had injured a guard, unprompted, two months ago. There were several eyewitnesses who confirmed so."

At that, Farthin stood. The man who had bullied her, mocked her, and beat her senseless the entire time she was a Royal Guard, glared at her with such ire that she would've flinched if she didn't hate him so much. That hatred made her stand taller, and she wished she could go back to when she had attacked him all those weeks ago. Where she had left him buried in a hole full of stones.

Kolfinna ripped her gaze away from him and Edwin. They were horrible people, and the way Nyborg spoke of her painted her out to be a lazy, deranged bully.

The king eased back in his throne and tapped the gilt armrest of his throne. "I see, I see," he murmured, looking pleased with himself. "It's becoming clear what kind of person Kolfinna is."

The rest of the crowd seemed to be in agreement as they nodded, glared, and murmured amongst each other.

"Then—" King Leiknir began.

The grand, gilded double doors of the throne room swung open and rattled against the walls in that exact moment. The whole room shifted toward the intruder. The sound of clothes rustling as people turned, stifled gasps, and the clacking of Sijur's heeled boots slapping the marbled floors pervaded the buzzing air. Kolfinna's breath, which had felt like it was stuck in her chest for the longest time, released raggedly at the sight.

Sijur was all smiles, despite being here at the last moment. His light gray, uncreased military uniform was out of place in the sea of luxurious dresses, shiny jewels, and Royal Guard uniforms.

"Apologies for being late!" Sijur announced with a wave to the crowd. When he was three feet away from the throne, he bowed animatedly to the king. Even to Kolfinna it seemed exaggerated, almost sarcastic. When he raised his head, his teeth gleamed in a grin. "Greetings, Your Highness."

"Sijur Bernsten." The monarch's eyes narrowed. The ends of his thin lips twitched into a scowl. "What are you doing here?"

"I have a request to halt this trial." He turned his head to Kolfinna and winked.

Kolfinna blinked in response, while someone audibly gasped. The king went unnaturally still while he peered down at Sijur with mildly veiled animosity.

She vaguely remembered that the Royal Guards and the king didn't get along with the military and the commander-in-chief. And seeing as how Sijur was the son of the commander, she could only imagine what rivalry brewed between the monarch faction and the military.

"On whose authority—" King Leiknir began.

"I'm glad you asked, Your Highness." Sijur unfurled a piece of paper from his pocket and held it up, as if he had been waiting for this moment. "On the authority of the commander-in-chief of the country, Commander Steffen Bernsten."

King Leiknir's hands clenched over the gold armrest of his throne until his fingers were bloodlessly white. "Excuse me?"

"Kolfinna is not within your jurisdiction to command, Your Highness." Sijur waved a hand to Kolfinna. "Did you not wonder why she wasn't wearing her uniform the day of the attack? Or why she was absent the week prior?"

Kolfinna flinched again, remembering that time with Hilda in the cabin. After that, she had been at Fenris's house to recuperate. Kolfinna wasn't sure what Sijur was getting at, but it was true that she hadn't been wearing her Royal Guard uniform the day of the attack and that she was absent the week before.

"She is with the military. She joined right around the time of the *Måneskin* ball." He pulled out another paper. It crinkled as he unfolded it. "She requested a transfer to the military under my branch, and *here*"—he pointed to something on the paper and

glanced at Fenris, who was watching the whole affair curiously—
"we have Captain Asulf's approval of the request, the commander-in-chief's signature to approve her instatement into the military, and my signature of approval for her to join my unit." He
stepped toward the throne and handed the papers to the king,
who took them with trembling hands. Sijur stepped back with a
sweeping bow. "Therefore, the Royal Guards are unable to question my soldier and her actions are to be assessed by the military. I
ask that you let my soldier go."

The king's lips pursed together and his cheeks reddened as he
stared at the papers. He flipped them over and scanned over the
scrawled contents. "Captain Asulf." The king held up one of the
papers. The rage in his tone was barely controlled. "Is this your
signature?"

Kolfinna had seen the look of confusion that had momentarily flashed over Fenris's face when Sijur had mentioned him,
but now he wore an expression of clear indifference, as if his
forged signature wasn't being waved in his face. "Yes, it is.
Kolfinna requested a transfer and I approved it, just like how the
Lieutenant General said."

"And you didn't think to mention it?" King Leiknir
ground out.

Fenris lifted a shoulder. "I apologize, Your Highness. I simply
...*forgot.*"

Nyborg gestured to Kolfinna's Royal Guard clothes. "Then
why is she in uniform? If she's now a soldier, then why dress like a
Royal Guard?"

"I wanted to wear it one last time," Kolfinna said, trying to
fight the smile stretching up on her lips. This was an unexpected
turn of events, even though Sijur and her had a deal. But still, she
hadn't thought it would turn out like this. Seeing everyone's
stunned faces was *almost* worth the stress and anxiety that had
built up to this moment.

Sijur smiled and smoothed down the front of his gray
uniform. "Since this trial isn't under the jurisdiction of the royal

family and the Royal Guards, I will be taking my soldier back to our base, where we will carry out our own investigation. If you have any questions, please feel free to send them to my father, the commander-in-chief."

No one moved and it seemed like no one breathed either. The king quaked in obvious rage, his face purpling. Sijur held his hand out to Kolfinna, a sneaky smile on his lips. "Come on, Kolfinna, let's go."

Kolfinna hesitantly stepped off the dais, her gaze flitting to Nyborg and the other guards, but when they made no move to restrain her, she closed the distance to Sijur. It wasn't until they began walking out of the throne room that movement and chatter erupted.

But it didn't matter to her anymore what they said—she was done with the Royal Guards and this blasted royal palace.

2

THIS WOULD PROBABLY BE THE LAST TIME SHE WOULD be in Fenris's office, Kolfinna thought as she shifted on her feet. She stifled a yawn with her hand—now gloveless.

Kolfinna barely slept that night. It was the last night she would be in her home, the last night she would be living in the capital, and the last night of her being a Royal Guard. Actually, the last statement was false. According to Sijur, she had left the Royal Guards three weeks ago. Which was now her truth. A truth that was hard to swallow because despite everything the Royal Guards had done to her—mocking her, bullying her, beating her —she had found friends and a place to be, even if that place was uncomfortable. She had been working toward a dream of living peacefully with everyone. She had been looking forward to spending more time with Eyfura and Nollar. She had wanted to make a place here for herself, and now it seemed like the five months of work she'd put into this position were in vain.

In the end, it didn't really matter.

"It's a shame."

She had been thinking it, but hearing the words out loud almost made her feel like Fenris was inside her head. But he was still sitting behind his desk, his gloved hands folded over a stack of yellowed parchment paper, and his gaze on the gold, lion-carved Royal Guard badge she had placed in front of him.

Kolfinna felt strange to be in his office in regular clothing—a thick wool dress with pockets and a particular heavy fur-lined cloak over her shoulders. Blár's scent barely lingered in its fibers, but it comforted her nonetheless and, she told herself, it was the only cloak she had that wasn't the Royal Guards' cloak—which she had been forced to give up. She would never wear the white gloves, the white pants with silver lines along the hems, the white buttoned shirt with silver buttons, the scarlet cape, or the scarlet cloak. The only thing she was allowed to keep were her steel-toed, black boots.

Fenris sighed and canted his head toward the window of his office, at the sprawling, bustling town down below. "A shame," he said once more, gaze flicking back to her. "That these people in the capital refuse to see your worth and your loyalty."

Her throat closed up and she stared down at her glossy boots, at the thick, corded rug, and the polished wooden floor beside it.

A shame indeed. All her hopes had been crushed. All those months of pining after a life in the capital—wasted.

"Captain Asulf—" Kolfinna began.

"Fenris." He leaned back in his gilded, velvety cushioned seat. "Now that you're not a guard under me, you can call me Fenris."

The casualness felt unfamiliar and awkward. "Fenris," she said, her voice sounding raspy from trying to keep the tears at bay. "Thank you for ... for trying."

Trying to protect her. Trying to stand up for her. Trying ... But ultimately failing.

He must've been thinking the same thing because there was a sharp movement on his stoic, handsome face. "No need to thank me."

"Also, thank you for, um, improvising yesterday." She rubbed the nape of her neck as she remembered Sijur waving Fenris's forged signature in the throne room. "If you had refuted his letter, everything would've been foiled."

He waved his hand dismissively. "It was nothing. Though, it *was* amusing to see the king flustered." The corner of his mouth rose, and then he added, "You didn't hear that from me."

Kolfinna laughed softly, and the room became silent once more. She stared down at her boots, trying to catch her reflection in the polish. "I actually also wanted to ask about ... Yrsa. Have you found her?"

She had told Fenris everything about Yrsa during her house arrest, but apparently, she'd been missing since the day of the attack on the palace. Maybe she had realized that once Kolfinna defeated her, her cover was up.

Displeasure crossed Fenris's face before smoothing out to indifference. "We still haven't found her, but rest assured that we will."

"I highly suspect she's a member of Ragnarök."

"I know. I believe you."

He was probably one of the few people left who did.

He eyed Blár's cloak draped effortlessly over her shoulders. "I'm surprised Blár Vilulf didn't show up yesterday at your trial. He seemed very distraught when you were missing, so I assumed ..."

That they were friends? Lovers?

Kolfinna wasn't even sure.

"I suppose he's busy." She inadvertently touched the wolf-pelt fur along the neckline, where Blár's scent of vanilla and spice barely lingered. "Being a black rank and all."

"Hm." Fenris tapped a finger over the crinkling papers on his desk. "You're leaving tonight, right? Have you packed your things?"

"Yes, some of them ..." She had only been able to pack her clothes and a few random things. She had years of experience with picking her life up, packing it into a small bag, and running to the next city, so it shouldn't have stung so much to repeat the process, but it did. She had thought she had finally found a place to settle down for good. She had bought things in her home that were there to stay—a few houseplants, a rug, furniture. But now she was leaving them behind to Nollar, who needed new furniture for his new apartment.

"I was surprised when Sijur Bernsten came to your rescue yesterday." It was more of a question than a statement, by the way he was staring at her with conflict brewing in his silvery gaze.

Kolfinna subconsciously rubbed the glittering gold rune-mark on her wrist, a reminder of their deal.

"Be careful about him." Fenris watched her unflinchingly. "Do not trust that man."

It was a bit too late for that.

The lively view outside Fenris's window drew Kolfinna's attention. She would be leaving all of this behind. The city, the Royal Guard life, everything. She had built nothing these past five months.

"I heard your wife gave birth a few days ago," she said to distract herself from the pang of sadness in her heart and the stinging of her eyes. "Congratulations."

Fenris's hard features softened. "Yes, we have another son now."

"That makes it two girls and two boys," she said with a soft smile. "You'll have your hands full."

He chuckled. "I've faced worse."

They remained in silence for a few more awkward moments. This would be the last time she'd be in his office, she realized. No more missions, no more meetings. Nothing.

Kolfinna gestured to the door. "I'll, um, head out then. Goodbye, Fenris."

"Goodbye, Kolfinna." Fenris rose from his seat. "It was a pleasure working alongside you. If you ever need anything, please feel free to contact me. I do sincerely hope that your position in the military will give you something positive, something the Royal Guards couldn't. Good luck."

Her throat closed up again as she nodded. "Thank you."

SAYING GOODBYE WAS THE HARDEST PART.

That hadn't been the case years ago, when Kolfinna and Katla had been constantly on the move, finding new cities, new villages, new places where no one would think too hard about them. Even a year ago, Kolfinna had been used to leaving old places for new ones. But leaving this time was different.

She didn't want to leave the capital, and she didn't want to say goodbye.

So even as she was sitting in her home for the last time with Eyfura, Nollar, and Magni, she couldn't bring herself to say the words.

"I can't believe—" Eyfura bit her trembling bottom lip. Her cheeks and nose were ruddy from crying so much, and every few seconds, her face crumpled together.

"I'll be fine," Kolfinna told her for the umpteenth time. She reached over and squeezed her hand tightly—reassuringly. "Fae are very adaptable, so I'll be okay."

"I know you'll be fine. You can handle yourself, but ..." Eyfura sniffled and turned to her younger brother, whose eyes were similarly red. "But we'll miss you."

Nollar nodded from his spot across from her and fiddled with the edge of the couch seat. His blond hair obscured half of his face while he looked down at his knees. "The military will treat you better, I hope. And if they don't ..." He raised his head to stare at her levelly. "You have to kick their asses."

Magni's eyebrow arched and Kolfinna laughed without meaning to.

"That's the plan," she said. Truthfully, that was the plan. She didn't intend to let anyone treat her like garbage. Not again. Not after how the Royal Guards treated her, and what good holding her tongue had done for her? "I'm just going to do my job and that's it. I won't give anyone time to bother me, and if they do"—she lifted her shoulders and gave him a ghost of a smile—"then I'll kick their asses."

Nollar finally grinned—the first real grin since stepping foot into her home that day. Eyfura chuckled, but that chuckle soon became an ugly sob again. Magni watched the entire affair with mild curiosity. He, very clearly, was not comfortable in her home, which she had expected. Although they had been in life-and-death situations several times—during the Eventyrslot ruins and the West Border mission—they weren't exactly buddy-buddy, and he appeared even more uncomfortable at all the crying. When he had arrived at her doorstep with the two siblings in tow, Kolfinna had been more than surprised to see him. She had never thought he would warm up to her in any way. But then again, he was probably only here for Eyfura.

Magni reached into the breast pocket of his white uniform, pulled out a crisp linen handkerchief, and held it out to Eyfura. "The military is definitely different than the Royal Guards," he said while Eyfura blotted her face with the handkerchief. "I believe they're more *tolerant*."

"Of fae?" Kolfinna snorted. She had dealt with soldiers back in the Eventyrslot ruins, and they hadn't been any different than the Royal Guards. "I doubt it."

"Many of the Royal Guards are still set in their old ways." He shrugged. "You have to keep in mind that the Royal Guards are very exclusive with whom they accept. The majority of the guards look down on those who aren't from certain affluent families. So it only makes sense that they would doubly look down upon a fae, whom most people think are beneath humans."

Eyfura's eyebrows pulled together. "The military is full of rough people. Do you really think they'll treat her any better?"

"It's *possible*." Magni raked a hand through his dark brown hair. "It really depends on the unit she's going to." His emerald-colored eyes flicked back to Kolfinna, and she could've sworn there was a hint of compassion in that flinty gaze. "Sijur Bernsten's unit isn't known to be rowdy, so I think you'll be fine."

"And if not"—Nollar patted his bicep and pointed to her—"you know what to do."

Kolfinna laughed again, but her smile faded as she realized that after leaving the capital today, she would be stuck on the western border for fifteen years with Sijur. It was possible she wouldn't see them again for many years to come. The very thought made the back of her eyes burn with unshed tears.

"This isn't goodbye," Magni said slowly, watching her carefully.

But it was.

"Yeah, we'll be able to visit." Nollar laced his hands together. "We'll maybe even be able to go on joint missions together. Wouldn't that be fun?"

"Yes! We can ask Captain Asulf to try to assign us to those types of missions!" Eyfura beamed and tightened her hold on Kolfinna's fingers. "We'll have so much fun."

Kolfinna could only nod. "This isn't goodbye."

"It isn't!" Eyfura's smile was so bright and hopeful that Kolfinna didn't have the heart to tell her otherwise.

3

THE RIDE TO THE MILITARY BASE WITH SIJUR AND HIS fae soldier, Joran, took a little over a week and by the time Kolfinna arrived at the tall, barricaded walls enclosing the fortress Løveslot, she didn't have room to be anxious—her exhaustion overrode everything. She wanted to collapse on a real bed, not a bedroll in the middle of the forest—which she normally would've loved, but due to the chill of winter, she wasn't a fan of. Her only consolation was that they were at the tail end of winter, so it wasn't *that* cold during their travel.

Along with sleep, she wanted to run to a private room and scratch her back because, for whatever reason, the past few days had rendered her back absolutely itchy. As if something had bitten her a million times over. The itchiness came and went in waves. She had been so caught up with the trial, her deal with Sijur, and Blár not being around that she didn't think too much about why her back had been so itchy the past two weeks. Maybe she had gotten an infection? Maybe her stress caused it? Maybe it was another strange change in her body, like her partially white hair? She didn't know. All she knew was that she just wanted to be alone to sleep and scratch her blasted back. And then *relax*.

Something she hadn't done in a long, *long* time.

The giant gates of the base opened and the trio urged their horses forward. A blocky, rigid, and monolithic stone building stood in the center of the fortress walls. Its edges were sharp as blades, the walls a boring gray, and the window slabs tiny and suffocating.

There were smaller buildings surrounding the fort, which she could only guess were the armory, hospital, and administration building. Everywhere she looked, there were soldiers. Either training in rows, sparring, or running laps. The sea of gray uniforms made her sick. It was so much different than the Royal Guards. Everything about the Royal Guards was fancy, bedecked in gold and finery, and polished. Here, it was the opposite: rough, stiff, and monotonous.

Sijur and Joran dismounted from their horses when they reached the stables and Kolfinna did the same. She threw her rucksack over her shoulder and stared at the looming, brutal building she would be calling home for the next fifteen years.

Sijur motioned toward Kolfinna and Joran after he handed the reins of his horse to a stable hand. "Joran, please lead Kolfinna to her room." He peered at the bright afternoon sky. "We've got about ... hm, three hours until the evening? How about you rest up and then you can meet everyone at dinnertime?"

Meet everyone?

Now that she had stepped foot in the base, with all the soldiers training around her, her stomach knotted itself into a tight ball and she didn't know how to act. She didn't come here to make friends—and she highly doubted she would—but the thought of making enemies, which was more probable, made her uneasy despite her and Nollar's earlier bold plans.

"Your new uniform will be in your room," Sijur continued, stretching his long arms as they exited the stables and the strong, eye-watering smell of manure, hay, and animal urine. "I'll see you both later tonight, then."

Joran bobbed his head and watched as Sijur walked toward one of the buildings. He then turned his golden-haired head to

Kolfinna, his vibrant green eyes appearing like two polished emeralds. "I'll, um, lead the way?"

If he was hoping to inspire confidence, Kolfinna didn't feel it. She waved for him to go forward and they approached the main building. Joran fiddled with the gray cuff of his sleeve, his shifty eyes flicking to the soldiers and then back at Kolfinna.

Most of the soldiers ignored them and were focused on their training—sparring and wrestling with each other—but Kolfinna noticed a few curious looks shot her way. Even at a distance, her white hair made her stand out.

She tucked a strand of white hair behind her ear distractedly.

"Are you nervous being here?" he asked quietly.

She tried to appear calm. "A little."

"You don't have to worry about ... um, people bullying you."

She stiffened. Did he know the Royal Guards bullied her? "Why do you say that?"

"No reason ... I can just imagine ..." He shrugged and stared straight ahead.

They were quiet for some time. The nearby soldiers trained with magic, splashes of water and streaks of lightning filling the space between them, while others trained with swords, the clash of steel against steel clanging all around. The air about the military seemed so much busier than it had been at the Royal Guards.

Kolfinna had hoped the inside of the building would be less cruel and brutal-looking and that it actually housed a cozy interior or even a coldly lavish one like the royal palace or the Royal Guards' headquarters—but she was disappointed by the stony gray walls, the cold gray tiles, and the tiny windows that didn't allow enough sunlight to filter into the hallways.

The only comfort she could find was that the floors and walls were made entirely of stone, which was perfect if she was in a battle inside here, since she had plenty of material to use for her stone magic. But she truly hoped it never got to that point.

When she glanced over at Joran, at the white badge stuck to his breast pocket and the way his burnt gold hair fell over his eyes, she wondered briefly if he could manipulate the stones better than her.

"You're not a white rank," Kolfinna said with a nod to his badge. White ranks were people without magic or with very little enhancer abilities. "Why continue to lie?"

Joran's eyes widened and he quickly looked around himself at the hallway, at the trickling of soldiers going in and out of rooms. "Don't say that out loud," he whispered. "*Please.*"

He was very obviously keeping it a secret that he was fae, and he was blessed with brilliant green eyes that could pass off as human if no one was looking or thinking too hard about how unnaturally bright they were, or that there were tiny threads of orange in them. Kolfinna should've respected his decision to remain hidden—after all, she had done the same her whole life—but it somehow prickled under her skin that he was able to walk around without fear of discrimination. That he could pretend to be human.

When they reached a door on the third floor with a simple 304 etched onto the dark wood, Joran knocked, waited, and then twisted the wobbly doorknob. The room was cramped with three beds neatly placed in a row. Each bed had a small nightstand and a trunk at the end of the bed. The nightstand on the left was cluttered with things—a stack of papers, a half-eaten hunk of bread, socks—while the nightstand on the right was neat and only contained a small stack of books. The bed on the left matched the nightstand in the way it was disorganized—the sheets were crumpled, undergarments were strewn on top, and a comb full of tangled fiery-red hair wrapped around the teeth sat in the center of it. The right side was, once again, the complete opposite. It appeared one of Kolfinna's new roommates was organized and one clearly wasn't. The bed in the center of the room was likely Kolfinna's. For a moment, she stared at it, her chest tightening. This was really happening. She was a soldier now.

Joran stared at the interior of the room with mild interest and jerked a thumb behind him. "The, uh, washroom is at the end of the hallway. You'll have to share it with everyone on this floor. Don't worry, though, this is the women's section of the barracks. The women have the first three floors on this wing of the fort, while the men have the upper three floors and the whole right wing of the fort."

Kolfinna quickly did the math. "So ... there are only one-fourth of women here in the military?"

"Um, yes, roughly. At least here in this base."

"What stops the men from coming to our floors?"

His gold eyebrows pulled together. "What do you mean?"

She glanced at the doorknob, which didn't have a lock. "Is there anything stopping the men from entering the women's rooms?" she reiterated. He couldn't be so dense as to not realize that women didn't usually feel safe surrounded by a slew of men from all walks of the earth.

Joran shifted on his feet and eyed the end of the hallway. "There's nothing like that here. Anyone can enter and go, even though they're not *supposed* to." He messed with the cuff of his sleeve again. "The men and women aren't allowed to go to the opposite gender's barracks at night, but there's nothing actually stopping them."

That wasn't reassuring at all. She could imagine a group of hunters in the military ambushing her in the middle of the night to seize her like Hilda had two weeks ago. The thought made her shudder.

Joran was already backing away from her. "If you need anything else—"

"Are there—" Her throat closed up and she looked out at the single window above the middle bed. "Are there any hunters here?"

Joran stilled, bright eyes flashing with *something* before he shook his head. "No."

Relief pooled in her chest. "Ah. Great "

"But there are people who don't like fae," he said slowly. "Many of the people we catch here are criminal fae running to the

Mistlands." He averted his gaze and messed with his cuff again. "I've seen ... I've seen some soldiers do some very cruel things to those we capture."

Her blood ran cold. Whatever relief she had felt dissipated, replaced with bone-deep apprehension. No matter where she went, she was bound to find people who hated fae, but the thought of living so close to them—and, when she glanced at the beds, potentially even sleeping in the same room as them—made her legs shake and her hands sweat.

"Your roommates will be back in a few hours. They can take you to the dining hall in the evening." He gave her a small smile before shutting the door behind him.

Now that he was gone, Kolfinna reached over her shoulder to scratch her itchy back. Her fingernails dug into the flesh and she ran her fingers over it, a wave of pain and relief washing over her. It was strange how itchy she had become.

It was also then that she was able to take note of the other details in the room. Like the rug beneath the left bed, with splashes of bright fuchsia, deep indigo, sunny yellow, and vibrant vermillion. On the right-hand wall hung a small tapestry depicting an expansive sea with ships and fish and sea-creatures in the water. The pop of color calmed Kolfinna somehow. As if there was life outside the slabs of gray stone all around her.

On top of the middle bed were folded gray uniforms. Kolfinna eased her rucksack on the empty bed and began unfolding her clothes from her pack and organizing them into the trunk. When all of her things were unloaded, she plopped down on the hard bed. It creaked against the stone floor and she made a mental note to buy a similar rug like the one her roommate had. The boring, spidery-cracked ceiling stared back at her, and even though the bed was stiff and the pillow was paper-thin, Kolfinna's eyelids fluttered shut.

THE SOUND OF A DOOR CRACKING AGAINST THE doorjamb jerked Kolfinna awake from her dreamless slumber. For a moment, her mind wandered to the Hunter's Association and Hilda, to that wooden room in the cabin and the sound of the door slamming shut, and the hunters laughing at her after they were done tormenting and torturing her. Before her eyes could even focus on the room around her, her heart raced and her palms grew sweaty. But then she was brought back to the room. To the stony gray floors and walls. To the two beds flanking her, to the single window lodged above her bed.

A woman had entered the room and stood a few feet away from Kolfinna's bed. A shocking mane of fire-red curls surrounded the woman's tanned, freckled face. Upon seeing Kolfinna, her brilliant blue eyes widened.

Someone clucked their tongue and Kolfinna looked to her left, toward the organized side of the room, where another beautiful woman sat cross-legged on the bed, a handkerchief clasped beneath an embroidery hoop in one hand and a needle in the other hand. Streams of bone-straight inky hair draped over her shoulder and reached down to her waist.

The dark-haired woman lifted her head from her embroidery. "You shouldn't be slamming the door so hard."

The other woman snorted and flopped down on her bed on the right, atop her clothes and disarray of sheets. "Whatever. It's not like this place is *mine*."

"Showing basic respect for—"

"Shut it, Inkeri. I'm not really in the mood to be lectured today."

Kolfinna expected the embroidery lady to be offended by that, but she only rolled her eyes and went back to her work. The other woman turned in her bed until she was facing the ceiling and covered her face with her pillow, a sigh escaping her lips.

"Aren't you going to ask *why* I'm not in the mood?"

"No."

The redhead shot up in bed. "Don't you care?"

"No."

She chucked the pillow at her, but it missed by a few inches. "*Bitch.*"

Inkeri eyed the pillow, which had sagged beside her lap, with an amused half-smirk before turning her soft-gray eyes to Kolfinna. She was hands down the most beautiful woman Kolfinna had ever seen, and if Kolfinna didn't feel so out of place, she might've had room to feel the stirring of jealousy.

"Hello, I'm sorry about Herja's attitude and how she awoke you." Inkeri shot the redhead an annoyed look but smiled when she met Kolfinna's gaze. "My name is Inkeri."

"I'm Kolfinna," she said, looking between Herja and Inkeri. "Nice to meet you both."

Inkeri opened her mouth to respond, but Herja snorted and flipped herself on the bed so she was lying on her stomach. "Yeah, I'm sure it's great for you to meet us, but it's not mutual, fae-girl."

Kolfinna had heard similar words so many times—fae scum, little fairy, heartless. She had heard so many of the same insults told with the same condescending tone. It was to be expected that the military wouldn't be any different than the Royal Guards when it came to bullying her.

Kolfinna sat straighter on the bed and stared at Herja, who was wrestling her comb out from the nest of sheets and clothes. "Why do you say that?"

"Hm?" Herja tilted her head to the side, her reddish-orange hair catching in the light. "Well, why do *you* think?"

"Herja—" Inkeri started, tone level.

"No, no, not you, Inkeri," Herja said. "You know exactly what this is about—"

"That's not fair to her."

"It's not fair to Brenda either." She pushed herself into a sitting position and combed her hair distractedly with rigid movements, ignoring Kolfinna altogether. "Or me."

Kolfinna's chest squeezed painfully slow; the next fifteen years would be spent like this. Maybe with the same two roommates, maybe different ones, and maybe in a different room, but fifteen years ... *like this*. With people who didn't like her. Or barely tolerated her.

At least when she was a Royal Guard, though, she didn't have to *live* with Gisela, or Farthin, or Edwin, or any of the people who didn't like her. If these two women planned on bullying her, she'd have no choice but to fight back because she wouldn't repeat the past five months.

Kolfinna's mana burned at her fingertips and she connected it to the stone floor just in case things got ugly. She fixed the red-haired woman with a level stare. "If you've got something to say to me, then say it."

Herja paused with combing her hair and gave Kolfinna a satisfied, snobbish look, as if she had been waiting for her to say that. "I don't like that you're my roommate and I definitely don't like how our previous roommate, Brenda, got kicked out to make room for you. I don't think it's fair and, quite frankly, I don't want you here at all."

"Herja ..." There was a warning in Inkeri's voice.

Kolfinna regarded Herja coldly. "I didn't kick out your previous roommate and I didn't do anything to warrant this reaction."

"From what the rumors say, you're a murderer"—Herja crossed her legs and ticked off one of her fingers—"you were kicked out of the Royal Guards for trying to attack and kill the other guards in the middle of a capital-wide emergency"—another finger ticked down—"and you have dubious, potential ties to Ragnarök." She nodded as if satisfied. "What about that list makes you think I'm comfortable having you as a roommate?"

Heat rose to Kolfinna's face. "You wouldn't understand—"

"Such a *typical* response." She rolled her eyes and got to her feet. "Just what I'd expect from a slimy murderer. Anyway, Inkeri" —Herja zeroed in on the pretty woman—"I'm not going to sit around and socialize with a murderer, so I'll be off. Do you want to come with me?"

Inkeri held up her embroidered handkerchief. "I want to finish this, but I'll see you at the dining hall."

"So long as you're okay being alone with a murderer." Herja gave Kolfinna a last, dark look before sauntering off and slamming the door shut behind her.

Silence filled the small space of the room and Kolfinna's face felt like it would burst in flames. She didn't know if what she felt was humiliation, mortification, or simply fury at Herja's abrasiveness. News of her trial seemed to have spread quickly if even people here on the western border knew of it.

But then she reminded herself that she wasn't here to make friends. If she couldn't find a place to belong in the Royal Guards, there was no hope of finding that here, in this military base full of unfamiliar, harsh faces.

"What rank are you?" Inkeri asked, breaking the tense silence.

Kolfinna was at least a yellow rank since the Royal Guards didn't allow anyone less than that to join, but she didn't have an accurate rank on display. It was only the military that plastered their rank on their chests. And by the reflective yellow lion badge clipped to Inkeri's breast pocket, Kolfinna knew her rank right away.

"I'm not sure." Kolfinna ran her fingers through her hair, untangling the worst of the locks that had knotted together on the side of her hair that was completely white before moving on to untangle the other side of her head full of dark waves.

"Is your hair like that naturally?"

It wasn't before, but after Hilda tortured her, it had somehow transformed into this half-white, half-black mess. Truthfully, she wasn't a fan of it. Not only did she stick out even more, but it was jarring to look at.

"Yes," Kolfinna settled with.

"Interesting."

Interesting indeed—it was something that bothered Kolfinna. Not just because of the way it looked, but because it made her wonder if it had anything to do with her uncertain bloodline. According to the book about magic beasts she had deciphered a few weeks ago that Fenris had given her, all elves had white hair and red eyes. If she truly was related to the half-elf commander in some way—likely a distant relative of the heir—then was this hair representative of that? And although her eyes weren't red, they were pink—and that was close enough, wasn't it?

Kolfinna shuddered to think of the cave she and her party had discovered on the west border mission, which foretold that the heir of the fae queen would release her. She didn't want to be related to the evil queen, or the half-elf commander, or the strange heir, but ... It was all too strange—the physical changes she was undergoing, her new ability to heal quickly.

She couldn't share any of this with anyone because if she truly was a relative of the half-elf commander's—and a relative of Queen Aesileif, his wife—then Ragnarök would come after her, since a blood relative of the queen's was needed in order to unseal the ruthless monarch.

Kolfinna didn't even want to think about what that meant for her, but she was absolutely sure she needed to keep that to herself.

Thirty minutes passed in silence; Inkeri worked on her embroidery, only occasionally raising her head to watch Kolfinna with a blank look, while Kolfinna distractedly combed her hair, reorganized her clothes and items again, and then combed her hair a second time. There wasn't much for her to busy her hands with.

Finally, when the sun began setting and their room filled with the soft orange-lavender glow of dusk, Inkeri set the embroidery aside on her nightstand and rose to her feet gracefully. "It's about time for dinner. Would you like me to show you the way?"

Kolfinna jumped to her feet, ready to leave the cramped room. "Yes, I'd like that."

"Wonderful." She waved her forward and they both entered the gray-toned hallway once more. Inkeri watched her with a knowing gleam in her eyes. "You were a Royal Guard before this, so I'm sure everything looks very drab to you."

Kolfinna almost laughed. "The Royal Guards paint everything in shades of gold and silver. And I mean that literally." She pointedly glanced at the plain gray walls and the stone-tiled floors. Even as they walked down the stairs and beyond the bends of the hallway, the brutally simple building design left much to be desired. The Royal Guards' headquarters had paintings on every wall, plush rugs and runners in every hallway and room, fancy carvings in the trim, and so many little ornate things that seemed unnecessary. Seeing this place made something sink in Kolfinna's chest. It almost felt like a prison.

Inkeri turned a corner just in front of her. "The Royal Guards might have more wealth and prestige, but the job sounds ... unappealing. Patrolling the city, catching criminals, and enforcing the law? Boring." She shrugged, and they passed a cluster of male soldiers hanging in the wide hallway; their laughter and conversation died down, and they stared at Inkeri as she passed by. "I prefer fighting magic beasts and exploring underground tunnels and running through beast-infested forests."

"It'll certainly be a new experience," Kolfinna said, glancing over her shoulder at the men. Had they not noticed her, or were they too entranced by the beautiful woman by her side?

"Oh, *certainly*." Inkeri smiled and this time it seemed to reach her eyes, as if passion was lighting her up. "It's incredibly fun, I think, the exploratory part of what we do here. I assume all the other military bases are different because they focus on different things, like protecting the border or hunting particular magic beasts. But since we focus on the border between Rosain and the Mistlands, we see so many strange creatures. *Especially* these past few months."

Kolfinna thought back to her last mission, where she, Blár, Magni, Eyfura, Nollar, and Yrsa were exploring the forest of Great

Divide in order to find the origin of strange magic beasts encroaching onto the lands. She thought of the horse creature, the Nuckelavee, they had faced, and how monstrously powerful it had been and how they had almost died.

She didn't find anything fun about that.

Even as she spoke, the Nuckelavee's heavy hooves sounded in her mind and its ghastly, skinless appearance made her shudder. "How has that been, by the way? Facing new creatures you've never seen or heard of before?"

Inkeri paused for a moment and her strides slowed. "It's unsettling, some of the things I've seen, but fascinating at the same time. I really do wonder why these creatures are suddenly coming out now."

It was still a secret that there was a rune barrier between Rosain and the Mistlands, and that Kolfinna's party had found a broken section of the barrier.

"But"—Inkeri tucked a strand of hair behind her ear—"it's fun discovering things no one has ever seen before. Like just last month, I saw a skeletal monster that was *moving* like it was alive."

"Oh. You mean a draugr?"

Inkeri's eyes widened and she stopped in her tracks. "You know what it is?"

"Yes." Kolfinna moved out of the way as soldiers passed them by, seemingly headed in the same direction as them. "When I went to the Eventyrslot ruins, I faced them and there were writings about them in the ruins." She shuddered to think about when she had faced those undead creatures and how she had seen them again during the West Border mission.

"See. That's *fascinating*." Inkeri shook her head. "I'd love to hear more."

As they entered a dining hall, Kolfinna noticed a few soldiers —particularly the men—glance at Inkeri surreptitiously from time to time, and it confirmed what she had suspected—Inkeri was probably the most beautiful woman in the military base.

The dining hall was similar to the canteen in the Royal

Guards' headquarters. Neat rows of tables filled the majority of the room, and it was completely packed with a sea of gray uniformed soldiers. They talked and laughed and ate, their conversations humming through the room. Inkeri guided her to the front of the hall, where cooks were ladling food into bowls and handing them to soldiers. A cook ladled a brightly red, steaming stew into a bowl, where chunks of beef, carrots, and beets floated to the surface, and handed it to Kolfinna and then another to Inkeri.

"The only downside to being here is having to work with certain people," Inkeri said as she grabbed a plate full of crusty bread, white cheese, and sliced strawberries from another cook, who handed Kolfinna a similar platter.

"I think that goes for every profession," Kolfinna said, thinking of the few times she had to work with Farthin and Gisela and the many times she had to work with guards who clearly abhorred her.

"Hm. I suppose." Inkeri maneuvered through the crowds of soldiers and set her food down on an empty section of the long table. A pitcher of water was already placed on the table, along with a few upside down cups. Inkeri flipped two, filled her cup, and then did the same with the other. "We'll be working together a lot in the future, since we're in the same little group."

Kolfinna took the spot across from her and sat on the worn, wooden bench. There were various people on either ends of the table, but they weren't close enough to be actually sitting with them, even if they were on the same bench and table. "By groups, do you mean like a unit?"

"Sort of. So we're all one big unit here since we're under Lieutenant General Bernsten. This is the main base for the western border, but there are two other forts the Lieutenant General is in charge of. We're the main force or the main unit. But within this unit, there are smaller groups that he has assigned us in. We don't move as a giant unit for every mission. Most of the time we go on missions with our small group."

Kolfinna tore a chunk of the bread and dipped it in her stew; the bread soaked up the oily red liquid instantly and when she ate it, the salty, meaty flavor exploded in her mouth. She stirred the stew with her spoon, her stomach growling. She had, admittedly, expected the food here to be bland, boring, and unable to compete with the delicacies the Royal Guards had, so she was pleasantly surprised to find it suited her palate.

She reined herself back into the conversation. Groups. Units. Being under Sijur Bernsten. "Are the groups designated by roommates?"

"Again, *sorta*." Inkeri folded cheese onto a piece of her bread and nibbled on it. "Our roommates are decided based on our group. So we'll only be roomed with our group members. Once again, it's not like an official group, so people get moved around all the time."

"Like Brenda." The woman Kolfinna had supposedly replaced.

Inkeri sighed. "Yes, like Brenda."

"She's still ..." Kolfinna lowered her spoon. "She's still here, though, right? Like, I didn't completely replace her, did I?"

"Oh, yes, she's still here." Inkeri waved to the room. "Somewhere, but she won't be working with our group anymore."

That was a relief—she didn't want to be the reason someone was kicked out. Not that it was even logical to think like that; the military wasn't like the Royal Guards, who limited who could become a guard. The military accepted just about anyone.

"Who is part of our group?" Kolfinna gave a sweeping glance at the crowds of soldiers milling about.

"You'll find out. I'm sure you'll meet them in the coming days."

"Do other people who aren't a part of our group join too?"

"Sometimes."

They ate in silence for a moment. Their spoons clanked against the rims of their bowls, and the conversations of the surrounding soldiers lulled over them. It was nice to have someone who didn't outright treat her like rubbish, but Kolfinna wondered why Inkeri was sitting with her, instead of acting like Herja. Why she was being civil—nice, even.

Thoughts of Yrsa infiltrated her mind. Yrsa, who had befriended her and then betrayed her. She then thought of Mímir, who had been kind to Kolfinna before and during the Eventyrslot mission, only to betray her as well.

Kolfinna was a bit wary of people being nice to her.

Someone's palm slammed onto the center of the table in front of Kolfinna, rattling the plates and bowls and jerking her away from her thoughts. Inkeri stiffened; a towering man stood directly behind her, his hunkering body leaned forward so his chest was brushing against her head, and his dark eyes were pinned on Kolfinna.

"Inkeri." The man moved his meaty hand off the table and rested it on Inkeri's shoulder, but when he spoke, he stared at Kolfinna. "Sweet thing, what in the actual hell do you think you're doing?"

Inkeri's lips thinned. "Unhand me, Bjarni."

"What are you doing?" The man, Bjarni, leaned down until his white-blond stubbled jaw was grazing her ear. "Fraternizing with the enemy?"

Kolfinna's hackles rose. *Enemy.* The uneasiness she had felt just seconds ago vanished. Yes, *this* was what was normal for her. Being treated like an enemy—the Royal Guards had taught her that much. And for some odd reason, it almost made her feel like she was back in the headquarters, ducking her head from the other guards, hoping no one would say anything to her.

Almost.

Inkeri's hold on her spoon tightened, her knuckles turning white. "I said *unhand me.*"

The surrounding people stopped talking and watched with a mixture of curiosity and surprise. Then the conversations at the other tables shushed to murmurs and Kolfinna became increasingly aware of everyone's stares—on her.

Bjarni released Inkeri, but not before dragging a finger down her arm. "Has this fae girl enchanted you with fae charm? Is that why you're sitting with her?"

Kolfinna didn't need to know Inkeri well to know that this looming man—who was at least four heads taller than Kolfinna—made her uncomfortable. To see the way her spine was stiff and how she angled herself away from his body, and yet he kept close. That alone infuriated Kolfinna. It wasn't so much the words—they were tamer than what she was used to.

The water in the glass pitcher rippled violently until a crack formed along the base of it, bleeding water onto the table. A water elemental, Kolfinna realized, glancing between Inkeri and the giant man. She wasn't sure which one it was, but if someone was losing control in this situation, it was probably Inkeri.

"I would appreciate it if you left me alone, Bjarni," Inkeri said icily. She set down her spoon next to her bowl with a loud clack. "What I do in my free time and who I choose to sit with is none of your concern. And, quite frankly, it's none of your business."

"Oh, don't be like that." He placed both hands on her shoulder and pressed forward again. "I'll—"

"Stop touching her," Kolfinna snapped.

Someone gasped. The man—Bjarni—paused and narrowed his eyes at Kolfinna. Even Inkeri looked surprised.

But the one who was the most surprised was Kolfinna. Because the fire in her—the fire of resistance and hot rage—had disappeared a long time ago. It was around the time Katla had died, or when Blár had defeated her. And even though Kolfinna had promised herself after the Royal Guards that she would resist more, snap at people, and speak up, it still surprised her to hear that anger. It was so foreign, but it felt *right*.

And it reminded her of when she had snapped at Edwin a few weeks ago, when that little fire of hers had grown enough to tell him to leave her alone. When she had decided she was done being a punching bag for the guards. Just like now.

"Stop touching her." Kolfinna dropped her spoon on the

table. He was still touching Inkeri, his thick fingers tightening on her thin shoulder.

"A murderous fae-demon telling me what to do? Something doesn't seem right about that," he purred, kneading Inkeri's shoulders as if to prove his point. The purple badge on his chest contrasted with Inkeri's yellow one. "You're not supposed to be here, fae-demon. You should be back in the capital with the rest of the royal bootlickers."

Inkeri slapped his hand away and tried to rise from the bench, but he grabbed her and shoved her back down. He pressed his weight on her, eyes flashing with irritation. "*Inkeri.*"

"*Let. Me. Go,*" she gritted out the words through clenched teeth, her hands tightened into fists.

"I'm still talking to the bitch. Don't interrupt me." Bjarni kept his tight hold on Inkeri's shoulder and leaned his head down to her ear. "Do you want a repeat of last week?"

Inkeri went still, the color draining from her face.

"Fae-demon." Bjarni turned back to Kolfinna. "You—"

Kolfinna couldn't hear what he was saying. She could only focus on Inkeri's bloodless face, on the pleading look in her eyes, as if to say *help me.*

If there was one thing the Royal Guards had taught Kolfinna, it was to protect people. It had been drilled in her every morning practice. Protect, serve, and help the people. It was a guard's duty. In the face of someone who needed protection, it was hard for her to turn away.

Kolfinna lurched to her feet. Her mana rushed through her body like a jolt of lightning, tingling her senses and warming her flesh. "Let her go."

She wasn't in the Royal Guards anymore. She didn't have to control herself for fear of losing her position. She didn't have to make herself small so everyone else could be comfortable. She didn't need to make friends. She didn't need to fit in. She didn't need anything here, so it didn't matter what they thought of her.

There was nothing standing in her way of beating the shit out of this man.

"Oh? The little fae bi—"

Kolfinna ripped a stone the size of her hand off the floor and chucked it straight at his face. It smashed right on target, the stone crumbling into smaller pieces. He stumbled back, blood gushing from his nose, and his arms flailed as he righted himself. It was all the time Inkeri needed to slip out of the bench and back away into the crowd—far from him and Kolfinna.

The silence in the room was deafening; everyone held their breaths. Waiting. Watching.

It felt *good* to smash the stone on his face. All the frustrations she had been feeling the past few weeks—the stress of the trial, the uncertainties of her future, losing her position as a guard, the weight of Ragnarök, binding herself to a man like Sijur—released with that single strike.

Never again did she want to feel like she had in the Royal Guards.

Never again would she let someone like Edwin, like Farthin, like Gisela—like Bjarni—push her around.

Bjarni brought a hand to the dust and blood smeared on his face. Scarlet dripped onto his fingers and spattered against the cold floor. At the sight of his blood on his hands, he brought his gaze slowly up to Kolfinna's. Murder danced within the dark depths of his eyes.

For someone so large, he moved quickly. He snatched a knife off the table and flung it at Kolfinna. She raised her arm, but her magic was too slow for the knife. It slammed into her forearm and stuck there.

She hissed as hot pain flashed over her senses, clouding her focus, but her mana was already working into the floor beneath Bjarni's feet. He ran toward her, lips twisted into a snarl when Kolfinna raised her hand and a spear of stone struck up from the floor. He tried dodging, but his body was too big of a target. The stone spear struck his shoulder and sent him reeling back.

Kolfinna stepped farther away from Bjarni; she didn't know what magic he possessed—Enhancer or Elemental, and which element he controlled—so she had to be wary and keep her distance.

Warm blood seeped down her forearm and created streaks of bright red on the drab gray floor. The other soldiers parted, clearing the area into a ring so they could watch better.

She grabbed the metal handle of the knife and wrenched it free from her flesh. She winced, more blood gushing from the wound. The pain made it hard to focus, but the rush of adrenaline dulled it with every throb.

Bjarni circled her. There was a smear of blood beneath his nose, tingeing his skin in pink. Bits of stone were still stuck to his shoulder, but he made no move to brush them away or yank them out. He had his hawkish eyes on her, watching her every move, looking for an opening.

Kolfinna launched another stone at him at the same time she threw the knife, but he ducked and rolled away. Another soldier caught the stone and it cracked in her hands.

They both kept circling each other, fingers flexing. He was probably an Enhancer, Kolfinna thought. If he was an Elemental —whether that was ice, fire, wind, lightning, or water—he would've been able to do long-distance attacks on her. But he wasn't: which only meant that he was an Enhancer and that she needed to be careful. If he caught her, there was a high chance that he would break her bones.

She wouldn't give him that chance.

Her mana worked into the floor, ready to rip a hole and drag him in—

Someone clapped loudly. Normally, it wouldn't have stopped her from a fight—especially since she was hyper focused on it— but at the same time, sparks of blue-white lightning synergized the air and surrounded her and Bjarni. Strands of her hair floated at the charged energy. Bjarni's forehead crinkled, clearly just as surprised as she was.

The clapping grew louder and the crowd parted. Sijur strolled into their circle with ease and grace and none of the rage she would've expected from her commanding officer. Instead, he appeared *amused*. His lips were curved up into a large grin, and those beady black eyes lit with laughter. Sparks of lightning buzzed off his fingertips.

"My, my, that was intriguing to watch," Sijur purred, rubbing his hands together. The crackle of lightning made Bjarni stand taller. A nervous look passed over his once arrogant face. "It's always so fascinating to see you fight, Kolfinna. As it is to watch you fight, Bjarni, but we can resume this match at a later time. Such as during a sparring match or a duel during training hours. But here"—he spread his arms wide and gestured to the room— "in the middle of the dining hall where everyone is trying to enjoy their meals? As much as I *love* the enthusiasm from you both, I will have to urge you both to stop."

He smiled wider and even though he made it sound like a request, It was anything but that. Kolfinna lowered her arms and released her hold on the stone flooring. She saw the fight leave Bjarni too.

"Bjarni, I'd like a word with you in my office." Sijur was still smiling, seemingly unaware—or unconcerned—about the way Bjarni's body went slack and his face turned ashen. "Kolfinna, why don't you go to your room and rest? Maybe get your arm checked out as well."

Kolfinna didn't need to be told twice to get lost. She moved toward the exit and the crowd of soldiers made way for her. Their expressions were a mixture of intrigue, confusion, awe, horror, and—what surprised Kolfinna the most   *respect*.

She had never seen that look before. Not when people knew what she was—a fae.

She spotted Herja by the exit. She was leaning against the wall, her muscular arms crossed over her chest and a violent grin on her face. She looked all too entertained, but there was that gleam in her eyes that told Kolfinna that something had changed. Like

Kolfinna had upgraded from a fae murderer to something more desirable.

When Kolfinna passed her, Herja whispered, "Looks like the murderer has some bite to her."

Kolfinna didn't respond as she left the dining hall. Away from the stares. Away from all the people and their confusing reaction to her. She was used to the horror and disgust, but not the other things.

She pressed a hand to the forearm Bjarni had injured. She hesitantly peeled back the bloody sleeve to reveal the smooth skin and the tiny pink scar that had been gushing blood just five minutes ago. Another wave of uneasiness washed over her. That was new.

Something similar had happened after she had left Hilda's torture cabin. And again after her fight with Yrsa. Although she was grateful for the healed wounds, concern filled her.

Why was this happening?

This wasn't normal for a fae or a human.

Was it maybe ... her body subconsciously using rune magic? That had to be it, she decided. It wasn't due to elf blood or elf magic.

She could hear Revna's voice in her mind. *The commander will come for this kingdom, and he will set our queen free.*

She banished those thoughts—she wasn't part elf.

She couldn't be.

4

Kolfinna dreamed that night of the Eventyrslot ruins. Of the voices that had whispered to her. Of Revna in the desert dimension as she taught Kolfinna how to use runes. Of the entire party as they ventured through the crumbling, ominous halls of the castle. But mostly, she dreamed of Blár. Of his ice-blue eyes that shone like a frozen lake. Of his wickedly handsome face, his sharp tongue, and his lean body. Her dreams shifted from the ruins to other mashed up memories that seemed clear but were strange at the same time. Her body pressed against his as they danced to random tunes during the ball. The feeling of nestling against his chest.

He was so beautiful, even in her dreams. And even in her nightmares, he was so wicked. So beautiful. So very much *not* hers.

It was that thought that woke her. Or maybe not because a glaring light burned her eyes from the window above her head, annoyingly streaming sunlight directly over her. Kolfinna slung an arm over her eyes and cursed softly.

She could almost still feel Blár's hands on her waist from the dream, and her face flushed with color.

Damn the stupid sunlight.

Pushing herself into a sitting position, she stared at her new room and her new roommates.

Inkeri slept to her left and Herja to her right. It was still strange waking up in a military base, instead of at her cozy home back in the capital.

Kolfinna slipped off the bed and quietly cracked her trunk open. The worn, wooden top creaked with the motion. Dressing herself as quickly as she could—so the two women wouldn't catch her partially naked—she put on the common military uniform. Dull gray pants and a long-sleeved gray top. It fit for the most part. The pants were perfect, but she struggled to button the top of her shirt. The material strained against her bosom and she hated how fitted it looked. How it drew attention to her.

"You're up at the ass crack of dawn."

Kolfinna whirled to face Herja, who was sitting upright in the bed. Her blanket lay over her lap and she yawned loudly. Her wild reddish-orange hair appeared even more like a mane as it stuck out in every direction. Herja scratched the nape of her neck and yawned again.

"You're up too," Kolfinna said, yanking on a pair of wool socks.

"Unfortunately."

A powerful, blustering wind howled beyond their window, momentarily distracting Kolfinna as she brushed her hair and braided it. At least winter was slowly pulling back. It wouldn't be long before she'd have full control of her nature powers again.

Herja began dressing herself as well, except she had no reservations about stripping herself down to her underwear and then donning the military uniform. By the time they were both dressed, Inkeri stirred.

"You—" Inkeri rubbed her eyes and stifled a yawn. "Is it morning already?"

"Sure is, princess." Herja detangled her hair with her fingers before working it through a wide-toothed comb.

Kolfinna washed her face with the basin water in the corner of the room and wetted down the frizzing parts of her hair. Today would be her first official day as a soldier; she had no idea what to expect. Would Sijur throw her in a forest and tell her to hunt a magic beast? Would she have to sit around the walls of the fort and wait for an attack?

"Let's get breakfast," Inkeri said after she stretched, slipped on her uniform, and washed her face. Her silken smooth hair tumbled over her shoulders effortlessly, not a single strand of hair out of place. When she caught Kolfinna staring, she smiled.

Neither of them had spoken about what had happened yesterday, and Kolfinna was thankful for that. She wasn't sure how to feel herself.

They all headed to the dining hall, which was still missing pieces of stone flooring from where Kolfinna had ripped it up, and ate a hot breakfast of barley porridge, scrambled quail eggs with melted, salty cheese, and a drink made of milk, honey, and ground strawberries. After breakfast, Inkeri took her to the training grounds where the military did their morning training. Around a hundred soldiers were on the grounds, and although they cast her curious looks, she didn't detect much hostility from them. Mostly curiosity.

The open field full of soldiers reminded Kolfinna of her mornings at the Royal Guards' headquarters. Where she would "train" with the other guards and essentially be mocked, beaten, and humiliated every morning.

She wouldn't allow the military to do the same to her.

However, by the third lap around the fort, Kolfinna keeled over, breathing heavily and feeling like she would faint. She was used to running—the Royal Guards had done the same—but the military made her sprint like her life depended on it.

So much for showing them how tough she was.

"You good?" Inkeri sipped water from her flask and watched Kolfinna with a worried crease between her brows.

She was in fact not good. Truthfully, she was sure she'd vomit her breakfast all across her new black boots any minute now, but she put her hands on her knees to force them straight as she stood up.

Inkeri didn't look convinced but grinned. "You'll get used to it."

"The Royal Guards must train like spineless rodents." Herja snickered to another woman, who hid her laughter behind her hand.

The laughter made the tips of Kolfinna's ears hot with embarrassment. The other nearby soldiers chuckled, but some were out of breath too, which assuaged *some* of her discomfort.

"All right, everyone, line up," a firm, monotonous voice called. The dark-haired man who had been giving orders came to stand at the center of the field. He wore a cloak of black feathers that gleamed under the morning sun. Dark circles rimmed his black eyes and he looked bone-weary, almost like the light had been leeched from him years ago. When he spoke again, it was void of emotion. "You half"—he gestured to one section of the soldiers— "will practice mana control by yourselves while you half"— another wave—"will do combat training. When I give the signal, you switch."

Kolfinna's section of the group was supposed to do combat. Everyone seemed to know what they were doing. Herja teamed up with another woman, and the others paired up as well. For a few seconds, Kolfinna wondered if she would be left out, but then Inkeri waved to Kolfinna with raised brows.

"Are you ready for combat training?"

Kolfinna glanced at the others. Some were already battling each other, flares of fire and water and lightning zapping the air and filling it with smoke. "Am I ... allowed to use magic?"

Inkeri gave her a strange look. "Of course."

The Royal Guards hadn't allowed Kolfinna to train with her magic, since Edwin believed she needed to be better at training with the sword before she could even think about using her magic. Kolfinna was sure it was just another tactic of his to keep her leashed and powerless.

"Why don't you practice with someone else?" Kolfinna asked.

Inkeri frowned and raised her hands. "Are you sure you want that? Because then you'll have no one to fight."

"But—"

Inkeri struck first. Wind slapped Kolfinna, shoving her a foot backward. Kolfinna stumbled on her feet and blinked at Inkeri in shock. She could've sworn Inkeri was a water elemental, but the wisps of wind circling Inkeri's outstretched hands confirmed that she *wasn't*.

Inkeri laughed at Kolfinna's shocked expression. "Come on, let's fight."

She didn't have thoughts for that. She readied her mana, feeling the familiarity of it coursing through her body like an adrenaline rush. The cobbled ground was made entirely of stone and she could use that to her advantage. She could also feel the plant life that lived beneath the stone ground, where tangled and gnarled roots lay dormant.

Inkeri beckoned her forward with a taunting grin. Kolfinna had never faced an air elemental head-on, so she didn't know what to expect, but she wasn't going to allow Inkeri the first move again.

Kolfinna hurled a stone at her chest, but the other woman jumped out of the way, raising her hands as she did. Wind slashed the air like a lash, hurtling in Kolfinna's direction. Kolfinna rolled away, but the wind followed her and slashed against her chest. She staggered backward, pain snapping over her body. For a few seconds, she was brought back to that cabin in the woods with Hilda, a leather whip in her wrinkled hands.

That had been traumatizing. And this? It was close to that, and the thought alone made Kolfinna's blood run cold.

But this is wind, she told herself and dodged the next attack by raising stone barriers. She couldn't allow herself to crumble every time something reminded her of Hilda and the torture she had endured.

Wind and stone ground against the other; the pressurized

wind howled against the grating and groaning of stone, neither relenting. Kolfinna threw stone spears, made stone walls, and tossed chunks of stone at Inkeri, but the woman easily dodged and countered with her own air strikes. They circled each other, neither paying attention to the booms of lightning, the charred smell of burning material, the slaps of water, or the crackling of ice. Everyone had dispersed across the courtyard, giving each other space for their respective fights.

Inkeri sent a barrage of wind slashes at Kolfinna, but she had expected that. She stomped a foot on the ground, pulsing her mana into it. In seconds, the wind crashed on Kolfinna just as the ground beneath Inkeri's feet rippled and broke. Inkeri yelped as she lost balance, her hands coming up to protect her face.

They both fell at the same time. Kolfinna, with her hair ripped from its braid from the wind attacks, and Inkeri with her hands and knees pressed against the uneven ground. Both of them breathed heavily and watched the other with wide eyes.

Inkeri pushed a strand of hair out of her face. "I'd say that's a tie, for now."

"We could keep going." Kolfinna made to stand up, but her legs quivered and she plopped back down. The other fights were slowly reaching their resolutions as well. A soldier to her left was lying on the ground breathing heavily, his uniform drenched with water while the soldier across from him was laughing. Another soldier to her right was pinned to the ground by an Enhancer. In the distance, Kolfinna could see Herja fighting a female soldier. Fire sputtered from her hands and cloaked her in brilliant violet flames.

"We *could*." Inkeri stretched her arms and winced, her fingers going to the shoulder where Kolfinna had flung a particularly clunky piece of stone at her. "But we could also just rest for a few minutes."

Kolfinna wiped her sweaty hands on her thighs and nodded. Resting sounded wonderful right about now. Especially since she was gulping in heavy mouthfuls of air and her muscles were quaking so badly she was sure they would break off her bones just like her stone attacks had crumbled on impact.

"Who's the man at the front?" Kolfinna jerked her chin in the direction of the raven-haired man with the cloak made of glossy black feathers. He couldn't have been older than thirty, but he looked like a man who had seen hell and come back.

Inkeri followed her gaze. "That's Eluf Larrsen. He's a rank above us and manages morning practice for our lot."

"There are other lots?"

"Certainly. You didn't think this was all our forces, right?" She waved to the hundred or so soldiers sparring with each other.

"I didn't think too hard on it."

"There are about four hundred of us here," she said.

Four hundred. She had expected more soldiers to be manning the border, but maybe magic beasts didn't incur the same threat as a bordering country did.

"Why does he look so ..." Kolfinna struggled to find the word. Monotonous? Glum? Dark?

"He's always like that." She sipped her water. "His brother is the complete opposite."

"You know his brother?"

"He's a soldier with us. He's part of our group." Inkeri scanned the crowds. "He's somewhere out there. I wouldn't be surprised if he and Herja are duking it out right now. They're both knuckleheads."

"Herja was fighting a woman last I noticed." Kolfinna caught sight of the redhead almost immediately. It was hard to miss her with the fiery explosion surrounding her in violets and blues. The only other person Kolfinna knew who used such powerful flames was Fenris. Herja was still fighting the woman and, by the looks of it, she was winning. "There."

Inkeri followed her gaze. "Ah. She's fighting Brenda."

Brenda was also a fire elemental, and although her flames weren't as colorful or powerful compared to Herja's, she was still putting up a fight. Herja didn't have room to relax; they both exchanged blasts of fire, their movements quick and their chest rising and falling in rhythm to their magic.

"Then Gunnar must be somewhere else."

"Is Gunnar Eluf's brother?"

"Oh, yes. Sorry, I should've mentioned that."

Silence stretched between them.

"In case you didn't notice," Inkeri said, "people who are the same rank have to fight each other. Under normal circumstances, you can't spar with someone that's a different rank."

Kolfinna hadn't noticed that, but now that she mentioned it, each fighting pair had the same badge color. Grays against grays. Yellows against yellows. Purples against purples.

"That's why I chose to fight you," Inkeri continued. "I kind of wanted to see what level you're at."

"Ah. And what level is that?"

Inkeri shrugged. "I don't know for sure. Maybe a yellow?"

A few minutes passed as Kolfinna breathed in the crisp, early morning air before Eluf's voice rang out in the courtyard, commanding them to switch. Soon, everyone on her side of the courtyard began practicing mana control by themselves. Herja contained a giant fire, her forehead creased in concentration. Another soldier shot lightning up in the air in multiple successions. An ice elemental tried carving into his ice. Inkeri created pressurized air in the form of a ball; sweat dribbled down her forehead as she did it.

Kolfinna watched them all uncertainly. She had never practiced her mana manipulation like they were doing. She vaguely remembered Blár telling her that he had done something similar to what these soldiers were doing.

But before Kolfinna could figure out a way to do something similar, she spotted Joran waving at her. He stood a few feet away from her, the white badge on his breast pocket seeming out of place next to all the colorful ones surrounding them both. His dark gold hair was brushed neatly to the side, revealing his vibrant green eyes. They shifted from her to the other soldiers.

"Joran," she said with a hint of surprise. By the looks of his uncrumpled, unstained uniform, he hadn't been training with them. She was fairly certain he was the only "white rank" in this section of the fort.

He smiled hesitantly. "Kolfinna. I, um, hope you're doing well this morning."

"I'm all right." She wasn't sure if she should keep talking to him or practice something. Maybe she could carve the stones into a statue like the ice elemental soldier to her left was doing.

"Uh. So, uh, Lieutenant General Bernsten wants to see you. It's about—" He looked at the soldiers in the distance who were fighting each other, and his voice became smaller and something akin to fear reflected off his fae eyes. "It's about your rank assessment."

It must've been hard for him to be in a fortress full of humans who probably wouldn't have liked him if they knew who he really was, but Kolfinna didn't have any sympathy for him. Not when she was living his fear.

Still, they were comrades here. Even if the others didn't know it.

"Right now?"

He nodded.

Well, she might as well get this over with too.

5

JORAN LED KOLFINNA INSIDE THE FORT TO A WING opposite the barracks. They went deep in the center of the building and then down multiple flights of stairs. Their final destination, it seemed, was an open basement a quarter of the size of the courtyard she had just left. The room was made entirely of grayish-beige stone. It was smoothed over, but there were dents and chinks missing from the ceiling and the walls, revealing either a fight or someone who had practiced with stone magic.

Kolfinna spared a glance at Joran, but his attention was on Sijur, who sat in the back of the room, munching on a plate of biscuits. When he saw Kolfinna, he rose from his chair of disjointed rocks and brushed the crumbs off his hands.

Sijur waved them forward and then gestured to the room. "Impressive, isn't it? I had this built a few years back when I first found Joran. I just knew that we needed to have a facility where fae can train. What do you think?"

Kolfinna could feel the stones all around the room; there were at least twelve feet of stones beneath the floor, above the ceiling, and beyond the walls. However, it made her stomach clench to think about training here and accidentally having the entire ceiling collapse on them. Or breaking a hole that was too big on the wall and having earth and soil flood the room.

But her uneasiness might've been unfounded fears because surely Sijur had built this room to last? And surely, she was only afraid because she didn't like the idea of being trapped in a room so far underground.

Instead of showing her apprehension, she tapped the solid floor with the toes of her boots. "It *is* impressive. I just hope it's not connected to the foundation of the fort?"

"No, it isn't," Joran said. "This was built separately."

Sijur chuckled. "Yes, yes. And besides, this is a basement level training room, so whatever happens here shouldn't affect what happens"—he pointed to the ceiling—"up there. Other than tremors, shakes, or the like."

"It's perfect for training with stone magic," Kolfinna trailed. He must've been planning this for a while, she realized. Building a room perfect for fae to practice in? It also made her wonder what exactly his plans were for her, and if he planned on having more fae in his army.

"*Earth* magic." Sijur smiled. "You fae use earth magic."

"Earth magic?" She arched a brow.

"Yes, it's what you fae use. You call it stone magic, but earth magic is the correct word."

She wanted to roll her eyes. Give it to a human to tell a fae what their magic was called. But she didn't call him out for that or give him a snarky reply like she wanted to.

Her footsteps echoed and bounced across the wide room. "It's perfect for training with *earth* magic, but not with nature-based magic."

Sijur eased back into his chair and balanced the plate of biscuits on his lap. "Yes, that's true, but I would argue it's better for the fae to train with earth magic and rune magic since that's more reliable than nature."

"Nature is everywhere—"

"Yes, it's everywhere," he said impatiently, "but can you use it during winter?"

That shut her up.

Kolfinna had been practicing with trying to feel the thread of dormant life in plant matter during the winter, in order to manipulate nature, but she had thus far been unsuccessful. She could occasionally grasp the threads, but they had always slipped through her fingers just as quickly.

Joran fiddled with the cuff of his sleeve at the sudden tenseness in the room. "Historically, the enemies of the fae would attack during the winter since our powers are weakest during that time. King Harald won the last battle in the Last Fae War during the winter. If it hadn't been winter, some say the outcome could've been different."

"Yes, but the fae and the humans were fighting for a long time, so if not that winter, it would've just dragged on to another point. The humans would inevitably win because the fae, after centuries of dominance, grew too arrogant." Sijur shrugged like it wasn't a big deal—but to Kolfinna, it was a big deal. There was so little she knew about the actual history between the fae and the humans. So much of it had been erased or changed.

Sijur ate another biscuit while Kolfinna inspected the divots and grooves along the surface of the floor, walls, and ceiling.

"We'll be assessing your power level today," Sijur said after he finished his biscuits. He placed the plate not-so-carefully on the floor and crossed a leg over the other. "We'll determine which rank you are based on your mana manipulation, how strong your attacks are, that sort of thing."

Kolfinna rubbed her suddenly clammy hands on her thighs. At least now she would finally know what her true power rank was. If she had been asked two years ago, she would've said she was very much a purple rank or even higher, since she had defeated Lord Estur, who had been a purple rank. And if she had been asked that question right after her defeat with Blár, she would've said she was a gray rank. But now? She wasn't even sure. Probably a yellow?

Joran walked to the center of the room and lifted his hand above the floor. In seconds, a circular ball molded out of the floor; a small hole where he had created it from remained behind. He did the same five more times until six hand-sized balls were lined up a few feet apart from each other. Kolfinna hid her surprise: even she couldn't mold stones to be *that* perfectly round.

Joran stepped away from the balls. "Please raise up the first stone."

Easy.

It took her less than a second to wrap her mana around it, raise it up, and allow it to plop back down.

"The second one as well."

Also easy.

She did the same, eyebrows raised. If this was all the test entailed, she'd pass it easily.

Joran only nodded, while Sijur braced his elbows on his knees and watched with intrigue.

"All six at once, please."

Kolfinna did as she was told, lifting the stones off the floor and then letting them fall back down.

Joran exchanged a glance with Sijur and gave a nod before he raised a hand and all six of the balls fell back to their respective holes. In their place, six formless boulders groaned from the floor, rising up as Joran added more details to them and pushed more stone into their creation. It took less than a minute for six humanoid statues to appear where the six stone balls had been. The statues had faces, arms, legs, and even the vague outline of clothes. At the center of their chests, he had carved a circular target.

She didn't have that level of control over her stone magic. Seeing that should've shocked her, filled her with awe at Joran's secret abilities, but it only angered her. He was a powerful fae, but he was content with pretending he was a white rank? His abilities were definitely at a purple level.

She reminded herself that the path she had chosen was one of visibility and authenticity, but she still couldn't help the anger that burned below the surface. She had it harder than him and they couldn't even commiserate together because he was going to keep pretending to be human. He was taking the easy way out.

And maybe it frustrated her because she secretly wanted that too. Where she didn't have to fight for her position. Where she wasn't seen as a threat at all times. Where the people around her just saw her as a normal person.

Joran's voice brought her back to reality. "I want you to raise up a stone and hit the third statue from your right. Please try to hit the chest, on the target."

Kolfinna carved a piece of stone from the floor and launched it at the third statue. It struck the chest and crumbled on impact. A cloud of dust rose from the attack and when it settled, she was satisfied to see a small crack indented on the statue's chest.

If Joran was impressed, he didn't show it. "Please attack all six at the same time."

"With ... different stones, right?"

"Yes. Raise up six stones and attack the target at the same time."

This wouldn't be that easy.

Kolfinna created six stones, but she hesitated before flinging them at the statues. She would have to keep track of which stone went where. She usually only worked with one or two stones at a time. She could certainly throw all six at the same time, but hitting the target? She wasn't so confident about that.

"Well?" Sijur asked from his spot at the back of the room.

She focused her mana on each stone and flicked them at their respective targets. Her mana strained and the rocks smashed into the targets. Four hit the statues on the legs, arms, or head, while only two hit the target on the chest.

Not perfect, but better than she had thought she could do.

The fae male stared at the statues. "Try again."

She did, but this time, half hit the target, while the other half hit the statues in a different spot.

"Again."

He had her repeat it ten times. Each resulted in something similar: each time she only hit half the targets in the chest.

"Keep in mind where the targets are," Joran said. "Turn around and hit them without looking."

She faltered at those words. "You want me to ... hit them while I can't see them? From *behind*?"

"Correct."

Kolfinna gave the statues a good, hard look and spun on her heels. Sijur was staring directly at her, and she felt a bit awkward to be facing him—albeit a few dozen feet away. It was easier to focus when she didn't have those beady, black eyes watching her every move and the sly grin that spread across his face whenever she used her magic.

She didn't dislike Sijur, but there was something about him that made her uncomfortable. She couldn't exactly explain it either. It was the same when she had asked him to dance at the *Måneskin* ball. Something about him had always felt wrong.

Discarding those thoughts, she focused on the task at hand. She formed six stones on the floor by her feet and tried to remember the positioning of the statues behind her. Her mana pulsed at her fingertips and she lifted both hands toward the stones. Without wasting another second, she sent the stones behind her. One of the stones cracked loudly, while the others popped off in the distance, likely hitting the ceiling or the wall at the end of the room.

She tentatively glanced over her shoulder. One of the rocks had broken off the head of the statue, while the other five were imbedded in the wall and floor. Warmth slowly clawed up her neck and cheeks. That was embarrassing.

Joran dusted off his clothes with a frown. "Your aim is still not perfect."

"Do you think *you* could do better?" Kolfinna didn't mean to snap, but the words came out like a challenge.

His vivid green eyes—which reminded her of dewy grass in the morning sun, of emerald leaves rustling in warm summer air, of dense moss growing on the sides of trees and rocks—shuttered and he looked over at Sijur. "I can."

Sijur grinned like a wolf, a gleam of mischief and amusement glowing in his dark gaze. "Joran, why don't you show Kolfinna your abilities? I think it would be very eye-opening."

Joran bobbed his head while Kolfinna clenched her teeth tightly. Was this where he showed her that he was so much better than her? He didn't exude much confidence and he certainly didn't carry himself like he was better than her.

He raised up six perfectly round stones from the ground and with a single flick of his wrist, they zoomed at the targets. The impact of stone grinding against stone sent a cloud of dust to settle in the air, and the loud crack of the stones echoed in the room. All six of his stones were deeply implanted in the statues' chests. Spidery fissures had formed around the indent in the statues, spreading down to the arms and legs like a broken mirror.

Kolfinna's lips pursed together. So he was better than her. "I'm guessing you can do the same when you're not looking at them?"

Joran shifted on his feet, a sheepish grin on his face.

She didn't want to hear the answer to that. She sighed and waved at the statues. "Well, now what? Is there anything else I should do?"

"Um." His smile faded and he pointed to the space between them. "Can you create a stone ball and make it float?"

Make the stone ... *float*?"

Had she heard right? Float? Like keep it suspended in the air? Most of her attacks with her stones required her mana to force the stones at a rapid speed toward whatever she pointed them at, but keeping them afloat? She could do something *similar* to that—like when she would create her rock armor over her body and keep it in place by various threads of mana—but she couldn't make anything stay afloat. It didn't even make sense with her magic.

Joran must've seen the confused expression on her face because he wordlessly raised his hand, and two dozen rocks and pebbles rose from the floor, going higher and higher. They spun in the air and when he turned his finger, each faceted stone was pointed at her. They all remained there for five, ten, twenty seconds.

Kolfinna couldn't rip her gaze away. "How?"

"You use your mana to suspend them. Like ... when you control the stones, you use your mana to wrap them up, correct? With the same concept, bring them up but don't release your mana from it. At least not until you're ready to hit your target."

She had never seen anything like it before—but that wasn't saying much since most of the fae she had known throughout her life weren't that good at magic like she was, or they were too afraid to practice it. Most of what she knew about stone magic was something she had learned through trial and error, since Katla hadn't been proficient at it and couldn't teach her anything related to it.

But here was frightened, little Joran, able to manipulate the stones and figure out something like this.

"How did you learn that?" Kolfinna worked her mana into a nearby stone and pulled it up with a string of her mana, and instead of releasing her hold on it and launching it somewhere like she was used to, she held it in place. Beads of sweat formed on her forehead and her mana wavered under the strain of the small rock. After a few seconds, her mana slipped from the rock and it slammed to the floor. She released a shuddering breath.

Joran settled the stones gently on the floor—all twenty of them. She could only watch in awe.

"I learned through reading about it," he said and a small, shy smile curved his lips.

"You have *books* here?"

"Yes, we have books." Sijur chuckled at her stunned expression.

She would've rolled her eyes if she wasn't so excited. "Books about fae magic?"

"Yes," Joran said.

"We're close to the border of the Mistlands," Sijur explained. "You'd be surprised how many relics we've come across. Particularly fae ones. And you'll be able to read them too, you know, once you get to a certain level of proficiency with rune magic."

And once I trust you more, she could practically hear him say. But that didn't matter. She could learn so much from those books, and maybe she could even learn about fae history. About her people. And maybe ... even about the half-elf commander, Queen Aesileif, and how Kolfinna was related to all of that.

She subconsciously rubbed the rune mark on her wrist. At least being stuck here would have its advantages. She could reconnect with her roots. The thought alone sent a myriad of emotions exploding in her chest.

"Anyway." Sijur clapped his hands together and rose to his feet. He smiled and waved a delicate hand at the array of upturned rocks, dents, and holes throughout the room. "That was a very impressive display of power, Kolfinna. Most fae aren't as capable of you and I'm thoroughly *impressed*."

Kolfinna wiped her dusty hands on her thighs once more. It wasn't often that she wished she were wearing her white Royal Guards' gloves, but with how clammy her hands were, she would've loved to have them here. Even if they felt sticky and gross at the end of the day.

Her lips felt dry when she spoke. "What's my power rank?"

"A solid yellow," Sijur said.

A ... yellow.

Disappointment crashed down on her chest, rendering her speechless for a few moments. She had hoped she was at a purple level. So many of the people here were purple—Herja and many others who had surrounded her during the morning training.

And it would have also meant she was closer to Blár's level. She had foolishly thought ... that maybe she could get closer to him that way.

A silly thought, since he wasn't even here.

Sijur studied her carefully. "You're disappointed."

Of course she was disappointed. She had thought she was stronger than that. It was probably the arrogance speaking, telling her that she was stronger than she actually was. Stronger than a yellow rank. But maybe she had to humble herself because she had thought she was stronger than Joran, and he had clearly shown her that wasn't the case.

She didn't like how Sijur and Joran were scrutinizing her, as if waiting for an outburst of some sort. Did they really think she would start screaming, crying, or demanding they rate her higher?

"I'm disappointed." Her voice wavered. "But it just means I have to work harder."

Sijur placed a hand on her shoulder in reassurance. "You're strong, Kolfinna, there's no doubt about that. I have faith that you'll only grow stronger! Especially considering how the Royal Guards wouldn't let you practice your magic. I have no doubt that with Joran's training, you'll reach his level in no time."

Reach his level. She hated how that sounded.

She didn't want to reach Joran's level. She wanted to reach *Blár's* level.

But maybe that was a stupid thought to have.

"Joran will train me?" Kolfinna asked, glancing at the golden-haired young man.

"Yes. He'll teach you." Sijur picked up a lock of her white hair and ran his fingers over it. A shiver ran down her spine, and not the same kind of shiver she had felt when Blár did the same thing a few weeks ago.

Don't touch me. The words were at the tip of her tongue, but she instead stepped backward until her hair slipped form his hand and spun to look at Joran. "When do we start?"

"Tomorrow," Sijur said.

"Tomorrow." She nodded. "Great."

"Do ... Do keep in mind," Joran started, his words coming out quiet, like he wasn't confident in himself, "that we only assessed you based on your earth magic, not your ... um, rune magic or nature magic, so you could potentially be a purple rank."

"Ah, yes, I forgot to mention that." Sijur clapped his hands together, the sound resounding loudly in the quiet room. "We'll have another reassessment in the spring to determine your true rank based on your nature magic. I don't plan on testing your rune magic because being good at rune magic doesn't necessarily mean you'll be good at combat, and our rank system is based on combat."

A tiny sliver of hope sprang up at those words.

Maybe she was a purple rank after all.

"I'll also have you train your combat skills. From my understanding, the Royal Guards didn't teach you that much when it comes to swordplay and close combat, yes?"

She hesitated. "They taught me ... but their version of teaching basically meant mocking me and beating me until I couldn't move."

"Ah. So they didn't actually teach you how to fight, only how to get beaten."

Kolfinna winced. She wished that wasn't the truth.

"No matter." Sijur rubbed his hands together and Kolfinna didn't like the excitement that trembled off his tall frame. "We'll have you train and become the best fae fighter we have. You like Inkeri, yes? I'll have her be your teacher. She's mighty good at combat. Probably the best we have."

"But she's a yellow rank." Kolfinna had nothing against the young woman—she actually liked her—but wouldn't it have been more productive for her to learn from someone much better than her?

"Yes, her magic is lacking at the moment, but she makes up for it with her skills in fighting." His grin widened and something unreadable flashed in those dark eyes of his—something that made Kolfinna pause and stare.

The prospect of becoming stronger and more proficient in her magic was enticing, but she couldn't help but feel uneasy. It shouldn't have mattered to Sijur whether or not she became strong. She somehow got the feeling that he was personally invested in her abilities.

She shook that thought aside.

"Now that we have that settled ... Joran, why don't you show Kolfinna that interesting contraption you set up with runes in your room? I'm sure she'll appreciate it."

A contraption made with rune magic? That piqued her interest, even though she didn't want to go anywhere with Joran. Especially after he had outdone her with his magic.

Joran jumped but then quickly nodded. "Yes, sir."

"Kolfinna, later this evening, I want to see you and Joran."

"For what?"

"A private matter."

Kolfinna didn't like the sound of that, nor the smile he gave her.

6

The walk to Joran's room was uneventful. They went up several flights of stairs to leave the basement training room and then went to the right wing of the barracks and kept going up until they reached the sixth floor. Kolfinna's legs were jelly by the time they reached the last door down the hallway. Her entire body was sore and throbbing after the morning exercise, and after the assessment Joran and Sijur had given her, the majority of her mana was drained as well. She was bone-weary and walking up those flights of stairs had used up the last drop of energy she had left.

When Joran hesitantly unlocked his door and motioned her inside, she could hardly care about whatever contraption he supposedly had up here. The room was neat and orderly, with a single bed in the corner of the room, a nightstand beside it, and a desk across the room next to another door. Dozens of papers were strewn on the desk, some with splashes of color that she could see from the doorway, and others indistinguishable.

"Um, here we are," he said, walking deeper into the room.

Kolfinna stepped inside and glanced around herself. The room itself was the same size as her room, but Joran didn't seem to have any roommates, which made his room seem vaster. "You stay here alone?"

"Yes."

"That's not fair," she grumbled.

"I ... I've been working with the Lieutenant General for some time now ..."

"Still not fair." She walked over to his desk and picked up a paper with a rough sketch of a woman drawn on it. Delicate gray lines filled her dark hair, and her eyes seemed to smile even through the drawing. It looked semi-realistic but with a subtle artistic touch. "This is beautiful," she murmured. "Is this someone you know?"

"Knew."

Kolfinna looked at him. He was sitting on the bed, his wide eyes searching her face and his cheeks slightly red. Embarrassment? Or something else?

Kolfinna lowered the paper. "Someone you knew?"

"She's dead."

"Oh."

There were several other sketches on the table. Some were colored, but most weren't. Horses, men, women, buildings—there was nothing consistent about his drawing, but the style was artistic in a way that made her smile. The Royal Guards probably wouldn't be a fan of it, she could imagine, with their fancy landscape drawings and boring portraits.

"These are amazing." She picked up a flimsy drawing of a gray cat with glaring green eyes and held it up for him. "You're really talented."

His cheeks further reddened. "Thank you."

Kolfinna dropped the sketches on his desk and rubbed the nape of her neck. As much as she enjoyed looking at these sketches, she would rather get to business. It didn't help that Joran's blushing made her uncomfortable. "So ..." she started. "What did you want to show me?"

He rose to his feet and crossed the distance to the other door in the room. "It's in here," he said as he turned the metal door-knob. He paused and turned to her hesitantly. "Um, please don't tell anyone about this. I'd rather keep it ..."

"A secret."

He nodded.

His constant submissiveness and quiet nature were still grating on her nerves, and she opened her mouth to ask him if he had any plans of revealing his identity as a fae, but she was silenced when he threw the door open. The room was ... plain. Anticlimactically plain.

A mirror took up one side of the small room, covering the entire expanse of that wall, and beside it was a small stool with glass jars and bottles. The floors slanted downward to the center of the room almost unnoticeably, and there were tiny holes in the ceramic tiles. The ceiling had similar holes clustered near the center. Drains? Or maybe something else?

It was then that she noticed the runes etched onto one of the walls. She ventured closer to it. *Hot. Warm. Cold.*

Kolfinna turned to Joran, who remained in the doorway. "What is this?"

"It's ... um, hard to explain. I made this so it's easy to take a bath. Except, you're not taking a bath, it's more like a ... shower of rain?" He quickly pointed to the ceiling and then to the runes. "I constructed it so that it connects to the water supply of the fort and those runes control the water temperature. There's ... a lot that goes into the construction of the pipes and adding runes to make it a continuous cycle of water when running ... Anyway, it makes it so that it's quick and efficient to clean yourself. It's run with magic."

She blinked, unable to wrap her mind around it. "You ... made this?"

"I got the idea from a book," he said quickly, waving his hands. "I'm not smart enough to come up with something like this on my own. Apparently, the ancient fae used contraptions like this and similar other inventions to make their lives easier.

When the humans took this country back, they destroyed those inventions because they couldn't use them without the use of rune magic, rendering them useless to the humans ... Unless they kept some of the fae around, which some nobles did, but the inventions themselves eventually died off because there was no one to make them and humans—" He clamped his mouth shut and then cleared his throat. "A-Anyway, yes, I made this."

"How do you turn it on?"

"You supply your mana into the rune." Joran pointed to the three runes on the wall. "And when you want to turn it off, you touch that rune." He entered the room and placed a hand on the adjacent wall, where she hadn't even noticed a rune that read *halt*.

The cramped room made her suddenly aware of just how close he was to her, close enough that she could smell pine needles and summer air. In the reflection of the mirror, her pink eyes appeared vibrant against the clash of her white-and-black hair. Next to her, he appeared more fae-like. His green eyes were more vivid and even his burnt gold hair appeared more vibrant. More otherworldly.

He was beautiful, like sunshine.

But that was only his appearance. His personality reminded her of clouds trying to cloak the sunshine.

"Um." Joran coughed. "You're free to use it. I'll be in my room."

"Oh, I don't know—" she started, but the thought of trying out a device that her ancestors had used was too tempting, so she shut her mouth and inspected the walls and the ceilings. It wasn't often that she would get a chance like this. She vaguely remembered Revna mentioning that fae civilization was more advanced than humans could ever be and that rune magic had been prevalent throughout her time.

"I'd like it if you tried it," he said. "I ... I would love to get your input on it, or if there's anything I can add to improve it."

She hid her enthusiasm by jamming her thumbs in the pockets of her pants. "Um, sure. Thank you."

"The soaps are there." Joran pointed to the stool with a set of colorful jars of different substances sitting on its warped, wooden surface. "I'll be in my room if you need me."

He backtracked, his eyes darting from her face, to her figure, to the rest of the room before he quietly shut the door.

Once she was alone, Kolfinna carefully stripped her sweat-drenched clothes off her body and tossed them on the floor. When she was completely naked and her hair was wrenched free from its braid, she placed a hand on the *warm* rune and sent a wave of mana into it. A spray of water rained down on her in seconds. She gasped at the unexpectedness of it, but her muscles slowly eased themselves as the warm water rushed over her hair, her sticky skin, and her face.

Her quivering muscles relaxed, the cuts and scrapes and bruises stopped throbbing, and her hair felt less weighed down with sweat and grime. She wanted to fall into a puddle on the floor.

Five minutes must've passed while she just stood under the torrent of water before she tried to find the soap. Joran, apparently, wasn't like a normal person who had a single bar of soap. He had jars of different-colored liquids; some were pink, others dark purple, and one that was strangely a murky swamp color. The pink one smelled like roses, the purple like lavender, and the third she wasn't even sure what it was, but it smelled pleasant too. Like citrus and moss.

Kolfinna poured the pink liquid into her palms and rubbed her hands together until there was a thick, sudsy layer on her hands. She lathered herself with it, slowly working it through her hair and then the rest of her body. She scrubbed at the cuts and scrapes along her body, at the debris and dust that had collected in her hair, at the rough patches of her skin—she polished herself until she was spotless.

When she finished, she placed her hand on the *halt* rune. The water instantly stopped when she activated the rune with her mana. The mirror was cloudy with condensation and without the warmth of the water, Kolfinna shivered.

Placing a hand on the mirror, she wiped at the steamy reflection, her pink eyes bright and her white-black hair soppy against her damp skin. She hesitantly turned her back to the mirror and twisted over her shoulder to glance at her back. Like she had suspected, something was wrong with the scars. Where there should've been two large, thick white scars on her upper back beside her spine in two identical cuts, the scars were raised and a blotchy red color, as if she had recently had her wings snipped.

What the hell?

That explained why her back was itchy but nothing else.

Was this ... normal? She truly didn't know anything anymore.

Even though the sight unsettled her, there was nothing she could really do about it but gawk and wait to see what would happen. Kolfinna looked away from the scars and searched for a towel.

She scanned the room, but it was bare of anything other than the jars of soap.

Kolfinna tentatively walked to the door and splayed her fingers against the fine wood, which had peeled and cracked at the corners, no doubt due to the water. "Um, Joran?"

Silence.

"Joran?"

Still, silence.

"Joran, I really need a towel."

When she was met with silence once more, Kolfinna carefully twisted the doorknob and poked her head through the opening. Joran was nowhere to be seen. A neatly folded white towel sat on his bed. She cursed softly to herself. Did he leave the room to give her privacy? Or was he hiding somewhere, waiting to ambush her?

The latter thought made her roll her eyes. There was no reason for Joran to attack her. Being with the Royal Guards and living her whole life in fear made those ridiculous thoughts like second nature.

"Joran?" She pried the door open a bit wider.

When it was clear that he wasn't in the room, Kolfinna padded toward the bed. Water dripped down her wet body and a chill swept over her figure. Her hands stretched out to grab the towel and—

Someone gasped.

Kolfinna turned to the suddenly open doorway, where Joran stood. He must've just opened the door, she realized. It all happened in a split second. His eyes were wide and they were trained on her sopping body. At the curves of her bare breasts and then ... they traveled down.

Kolfinna screamed something unintelligible, grabbed the towel, and quickly wrapped it around her body. Joran's eyes widened even further and his mouth fell open.

"J-Joran!" she said, tightening the plush material over her chest. She stumbled back, face aflame. "W-What the hell? *Get out!*"

"S-S-Sorry!" Joran's face had turned beet red, but he didn't rip his gaze away from her. The sensible, polite thing to do was to look away and leave the room. But he was rooted in place and he didn't make any move to leave. He was either too shocked or he didn't want to leave. Regardless, Kolfinna wanted him *out*.

"You could've knocked—" she started.

"I didn't know! I just went to the bathroom—"

"L-Leave!"

"S-Sorry!" She finally noticed the bundle of gray clothes in his arms, which he quickly placed on the floor. "I'll just leave this here," he said, his ears a deep shade of scarlet. "It's an extra uniform."

Without another word, he shut the door behind him. Kolfinna's heart hammered in her chest loudly, the blood rushing to her face. He had seen her *naked*.

She had never felt so mortified. Especially since he had kept staring.

Her heart kept racing, but not in the way that reminded her of butterflies fluttering in the pit of her stomach, but the sick type of heart palpitations. The type that happened right before a fight or right before facing danger. She hated that he had seen her in such a vulnerable position.

No one had seen her butt naked like that, and the first person to see her was ... *Joran*? Joran of all people?

It was a mistake, she told herself as she jammed her legs into the pants of the uniform. There was no way he had done that on purpose, and truthfully, she should've thought twice about trekking through his room. She should've waited for him to come back. She should've taken longer in the bathing room. She cursed herself and then cursed him. He should've knocked. He should've left as soon as he saw her. He should've ... He should've been more careful!

Once dressed, she reluctantly opened his door to find him pacing the corridor, his face still the same red it had been minutes ago. When he saw her, he stared down at his boots.

"Sorry about that," he whispered.

"Let's pretend it didn't happen." Kolfinna winced at the harshness of her tone, while he flinched. A mistake, she told herself. She softened her tone. "Err, I'll see you later then."

"I'll fetch you after dinner ..." Joran chewed on his lower lip.

Kolfinna nodded, keen on finishing their conversation. "Great, I'll see you then." When he opened his mouth to speak, she added, "No need to escort me. I'll go to my room by myself."

"O-Okay—"

She was already heading down the hallway. She had no plans of spending more than a few seconds alone with him.

Kolfinna had expected Sijur's office to be militaristic but still bedecked in luxury, like with glass chandeliers and intricate paintings of battlefields hanging on the wall, and swords and various weaponry on display. It was what she imagined for the son of the most powerful man in the country. But instead of violent war art and gilded furniture, his walls were full of bookshelves jampacked with books, there were two velvet couches across a snug fireplace, and the room had the woody vanilla scent of old books.

Sijur sat behind his desk, riffling through a thick, yellow-paged book. When he saw Joran and Kolfinna, he rose from his seat. "Come in, come in! Kolfinna, I'm hoping your mana replenished during the time you've been resting?"

"A bit." Between the embarrassing bath scene, curling up on her bed in mortification, and having dinner, her mana had refilled itself to the point that she wasn't nearly dried out, but the day's exhaustion still persisted.

"Good. Good." He rounded his desk and came to stand in front of them both. "How are you feeling in terms of your magic?"

"I'm okay." She could feel Joran burning holes into the side of her face. She hadn't spoken to him since the bath incident and all he had done was stare at her and wait for her to speak first.

"Do you feel confident in your abilities?"

She had such a strange relationship with her confidence; sometimes it was high, sometimes it was low, but it was mostly all over the place. "I feel all right. I think I'm stronger than most fae."

"What about your rune magic?"

"I think I'm pretty good at it," Kolfinna said truthfully. She still had a long way to go, but she didn't think she was terrible, and the last few times she had used rune magic had good results.

"Good, good." He clapped her shoulder. "That's just what I want to hear."

Kolfinna absentmindedly touched the rune mark on her wrist. At least Sijur seemed interested in how she was doing at the fort. The two days that she was here, he had shown more compassion about her situation than Fenris did the entire five months she was with the Royal Guards.

Despite that ... she hadn't felt uneasy with Fenris like she did with Sijur, and she could still hear Fenris's warning in the back of her mind.

Fenris also wasn't this touchy-touchy, which she had been grateful for.

Sijur removed his hand from her shoulder, as if sensing her discomfort, and strolled over to his desk. He leaned against the edge of it and folded his arms over his chest. "I forgot to ask this earlier today, but how is your arm doing?"

"My arm?"

"Yes, your arm," Sijur said slowly, his gaze flicking to Joran and then back at her. "Didn't you injure it yesterday?"

Right—the fight with Bjarni, where he had thrown a knife at her forearm, and how it had subsequently healed.

"Oh, that! I'm fine," she said with a dismissive wave. "It was just a scratch! It looked worse than it actually was. I'm fine, really." Kolfinna pushed a strand of hair behind her ear and tried to appear nonchalant, but she was sure she was failing as the two men looked at her with raised brows. "A-Anyway, what did you need from me?"

Kolfinna really, *really* hoped Joran hadn't noticed that her arm was completely healed when he saw her naked. Hopefully— and she couldn't believe she was even thinking it—he had been too focused on her breasts to notice her arm.

"Right, let's get to business, then." Sijur jutted his chin toward the door. "Joran, can you please bring the woman inside?"

Joran's spine went rigid and for a moment, panic flashed over his face momentarily. It was so short of a second that Kolfinna almost thought she imaged it. But the stiffness of his posture as he jerkily went to the door told her she wasn't imaging things. He appeared ... scared, almost? Uncomfortable?

Kolfinna shifted on her feet and the polished, wooden planks squeaked with the motion.

"So," she said, "who is Joran bringing?"

"You'll see."

Sijur stared out the window overlooking the courtyard below.

The distant sound of someone screaming jolted Kolfinna to stand straighter. She opened her mouth to say something, but Sijur appeared unfazed and was picking at something beneath his nail. Completely unperturbed.

Strange. Had she heard wrong?

But then she heard it again, louder this time, like it was growing *closer*.

As the seconds ticked by, the screaming continued. A wave of goose bumps rose along her flesh, making the hairs on her arms and the back of her neck stand straight. Still, Sijur appeared calm and unbothered.

She couldn't take it anymore. "Don't you hear that?"

"Hm?"

"The screaming."

He gave her a strange look. "What screaming?"

"I ... Never mind."

More minutes ticked by, and this time, the screaming grew even louder. Sijur clucked his tongue and grinned. "Ah, *that* screaming."

"You can hear it?" Kolfinna wasn't sure if she should feel relieved that he could hear it because it was too bizarre in the first place.

"Oh, I certainly hear it now." Sijur pushed himself off the desk, but still, he appeared unsurprised.

The office door burst open and Kolfinna nearly jumped in shock as Joran wrangled a blond woman inside, his grip on her forearm leaving pale indents whenever his hands slipped. The woman tried wrenching away, tears and snot streaming down her dirt-streaked face.

"Please, please! I beg of you—" the woman pleaded as Joran released her at Sijur's feet.

She wore a thin, ragged dress that showed off her bony, dirty body. The skin on her wrists was peeling, red, and chafed from what must've been tight ropes. Her hair fell over her shoulders in greasy tendrils and her eyes—they were hollowed and wild, like a desperate, cornered, starved animal.

Kolfinna's mouth went dry and she suddenly couldn't move.

The woman latched onto Sijur's legs with broken, bloodied nails. "Please, I beg of you, I won't do it again—"

"Now, now, Olia, you should know better than to beg like that." Sijur smiled down at her thinly, unaffected by her tears or the desperation in her voice.

Kolfinna turned to Joran to see his reaction, but his gaze was downcast and he was fiddling with the cuff of his sleeve. A typical Joran behavior, she was soon finding out.

This had to be a joke. Maybe it was a test? To see how Kolfinna would react? Because there was no other explanation why someone was in this state in front of them. Unless she was a criminal? Unless she had done something heinous? Unless ...?

The woman, Olia, cried and beseeched some more, while Sijur tutted his tongue and spoke to her casually, like he was scolding a child. As if she wasn't a clearly emaciated prisoner begging for her freedom. Kolfinna stood still, waiting for something to happen, but when the begging continued, she couldn't stop herself anymore.

"Lieutenant General, what the hell is going on?" Her voice betrayed the confusion and horror she was feeling. The woman turned to her, as if seeing her for the first time. "Who is this woman and why—"

"Please, help!" The woman crawled to Kolfinna and grasped her legs, her dirtied hands leaving smudges of blood and grime against Kolfinna's pants. "Please help. I won't steal again! I promise! I was hungry—"

"Olia." There was a warning in Sijur's tone.

Tears filled the woman's eyes. "*Please.*"

Kolfinna couldn't move. Couldn't breathe.

The office suddenly felt too small. The smell of defecation, urine, vomit, and blood was too strong. The desperation, the crack in the woman's voice, the tears—it reminded her too much of her time with Hilda, stuck in a windowless room full of torture. Kolfinna's stomach continued to twist and churn. Her vision tunneled, everything blurring except for the woman—the ragged clothes hanging off her wire-thin shoulders, her brittle hair, the faint yellowish bruises over her neck.

Sijur grabbed the woman by the shoulder and yanked her backward until she fell in a heap on the floor. He grimaced at his hand and wiped it against his thigh distractedly. "Anyway, let's get to business, yes?"

"Business?" Kolfinna's voice was barely a whisper. Her stomach was so knotted she was sure she'd vomit right then and there. Her mana begged to flare to the surface, but she also wanted to run away as far as possible. Away from the tragic woman who looked too similar to how Kolfinna did just mere weeks ago.

"Yes, business."

"No, please—" Olia sobbed.

"*Olia.*" The smile on Sijur's face disappeared and was replaced with a stern, firm-lipped expression.

The woman covered her mouth. Her silent sobs wracked her weak shoulders.

Kolfinna swallowed down the bile clawing up her throat. *Breathe,* she told herself.

"What business are you talking about?" Kolfinna said through clenched teeth.

Sijur tapped his wrist and clucked his tongue. "Come now, Kolfinna, you didn't expect that you would do nothing here?"

She followed his gaze to the crescent moon rune on her wrist. "I ... I don't understand?"

"We'll be putting your powers to use here." He motioned to

Joran and then leaned against the edge of his table. "You both are fae with powerful rune magic. We'll be putting those abilities to the test."

Testing her abilities? To do *what*?

Kolfinna looked between the withered woman and Sijur. From the corner of her eye, she could see Joran was still fussing with his clothes. When no one supplied an explanation, she whispered, "What does that mean?"

Sijur sighed, long and hard.

"*Kolfinna*"—there was almost a scolding tone in his voice, like he was explaining things to a small child who didn't understand a simple task—"I need you to test your rune magic and see how far runes truly go."

When she didn't say anything, he continued, "Don't you ever wonder what society was like before the humans defeated the fae and killed them to near extinction? I've had Joran decipher old books and we've learned so much over the past few years. So much development that could advance our society." Sijur's voice quickened in excitement and he stalked forward, his hands waving around animatedly. "The fae had made drastic developments in engineering that make our systems look rudimentary! They had bathtubs that filled themselves even though they weren't water elementals! They had stoves that would create fires without a fire elemental, without flint and fire steel! They had prisons that were inescapable! Items that rendered people magicless! So many inventions that are lost and artifacts now. So many methods that are lost to us."

The last part came out with a hint of sadness.

Kolfinna's palms grew clammy. It was information she had already known. Information she had gleaned from the Eventyrslot ruins, from Revna. "And?"

He dragged his finger across the worn leather of one of his books. "Queen Aesileif had many rune-marked slaves that would do her bidding."

Rune-marked slaves.

Kolfinna inadvertently traced the mark on her wrist. "Why ..." Her throat closed up and she couldn't rip her gaze away from the weeping, terrified woman. "Why are you telling me this?"

"Kolfinna." This time it was Joran. His voice was small and hoarse, and he continued to stare at the dark, hardwood floors. "She's not a good woman."

Kolfinna laughed bitterly. "And so what? That gives us the excuse to ... to *enslave* her? With *runes*? Is that what you're getting at here?"

This had to be a joke. A sick, sick joke.

But neither Sijur nor Joran said anything. Only stared at her like *she* was the ridiculous one.

"Is that ... Is that really what we're going to do?" Kolfinna clenched and unclenched her fists. "We're going to enslave her? To who? *You*?" She jerked an accusing finger at Sijur. "Is that why you wanted me in your army? So that I can join you and Joran in enslaving other people? What the hell are you thinking?!"

Sijur sighed and dragged a hand over his face. "Kolfinna, calm yourself—"

"I am calm!" She placed a steady hand on her chest. "I'm calm as can be, but this is just so ... so offensive to me and to the fae and to our abilities. We are not all heartless enough to enslave someone against their will with runes! And I'm shocked that you would even think about that! Or that you"—she sent a daggered glare to Joran, who flinched—"would be willing to do such a thing!"

"Kolfinna—" Joran squeaked.

"No! It's not right—" she started.

"Don't you want the advancement of fae society?" Sijur asked with raised brows. "Don't you want the fae to live in our society, side by side with humans and to be treated equally? That's what I'm aiming for. That's what I'm fighting for. The fae have such extraordinary abilities that it would be a waste to let them die! People are so naïve to not see the fae as assets. As *allies*. Kolfinna, you'll have to dirty your hands if you want to create a better world for yourself, your people, and your future children."

"And how will enslaving this woman"—she thrust a hand in the woman's direction—"accomplish that?"

"It's the first step in making the nation realize your worth. In the worth of *befriending* the fae."

Kolfinna couldn't believe him. "And you think *you* can single-handedly change society? And that I will be a proponent in that so long as I listen to you?"

"I'm the son of the commander-in-chief. I can change many things, like that trial you had. Do you really think, under normal circumstances, you would've been able to survive that without me? Certainly not." He smiled coldly. "But change needs to be small and gradual. Once people start seeing that the fae are allies and are useful, they'll start accepting them more."

Suddenly, she wasn't in front of Sijur and Joran and the crying woman. She was in front of Revna, saying the same thing. Telling Kolfinna that if she followed her, they would be making a better world for the fae. That all it would require was to dirty their hands. To push other people beneath them. And if Kolfinna didn't agree, she was then against the fae.

Her blood boiled in her veins, her breaths coming out shallow with barely controlled rage. "You want to use the fae for your own selfish desires. Enslaving people does nothing but benefit you!"

She could imagine Sijur with hundreds of rune-marked humans and fae alike, completely bound to his will.

"Now, now, Kolfinna. You're jumping to conclusions." The air around Sijur was still calm and collected, and that further infuriated her. "I'm doing what's best for our society. These people —" He gestured to Olia. "These people are not benefiting society in any way, so wouldn't it be better to see what they can do for us? To use them to test the runes? What's the harm in learning more about your abilities? About the extent of runes?"

"The harm?" Kolfinna laughed mirthlessly. "The harm is right in front of you!"

He made an incoherent sound. "Kolfinna! You're still a child, I see, with a childish mentality. You don't seem to understand that we adults sometimes have to muddy our hands for a brighter future."

"Don't patronize me," she snarled.

"This is just to test out what your abilities are made for. That's it." Sijur lifted his shoulders.

It wouldn't stop here, would it? He was a soldier. A top official in the military. He would certainly use any chance he could to enslave people under him. How many more rune slaves did he want to make?

Maybe it was something the fae did in the past, but that didn't mean she wanted to be the reason someone was bound to Sijur.

"I'm not going to do it," she said firmly.

Joran stiffened while Sijur's eyes narrowed. The woman had stopped crying and was watching the exchange with wide, teary eyes.

"Kolfinna." There was a warning in Sijur's voice.

"I'm not going to. This goes against what I believe in." Kolfinna broadened her stance. She wasn't going to be the cause of any injustice. It was the same reason she didn't want to join Ragnarök—she didn't want to enslave the humans beneath the fae. She didn't want to oppress anyone.

Joran tried to tell her something with his eyes, but she couldn't read them. She didn't really have to, to understand that he was on Sijur's side.

Sijur exhaled loudly—almost dramatically. Like he was bone-weary. Like Kolfinna was a child dragging her feet around him.

She hated the way he appeared so dismissive and annoyed with her.

Suddenly, Fenris's warning whispered again in the back of her mind. *"Do not trust that man."*

He had been right, but she hadn't realized the scale of Sijur's ambition and Kolfinna's role in it.

"Kolfinna." Gone were the smiles and the frivolities. "You will do as I say. Now, take the woman by her hand and put this rune on her. The rune will say—"

"No—" Kolfinna began.

She couldn't even finish her sentence before a jolt of fire ran up her wrist to her chest. The sheering, blistering pain pushed her to her knees, her hands clutching her chest and her breath stolen from her lungs. She couldn't breathe, couldn't speak, couldn't see beyond the blackness of her vision, beyond the crippling white-hot pain searing her entire body.

Kolfinna tried breathing, tried lessening the burden of fire coursing through her veins, tried to see Sijur's disappointed expression, but it was difficult to keep her eyes open. Difficult to say anything beyond the silent scream dying on her lips.

Breathe, breathe—

It was so hot. So unbearably hot.

Like she had jumped into a fire. Like she was being shocked by dozens of lightning strikes.

Breathe! Breathe!

Beyond the pain, someone grabbed her shoulder. She peeled her eyes open to find Joran's wide eyes staring at her. His mouth was moving, but the words didn't register to her.

Tears filled her eyes. She wanted it to stop. She needed it to stop.

Minutes passed. The pain intensified, but at the same time, the world was starting to become clearer. Her blurry vision was righting itself.

She needed to focus on how to stop it.

Focus—

"—just listen!" Joran's voice penetrated through the pain. "Listen to what he says!"

Her rune burned hotter and hotter. She looked at Sijur. At the dissatisfied, apathetic look on his face. And then at the woman, who was cowering by his office desk, her threadbare skirts barely concealing her bruised ankles. And then at the rune glowing on Kolfinna's wrist.

Kolfinna would die if this kept up, she realized.

When she had sealed her fate with this rune, she hadn't realized what she had signed up for. At this very moment, she was bound to Sijur's will. What had he told her when they made the deal? That she didn't want to find out what would happen if she disobeyed?

This was what he had meant.

"Kolfinna, pick yourself up," Sijur said. "And then you'll stop feeling the pain."

Kolfinna tried climbing to her feet, her thighs and ankles giving in to the floor, but Joran wrenched her up by the elbow. Almost instantly, the pain ebbed away. She trembled in relief as the violent magic released its hold on her, as the rune on her wrist stopped its oppressive, pulsing punishment. Tears streaked down her cheeks and she made no move to wipe them away.

Sijur braced his hands behind himself on the edge of his table and watched her with half-lidded, snake-like eyes she wanted to gouge out. "Kolfinna," he spoke softly. "Stand tall and grab Olia's arm."

"No."

Again, a white-hot pain overtook her body and she doubled over on the floor. A scream ripped from her throat and she couldn't see or hear anything past her own pain. Before she knew it, Joran yanked her back to her feet and the dizzying pain slowly receded.

Her vision was dark, but she could make out Sijur's disappointed expression.

"Kolfinna," Sijur said again. "Grab Olia's arm."

"No," Kolfinna gritted out.

She fell back to her knees as fire roared from her skin, the rune burning her. Twenty minutes must've passed with the same enactment: Sijur would tell her to grab Olia, she would refuse and be in excruciating pain, and then Joran would pull her out of it. But by the sixth time, she couldn't stop trembling.

It was too painful.

Sijur must've realized that something broke in her—her tolerance for pain, maybe—because the corners of his mouth rose into a sharp, victorious smile. "Kolfinna, grab Olia."

For a moment, she didn't want to move, but the phantom pain sizzled beneath her skin and she walked rigidly to the woman. Shame and guilt ate at the core of her being, but she couldn't stop from putting one foot in front of the other.

Olia scooted away and shook her head. "No—"

"I'm sorry," Kolfinna whispered through stinging eyes. She gently grasped her by the bicep, while the weak woman tried to tug away, her shouts falling on deaf ears. Kolfinna wanted to stop and cry herself, but her body moved on its own.

She hated Sijur with all her being. How dare he force her into this? How dare he?

But she also hated herself for being a part of this. For not being strong enough to stop herself.

Olia squirmed on her feet, crying and screaming and trying to jerk away, but Kolfinna held her in a tight grip. Joran joined Kolfinna and grabbed Olia's other arm. He didn't look as defeated as Kolfinna did, but the hardness in his mouth told her he wasn't enjoying this either.

Sijur clapped his hands together, smiling. "Perfect. Now, Kolfinna, I want you to place a rune on Olia that says she must obey my will and never disobey me."

Kolfinna hesitated. She couldn't do this—

Sijur's frozen smile made her flinch.

She didn't have a choice, she told herself.

"Where—" Kolfinna croaked. "Where should I put it?"

"Anywhere. It doesn't matter."

Kolfinna gently grabbed Olia's thin wrist. The woman had stopped fighting and was now staring at her with bleak, teary, and defeated eyes. It haunted Kolfinna—the black depths of despair in her gaze.

Mana flared beneath Kolfinna's fingers and she closed her eyes. *Olia will obey Sijur's will and never disobey him.* Just thinking the words made her stomach flip. She wanted so badly to run away from all of this. If only she hadn't involved herself with Sijur. If only—

Her magic pulsed at her fingers. She normally loved the feeling of her mana bubbling beneath her skin, ready to be used, but now it felt traitorous. It felt wrong.

She opened her eyes, but no runes were etched onto the woman's dirty, peeling, raw skin. She tried again, forcing her mana into the woman, but again, no golden runes bloomed beneath her grasp.

"It's not working," she said, unable to hide the relief in her voice.

Sijur's smile fell. "That's very unfortunate. Joran, try to help Kolfinna."

Joran tentatively reached for Kolfinna's free hand. "I'll try to channel my mana to you."

Kolfinna only nodded. He slipped his hand into hers, his fingers lacing through with hers. His hand was soft and uncalloused, so unlike Blár's rough and scarred hand, which showed years of training. Kolfinna closed her eyes and focused on the rune again.

Joran's mana prodded at her hand, as if requesting for Kolfinna to take it. It was such a foreign feeling, so unlike when Kolfinna had dipped her fingers into Blár's expansive cold mana. Back then, she had been the one to search for it and take what she wanted. But here, Joran was offering it to her and moving it toward her. He was a fae, so it was only natural that he could move his mana in such a way, but it still unsettled her. Like something was crawling under her skin.

She allowed his mana to enter her stream, even as a small voice in the back of her mind told her that opening such a channel would allow him to do the same—to steal her mana.

She silenced that voice.

Joran's mana was nowhere near as large as Blár's, but unlike Blár's, whose mana had been like winter itself, frigid and violent, Joran's was full of warmth, like standing under sunlight. Like feeling the trees whispering above her head. Like bathing in warmth.

She didn't like it at all.

Kolfinna pulled at his mana and focused on Olia's arm. On formulating the runes.

Olia will obey Sijur's will and never disobey him.

The rune didn't appear.

She tried again, tugging at Joran's mana once more. She added her own mana to it, and tried again.

Nothing.

And again.

Still nothing.

"It's not working," Kolfinna whispered.

Sijur's lips pressed together in displeasure as he looked between her and Joran. "Truly?"

"Yes," Joran said with a wince. "We used both of our mana, but it didn't work."

Sijur rubbed his clean-shaven jaw thoughtfully. "Hm. I wonder if it's a matter of the strength of your rune capabilities or the fact that she's human? No, that can't be. The last fae queen had many human rune-marked slaves. It must be that you both are not strong enough." He shook his head, sighing. "Well, we'll have to do more research, Joran. In the meantime, you both need to become even stronger."

The pit in Kolfinna's stomach ripped open wider and wider like a gaping wound stretching painfully. She knew Sijur would never let this go and eventually, she and Joran would succeed in binding someone to him. If he was correct and that all they needed was to become stronger, then it would definitely happen. And when it did—Kolfinna would be complicit in someone's oppression. She would be the one shackling someone to Sijur's will—or her rune magic would kill them if they disobeyed.

She couldn't look at any of them—not the sunken woman on the floor, not Sijur and his determined resignation, not passive

Joran. She felt sick to her core. Everything she knew about herself felt like a lie.

She had thought she was stronger than this.

She had thought she was smarter than to have her hands tied behind her back.

She had thought she was *better* than this.

"Kolfinna?" Joran touched Kolfinna's elbow lightly and jolted her back to reality.

His vibrant forest-like eyes were trained on her, hints of worry coloring the threads of gold in his gaze. It disgusted her that he was apprehensive about her when he was a part of all this. He followed Sijur. He hid the fact that he was fae from everyone. Meanwhile, he participated in this sick experiment.

Sijur slumped in his chair and flicked through the papers strewed on his desk. He no longer seemed interested in the three of them. "Both of you are dismissed."

Kolfinna turned to leave but then stopped mid-stride. "What about ... her?"

"Don't concern yourself with that. Go." He waved them away with the paper in his hand. "Both of you."

When they both left the room and the door clicked shut behind them, Joran turned to Kolfinna. "Are you okay?"

Was she okay?

She would never be the same again.

She stiffened as a half-sob escaped the room behind them. It was a reminder that Sijur was a monster in disguise. That he had ulterior motives. That he was going to use Kolfinna for *fifteen years*.

Kolfinna pushed past Joran and didn't bother to answer him. Not when he jogged after her and tried to speak again, and not when he tried grabbing her arm once more.

"Don't talk to me," she hissed when he touched her shoulder. "I'm so incredibly ashamed to be next to you right now."

"Ashamed?" The dim lighting of the hallway they were in warped with the flickering flames in the wall sconces, casting shadows over his stricken expression. "Why would you be ashamed?"

Kolfinna's voice rose in volume. "You didn't even care that he—"

"We don't have a choice," he said quickly, glancing around themselves. There was no one in the corridor. Sijur probably didn't want anyone finding out about whatever sick experiments or horrors he inflicted on that woman—and whoever else was imprisoned by him. Joran licked his lips. "Kolfinna, please. I didn't want to do it."

She spun around when he grabbed her wrist, the one where he had stamped the rune on her over a week ago. She wrenched her hand away from him. "Don't touch me."

"B-But—"

He wanted forgiveness. She could read it all over his face. He didn't want her to hate him, even though that was what she felt in that very moment. Later, she would probably try to dissect her feelings and maybe realize that she was misplacing her hatred of Sijur and her own uselessness onto him, but right now all she saw was a fae who was a part of all this.

Kolfinna moved away from him and stomped down the hall.

Her mind was made up.

She needed to find a way to break the rune on her wrist. It almost burned as she thought about it, and she looked down at the gold crescent moon. She would have to find a way to break free because there was no way she was going to be a cog in Sijur's plan.

She would have to find a way.

Thankfully, Joran didn't follow her this time.

7

<hr>

Kolfinna slammed into the sandy ground for the hundredth time that morning. But unlike the laughter and sneering she was used to at the Royal Guards, she was met with silence. Silence and potential disappointment.

She pushed herself up to her elbows and met Inkeri's thoughtful gray eyes. Kolfinna wasn't sure what she saw in Inkeri's gaze—pity or guilt—but she didn't like it.

"Come on, let's do another round," Inkeri said, beckoning her forward.

They were in a small, fenced in training area with yellowish-white sand, separate from the other training grounds, where she could see soldiers running around the perimeter of the fort or sparring with magic off in the distance. This place was tucked away in a far corner within the tall walls of the fort.

Inkeri had dragged her here after their morning drills and had handed her a sword. They had been sparring for the past hour and Kolfinna hadn't beaten Inkeri even once. She was too fast on her feet and she moved gracefully but also brutally. She knew where to move, where to jab her wooden sword, and how to trip Kolfinna up and make her faceplant a hundred times.

As much as Kolfinna disliked being beaten over and over

again, it was something to take her mind off of Olia, Sijur, and Joran. Of the brutal scene she had witnessed yesterday.

Kolfinna pushed herself to her feet and rolled her aching shoulder. Her gray uniform was already drenched in sweat and she had discarded her navy-blue cloak a long time ago, where it was draped over the three-foot-tall black fence. The biting wind didn't even faze her. In fact, she wished it were a bit colder.

"You drag your feet too much," Inkeri said while Kolfinna yanked her wooden sword out from a mound of sand. "Try to move your feet with your attacks. This way when you jab, and that way"—she moved to a different position—"when you strike."

"Got it." Kolfinna breathed out and rubbed the grains of sand off her clammy palms.

"You're improving," Inkeri said.

"Am I? I feel like I'm just making a fool of myself." It had been the same feeling when she was in the Royal Guards. Almost everyone had mocked and belittled her. She could still hear Farthin, Gisela, and Edwin sneering at her.

Too slow, they all said in unison.

Look at her flailing to the ground.

She tried to silence the voices and raised her sword again. She concentrated on Inkeri's slight frame, the way her sword was positioned, and the angling of her feet. She tried to read her movements as she shot toward her. Slash, strike, slash. They fell into a rhythm of exchanging blows. Their swords cracked against each other. Inkeri's moved more gracefully, Kolfinna's desperately.

Look at how her legs tremble. That was Farthin's voice.

Kolfinna jabbed her sword forward.

Gisela laughed. *Look at the face she makes when she concentrates!*

Inkeri side-stepped, dodging the jab, and slammed her sword to Kolfinna's side, sending her skittering to her left. If her legs weren't quivering and leaden, she might've been able to right herself, but she stumbled instead. Inkeri raised her sword to strike again, but Kolfinna was already tripping falling backward.

How pathetic, little fairy!

Kolfinna remained on the ground, her sword still in her hand, and she stared at the white clouds floating around the bright sky. She just lay there. A part of her recognized that she wasn't good at swordplay but that it was okay—because she would learn and become better—but the other part of her, the part that was drowning in negativity, told her that it was pointless. She would never be good at it.

"You okay?" Inkeri was in front of her, her hand outstretched and her dark eyebrows knitted together in worry.

There was no mockery. No jeering. No laughter.

Just concern.

Kolfinna breathed out deeply. She wasn't in the Royal Guards anymore.

"Thanks," she said, letting Inkeri haul her to her feet. She quickly dusted her hands on her shaking thighs, but more grains of sand were now stuck to her sweaty palms from the fall. "How are you able to move so quickly? I'm jealous."

The other woman laughed. "Practice. Lots and lots of practice. Eventually, your body moves on its own."

"I get like that when I use my magic," Kolfinna said. "But not with ..." She twisted her sword in her hand and frowned. "*This.*"

"It takes a lot of time. You're doing a lot better than most people—trust me."

"It doesn't feel like it."

"I think you're ready for tomorrow, even if you don't feel like you are."

Kolfinna paused. "What's tomorrow?"

"Oh?" Inkeri tilted her head to the side, the light catching off the tiny, crystal earrings adorning her ears. "Nobody told you? We'll be going on a hunt tomorrow with you, to test out your abilities and get you used to the regular military life here. We'll be going as a team with Herja and the others."

Something akin to excitement bubbled up in her chest. A mission. A magic beast hunt. Finally, *something* she could do that wasn't simply training. Something that could get her mind off the gold rune on her wrist, the threat of further torture hanging over her head, and something to stare at that wasn't just monotonous gray walls.

"You'll have to be really careful, though." Inkeri took that moment to slide her wooden sword into the belt around her waist. She undid the ribbon holding her inky hair and raked a hand to loosen the straight strands. "You still have a lot to learn about different magic beasts, what magical properties they have, their weaknesses, that sort of thing. Knowing about the beasts helps immensely instead of being thrust in the thick of battle, unsure how to kill it."

Kolfinna knew exactly what she meant. Facing the Nuckelavee, the skinless half-horse half-humanoid monster, over a month ago had shown her just how important it was to know about the enemy. Herself and the team—Magni, Truda, Blár, Nollar, and Yrsa—hadn't known that the Nuckelavee was able to render them magicless. If they had been more prepared, maybe Magni and Blár wouldn't have gotten so injured.

"Do you know anything else about the mission?" Kolfinna asked. "Like who's going? What the objective is?"

"It's going to be a small party." Inkeri combed her hair with her fingers. "Me, you, Herja, Eluf—you remember Eluf, right?"

The name sounded familiar, and the more she thought about it, a hazy image appeared. Raven-colored hair. A cloak made of feathers. Dark circles rimming tired black eyes. "He's ... That purple rank, right? The one who looks gloomy all the time?"

"Yes. He's a rank higher than us too, so he'll be in charge of us. He's actually almost always in charge of our group." She smoothed down the front of her dark gray uniform. "His younger brother, Gunnar, will be with us as well. Along with—"

"Look what we have here." A male voice carried into their

conversation, clashing with whatever Inkeri was saying. "I'm surprised you're her teacher in this."

A young man with a purple badge pinned to his breast pocket was leaning onto the fence, his forearms casually folded and braced on the wooden railing. Curly chestnut hair brushed his shoulders and a jarring pair of heterochromatic eyes stared at her—one eye a sea-green with specks of blue, while the other was ocean-blue with specks of green. His lips twisted into a smirk while Inkeri's smile faded.

"Ivar," she said flatly, annoyance flitting over her face.

"The one and only." His strange eyes flicked to Kolfinna. "You're the fae everyone's been talking about. Kolrinna, right?"

"*Kolfinna.*" She shifted the training sword to her other hand to at least do something. She wasn't sure what she felt about this intruder. On the outside, he looked harmless, but there was something about him that pricked her senses. Like he was dangerous.

"Kolfinna. Got it." He flashed a white-toothed smile. A hint of feral glee gleamed in his unmatched eyes. "I liked what you did the other day, smacking that big oaf with that rock."

That made her smile at least. Throwing that piece of stone at Bjarni's face had been satisfying, to say the least. She had seen him once or twice in the dining hall, but he hadn't said a word to her and had only glared from the distance. No doubt Sijur had given him a stern talk. Especially considering how Sijur needed Kolfinna for his grand plan of creating rune-marked slaves.

The last part made her smile fall.

"What do you want, Ivar?" Inkeri gave him a pointed look. "We're training here. Don't you have something better to do?"

"There are a hundred things I can list off that would be better than watching you dance with that sword. None of which I can do at the moment, unfortunately." He watched her with an unreadable look before turning to Kolfinna. "I've been given the task to watch over you two to make sure you"—he pointed to Inkeri—"don't screw up."

Splotches of red bloomed on her cheeks. "What would I mess up on?"

He lifted his shoulders. "You don't have a good track record."

"Stop screwing around, Ivar," she snapped. "I know Lieutenant Bernsten didn't send you here."

"Hm." He didn't deny it. "What I've seen of you two fighting has been pretty ... *boring*. Didn't the Royal Asses teach you anything?"

Kolfinna bristled. She was starting to become embarrassed whenever people gawked at her lack of skills with the sword. Even though it was technically the Royal Guards' fault for not teaching her enough, it still was a jab at her.

"We're in the middle of training," Inkeri said through clenched teeth. "Feel free to screw off."

"*Middle* of training? Looks more like the end of training, if you ask me—"

"We didn't *ask* you."

He propped his chin on his palm and leaned on the fence lazily. "Don't be like that. I've come to help."

Kolfinna watched them exchange heated looks. Ivar looked more pleased and amused than furious, while Inkeri was all shades of anger and annoyance.

Ivar's grin only made Inkeri simmer. "I'll be helping out occasionally, so no need to look so angry. She's a member of our team, isn't she? So it only helps all of us if she's trained well and, judging by her lack of training, I'd say she needs all the help she can get."

Kolfinna rolled her eyes. "I can handle myself just fine. I might not be the best swordsman, but I'm not a lousy fighter."

She had fought several people in the past year or two. Lord Estur, a purple rank. A handful of Royal Guards when Fenris had chased her down before the Eventyrslot ruins. Draugrs, drekis, the Nuckelavee. When needed, her instincts had always kicked in.

Not that she didn't need the training—she knew better than anyone else that she did—but it annoyed her that everyone was treating her like a weak fae who couldn't fight back.

She certainly could.

Ivar raised an eyebrow. "Really? That's news to me."

"You don't even know me," Kolfinna said slowly. "Am I to believe that you're basing my fighting abilities off ... the fight with Bjarni and"—she waved her hand at the dents in the sand where she had fallen and then to her sword—"all of this?"

He watched her carefully. "All of this, yes. But also when you were sparring earlier today and yesterday during morning drills. I wasn't entirely impressed, if I'm being honest. Don't get me wrong, I certainly think your magic abilities have potential, but do I think you can rival me or ... Gunnar? Or Eluf? Or Herja? Certainly not." He pointed an idle finger to Inkeri. "Do I think you can rival her? In a week or so, yes, I think so."

Inkeri's lips flattened to a straight line while Kolfinna scowled.

He raised his hands. "Hey now, you both don't need to look so offended. I'm just giving you my opinion—"

"Which we didn't ask for," Kolfinna said, rattling off what Inkeri had said earlier.

"You sort of did." He flashed another wolfish grin.

"Leave. You're only distracting us." Inkeri unsheathed her sword and turned her back to him. "Come on, Kolfinna, let's continue."

Kolfinna raised her own sword, but Ivar's voice snaked between them again.

"You shouldn't train her too hard. Wouldn't want her to be so sore that she trips and gets killed by a green-skin, you know?" Ivar picked at a splinter in the fence cap. "Tomorrow's mission is more for her than us."

Inkeri lowered her training sword while Kolfinna hesitated. She *was* sore. Not to mention she still had another training session to go to after dinner—her unfortunate training session with Joran. Just the thought of it soured her mouth. But she wasn't the teacher in this; she had to listen to whatever Inkeri decided.

Inkeri must've been thinking something similar because she

too hesitated for a minute too long. It was enough time for Ivar to continue, "She just got here a few days ago. Give the lady a little rest, sheesh. You do realize that if you push her too hard and she cracks, then it all falls on you."

"That's not fair," Kolfinna interrupted, eyes narrowing. "Why are you trying to put pressure on her like that? I can handle myself, all right? This isn't my first mission."

"You ever faced a green-skin before?" He grinned again, and it annoyed her again.

Despite her annoyance, she asked, "What the hell is a green-skin?"

"Short, humanoid thing. Kinda cute-looking," Ivar spoke smoothly. "If you look past its yellow sharp teeth and its bulging eyes. And that it usually walks around with rags that barely covers its—"

"It's a magic beast that showed up a few months ago in this area," Inkeri cut him off. She jammed her training sword into her belt. "Like its name implies, it has green skin."

Kolfinna vaguely remembered facing something like that when she had gone to the West Border mission. According to the texts she had translated from rune writing, it was called a goblin. This was *if* she was thinking about the same thing they were.

"*Anyway.*" Inkeri blew out some air. "I think it's best to end this training session—"

"Told you so."

Inkeri flicked her wrist and a gust of wind slammed into Ivar. But his quick hands seized the wooden railing before the wind could hurtle him backward. His chestnut locks blew backward with the force and a flash of surprise crossed his face.

Kolfinna snorted, while Inkeri smiled for the first time since he arrived.

He muttered a string of curses under his breath. "What was that for?"

Inkeri ignored him and jerked a thumb at the fort. "Want to

go inside? We should take a bath and maybe I can show you some books about magic beasts? It'll be helpful for tomorrow—"

"You might want to be careful about that." Ivar ran a hand over his wind-blown hair with a scowl, his unsettling green-blue stare on Inkeri. "All the ladies in there are rushing to bathe and get themselves groomed. Might be a bit tight this time around."

Kolfinna quirked an eyebrow.

Inkeri looked just as confused. "Why?"

"All those ladies got their panties in a twist," he sneered. "Rumor spread this afternoon that the mighty Blár-freaking-Vilulf will be here in a few days."

A jolt ran through Kolfinna's body and she forgot to breathe. Blár.

He was coming here? Why?

It didn't actually matter why. The only thing she could really focus on was that he would be here, soon. Much sooner than she had thought they would meet again. She had thought they wouldn't see each other in months or years, considering how Blár had been absent from her trial and how he was obviously too busy for her. Her confusing feelings for him also played a factor in her excitement and the unknown. She didn't know what he felt about her, but it was clear that he didn't feel that strongly for her if he couldn't even be there for her when she needed him the most.

Ivar picked at another splinter on the fence, his watchful gaze on Inkeri the whole time. "Brenda overheard Lieutenant Bernsten mentioning to a soldier to get the black rank room ready since Blár will be occupying it once more. Then Herja asked the lieutenant to his face, and well, looks like he's been stationed here."

"Is it because of ..." Inkeri didn't finish the question, but Ivar seemed to know what she meant because he nodded.

"I think so."

Kolfinna looked between the two of them, hoping her face showed indifference. Did they know Blár? He had once been stationed here; she remembered him mentioning that he had been stationed on the west border under Sijur, but that he didn't like being here. And he certainly didn't like Sijur.

Why was he coming back? She would've foolishly thought he was coming here for her—just like how she had foolishly and secretly hoped was the case during the West Border mission—but the way Ivar and Inkeri were exchanging glances, she wasn't sure.

They knew something she didn't.

Inkeri eyed Kolfinna's cloak that was draped over the fence just a few feet away from Ivar, and then she gave Kolfinna a tight-lipped smile. "Come on, we should go inside."

Kolfinna was happy. Nervous. Scared. Unsure. All of that swirled in her core; it felt like a nest of butterflies was caged within her, but it also felt like a pit of snakes in her stomach, twirling and twisting and brewing with venomous apprehension.

She had questions for him and she wasn't sure if she wanted the answers.

8

Kolfinna had been on two missions before, so she wasn't a complete novice when it came to magical battles with impossible tasks or fighting a legion of dead magical beasts. But despite that, her nerves were rattled when she got ready that morning and marched off with an excited Inkeri and a sleepy Herja into the courtyard outside the east gate of the fortress and near the stables. The smell of earthy hay, manure, and woodchips pervaded the dry, frosty air.

Their small group consisted of only seven people. She recognized Eluf, the man with the dark circles and the feathered cloak, and Ivar, who had curved double blades that shone sinisterly in the morning light. The only person she didn't recognize was a muscular man with dimpled cheeks and a boyish grin that looked all too similar to Eluf, but a happier, younger version of him. One that didn't exude the vibe of smoke and shadows and raven wings. What was his name again? Gunnar?

Eluf glanced between each member of the party carefully. His eyes—which had looked black in the distance—were actually a deep brown, and beyond the hardness, she found kindness in them as he gave her a nod. "Kolfinna, was it?"

"Yes, sir." She gave a short nod, but he was already shaking his head.

"Please, call me Eluf."

"Are you sure?" From what Inkeri had said, he was a rank higher than her, and she knew the military was a stickler with rank.

"I am. Did Inkeri or Herja fill you in about the mission details?"

"No." Kolfinna shot her roommates a look, but they were chatting with each other about something else, completely unaware of her annoyance. Were they supposed to tell her something? Kolfinna wasn't foolish enough to think that Inkeri or Herja were her friends. Yes, Inkeri was civil and nice to her, but that didn't mean much. Especially considering how Yrsa had also been kind to her, and that hadn't worked out well.

"Hm." Eluf frowned, turning his head just as a gust of chilly air blew through his dark locks.

"I don't know the details either," Ivar said, casually propping an elbow on the dimple-cheeked man. "Gunnar here didn't fill me in about anything."

Gunnar chuckled and shoved his arm away without malice. "Probably because you were falling asleep or not paying attention anytime I brought it up."

"Hey now, you can't *blame* me. Whenever you talk about important shit, you sound boring as hell."

Gunnar struck him in the abdomen, but Ivar dodged just in the nick of time, snickering all the while. "You need to be faster than that, birdbrain."

"You—"

The two exchanged mock blows, which seemed to catch Herja's and Inkeri's attention; neither girl looked impressed, but Herja laughed. Kolfinna didn't know how to react. Wasn't the military supposed to be ... trained? Hardened? Not like ... this? With laughter, with casualness?

Eluf stepped between them and smacked Gunnar in the back

of the head, sending the younger man nearly faceplanting to the ground had he not righted himself on time.

"Hey—" he started, his breath steaming in the frigid air.

Ivar laughed and that earned him a smack on the back of his head as well. Inkeri grinned widely at that, and even Kolfinna had to hide her chuckle with a cough.

"We'll have to do a team debriefing," Eluf said while the two men rubbed the back of their heads. From what Kolfinna had gathered during the past morning practices, Eluf was an Enhancer, so she could only wonder if he had smacked them with magic or without.

"We're traveling to Egetrae village. It'll take four hours by horse ride. There's been an increase of green-skins attacking the village despite the soldiers stationed there. It's too much for them to handle and the green-skins are becoming bolder and infiltrating in the middle of the day. We think they've settled near a cave in that area. Our goal is to eradicate their hideout completely and to kill as many of them as we can."

A shiver ran down Kolfinna's spine at the thought of a mission like this—of hunting magic beasts and actually making a difference. But then, another thought dampened her mood: was this really what she should've been doing? Instead of freeing herself from the rune marked on her wrist?

If she wanted to get rid of the mark, she needed information, and so she should've been hunting for that rather than magic beasts. If Joran had information on how to build a rune-based bath and to bind people with runes, he had to have gotten it from somewhere—like a book. If she could find those books ... There was a high chance that it would reveal more about runes and possibly a way out of them.

That was what she should've put her focus on. Not this.

But she didn't have a choice. She had to play the part of a loyal soldier. And even if—when—she freed herself, then what? Where would she go?

She pushed that thought aside. She'd have to think about all those big questions later.

"Does anyone need a minute before we leave?" Eluf turned to the party. When no one said anything, he motioned them forward. "Then let's go."

TRAVELING THROUGH A FOREST WITH THE GROUP reminded Kolfinna of the West Border mission, but instead of traveling with a few of her friends, she was with a group of strangers. One of which didn't like her. and the rest who were completely indifferent. Almost immediately, Kolfinna felt the difference between the Royal Guards and the military.

"Your name is Kolrinna, right?" Gunnar slowed his horse so that he was beside her. His dark brown eyes matched the semi-frozen trees surrounding them. "Ivar told me—"

"*Kolfinna*." She gave him a tight-lipped smile. Was he purposefully botching her name? Ivar had done the same yesterday.

He blinked. "Oh. Kolfinna, then."

"Yes, *Kolfinna*," she repeated.

"Huh. I could've sworn it was Kolrinner."

"Kolfinna," she repeated. "You've said it wrong twice now."

"Kolfinna. Kolfinna." He bobbed his head, seeming to be thinking out loud. "Kolfinna."

"Repeating it won't get through to his thick skull," Ivar called from behind them.

"You're the one who told me it was Kolrinna yesterday." Gunnar narrowed his eyes at Ivar, who gave him a look like he didn't know what he was talking about, but the gleam of mischief in his unmatched eyes told her otherwise.

Herja rolled her eyes as she brushed snow off the mane of her dappled horse. "Can you all just focus on the road? We're almost there—"

"Why are *you* so annoyed?" Ivar raised an eyebrow. Sunlight filtered through the canopy of barren tree branches above their heads and cast slashes of light and shadows over his face. "Shouldn't you be excited to chop up some green-skins?"

There it was again—green-skins. She wondered, not for the first time that day, if he was referring to goblins.

Herja scowled and turned back to the forest. Her fiery red hair stood out against the melting snow and mahogany-colored trees. "I would be, if I wasn't stuck with you buffoons."

"Don't lump me with them," Inkeri said with a look of disgust.

"You're lumped in with us whether you like it or not." Gunnar laughed and his dark eyes twinkled. "And forgive me if I'm wrong, but weren't you excited to go on this mission today?"

"To boost your rank, hm?" Ivar added with a snicker.

Inkeri's cheeks reddened and Kolfinna watched the interaction with raised brows. This was all new to her. There were people in the Royal Guards who were friends with one another, but she had never been in on the jokes or the interactions. Whenever she was around, they became ice-cold to her and would stop talking.

"*Focus.*" One word was all it took for everyone to straighten on their horses. Eluf looked over his shoulder from the head of the party. "We're reaching the caves where we think the creatures reside. It wouldn't be abnormal to stumble upon a few of them. I need you all to focus and stop with the games."

The horses' hooves clopped over half-frozen earth, gnarled roots, and twigs. Kolfinna flexed her hands and felt the familiar flare of mana beneath her skin. There were various stones hidden within the earth, some deeper and some closer to the surface. It wouldn't take her too long to wrench those stones and smash them into a goblin's face if it came at her.

Eluf and Gunnar were both Enhancers, Herja was a fire elemental, Inkeri was an air elemental, and Ivar was a water elemental. That meant that along with Kolfinna, Inkeri, Herja, and Ivar would be in charge of any long-distance attacks. If a green-skinned goblin did show up, it was their job to take care of them before the monsters reached the party.

Simple enough, but Kolfinna still felt nervous as she scanned the trees for movement. Having green skin meant that the beasts could blend in well in forests, but that wasn't the case in winter. According to Eluf, these creatures were supposedly more active during the nighttime, probably because they could blend in better.

A rustle of trees to her right caught her attention. Twelve feet away, a three-foot-tall green-skinned creature was swinging on branches, its red eyes glowing and its mouth full of rotted, yellowed teeth. It was the same creature she had seen in the West Border mission.

It opened its mouth to snarl, but Kolfinna was quicker. She raised a hand and shot a large stone at its face. The creature swung to another branch and her stone crashed into a tree, snapping several branches in the process.

Kolfinna cursed and wrenched more stones from the earth. But in mere seconds, a boom and flash of blue fire blasted the creature. It didn't even scream as it fell to the ground. The remaining fire licked the nearby trees and melted the snow. A wave of heat hit Kolfinna and she gritted her teeth as a charcoal-like, burning flesh type of smell rolled over her.

Herja laughed loudly. "Beat you to it, fairy-girl. You gotta be much faster than that. *And* accurate."

Kolfinna's eye twitched.

This wasn't a competition, but she swore she'd get the next one.

Ivar waved his hand and the nearby clumps of snow clinging to the branches shifted as he drew the moisture out of them. Suddenly, a streak of water glittered in the air. He flicked his wrist and the water swirled over the fires, putting them out effortlessly.

"My water is still stronger. If it wasn't, your fire would still be roaring," Ivar said snidely. "No need to act all cocky with the new recruit."

Herja frowned, and Kolfinna could've given him a hug for that—dampening Herja's mood was worth being around the sly and mocking man. He certainly earned a brownie point from her.

"Whatever," Herja muttered, urging her horse forward.

"Good job spotting that thing," Gunnar said between glances at Kolfinna and the blackened corpse of the creature.

"Thanks," Kolfinna muttered. She still had missed, even if she was one of the first to act, so there wasn't much glory in that. After her training session with Inkeri yesterday, her practice with Joran had proved to her that she still had a lot to practice when it came to striking moving targets. Even as she thought that, her mood further soured. She hated thinking about Joran. For many reasons. One, he reminded her too much about the mark he had sealed on her wrist and everything it signified. Two, she hated how he hid that he was a fae and that he couldn't commiserate with her —it would've definitely been better to know that she wasn't the only one struggling with survival. And three, she simply hated that he had seen her naked and seen that vulnerable part of her.

Their party moved forward, more alert than before. Kolfinna raked her mana over the passing stones, her mana gripping them and releasing them when she moved forward. She would be ready for the next one, she told herself. And this time, she didn't plan on missing.

A blur of movement to her left caught her attention. A goblin sat on one of the branches a few dozen feet away, watching them. A wooden club was slung over his shoulder.

Their eyes met.

Kolfinna raised her hand and chucked a stone at the creature. Her attack struck it on the shoulder and it lurched to the side. An ugly scream emitted from the creature as it fell, sharp branches scratching and tearing its body. Kolfinna was about to launch another stone at it, but the creature was already running away.

It didn't get far.

Water swirled around the creature so quickly that Kolfinna only blinked and it was there, completely encapsulating the magic beast in a ball. The beast flailed within the floating water and a rush of it filled its mouth. More and more until the ball grew smaller and smaller. It took Kolfinna a horrified second to realize that Ivar was drowning the beast and filling its lungs with water until it would burst.

And that's exactly what happened. Meat and organs splattered in seconds, splashing over the barren trees with bright blue blood. The goblin's chest had blown apart and its limbs lay in a pile of its blood and guts and bones.

Kolfinna frantically tried to stop her horse before she leaned over its side and vomited.

She had never seen a water elemental use their magic like that. She hadn't even known it was possible.

Because how ... how could someone *do* that?

She definitely had a new fear unlocked, she realized as she finished retching from her spot in the middle of their party. She gave Ivar a wary glance.

He only raised a sardonic eyebrow.

"You good?" Gunnar asked.

"I've ... never seen anything like that." She wiped her mouth with the back of her hand. Her stomach twisted once more and she looked away from the gruesome scene.

They were met with a few more goblins after that. For whatever reason, Kolfinna was able to spot them before anyone could, but she only killed two of them. The others she either missed or her stones hadn't been able to deal the finishing strike in one hit.

After the seventh goblin, which Inkeri managed to kill by slicing it in half with her air magic, she turned to Kolfinna with a wide-eyed stare. "How are you able to see and hear all these things before us?"

Gunnar flexed his wool-gloved hands. "Yeah, that's really impressive."

All at once, everyone was looking at her in a new light.

Kolfinna could only blink at them slowly. Heat crawled up her neck at their stares; she didn't like having all the attention on her, especially since she couldn't answer their question.

Frankly, she had no idea why her reaction time was faster than theirs. Especially since they were trained soldiers and she was an ex-Royal Guard who, apparently, wasn't trained that well.

In the Royal Guards, during the Eventyrslot runs and during the West Border mission, she hadn't seemed that much faster with her reactions.

But—

That was *before* those shadowy things sprang out of her body. *Before* her body started healing itself rapidly. And *before* her back became insufferably itchy and blood-red.

"I don't know what to tell you guys." She shrugged, hoping she came off as nonchalant as Ivar was. She needed to borrow some of that confidence, borderline arrogance. Maybe that would earn her some respect. "Maybe you guys just aren't up to speed with me?" She shot Herja a gloating look. "Might want to be faster than that, human girl."

Ivar snorted a laugh and Gunnar joined him, while Herja scowled.

"Hey now, I admit that you're faster at reacting than me— which in itself should be a big feat for you—but that doesn't mean you've been able to follow through." Herja cracked her knuckles. "How many of those things have you killed? One?"

Eluf raised a scarred hand, dark eyes set forward. "All of you, quiet."

Everyone shushed immediately and went on the defensive. After a moment of nothing, he urged his horse onward. "Let's keep moving and don't forget that this isn't a competition." He gave Herja and Kolfinna a long look over his shoulder, and she had to look away to not feel like a scolded schoolgirl. "Herja, you should know better—"

"Oh, come on, Eluf. You know what we're like." Gunnar pressed his horse forward until it was beside his older brother's.

"When have we ever failed a mission before, huh? We can't all be glum, ya know? We need some healthy competition from time to time. Know what I'm saying?" He glanced at the others, his dimples indented deep. "It'd be boring if we only shut up and never said anything."

Herja laughed as she dusted snow off her blazing-red hair. "Yeah, I agree with the village idiot. It's healthy to talk shi—"

"*Village idiot?*" Gunnar's mouth hung open. "You too, Herja? I'm offended."

"That's Blár's line." Ivar rolled his eyes.

Herja shrugged. "It's fitting."

All at once, Kolfinna felt uncomfortable. Even as Inkeri chuckled and Eluf sighed loudly. As Ivar ducked from Gunnar's fist, as Herja galloped forward to avoid Gunnar's ire. It was all too much for Kolfinna in that moment.

They all knew each other. Were friends, even. And then there she was: intruding.

She had to tell herself that she wasn't here for friends. Actually, she wasn't even sure why she was here anymore. In the Royal Guards, she had been looking for her own place in the world. She had only come here to save her skin. But what happened now? Was she supposed to just find her place here while being rune-marked and forced to obey Sijur Bernsten for the next fifteen years? Or was she supposed to break from her runes, escape—because Sijur likely wouldn't keep her around if she broke her bond with him—and then find her place somewhere else?

Her head began to throb at those thoughts. At what she would be throwing away if she decided to destroy the rune marking her and leave the military. Her chance at having a place in society. The ability to change society.

And that wasn't even including the problems she had with Ragnarök, the heir business, or why her body was going against her—with her hair and her skin—and all the other changes she was going through.

She was confused and as she watched the others clown around her, she realized she had no one to talk to about it.

THEY ARRIVED AT A CAVERNOUS SITE IN THE FOREST about a half mile away from the village Egetrae. Trees hung over the dark gray cave opening and shrouded it in shadows. The opening was only four feet tall and Kolfinna couldn't imagine squeezing through there to find anything useful, but she could feel the stones connecting below the cave and opening it into a large network in the ground.

Herja stiffened at the sight of the cave opening and then turned to Inkeri with wide eyes. "Are we ... going inside that?" she whispered, but Kolfinna could hear it even though they were at least seven feet apart. No one else could, judging by the way they were jumping off their horses and speaking to one another.

Strange. Maybe her hearing had improved?

"You'll be fine—" Inkeri was saying, her voice low.

"But you know I hate small openings like that."

"I'll be right beside you."

That was also strange. Kolfinna hadn't expected Herja, who seemed tough and rough and untamed and wild, to be claustrophobic. It almost made her feel bad for eavesdropping, but it wasn't like she was doing it on purpose, she told herself. They were just speaking ... loudly? Quietly? She wasn't even sure why she could hear them.

"You sure this is where those green-skins are coming from?" Gunnar asked, tying his horse to a tree.

"A soldier from the village reported that when he tracked one of them, this is where it went." Eluf tied his horse as well. His movements were slow and cautious. "They probably have a huge gathering here."

"And the six of us is enough to take down their whole base?" Ivar raised his eyebrows. "Now, don't get me wrong, I've got a lot of faith in ..." He glanced at the party and then shrugged. "Myself, honestly. But a whole base of green-skins? I'm not sure those odds are looking *super* favorable."

Gunnar laughed. "I'll take care of most of them."

"Like hell you will." Ivar rolled his eyes.

"Is it a good idea to leave our horses so close to the cave?" Inkeri placed a gentle hand on the black mane of her steed. "I would be devastated if one of those creatures did anything to them."

Eluf opened his mouth to say something, but Kolfinna was already moving forward. She stopped in front of the cluster of horses tied to the trees and raised her hand. All at once, mana gushed from her and seared the ground in flashes of gold writing.

Gunnar cursed softly. "Her eyes are glowing *gold*."

Runes danced on the ground around the horses in a ring. *Nothing shall pass through here to hurt the horses. Nothing with magic will cross inside here. All the horses will be protected within this ring.*

"There." She followed the circle around until she was sure it was complete before turning to the party. "The horses will be safe so long as they remain in the circle."

"What ... Is this?" Ivar's eyes were wide as he tentatively poked the runes with his foot. When his foot didn't go inside the ring, his eyes widened further and he looked up at the group. "I can't even put my foot in. It's like there's an invisible ... *wall*."

"What did you do?" Herja asked, voice rising an octave in panic. "Is my horse okay?"

"Is this ... fae magic?" Inkeri looked both thrilled and nervous.

Eluf hadn't moved. "What ... is that?"

They had probably never seen rune magic, Kolfinna realized. Most reports from the Eventyrslot ruins weren't made public or even shared within the military or Royal Guards outside of the higher officials, so it was no wonder they didn't know.

"It's rune magic," she said with a shrug. "I made it so that the horses are safe within the circle I created with my magic. The horses are fine."

"How does that work?" Inkeri tilted her head curiously, looking between Kolfinna and the row of curved glowing runes.

"It's a long explanation," Kolfinna said. "But essentially, runes put commands or rules or conditions in place that my magic carries out. It's a bit complicated and I don't understand it completely, but it's an ancient fae magic. I'm still learning, so I'm no expert."

"I didn't even know fae could do that," Ivar said, still trying to poke the runes.

"There's a lot you probably don't know about the fae." Kolfinna tried to smile, but she couldn't, not when everyone's attention was zeroed in on her. "Anyway, are we going inside the cave now or ...?"

Eluf nodded. "Yes, let's all go."

They all headed inside the cave. Herja was the first to enter; she acted confident, with violet fire roaring in the palm of her hand, and to everyone else, she probably seemed unbothered. But Kolfinna knew the truth. She could hear her shallow breaths—breaths that Kolfinna shouldn't have been able to hear. Herja was trying to calm herself—trying to breathe in and out, in and out. Kolfinna recognized the strategy—it was something she had done too in the face of fear and anxiety. And yet Herja still appeared confident. She walked forward and led the party through the narrow opening of the cave as everyone filed in behind her. Her fire shifted to a bright white, better illuminating their path.

The slender opening slowly expanded and eventually stretched out until it was at least eight feet tall. Herja's breathing had calmed down when they were no longer squeezing through the narrow cave. The hallway slowly descended down. Crude steps led them deeper into the network of paths that Kolfinna could feel with her stone magic.

She could hear movement even better down here, where the

breaths of the forest—the swishing of branches and the scampering of rodents—weren't as deafening. She could hear the small scurries of mice flitting across the ground and above the tapered structure at the roof of the cave. She could hear footsteps in the distance. She could hear everyone else's breaths.

It was both bizarre and fascinating—how much clearer everything suddenly became. This must've been a new development for Kolfinna because she was certain she didn't have this level of hearing a few weeks ago.

When they went deeper into the cave, they no longer needed Herja's fire because crude sconces along the bumpy, cavernous wall held flickering fire that bathed the hall in shades of dark shadows and deep orange.

Herja still kept her flame in hand, the color shifting between violet and white and blue, each different flicker of color changing the temperature in the hall.

Footsteps neared them. One? No, three sets of footsteps. They shuffled, slowly.

Kolfinna's eyes narrowed. They were coming closer. Maybe fifteen seconds away. The hallway bent at the end of the hall about four feet away. Was it a group of goblins? Or something else?

She grabbed Herja's elbow, halting the woman. Kolfinna hadn't realized how tall Herja was until she was peering down at her with sapphire eyes, threads of silver running through them like the white fire in her hand. Ivar looked over at them and was about to say something, but Kolfinna's expression stopped him.

Kolfinna raised three fingers and pointed to the end of the hall.

Understanding flickered in the other woman's face and she nodded. Kolfinna turned to the others and was about to relay the same information, when the footsteps came to the bend and stopped abruptly.

Three green-skinned goblins wearing thin rags over their groins stood at the end of the hall. White, wispy hair hung over crinkled, leathery skin. Their stomachs protruded slightly, and they held crudely shaped wooden clubs. At the sight of their group, they charged them.

An ugly battle cry left one of their lips, but Herja was already on the move.

Fire blasted the hallway in crimson, sending waves of heat behind Herja. Kolfinna found it hard to take a breath of that remaining hot air. The fire died out just as quickly as it sprang forth. The unexpected heat in the cave remained, clinging to the once-cold walls. Kolfinna exhaled deeply. The three goblins were dead on the ground, their bodies black, and the smell of burning flesh came off their corpses so strongly that Kolfinna almost retched on the side of the hall.

Herja grinned. "I am too good."

"Save that for when we're done with this mission." Water twirled around Ivar's hands. Water he had probably pulled from the dew drops on the stalactites above their heads.

"Three for me, and zero for all of you." She grinned even wider. "Thanks for the heads-up, fairy girl."

Kolfinna frowned. Maybe she should've taken care of the goblins herself and not warned the others. But no, she couldn't think like that. This was supposed to be a team effort. Even if there seemed to be a competitive streak between everyone.

"How many missions have you been on before?" Gunnar asked as they moved forward.

"Two." Kolfinna kept her ears open for any more noises, but it was hard to cancel out the miscellaneous sounds—of mice, of insects, and of the wind blowing against the tiny crevices all along the cave.

"You're ... better than I thought you'd be," he said. "Ivar said you were lousy—I mean, *untrained* in a swordfight."

Kolfinna shot Ivar a look, but he either didn't see or ignored her. "I'm decent with my magic."

"And your reflexes," Gunnar said. "You notice—"

"Shouldn't we be focusing?" Kolfinna quirked an eyebrow. "Instead of trying to get to know one another?"

Gunnar chuckled as he stepped over the burned bodies of the goblins. "Huh, is that how you work? I'm better at taking things easy. I work better than way."

"We should be prepared for—" Kolfinna started.

He groaned, "You sound like my brother."

Inkeri moved up beside Kolfinna, her hands raised for an attack as she watched her surroundings. "I agree with Gunnar. You're better in action than you are when you're training. I mean that as a compliment, by the way."

"Some people are great at practicing with their fancy swords, but when it comes down to actually killing and doing something" —Ivar glanced at Inkeri—"they fail."

Despite the dim lighting, Kolfinna could make out the redness of Inkeri's cheeks. "Screw off, Ivar. It was *one* time."

"One time that almost cost us—"

He didn't get to finish because four more goblins appeared at the end of the hallway. Inkeri pushed past him and sent a powerful blast of air to shove the goblins off their feet and slam into the wall. Dents formed along the wall and they fell in a heap on the ground. Blue blood spotted the ground, but two struggled back onto their feet, their murderous red eyes focused on them. Kolfinna lifted a hand, her mana moving quick as lightning across the distance between herself and the wall behind the goblins. They moved forward, but not before a chunk of the stone wall lurched forward and grabbed each one by the midsection. Kolfinna flicked her wrist and the goblins became one with the wall. She covered their mouths with stone to keep their screams muffled, crushed their bodies with the stone, and then had the stones spit them out onto the ground.

Gunnar lowered his fists. "Impressive. Brutal, but impressive."

"And you puked your guts when you can do *that*?" Ivar laughed while waving to the blue-blood-drenched corpses.

Kolfinna grimaced. It was probably a bit hypocritical to think his magic use was vicious while she did something similar with her stones. Though she did think there was a difference in the level of brutality between crushing something to death and imploding something to death.

"Look, your magic ... literally burst those goblins up from the inside out," Kolfinna countered, her stomach clenching uncomfortably as that memory resurfaced. "This is a bit brutal, yes, but it's a lot more ..."

Ivar quirked an eyebrow, waiting for her to finish.

She wasn't sure how to finish. "Humane?"

"Fairy girl, I'm pretty sure yours are just as dead," Herja said with a grin that showed a hint of respect—but it morphed into grimness much too quickly.

Eluf stepped toward the corpses quietly. His footsteps were light and featherlike, despite his tall and muscular frame. He touched one of the crumbling pieces of the wall she had used. "Can all fae use earth like this?"

"We have the ability to, yes." It all came down to proficiency and skill after that.

"What did you call that thing?" Gunnar asked as they continued down the hallway.

"A goblin," Kolfinna said. "I've read about it in old fae texts. It's a creature from the Mistlands."

"What's it doing all the way here?" Inkeri asked, confused.

"It's ..." Where to even begin? That Ragnarök and Revna had destroyed a hole in the barrier between the Mistlands and Rosain? Or did she have to first explain the barrier and rune magic? Or that Blár had erected an ice wall so it shouldn't be a problem? But first of all, could she even talk about it, or was it confidential? It wasn't like she was a Royal Guard anymore. "It's a long story."

Gunnar dragged a hand across the rough wall of the cave. The corpses were already out of sight behind them. "What did you read about them? All the information we have is what we've gathered these past few months."

Kolfinna wracked her brain for characteristics of goblins and their personalities. She had read and reread so many passages of that book on magical creatures, but she hadn't focused much on the simple monstrous creatures. Her focus had been on the sirens, the mermaids, the elves, and all the interesting humanoid creatures.

"Goblins are intelligent." She nodded at the sconces. "They live in communities much like humans do, but they lack empathy. The book described them like a colony of ants, except they don't have a queen, they have a king. They also enjoy eating ... children. Whether that's human children, fae children ..." Or elf children, but she didn't want to include that since they likely didn't think they existed. That and she didn't want to remind herself of elves and what it meant for her.

"What about weaknesses?" Herja asked.

"They're physically stronger than humans, so you can only really kill them with magic. Whether that's an Enhancer or Elemental." She shrugged. "But if you're asking if they have something in particular that they're weak to, then no."

"Hm." Ivar frowned. "So are you sure these goblins are the same thing as these green-skins?"

"I think so. Everything sounds the same so far."

"These *goblins*," Eluf said, "might be weak compared to us, but we still have to be on our guard. They have the advantage of numbers."

His words and a new sound made uneasiness wash over Kolfinna. Finally, she realized what she was hearing were muffled grunts and screams from somewhere—below, maybe? But the more they walked through the winding hall, the less sure she became. They didn't meet any more goblins, which was also strange. If Kolfinna and her group were at the hideout of these creatures, shouldn't it have been teeming with the creatures?

Something shuffled behind her. Kolfinna spun around, hands raised and mana flaring, but there was nothing. The fire in the sconces flickered, illuminating the empty hallway they had come from. Kolfinna narrowed her eyes at the walls and then up at the stalactite-covered ceiling and the small holes along it.

The group had stopped moving and was now watching her. Herja's palms were blazing with bluish fire, water was dancing on Ivar's fingers, Inkeri had air swirling over her arms, and the two brothers had their fists raised for battle.

"It's nothing," Kolfinna said. "I just thought—"

The ground began to crack. Fissures formed in the center of the hallway, widening in seconds. Kolfinna tried jumping from the suddenly uneven, cracked ground, but it was too late. All at once, the ground collapsed beneath their feet and she was plummeting. A scream ripped through her throat. Her mana flailed, trying to latch onto something, but she was falling too fast to get a good bearing on her surroundings. Finally, she slammed onto something hard, the wind knocking out of her. Immediately, her ankle throbbed. The stalactite-filled ceiling—which had been the ground just seconds ago—gaped above her. She must've fallen at least two stories.

Clothes rustled, steel clanked together, and crumbling rocks peppering the ground filled her ears.

Kolfinna blinked and shoved herself into a sitting position. The rest of the party was similarly sprawled on the ground. But they weren't groaning and holding onto their sore bodies. They were instead staring at the room. The hall, really, because that's what it was. A giant hall full of crude wooden tables with slabs of raw, bloodied meat at the centerpieces.

They weren't alone.

Hundreds of bulging blood-red eyes were on them. The goblins were all around the hall, their weapons haphazardly left on the tables beside their meals.

Ivar rose to his feet, glancing at the horde of goblins. "Oh shit."

It happened so fast—an earsplitting screech pierced through the air from the closest goblin and everyone sprang into action. Goblins grabbed their weapons and screamed their battle cries, which coalesced together into a horrifying cacophony of grunts and squeals and monstrous sounds.

Kolfinna scrambled to her feet. Her heart was already pounding, adrenaline rushing through her veins and her magic warming her core.

The closest goblin grabbed its club off the table and charged at her. Kolfinna didn't think. Her body moved on its own. She chucked a hunk of the broken ceiling at it, cleaving its head off its shoulder with a single strike. A spray of blue blood arced through the air and another goblin was already on her.

Kolfinna moved her arms, directing her mana to flow into the stones by her feet and slam at her targets. She didn't have to worry too much about accuracy due to the sheer number of goblins. If she did miss, it ended up striking another one, so it didn't really matter. The only thing she had to make sure of was that she didn't accidentally hurt any of her comrades.

In her peripheral vision, between piercing the magic beasts with stone spears and huge chunks of the walls, she could make out Herja's blue fire blazing in giant streaks. Gunnar and Eluf were fighting with their backs against each other, both of their fighting styles mimicking each other. They were both Enhancers, and their punches and kicks sent the creatures flying across the hall. Inkeri had drawn her sword and was fighting with both air and steel, her movements lithe and graceful. Ivar kept close to her side, his water viciously shoving the creatures away and making them burst in seconds.

Kolfinna fell into a rhythm. Spread her mana through the ground, create stone spears from the ground, and pierce the goblins before they could get close to her, then repeat. She kept a close eye on the goblins but also on her comrades. Anytime Herja had her back turned and a creature was coming up behind her, Kolfinna would raise a pointed stone from right below the creature's feet, slowing it down enough that Herja had time to turn and burn it. Eluf and Gunnar fought seamlessly together and didn't give the goblins an opening. Ivar filled all of Inkeri's openings. Only Herja had no one to watch her back, not that it seemed like she needed the help—she was laughing and launching her fire wildly, but *precisely*.

When Kolfinna had been at the West Border mission, she clearly remembered Yrsa losing control and burning Eyfura and the surrounding trees, and how Magni had reprimanded her. *Our magic is the most volatile magic there is. It's incredibly easy to hurt someone with fire. Whether yourself or your teammates. As fire elementals, we have to be extremely careful of our surroundings. We don't want to burn other people or cause unnecessary collateral damage.* But Herja, despite her flashy display of blue-violet flames, was deliberately ensuring that not even a spark of fire touched her teammates.

It only made sense that Kolfinna watched her back for her. So, in reality, Kolfinna was the only one who had no one to watch her back. It was fine, though. She could handle herself.

Her mana seeped out of her unreservedly. It spread to the ground, to the stray rocks, and pulled apart chunks of stone to chuck at the creatures. Adrenaline rushed through her system, making her go faster, more efficient. Sweat formed on her brow. She had forgotten the thrill and excitement of battle.

She tried not to move too much, since her ankle throbbed from the fall, but the longer the battle progressed, the less it throbbed. Until, eventually, it stopped altogether. She didn't understand how her healing abilities worked, but even in the thick of battle, she seemed to be healing herself.

The entire battle must've taken fifteen minutes, but it only felt like a few. Kolfinna was moving stones so fast and without hesitation. She was completely in the zone—strike, strike, strike. She didn't stop until there were no more goblins lefts. Until only a sea of corpses filled the hall.

Inkeri yanked her sword out of a goblin's chest. The steel of her blade dripped with sapphire blood. "Is that all of them?"

Ivar cleaned the specks of blood off his hands with a wave of his water magic.

The ground was bathed with splashes of blue and bits of guts and entrails. The corpses closest to Inkeri and Ivar had gashes from her sword or were drowned, while the corpses by Herja's feet were black husks, and the ones near the two brothers were broken and twisted in strange positions. Kolfinna glanced around the hall. "Looks like it."

"Is anyone hurt?" Eluf flexed his fingers and kicked a twitching goblin in the face. Its head snapped off its body and smashed into the wall, where it stuck among the splatters of blue blood.

Gunnar winced and brought a hand to his hip. "I fell in a weird position and my hips are killing me."

"You were fighting fine just seconds ago." Even though he said that, Eluf gave him a once-over, worry creasing his forehead.

"I doubt that's the last of them." Ivar jerked a thumb at the wide cutout in the cavernous wall that seemed to serve as the exit and entrance. "Looks like this place is bigger than we thought. I think we took care of most of them, but I wouldn't be surprised if there are more hiding somewhere."

Kolfinna stepped over the mangled corpses to get a better view of what the goblins had been chewing on before their party had unceremoniously dropped from the ceiling. Her stomach twisted at the bloodied meat on the table. Red blood stained the wooden tables and bits of flesh was imbedded in the cracks of the wood. Most of the bloody shapes looked like animals, but a few of them appeared ... humanoid.

Her stomach twisted and she fought the urge to vomit again.

"We have to keep moving forward." Kolfinna turned away from the goblins' feast. "From what I've read, goblins like to keep humans and children until they're ready to ..." She didn't even want to finish her sentence.

Ivar's mouth hung open. "Holy—" He cursed and looked at the tables of meat with renewed disgust. "You're not saying that ... that these creatures keep them *alive*?"

"Until they're ready to eat them?" Inkeri paled.

Eluf had gone very still.

"There might be some humans left alive here." Kolfinna nodded. "How many children have gone missing from the village?"

Gunnar licked his lips. "Eluf?"

"Fourteen." Eluf clenched his fists together, dark eyes growing darker. "If there's a chance we can save them—"

"*If* they're alive." Herja gave him a careful look. "We've already taken care of most—"

"We don't know that. For all we know, this could be the tip of the iceberg." Eluf breathed out shakily.

Kolfinna watched the way his hands trembled just slightly. She too could barely tolerate the thought of children being kept in a goblin's horde, starved and waiting to be feasted upon. Even thinking about it herself had her stomach twisting once more.

"But this place is huge." Gunnar spread his arms out to the hall, which was at least twice the size of the royal palace's throne room. "How many more halls and rooms are out there? What if we can't find them?"

"We can still save them," Kolfinna said. "We have to try."

Everyone was staring at her and this time, instead of balking at the attention, she tried to use the moment to bolster everyone's confidence—and her own. "I can feel the network of stone passages. So don't worry about missing a spot or two. I can find them. Trust me."

Herja whistled as she wiped bits of goblin flesh off her sleeves. "You can do that?"

"Yes." Kolfinna tried to smile, but the smell of raw meat and burning flesh made it hard to not feel the grimness of the situation. Especially since she could *taste* the iron in the air.

Without another word, they all wove their way through the sea of corpses until they entered the hallway outside the feasting hall. The hallway split into three hallways, each of them lit with fire sconces.

"Our priority right now is finding the children," Eluf said.

"We'll split up here. Scour every single room and every hall. Make sure not a single green-skin makes it out alive. Kill the bastards and save the kids. Understood?"

"What if we get lost?" Herja rested a hand on her hip. "If this place really is as big as we think it is, what if—"

"Kolfinna will come and find us then." Eluf nodded to her. "Isn't that right? You can feel all the networks, so it wouldn't be too much of a stretch to say that you can find us if we get lost, right?"

From what she could feel of this place from the stone passages, the cave extended in many directions with different halls, some going deeper underground and others coming up close to the surface. She could navigate it without much problem, since she could, if need be, create a new path to the surface. However, just because she knew where everything was mapped out didn't mean she knew where anyone would be located. She would still have to scour every nook and cranny of the place.

And this place was ginormous. It could very well take days.

But she didn't need to tell them that.

"Yes, I can find you all." *Probably.*

Eluf seemed satisfied with that. "Gunnar and I will take this hall. Herja and Inkeri, take the middle. Ivar and Kolfinna, you take the last one."

Their group broke apart and each pair headed down their designated corridor. Kolfinna dragged a hand over the bumps and divots in the cavernous wall; she threaded her mana through the stone and tried to feel the bends in the path ahead and the various interconnected hallways and dead ends.

Ivar's footsteps were heavy against the stony ground. Kolfinna picked up the noise of all the tiny pebbles he crushed beneath his steel-toed boots and the sound of the rubber tread on the bottom of his boots gripping the ground. She could also hear the distant drip of dew falling off the sharp ends of the stalactites in the ceiling. The scuffling and squeaks of mice down the hall.

Her head began to throb with the overload of her senses.

"I noticed you were sticking close to Inkeri," Kolfinna found herself saying. At least if she talked and she focused on their voices, she could ignore the hyper focused sounds her ears were picking up.

Ivar's steps slowed and his jarring green-blue eyes skated to her. "Was I?"

"You were." Kolfinna tucked an errant strand of white hair behind her ear. "For someone who's so rude to her, you sure seemed worried—"

"She's the only yellow rank in the group," he started.

"The *only*?" Her eyebrows rose and she pointedly tapped at the reflective, yellow badge pinned to the breast pocket of her gray uniform.

His lips pursed together. Something akin to annoyance flitted over his face. "That's just the dynamic of our group. Eluf and Gunnar stick together since they're brothers and know how to fight well with each other. Herja likes to go off on her own and burn things up. And then I'm tasked with making sure Inkeri doesn't get killed due to her lack of skill."

"She's not weak." Kolfinna frowned. She had seen Inkeri fight and had sparred with her countless times these past few days. Even though she was a yellow rank, Kolfinna surmised Inkeri was on the cusp of becoming a purple. It was only a matter of time.

Ivar was quiet for a long time. She couldn't read the expression on his face and she didn't know him well enough to know what the twitch at the corner of his mouth meant. Or if he was slowing down because he was thinking too hard or he was annoyed or because he didn't have an answer.

The slight noise of air escaping at the end of the corridor caught Kolfinna's attention. She ripped her gaze away from Ivar and focused on the sound. Another ragged breath. Could it be a child? Or a goblin?

The corridor curved and she could make out small cutouts in the cavernous tunnel-like cave—rooms, perhaps.

Kolfinna's mana tingled at her fingertips. Ivar read the shift in her demeanor and narrowed his eyes at the darkness down the hall.

"How many?" he whispered.

She raised a single finger.

He bobbed his head and they both neared the first doorway. Suddenly, a green-skinned creature hobbled out into the hallway, completely unaware of them. When its eyes landed on Kolfinna, they widened. She didn't think, she moved. Her mana ripped a pointed stalactite off the ceiling and slammed it right at the creature's heart, pinning it to the curved part of the hallway. The goblin's head lolled forward, dead.

Ivar jogged over to the doorway and he peeked inside while Kolfinna followed behind him. "Seems like a bedroom." He sighed. "Nothing important."

The room had a bundle of blood-tinged furs on the ground that probably served as a bed and a small cluster of brittle bones in the corner.

"Doesn't it make you feel uneasy seeing that these creatures are intelligent?" Kolfinna asked as they continued down the hallway once more. "Like, they have their own dining hall, makeshift tables and beds ... And yet they hunt humans. *Children.*"

He cast her a sidelong look. "It's creepy, don't get me wrong, but you have to keep in mind that if we don't kill them, they *will* kill our most vulnerable population."

Of course she knew that, but it still unnerved her that these creatures had their own mini civilization here, and they were hunting them all down.

"At the end of the day, they're monsters." He poked his head into another room. It was decorated like the other room but empty.

"The fae are considered monsters," she said.

His sea-like eyes found hers. "You're not thinking that you're the same as them, are you?"

"My people are hunted the same way." She tried not to shiver, but coldness swept down her spine and she involuntarily shuddered. She didn't think goblin hunting or monster hunting was the same as hunting fae—but what if these soldiers thought of it as one and the same? She could see the difference, but not everyone could. Most people branded the fae as monsters. The same as these goblins.

He blew out air. "The fae are much more intelligent, for one. And they look like humans too." He eyed her white hair and then met her pink eyes. "Well, sorta. But you're close enough to human-looking that I think there's a big distinction. Plus, the fae can fu—" He cleared his throat with a laugh, as if realizing he was talking to her. "Well, let's just say you guys can procreate with humans, so you've got the same kind of hardware down there."

She could already feel the heat clawing up her neck.

"I'm sure there are people who think you guys are no better than these green-skins," he said as if reading her initial discomfort. "But they're either blind or lying to themselves if they think you're *actually* at the same level."

It was oddly comforting to know that he didn't view her as a heartless monster like these goblins. He might've been rough around the edges, but at least he wasn't hunter material.

They continued down the corridor, looking through every dark room they passed. Occasionally, they came across a random goblin or two, but they took care of it with ease. Ivar let her do most of the killing, citing that she needed the experience.

Kolfinna halted in her steps when she heard in the distance the distinct sound of a child sobbing and the screech-like cackling of a magical creature—it sounded similar to when a goblin grunted before it died or before it readied itself to attack. Her blood ran cold.

She didn't think, she just ran.

Ivar ran behind her, his gaze cutting to the various open doorways they passed. "What's going—"

A goblin shot out from one of the rooms and slammed right into Kolfinna. She knocked into the wall. Her temple cracked against one of the rocky protuberances along the wall and her vision danced with shadows. A club struck her shoulder at the same time she hit the floor.

Gritting through the pain, she reached for her mana and touched the rocky wall as the goblin raised its club again. One of the stones burst from the wall and she hit the goblin across the face. It skittered backward and Ivar wrapped a ball of water over its face. The creature clawed at its throat, eyes bulging and mouth flapping open in shock.

"What—" Ivar was saying.

"Go, *children*." She blinked past her starry vision and pointed to the end of the hall. "Now."

Ivar bolted in the direction she had signaled to. Kolfinna rubbed the side of her face and tried to stand, but her vision was still blurred at the edges and darkening like blots of ink. She blinked back and calmed her breathing. Ivar would save the child. She trusted in his abilities. She just hoped she could right herself in time so she could join him and help.

She pushed herself to her feet. Her vision still danced with blotches of black and she had to hold the wall to keep herself upright. She squeezed her eyes shut and exhaled deeply. She knew it would only take a minute or two from her past experience of healing herself. Then she could spring into action and help.

Across from her, something breathed loudly. Unevenly.

Kolfinna turned her head just as a creature lumbered through the doorway. Unlike the small goblins who had hobbled forward and were only three to four feet tall, this thing was at least seven feet. It had to bend its green-skinned bald head to fit through the doorway. Its belly was distended and round, like it had eaten far too much, and its muscles bulged. Razor-sharp teeth stuck out of its mouth and its beady red eyes found Kolfinna's instantaneously.

She raised a hand to bring forth her mana, but the creature, despite its size, was faster. It rushed her and Kolfinna tried to shove herself off the wall and away from its attack, but it was too late. Its fist connected with her shoulder and it swatted her away like a fly. She tumbled and rolled across the hallway like a rag doll. Her vision spun, her shoulder and back ached, and she kept rolling until she slammed into a wall.

She raised her wobbly arms. She needed to get up and fight—

It was on her again. It kicked her side and she flew again, tumbling and cracking her shoulder against the ground. Fierce pain shot through her core. Her wet gasps told her she had at least one broken rib.

Up—

Get up—

Kolfinna barely pushed herself to her elbows. All she could see was spinning black and blurs of indistinguishable color.

Again, something struck her stomach—a foot, maybe—and she hit the wall. Iron blood filled her mouth. She pressed her palms against the rough structure behind her and caused the stone to wrap in front of her in seconds. Another fist—or foot— slammed into her makeshift armor, but it was enough of a barrier for her to fall into the room behind the wall. She stumbled back, repairing the wall with a hand to make sure the creature stayed in the hall.

It roared and slammed into the stone she had replaced. Pebbles littered the floor and she could feel the sandy debris dusting her face every time the creature punched her new wall. She blinked rapidly, trickles of warm blood slipping past her lips.

That would keep it away for a minute. Enough time for Kolfinna to find her bearings.

A few seconds passed; the creature continued to pound on the wall. Kolfinna's vision started to return to normal and she could make out the dark room. There was a doorway that seemed to lead to another hallway, but running wasn't an option. There were humans inside this place and if she let this monster run amuck, she would be putting them in danger.

She needed to kill it—now.

Kolfinna touched her chest tentatively and gasped raggedly. Three broken ribs.

She didn't know how long it took her body to heal itself, but it wasn't happening fast enough.

The walls shook and all Kolfinna could do was back away farther into the darkly lit room. Just as she did, the creature barreled through. Stones and bits of rocks flew across the room. Kolfinna aimed a pointed stone spear at the large goblin's face and shot it forward. The creature ducked in the nick of time and charged like a bull. She dove to the ground, away from its attack. Her chest screamed in agony and she tasted more metallic blood.

The goblin grunted loudly and picked up a piece of the crumbled wall and chucked it at her with all its might. Kolfinna raised her hand and a thin barrier of stone erected itself in seconds in front of her. The stone ground against her barrier and cracks formed all along it like a broken mirror. Kolfinna rolled in time as the creature struck the barrier with its muscular, green-skinned arm.

They circled each other. Kolfinna's ribs throbbed painfully and her vision waned with every passing second. Broken bones seemed to heal slower than wounds on her flesh, she realized, since she could still feel the broken parts of her ribs. Moving hurt and breathing hurt even more. The rush of adrenaline couldn't completely mask her pain.

Kolfinna continued to throw stone spears and slam pieces of rock at the monster, but for whatever reason, it was unfazed. It didn't falter and only pushed aside her attacks like they were buzzing flies.

It also didn't help that every passing second felt like her last.

Kolfinna finally wrenched her sword out of its sheath. She wasn't as good with a sword as she was with her stone magic, but considering how her magic wasn't putting a dent on the creature, this was her only option.

She charged forward, sword raised. The creature backed away and dodged her attack with a roar. They rounded each other again, the goblin breathing in and out deeply while Kolfinna tried to calm her uneven breaths. She needed to finish this quickly.

Right when the creature lunged, Kolfinna brought down her blade. Her sword sank into the goblin's forearm. But only an inch.

Her eyes widened. In slow motion, it smacked her face and she tore to the other side of the room. She crashed into the wall and could feel the rough textured wall ripping through the skin of her face. Her chest felt like it had cracked open and more blood filled her mouth and nose.

She couldn't die here.

She turned and tried to pull herself up. Tried to look past her distorting vision. Tried to use her mana to attack. But her movements were sluggish and she could barely move.

She didn't want to die. Not like this. Certainly not by this creature.

She could already see its feet lumbering toward her motionless body. She could hear its jagged breathing. It knew she was done for.

Where was Ivar? Where were the rest of her teammates when she needed them?

No, he needed to save the children. It was probably better that she was alone here.

But she didn't want to die.

Not like this. Not now.

The goblin's breath fanned across her face and smelled like rancid meat. Right when it reached to grab her, Kolfinna's magic flared and her mana came to life all on its own. Black shadows ripped through her chest and burst over the creature's skin. The creature reared back with a scream, its arms flailing as black flame-like shadows spread over its body. The shadowy tendrils whipped out of her body with a life of their own. They seized the creature, wrapping it up tightly. The smell of burning flesh and the creature's screams filled the air, and an ice-cold chill emitted from the shadows, writhing out of her hands and feet. Inky black splotches filled the ground and stained her hands with black.

Kolfinna watched in horror as the creature fell to its knees, the shadows consuming it with swathes of ominous black. She remembered the looks on the faces of Hilda's lackeys as they had died in the same way. Seconds passed and the creature finally fell to the ground. The shadows slowly receded from the ink-stained corpse and flitted back toward Kolfinna. She tried pulling away from them, but they slithered and disappeared into her skin in seconds.

9

Kolfinna lay on the ground for several minutes. Just breathing, thinking, and allowing her body to heal itself. The cuts inside her mouth healed first; that only took a minute. Her face took at least two minutes. But the rest of her body took longer. Her ribs continued to throb, but not as painfully as before, and she could at least breathe without feeling like she would lose consciousness.

Her mana was close to being drained completely. She guessed she had about ten percent left. Not nearly enough to continue fighting, so she would have to rely on her sword skills. Speaking of the sword, it was lying on the ground several feet from her. A thin crack ran along the middle of the blade. *Great.*

Her hands were still stained with inky shadows and no matter how much she rubbed them against her pants or the front of her uniform, they didn't smudge at all. She couldn't remember how she had washed them off last time. After she had left Hilda's torture cabin, she had stumbled into the bakery Fenris's wife, Malene, owned. Everything after that was a blur, but when she had awoken at Fenris's estate, she hadn't noticed any inky stains on her hands.

These stains were probably remnants of her magic. Time would probably fade them.

Her ears nearly twitched as she caught soft footsteps headed her way.

"Kolfinna? *Kolfinna!*"

She paused—it was Ivar. Judging by the sound of his voice bouncing off the stony, craggy walls, he was at the end of the hallway, maybe, where she had been before the monstrous goblin had attacked. His rushed footsteps echoed in the distance.

Kolfinna hurriedly pulled herself into a sitting position. Her teeth gnashed with each other from the effort, and her hands scrambled against the dusty ground and the bumpy walls. Although the worst of her injuries were healed, she was still sore and her ribs weren't completely healed. She could probably walk, though, and not black out.

She needed to get out of this room before he stumbled upon her and saw everything she couldn't explain—the obvious scuffles of a hard-won battle, the black stains all over the ground and the goblin monster, and her miraculously healed body despite the fresh blood on her uniform.

She pushed herself to her hands and knees.

Just a bit more—

Too late.

Ivar stepped through the hole in the wall carefully. "Kolfinna?"

The first thing Kolfinna noticed was that he was holding a little child. A young red-headed girl was tucked into his chest, her face pressed against the crook of his neck. Her tattered dress was covered with grime and dirt, but he didn't seem to mind. Kolfinna's nose crinkled at the overwhelming scent of urine.

Ivar halted in his steps and his blue-green gaze roved over the room, at the goblin monster covered in black stains, at the dents and missing chunks of stone from the walls and ground, and then it settled on Kolfinna. Questions brewed on his face and before he could open his mouth and voice them, Kolfinna beat him to it.

"Is she okay?" She rose to her feet and dusted off her pants distractedly with trembling hands. She didn't want anyone to find out about her strange abilities and connect it to something else. Something like those strange rune writings during the West Border mission that foretold an heir who would free the queen. Because Kolfinna certainly wasn't the heir, but there was a chance that she was related to the heir. And with these strange abilities showing their face, her fear and confusion intensified. She didn't need more questions.

Ivar laid a gentle hand on the child's quivering back. "Terrified, speechless, and starving, but otherwise safe and uninjured."

Kolfinna could only imagine how frightening this whole ordeal must've been for the little girl. She couldn't have been more than five years old.

"That thing is *massive*." Ivar stared at the dead goblin three feet away from Kolfinna. "Did you defeat it?"

"Yep." She headed toward the opening in the wall. "How about we—"

"Are you going to explain"—he waved his free hand at the room with raised brows—"any of this?"

"Fae magic," she lied smoothly. "Rune magic, to be specific."

That seemed like a good enough answer, especially since he didn't know any of the specifics of rune magic, but maybe it was because he was a trained warrior that he didn't seem to buy it. Kolfinna held her breath as he continued searching her face. Finally, he shrugged. "I see. Well, remind me not to mess with you."

She forced a laugh and hoped it sounded genuine. "Let's go and find the others."

"You're bleeding. Maybe we should take a break—"

"They're shallow cuts." She walked into the open hallway and looked over her shoulder at him. "We should try to save as many humans as we can. So let's go."

She moved quickly down the hall, hoping he wouldn't ask any more questions.

It took their party two and a half days to completely clear out the cave of goblins and find all fourteen children. They had found the children within the first day, but since Eluf didn't want to miss any child or person who hadn't been accounted for, he had made Kolfinna and the rest of the party scour every nook and cranny of the caves. And, of course, to make sure they killed each and every last goblin.

When they finally left the village after reuniting the children with their families, Kolfinna was exhausted down to her bones. They traveled on horseback to the fort. Everyone chattered happily and cheerily. After all, the mission had been a success and they had managed to save all the children—children who the villagers had thought were long dead—so of course everyone was happy.

Everyone except for Kolfinna.

She was satisfied with how the mission had turned out and something inside her had warmed at the sight of the children reuniting with their families, but there was something that was bothering her.

She had changed. A lot.

Ever since those shadows had first emerged from her in her fight with Hilda's underlings, she was morphing. Her hair had changed, her hearing and sights and smells had improved, her body was able to heal itself, and she had strange shadow magic.

She also remembered what the book of magic creatures had said about elves. White hair. Red eyes. And magic that entailed healing, shadows, and light.

All of which, except the red eyes and the light magic, Kolfinna seemed to have developed.

She didn't want to face what that meant: that she was part elf. That she had something to do with the half-elf commander. That she was related to the heir. That she ... was something more than just a regular fae girl trying to survive in a world that didn't want her around.

If anyone found out about this—that she was somehow related to the heir—then they would kill her. Point, blank, period.

Because if she truly was related to the heir and thus had the power to awaken the queen, then it would've been easier for everyone in Rosain to kill her and effectively kill the only chance Ragnarök had at freeing their queen.

And as much as Kolfinna didn't want Ragnarök to succeed, she also didn't want to die.

The only good thing she had going for her was that Ragnarök didn't seem to have any idea who she was.

If she was related to the heir. The only evidence of that was that she had been able to wield the *Død Sværd*. But there could've been a reasonable explanation for it all. Like maybe Revna and everyone's understanding of the ancient sword was wrong. Maybe anyone could wield it if the sword allowed them to?

But the last three days had solidified a plan in her head. She needed to leave. Where she would go, she had no clue, but the more she remained here, surrounded by soldiers who could potentially figure out that she had different powers, she had to leave.

First, she had to find a way to get rid of this blasted rune etched onto her wrist. Then she would secure an escape plan. And probably hide out for the rest of her life.

She didn't like the latter part of her plan. Her whole reasoning behind joining the Royal Guards had been to make a place for herself in society. But that plan had fallen through and she doubted the military could offer her a semblance of that—especially not with the Hunter's Association now a part of the military and with Sijur's sinister plans for her.

As much as she hated to run away from all the work she had done, she didn't have a choice. She'd rather be alive than not. And she would rather hide away somewhere than be forced to enslave people.

All those thoughts swirled in the back of her mind. In order to figure out how to break the runes, she'd have to get close to Joran and ask him about the books he had read and learned about rune magic through. There had to be something that she could learn from them. A clue.

Kolfinna was so wrapped up in her thoughts that when they arrived at the base, she didn't notice the iciness of winter's clutches over the fort, even though the weather had warmed now that they were in the tail end of winter. Even when she stepped into the lobby of the fort, the rest of the group with her, she didn't notice the familiar chill inside the building. It wasn't until Herja squealed and ran past her that she snapped out of her thoughts.

Her gaze drew to the center of the lobby and her breath caught in her throat.

Blár Vilulf was here.

He was speaking to another soldier, but everything surrounding him distorted away until all Kolfinna could see was him. His midnight, tousled hair, his ice-blue eyes that reminded her of a frozen lake, his muscular frame that filled out his dark bluish-gray uniform. Her breath stole away at his beauty. At his unexpected visit here.

That image shattered when Herja flung herself into his arms. He stumbled back while she giggled, hugging him tightly. His eyebrows arched in surprise, and his hand rested casually on her upper back as he gave her a pat.

Then, to make matters worse, Herja went on her tiptoes and *kissed* him on the cheek.

He didn't push her away. Didn't even look disgusted. Only looked down at her with dark lashes. Not a flicker of surprise lingering on his face—like he was used to this.

Herja backed away and laced her hands together in front of her. Her cheeks were rosy as they began talking. Kolfinna couldn't hear what they were saying. She felt like someone had splashed cold water all over her face.

Kolfinna's chest tightened painfully—more painful than her broken ribs had been two days prior. It felt like someone had stabbed her with an ice-cold dagger and had twisted, twisted, and twisted until her heart couldn't take it anymore.

This must've been the reason Herja didn't like Kolfinna. It must be the reason Blár had come back here. He must've been in a relationship with Herja. There was no other reason why Blár Vilulf wouldn't push her away at the kiss. He had hugged her back. He had *allowed* her to kiss his cheek.

The Blár she knew didn't like people invading his personal space. He didn't like casual touching. He didn't like people hovering over him.

Ivar clapped Blár on the back, and Blár *grinned* at him. Gunnar hugged him too, and Blár shoved him off, laughing all the while. Inkeri nodded at him and said a few words, and then Eluf gave him a hug too, which Blár reciprocated. He was smiling at them all. He looked … happy. So unlike the brooding man she had known these past few months. He didn't smile like that around her. He didn't laugh like that. She didn't … know him like *that*.

Finally, his cold, cold eyes landed on her and she froze all over again. Her mind came to a stuttering halt when his eyebrows pulled together in confusion. He blinked, and she blinked. And then the moment passed.

"Kolfinna." His smile faded and so did the warmth in his voice. "What … What are you doing here?"

She could feel the pieces of her heart cracking.

"Kolfinna?" This time it was Inkeri. Her dark brows were knitted together in worry. "Are you—"

"I'm fine," she said with a tight-lipped smile. All she could see was the empty seat in the trial room. He should've been there with her and she had foolishly given him a hundred excuses, but now things were making sense. He hadn't been there when Kolfinna needed him the most because he had a life and he had things that were more important than Kolfinna's potential doom.

One of them being ... *this*, apparently. Herja, maybe, and the others in the fort.

She noted the way Herja kept to his side, her hand lightly grazing his forearm. Like it belonged there. Like *she* belonged there beside him.

"Kolfinna—" Blár stepped forward and the usual comfort she found from the ice-cold chill that clung to him was nowhere to be found.

"Nice to see you here," she said politely, distantly. "I didn't expect it."

"Likewise." He glanced at the cloak she wore—*his* cloak.

She wanted to rip it off and fling it at his face for making her feel like a fool. Like a lovestruck fool who thought she had meant something to him. But all the facts were in her face: running across the lake, dancing at the ball, and hugging her at the end of the battle—all of it didn't mean anything because he wasn't in love with her. He had just strung her along, and for what?

Her mind was too scattered to be able to think clearly. The back of her eyes burned and she blinked them rapidly. "Well then, I'll see you later," she said with a nod. "I'll—"

He reached forward as if to grab her by the arm, but she was already stepping back.

"We just got back from a long mission." The others didn't seem to notice her discomfort, other than Inkeri, who watched her with concern. "I'm going to wash up and rest for a bit." She then turned to Blár with a shuttered expression. "It was good to see you."

His forehead crinkled. "Why—"

She didn't let him finish and instead shoved past him down to the hallway that led to the women's quarters. She had been so excited to see Blár, but now all she wanted to do was hide.

10

Kolfinna didn't have time to weep into her pillow or do anything dramatic because Inkeri entered the room soon after she did, and the tiny sliver of privacy she had was gone. So she instead washed up like she said she would. She stripped out of her dirtied, bloodied clothes and put on a clean uniform. She brushed out her hair and cleaned her face with the basin water until she was presentable. She just needed to do something to busy her hands so she didn't have to think about anything.

She so badly wanted to curl away somewhere and cry out her feelings. To sort through her thoughts and come up with an outline of her frazzled emotions. But Inkeri was there and she didn't make a move to leave.

"Are you going to wear that to dinner?" Inkeri was combing her silken hair. She had also washed the grime off her body.

Kolfinna looked down at her clean, gray military uniform. It still smelled fresh from the dried, pressed jasmine petals she had placed in it like the rest of her clothing in her trunk. "What's wrong with my uniform?"

"Nothing." Inkeri shrugged with a slight frown. She had put on a simple, sleeveless black dress with a square neckline that showed a hint of cleavage. "Usually, after a mission, we get the whole evening off and our group has dinner together in one of the more private rooms. It's to help us bond and go over the details. And since Blár is back, we'll probably have dinner with him."

Kolfinna eyed the silk dress she was wearing. "And that requires you to dress like that?"

Inkeri's cheeks reddened. "No, but I like to dress nicely." She tucked a strand of hair behind her reddening ear. "It's not often that we get to dress up."

Kolfinna wondered if it was because Blár was there. She could already hear Ivar's snide remark. *All those ladies got their panties in a twist.*

Maybe Inkeri also liked Blár? That thought further soured her mood.

"I think I look fine like this." Kolfinna smoothed down the front of her uniform. If she wore anything else, she was sure she'd be uncomfortable. Facing Blár without first facing her messy feelings required her to wear a soldier's uniform. Not something flirty that would confuse her. This was a battle in itself.

"If you say so."

Herja bounced inside the room soon after, her cheeks flushed with color and a giddy grin on her face.

Kolfinna couldn't look her in the eyes, so she busied herself with picking at the dried blood stains on her crumpled clothes from the mission while the red-haired woman cleaned herself and dressed in an emerald green sweeping gown.

"Can you help me with my hair?" Herja's voice was high-pitched, girly, and *breathless* with excitement.

Of course she was excited.

Bitterness filled Kolfinna's mouth like vinegar-soaked tart berries. She didn't want to go to any dinner where she'd have a front row seat to Herja and Blár flirting together. Or whatever they did together.

Inkeri helped her with her hair, both of them chatting freely.

"I invited Brenda over," Herja was saying. "I'm sure a few

more people want to join us too, but Blár said he'd rather have limited people."

"Hm." Inkeri finished brushing out Herja's curls and began twisting and braiding them until she had an elegant bun in the back of her head. She rested her hands on Herja's shoulder and inspected her handiwork. "There, you look great."

Kolfinna's own hair looked like a fluffy rat's nest compared to hers. Even though she had brushed it, her curls had frizzed in the cold and didn't look right. She hastily began to braid it right when the two women rose up to leave.

She followed after them, her fingers deftly working to tie her hair together, even as her heart sank and sank like an anchor, except it never stopped. It kept sinking and sinking and even as they reached the dinner room, her heart had not yet reached the bottom.

They entered a smaller room close to the dining hall, and Kolfinna was immediately overwhelmed with the smell of baked goods, roasted meats, and mouthwatering delicacies. Unlike the rest of the fort with its monotonous gray, this room seemed to be the exception. Stepping foot inside the private dining room was like stepping into a different fort altogether. Gone were the boring floors, replaced with shining marble with red-veined tiles. Gone were the slabs of gray walls and in their place were wooden paneling and silvery, embossed wallpaper. One of the walls opened up to glass doors and a stony white balcony, and another was comprised completely of glass and overlooked the courtyard down below.

There was a long serving table full of meaty broth, buttered bread, honeyed oatcakes, varieties of cheese and jams and fruits, roasted duck and chicken, and various other delicacies. Four smaller circular tables with silk tablecloths were scattered in the room.

Kolfinna had to pause and stare at everything for a moment. If she didn't know any better, she would've thought she was in a different place altogether. Why hadn't anyone put this much attention to the rest of the fort? Or maybe that was just the Royal Guard side of her talking—the side that had gotten used to having fancy rooms as a default.

A dozen people were already inside, including Blár, Eluf, Ivar, and Gunnar. The four men occupied one of the tables and they didn't seem to care much for their appearance compared to the two women by Kolfinna's side because they wore their uniforms. They were clean, she was sure, but that was it. Nothing else.

Kolfinna would've been relieved at that, if it wasn't for the fact that every woman was dressed in some sort of gown. She stood out like a sore thumb, even more than usual.

"Looks like a few people also finished their missions around the same time—" Inkeri started, but Herja was already bounding to Blár, a large grin stretching over her face. Her green skirts fluttered behind her with every bounce.

"She's excited." Inkeri gave a short laugh.

Kolfinna watched as the redhead planted her hands on the table and announced her presence. She wanted to turn around and leave the room, but that would attract more attention. Maybe she could make an excuse that she was tired? They had been traveling for a long time before this, so it only made sense that she would be tired from the journey and not exactly pleased to be thrust into a social event so soon.

But Inkeri was already moving toward the table, and Kolfinna's stomach grumbled at the various smells and the thought of decadent food. She followed behind begrudgingly. She couldn't help but glance over her shoulder at the entrance. The dining hall was nearby and although the food might not be as great as here, she was prepared to make do with it if necessary.

When they reached the table, Brenda rose from her seat beside Gunnar and gave Inkeri a hug. "You look amazing."

"Thank you."

Kolfinna awkwardly hung behind the two hugging women. There were two empty seats left; one beside Ivar, and the other next to Herja. She noticed the way Ivar's gaze flashed at the sight of Inkeri and roved over her figure, and how his sea-colored eyes flitted away just as quickly.

Interesting.

She took a seat beside him while Inkeri sat next to Herja. Herja had to take the spot beside Eluf, instead of next to Blár, since Eluf and Gunnar were currently occupying those seats. It was a small victory—at least Kolfinna didn't have to be front and center of it all—but the expectation on Herja's face still soured her stomach.

The kiss replayed in her mind and her insides clenched painfully.

Between the girls greeting each other, Blár's eyes found Kolfinna's. The silvery-white fur lining of his cloak made the blue of his eyes stand out vividly. With a single stare, the breath of winter breezed past, sending a shiver down her spine.

Kolfinna forced herself to be as expressionless as she could be —as if his appearance didn't bother her in the least. Like she was unaffected by all of it—the hugging, the kiss, the smiles and laughs he gave.

"How have you been?" Inkeri asked him as she settled into her seat and folded her hands over the white, shimmering silk table-cloth. "It's been a long time since you've been back at this base."

"I know." Blár picked up his knife and cut a piece of his roasted duck from his ceramic plate. The silver edge of the knife gleamed in the bright lighting of the room, and it took Kolfinna a second to realize that he wasn't using the cutlery—he was using a dagger. "You know why I left."

It almost made her smile—the crudeness was so like him, but then she remembered the kiss and the fact that he hadn't been there at the trial, and her twitching lips stilled.

She folded her hands on her lap and stared at the flower arrangement centerpiece at the table. She tried to name each one —pink roses, purple Astrantias, and soft-green eucalypts—to keep her mind occupied.

"Because you couldn't stand the lieutenant?" Inkeri asked.

"Damn right." Blár popped the meat in his mouth and chewed. He was staring at Kolfinna, but even as she felt his gaze boring into her, she stayed focused on the flowers.

"And here I thought you couldn't stand Gunnar and that's why you left," Ivar said as he dragged a finger over the rim of his wine glass. His lips formed a subtle smirk, while Gunnar snorted.

"I'm the only reason he stayed for so long," Gunnar said. "I thought for sure he couldn't stand living with your dusty ass."

Eluf lowered his bone-in chicken thigh and fixed a disappointed look at the two men who continued to bicker. "I'd prefer to have a *quiet* dinner that doesn't involve your childish antics. Either of you."

Kolfinna almost laughed, while Herja braced her arms on the table and leaned forward in Blár's direction. She was seemingly immune to the conversations around her. "But the bigger question is, are you back for good?"

Blár stabbed another hunk of meat with the tip of his dagger and lifted his shoulders at the same time. "No clue. That depends."

"On?"

Kolfinna didn't even realize she was drumming her fingers on the table until Inkeri suddenly placed her hand atop hers.

"Are you okay?" Inkeri whispered, a hundred questions reflecting within her kind, gray eyes.

"Oh? I'm good—"

"Are you hungry? I'll get you a plate."

"No, I'm fine—"

But Inkeri only shook her head and left the table. Had she noticed the conflict on Kolfinna's face? Was Kolfinna not doing a good enough job at appearing aloof? Or maybe Inkeri thought she was too hungry to socialize well?

It could've just been that Inkeri was being kind. She hoped that was why because she didn't want to think about the woman knowing her vulnerable secret—that she had feelings for Blár and that she was *hurt*. Hurt and betrayed.

Brenda folded her arms together on the table and watched Inkeri at the serving table. "So ..." Something lit in her eyes and she pressed forward like she was sharing a secret. "Is it true about Inkeri?"

"About what?" Herja tilted her head to the side.

"Come on, you know what." Brenda grinned. "Is she going to accept that date with Asger? They'd make a beautiful couple, don't you think? *He's* gorgeous, *she's* gorgeous. They'd be the power couple of this fort."

Herja lit up. "Ah, *that*. I haven't asked her yet what her response was."

Ivar's lip curled back and he reached for his drink. "Oh, they'd be the perfect bloody couple all right. The image of virginal, pure love." He downed his drink in seconds.

Perhaps Kolfinna wasn't the only one nursing a wounded heart.

Inkeri returned a minute later with two plates full of steaming food. Kolfinna picked at the roasted lamb, chicken, rosemary potatoes, crumbly cheeses, and herby vegetables on her plate. She couldn't taste much and didn't try to converse with anyone either. They all talked about the mission, about the goblins, how they fell through the ceiling, and about the children, and every other detail that fascinated them. Blár ate and listened, laughed and smiled, and offered his own words now and then.

Kolfinna could barely look at him.

She could feel his glacial eyes roam over to her from time to time, but she only stared at her plate and then at the exit. She picked at her food distractedly. It was a sumptuous, delectable meal—she could tell by just looking at—and she wished she were more capable of appreciating it.

"Do you want to try the desserts?" Inkeri asked her. She had finished everything on her plate and was dabbing her mouth with a linen handkerchief. "They have honeyed oatcakes and rice pudding—"

"I think I'll actually be heading to my room," Kolfinna said, rising to her feet. She gave a small nod to the rest of the group, who were too engrossed in their conversation with each other to give her more than a wave. "I'm pretty tired."

Kolfinna hated the pity she found in Inkeri's eyes. "All right then. I'll see you tomorrow at training, yes?"

"Sure." Kolfinna departed from the table, keen on escaping up to her room, curling up in a ball, and clearing her mind. It was probably better this way, she told herself. If she was planning on leaving this place for good, it was better that she didn't have attachments to anyone—especially Blár. Romantic feelings had never been on the table for her.

Two steps away from the exit. She could go to her room and cry—

The air shifted with a cool breeze before Blár even said her name. "Kolfinna."

She faltered and turned. He was a few feet away from her and now that she was looking at him, she noticed a few things she hadn't before—like how his mussed hair was slightly damp, how he smelled like vanilla and cinnamon and clean soap, how his blue eyes appeared almost silvery blue against the moonlit sky behind him through the wall of windows.

Between him and the exit, she would've rather stayed with him, but then the image of Herja kissing his cheek twisted her heart painfully, and she turned to the door. "I'm tired, Blár, and—"

The excuse fell away when he touched her arm gently. "Why are you acting like this?"

She could feel the eyes on them without having to look at their table. Could practically sense the daggers Herja was sending her way. Kolfinna stared at his hand pointedly, and he removed it. "Look, Blár—" Sure enough, she caught everyone at their table watching them.

He followed her gaze to the table and frowned. "We need to talk."

"No—"

"Come with me." He didn't wait for a response and left the room.

Kolfinna hesitated for a second longer before following after him. They didn't go far. Across the hallway, Blár opened the door, peeked inside, and then ushered her forward. It was a small conference room, by the looks of it. A round table took up the center of the room and there were a dozen chairs circling it. Two square windows took up one of the walls, casting the room in a silvery glow, which battled with the waning orange fire smoldering in the hearth.

The door clicked shut behind Blár while Kolfinna ventured deeper into the room, putting as much distance between them as she could.

She dragged a hand over the rounded ears of the chairs as she passed them by. "So? What did you want to talk about?"

Blár mimicked her movement but from the opposite end of the table. His hands gently rested on the back of one of the chairs. "Why are you avoiding me?"

"I'm not—"

"You're a terrible liar, so don't even try it." He pinned her with a slightly confused stare. "What's bothering you?"

The lies she was prepared to say died on her tongue. She didn't like how he knew that about her. That observation that nobody else seemed to have picked up on. Not even herself.

"Kolfinna, what's wrong?" Gone was the confidence of a black rank. The arrogance, the laughter, the fun. His eyes searched her face and her body tensed.

She hated the effect he had on her. Her heart was already racing, her thoughts a blur. But the ache in her chest only intensified. Still, she didn't talk.

"Kolfinna." He rounded the table, drawing closer to her with slow, tentative steps. "Did something happen? You've been acting very distant."

She stared intently at the flickering flames in the hearth. Many things had happened. He hadn't shown up at her trial. He had strung her along. He had allowed Herja to kiss him. He had played with her feelings. And worst of all—he had made her a hopeless, naïve fool during all of it.

Blár closed the distance between them and rested a hand on her bicep, his head tilted so he could get a better look at her. Concern laced his words. "Talk to me," he said softly.

"You didn't show up at my trial." Her throat closed up and she didn't even try masking the hurt from her voice or her face. She didn't want to show him any more vulnerability than she already had, but she couldn't stop herself. The wobbly words tumbled out freely. "I expected you to be there. I was waiting for you to show up and … I don't know, help me? To show everyone that you're still on my side. I thought …"

Now her words dried up. She thought she had meant something to him.

Blár raked a hand through his hair. "I was busy."

She flinched and he had the decency to look slightly ashamed.

"You were *busy*?" The fissure in her heart deepened.

"That came out wrong." He winced at her sharp tone. "I had to do something really important. The details—I can't really explain."

She clenched her fists together. "Okay, so you were busy with something, so busy that you couldn't show up at my trial. In which I was being tried by the Royal Guards and the king for *treason*. And you were … *busy*."

"Is that what's bothering you?" Blár watched her carefully. "That I wasn't there for you?"

Her cheeks warmed with embarrassment; he said it like it was such a trivial thing. They weren't anything more than friends, so she shouldn't have expected anything more. Even her actual friends—Eyfura and Nollar—hadn't been able to make it to the trial since it was only allowed for higher-ups, but she had thought that Blár would've been able to come. That he held enough sway to change her fate.

Kolfinna blew out air. "Blár, what are we?"

"What?"

"What are we?" She flicked a hand between the two of them. "Me and you. What are we? Because you said a few weeks ago that we're friends, but we also ran across that frozen lake and laughed our asses off. We danced at the ball. We *flirted* with each other." Her voice dropped to a whisper. She truly hoped he didn't come around and say that it was all a lie. That her version of the truth wasn't his. "So what exactly are we? *Friends*?"

Blár was quiet—too quiet. Like he didn't know what to say.

When he didn't answer, Kolfinna continued, "So we're just friends. All right. Got it." She blinked back the tears burning her eyes. "I was just ... shocked, to say the least, when I saw Herja kiss you. Since you're in a relationship, I don't think it's appropriate for you to flirt with another woman—"

"Wait. Wait." The shadows in the room played across his face as he canted his head. "I'm not in a relationship with anyone."

"But ... You kissed her."

"I didn't kiss her. *She* kissed me on the cheek—that hardly counts as a kiss. Herja just greets people that way." He rested a hand on the back of one of the chairs. "We're not together in any way. I'm not interested in her like that."

Herja most definitely didn't greet everyone like that. Kolfinna had never seen her kiss Gunnar, or Eluf, or Ivar, or any of the other soldiers in that way. Herja had lit up at the sight of Blár; there was no doubt in Kolfinna's mind that Herja was in love with him—or, if not in love, she would soon be. He was either too stupid to see that or he was lying to her. She really hoped he was being stupid.

"I'm not interested in Herja," Blár said slowly, drawing closer to her. "She's a good friend of mine from when I was stationed here over two years ago, but I don't have those kinds of feelings for her."

Relief pooled in her chest, but it was short-lived. She couldn't shake her unease at seeing a side of him with everyone here that he had never shown her before. It also didn't help that whatever was going on between them was unresolved. She liked him. She knew that for a fact. But did he like her beyond just flirting and being friends? She had no idea.

"You're good friends with all of them," she said instead of confronting those feelings.

"I am." He rubbed the nape of his neck. "Gunnar and Ivar are my best friends, and Eluf's my brother-in-law."

Brother-in-law?

He must've seen the question on her face because he winced and softly said, "He was married to my sister."

His sister, who had been killed with the rest of his family. Kolfinna could barely hide her shock. "I'm ... I'm so sorry."

She was suddenly reminded about how everything about Eluf seemed so bleak. The dark circles, the lifeless stare, the gloomy air around him. It all made sense now.

"Sylvi and him were expecting a child when ..." He didn't need to finish his sentence. She caught the slight rise and fall of his voice and the momentary pain flashing in the icy depths of his blue eyes. It was gone in a split second. Like a mask clicking in place, he continued, "Gunnar has been my best friend since childhood. All three of them are good friends of mine."

"Blár, I'm so sorry." Kolfinna didn't know what else to say. She momentarily forgot about the betrayal she had felt, the pain that had seized her heart. She wanted to comfort him somehow, but she had no idea how to do that.

He waved a hand, dismissing her words. "Forget about that. Why are you upset? Did someone in the group say something? Did they treat you badly?"

The hardness in his tone didn't go unnoticed by her. "No ... They've been treating me well."

"Then what is it?"

You.

Kolfinna sighed loudly. Her feelings were messy and she needed to decompress everything that had happened in these past few hours. The kiss, the hugs, the fact that their relationship was muddy at best, her feelings—there was a lot to unpack. "I don't know, Blár. I'm just ... confused."

"About what?"

Us.

"Everything." She shrugged and picked at a dent in the wooden chair in front of her. "I'm in a new place with new people and new duties. It's a lot to take in, I guess."

"Why are you even here? Shouldn't you be with the Royal Guards?"

"You would know," she said suddenly, her voice sharp, "if you had gone to my trial."

He blinked back, as if not expecting her ire.

"Aren't *you* supposed to be at the eastern border?" Kolfinna countered.

"I transferred here."

"Why?"

He lifted his shoulder and looked out the window. His jaw was set tight. "Reasons."

"I ..." Kolfinna felt foolish for even thinking it, but she had expected more from him when he first saw her. She had expected him to be happy to see her. The image of his surprised face made her insides twist painfully. He had looked displeased. "*What ... What are you doing here?*" he had asked.

She pushed those thoughts away. "I'm happy to see you here, really." Kolfinna's smile came out somehow strained. She would just have to smile and be a friend. She had never thought the word *friend* could sound so bitter, but since she was planning to escape Sijur's clutches and leave this place behind, it was better this way. She would be a good friend and depart from him on good terms.

Blár watched her carefully. His gaze trailed from her tight smile to her white-touched hair. "It's good to see you too," he murmured, reaching forward and grazing a knuckle along her cheekbone. Her breath caught in her throat as he pushed a strand of hair behind her ear.

Kolfinna backed away even as her heart raced and even though she wanted to lean into his touch. She clasped her hands together tightly behind her back and tried to laugh casually, as if that little moment hadn't made her stomach flutter with a cage of butterflies. She would have to keep her distance from him if she wanted to make it easier for her heart to leave.

"I really should go now." She glanced at the doorway. "I've had a long day and I really just want to knock out in bed. So ... yeah, I'll see you around?"

"Prob—"

"Great!" She zoomed past him to the door. She had wrenched open the door three inches when he called out from behind her.

"Hey, sweet-cheeks."

Her ears reddened at that nickname. She had thought he had forgotten about that.

"Hm?"

Blár was leaning against the table, his grin subtle. "It really is good to see you."

Words failed her and she could only nod. Distance, she told herself. She really needed to keep her distance. He was far too dangerous for her heart.

11

Training with Joran was tiresome. As she manipulated stones in the rocky basement with the male fae, she couldn't meet his gaze. She didn't really want anything to do with Joran. Her anger toward him had sizzled out days ago, when she realized that he probably wasn't any more involved in Sijur's mess than she was, and that he probably had no choice like she did, but that still didn't change that she didn't particularly like Joran.

Joran wasn't actually doing anything wrong, per se. He was just trying to survive. No other fae in their right mind would reveal they were fae, since the current society wouldn't allow them to. They'd be hunted down, Kolfinna reasoned. Which was especially true since the Hunter's Association was reinstated. So it wasn't his fault that he was acting out of survival like the rest of their race. But it still bothered her. She hated that he could pretend to be human and she couldn't. And that he didn't have to face the criticism and hatred like she did.

But if Kolfinna wanted to find out what he knew about rune magic and how he had learned about it, she needed to befriend him. It also helped that she saw him almost every day for their stone magic training.

Joran had her mainly practice three things every training

session. One, aim her stones at immovable statues he erected. He would make her practice hitting them with multiple rocks, with her eyes closed, and while running laps around the training room. Second, carving into stone to make intricate patterns. Apparently, it helped with mana manipulation, and she had to agree because it wasn't as easy as it looked. Thirdly and lastly, he made her try to levitate the stones without throwing them anywhere. That was probably the hardest part of her training. She could make rocks float for five seconds, and that seemed about all she could do at her current level.

That was what she was doing right now. Kolfinna kept trying to raise her current rock—which she had carved into a very crudely cut mushroom—but holding it in place was straining her already drained mana. Joran sat cross-legged on the floor a few feet away from her, watching her with meadow-like green eyes.

The rock fell to the floor after five seconds and she blew out air. Sweat trickled down the nape of her neck and she could feel it uncomfortably collect down her itchy spine.

"You're not focusing too much on control," Joran said in that soft, soft voice of his.

She pushed a sweaty tendril of hair off her damp face. "How would you know that?

He winced at her harsh tone as if she had struck him. "I can't know for sure, but I can sort of tell."

"Really? Can you tell what I'm thinking then?" She almost rolled her eyes. Not everything came to her effortlessly. Raising this stupid rock up in the air was one of them. How Joran—spineless little Joran—could raise a dozen rocks and keep them afloat for minutes at a time was beyond her comprehension. And it irked her.

"You're probably thinking that you want to punch me."

"Close."

Joran sighed. "Kolfinna, I'm not your enemy ..."

"Mhm." She wrapped her mana around the rock once more and lifted it up. Her mana naturally wanted to let go and launch it somewhere, but she held on to it tighter and poured more mana over it. Just a bit more. Just a bit—

It slipped and fell once again.

Kolfinna muttered a curse and tried again.

"You're focusing too much on adding your mana to the stone and too little on controlling your mana. You don't need much. You only need a thread of mana to keep it afloat. Smothering it with heaps of mana isn't going to make it float."

Kolfinna hesitated and released her hold on the stone. "What do you mean? I'm exerting a normal amount of mana over it."

"I suspect ..." He traced a circle on the floor. "I suspect you use too much mana when you use your stone magic. You shouldn't be that drained by the end of our training sessions, but you are. So I think ... use less."

She blinked back. *Use less?* Was he being serious? Did he really think that she wasn't using her mana efficiently? Whatever annoyance she was feeling earlier, flared and spread down to her toes.

"You don't know that—" she started.

Joran raised his hands. "I know. I know. I'm just saying what I think."

She pursed her lips together. When she trained with Inkeri, it didn't bother her when the young woman told her where and how to improve, since she knew her combat skills were lacking. But hearing the same thing from another fae concerning her magic? It angered her. She knew how to use her magic. She knew how to fight. She knew how to manipulate her mana and didn't need him to tell her she was doing a bad job.

The flash of emotions crossing her face made Joran shrink back; it wasn't enough to pacify her annoyance. Because this sniveling, flinching man was better than her at stone magic.

Kolfinna breathed out deeply from her nose.

She wasn't one to lose control over her emotions. She had endured Edwin's bullying. She had endured the Royal Guards' nasty words and mean stares. She had endured endless criticism from the denizens of the capital, the royal family, and the nobility.

She could handle her emotions here too, even if she was facing criticism.

He only wanted to make her stronger, she told herself. Sijur needed her to be strong for the rune magic they'd be doing, so it was Joran's duty to ensure she got to that point. Everything he was saying was for her benefit—and Sijur's.

With that in mind, Kolfinna pushed her ego aside and focused on the rock in front of her. She usually used a good amount of mana to wrap around stones and rocks, but instead of using what she would normally use to get a good grip, she used less than half.

To no one's surprise, the rock barely lifted an inch before falling.

"See?" She thrust a hand at her rock. "It went nowhere."

"It's because your control is lacking. You're not efficient enough at mana manipulation to use less mana to yield the same results. Try again."

Kolfinna didn't want to try anymore and would've rather gone to her room to retire for the evening, but giving up wasn't an option. Not until Joran said it was.

While she tried expending less mana on the rock, Joran spoke again. "So ... Blár Vilulf is back."

Kolfinna's stomach flipped at the sound of his name; she had been avoiding him all week. She woke up earlier than before to make sure she didn't see him in the dining hall. She went to dinner only after Herja returned to their room—because Herja made sure she went to dinner on time to catch Blár, so Kolfinna's best bet to avoid him during dinnertime was to watch Herja's schedule.

"I read the reports, you know." He picked up a rock and began whittling at it with his magic distractedly. "I know he hurt you."

She didn't like thinking about that fateful summer day over a year and a half ago, when Blár had faced her and attacked her with his ice magic. When his ice had shattered her leg and ankle in multiple places to the point that she had a permanent limp—until

Revna had healed her. She didn't like thinking back to those days when she only saw him as a nightmare.

The past Kolfinna would be shocked that her present self didn't see him that way anymore and that her thoughts strayed to a more dangerous realm than nightmares.

"He hurt—"

"I know," she said quickly.

She couldn't pinpoint what emotion was playing on his face, but it was a mixture of guilt and pity and sadness and maybe even anger.

"I'm friends with him." Kolfinna focused on the rock and raised it up. "We have had our differences, but we've also worked together a few times and I guess we got over it."

"But he tried to *kill* you."

"I'm aware," she said dryly.

"And you forgave him?"

"Joran, it's not that simple."

"But ..." He sighed loudly, tossed the carving of a miniature tree he had made in the rock, and raked a dusty hand through his golden hair. Debris from the stone colored his burnt golden hair in a pale powdery beige color. The image of him frazzled momentarily paused her from her training. It was strange to see him look anything but small, quiet, and docile. "He *hurt* you, Kolfinna. And you can just ... forgive him? Why? I don't understand."

"You don't have to understand." She turned away from him and the rock fell, joining her other failed attempts. She tried to focus on all the imperfect rocks surrounding her and tried to raise another one, but her mind was too jumbled. "It really isn't your business."

Joran was quiet for a few seconds. "Why are you able to forgive him but not me?"

"Excuse me?" She spun to face him.

"Yes?"

They stared at each other for several seconds. Kolfinna finally sputtered, "Forgive you for what?"

"Why don't you tell me that? Because, clearly, I've done something wrong for you to hate me." Joran brought his knees to his chest and watched her with intense, green eyes. Against the backdrop of monotonous, earthy, reddish-brown rocks, his eyes appeared vivid. "Is it because I saw you that day? In my room? I'm really sorry about that. I just left to grab an extra uniform for you because I figured you wouldn't want to wear your sweaty, dirtied clothes. I truly had no intention—"

"That's not why." Her face flamed and she brushed off the dust from her hands to keep them busy. She didn't want to think of that day.

"Is it because of what happened in Lieutenant Bernsten's office? I'm just as bound to listen to him—"

"*Joran.*" Kolfinna bunched her hands together. "Look, it really doesn't matter—"

"It does." He rose to his feet. "It matters to me."

She blinked. She didn't like the way he was staring at her. The expectations on his suddenly determined face. "*Why*? Why do you care what I think about you? We don't even know each other—"

"You're the first fae I've met in a long, long time. I want to be friends. I want to ..." Joran stared down at his scuffed boots. "Connect with someone who knows the *real* me."

Everyone knew him as the white-ranked soldier, but no one knew the fae Joran. Except her.

"You could tell everyone—" she started.

His eyes widened. "No. Why would I do that?"

"So people know the *real* you."

"No." Joran shook his head and twiddled his fingers together. "Kolfinna, I want to be friends with you—"

"And *only* me?" She sighed loudly. "Just because I'm fae like you?"

He didn't say anything and chose to peer down at his feet, with his gold locks obscuring his face.

You need to be friends with him, a voice whispered in the back of her mind. She had almost forgotten about her objective: get information on runes so she could free herself. This was the perfect chance for her to swoop in and say that they were friends already, and that he had nothing to worry about. But Kolfinna couldn't even open her mouth to utter those words.

Joran finally raised his gaze to meet hers. "I don't have many friends and since we will be together for a while ..."

For fifteen years, if she couldn't break the mark on her wrist. The thought alone made her internally cringe, and it was what finally opened her mouth.

"I understand," she said.

"Really?" The relief in his voice cracked at her consciousness.

"Yes." Kolfinna licked her lips. "Joran, like you said, we'll be spending a lot of time together because of"—she raised her wrist —"this. How did you even find out about runes and how to bind people to contracts?"

Joran hesitated and glanced between her and the golden rune on her wrist. An uncomfortable look passed over his face. "By reading books."

"Where did you find those books?"

He rubbed his neck. "The lieutenant found some of them. Others ... *you* found."

Kolfinna paused. Waited. And when he didn't elaborate, she whispered, "*Me?*"

"The Eventyrslot ruins." Joran watched her. "There were hundreds of books there because it was a school, right? So ... the lieutenant got some for me."

It was all confidential, classified, and sealed away by the king. Or so Kolfinna had heard. Even Fenris hadn't been able to acquire that many books for her. To hear that Joran had found out how to use his rune magic because of her ... filled her with a strange, sick feeling. She had been the reason he had somehow learned about rune magic and how to bind a soul to another.

But it also meant that she needed to get her hands on those books.

Her mind raced to Joran's room and she tried to remember if she had seen some books there, but she kept drawing a blank.

She would have to sneak in at some point and see for herself, she decided. But not now. If she did it too soon after this conversation, he would obviously become suspicious.

"That's amazing," she said instead with a forced smile. "You were able to learn so much from just books. Really, that's amazing."

A blush crept up his cheeks. "T-Thank you. Um, let's get back to training now?"

Kolfinna turned her attention back to levitating the rocks, but her mind wouldn't remain focused. A plan was already formulating in her mind: sneak into Joran's room and find those books.

12

THE EARLY MORNING LIGHT STUNG KOLFINNA'S EYES, but that wasn't what had her blinking up at her crackled, gray ceiling. Her heart was racing a million beats a second and she subconsciously thanked the morning light for waking her from her nightmare. She tried to calm her breathing, but the images of the nightmare flashed before her eyes. She had dreamed of Olia, Sijur's imprisoned woman. Olia had been screaming and crying, chained up and covered in a mapwork of rune marks over her emaciated body. Beside Olia, there had been hundreds of thousands of similar men and women. Withered and covered with runes.

And then there was Kolfinna, bowing down beside Sijur as he looked upon his little army with a wide, calculated grin.

The dream was too close to potential reality. It reminded her that she was being too idle. She hadn't figured out anything about how to break herself from the runes and she hadn't tried hard enough. She had figured she'd give herself some time before sneaking into Joran's room to find the books, but now with this dream fresh on her mind, she wondered if it was best to work as fast as possible.

Kolfinna didn't have to glance at Inkeri or Herja to know that they both were fast asleep; she could hear their soft, gentle breathing. Kolfinna laid an arm over her eyes. She had soon realized that the middle bed was the worst bed in the room because the window was directly above her and every morning, without fail, nearly blinded her awake.

With the quiet of the mornings, she was able to focus on the noises of the fortress. Her ears picked up the distant sounds of people walking the halls, the soft hums of voices down below, the stirring of the wind against barren branches. At least focusing on that made the nightmare recede in the back of her mind.

Kolfinna pushed herself into a sitting position and shoved the thick blanket off her body. She would've loved to remain in bed, curl up in a ball, and fall back asleep—hopefully without a nightmare this time—but now that she was actively trying to avoid Blár, it was better to wake up at this time, eat, and start her day. Besides, it was easier to squeeze in a bath this early, since most of the women didn't wake up for another half hour.

She ran to the end of the hall for a quick bath. Thankfully, there was no one waiting, so she took her bath, dressed in her drab gray uniform, and brushed out her damp curls back in her room. After pinning the yellow badge to her breast pocket, she was ready for the day. Herja and Inkeri were still fast asleep when she left her room.

Her mind was so focused on breakfast that when she entered the dining hall, she didn't even notice the shift in the temperature, the slight chill that settled down on her skin like dew. It wasn't until she heard his voice that she realized her mistake.

"There you are."

Kolfinna looked over her shoulder, eyes wide. Blár was leaning against the wall beside the double doors. His black hair was tousled and slightly damp, likely from an early morning bath, and the white fur collar of his cloak brushed over his cheeks and made the blue of his eyes look even sharper, like silver-blue steel.

Kolfinna's chest tightened and she ignored the fluttering in the pit of her stomach. She should've been disappointed that she had failed at avoiding him, but she wasn't. There was a small part of her that warmed at the sight of him, that wanted to lean in closer to him. But the more logical side of her calmed the racing in her heart.

Blár was beautiful, yes, but he was also trouble. He didn't like her the same way she did, and he was more interested in … flirting, it seemed. She didn't need that kind of relationship, not when she was planning on escaping from this fort anyway.

She steeled herself with resolve and gave him a curt nod. "Blár. Good morning."

"And a very good morning to you," he said dryly before waving at the mostly empty hall. "Care to eat with me?"

Kolfinna's stomach rumbled, and she lost the opportunity to deny. "Lead the way."

Blár sauntered over to the serving table and grabbed himself a ceramic plate. He handed one to Kolfinna and moved to the array of flaky bread, smoked meats, cheeses, olives, jams, and dried fruits.

"You've been avoiding me," he said while piling bread and meat on his plate. He didn't even look at her as he spoke and said it so matter-of-factly that she couldn't even deny it. He grabbed the tongs sticking out from the assortment of white and orange cheese and picked a few slices before moving on to the dried cherries. "I've been here for two weeks and I've only seen you twice."

Kolfinna ladled barley porridge onto her plate. "I've been training a lot—"

"With Inkeri." Blár glanced at her. "At the same time I have my training."

She focused on pairing fruits atop her porridge. "That's purely coincidental."

"Is it?" He cocked an eyebrow. "You also eat breakfast and dinner at a different time than everyone else."

Kolfinna drizzled honey over her meal and gave a lighthearted shrug. "Why does it matter what time I eat?"

"I can only see you a few times between my own missions and orders."

"Careful," she muttered. "If you keep talking like that ..." *I'll get the wrong idea.*

"I'm not stupid. I can tell you're avoiding me."

Kolfinna placed the spoon back into the jar of honey and then moved to grab a piece of bread. "Blár, I'm—"

"*Not avoiding you.*" He snorted. "Is that what you want to say? No need to lie, Kolfinna. I can see right through you. You're not a good liar at all." He grabbed her plate from her hands, led her to a vacant table, and they both sat down.

Kolfinna took her plate from him. "You don't need to carry my food."

"I was trying to be polite—"

"Well, thank you, but I can carry my own plate." She picked up her spoon and stirred the thick barley porridge with it.

Blár gave her a long stare. "I know you can carry your plate. I was trying to be nice."

"You and nice don't exactly blend together."

"Do you want me to throw your damned plate on the floor then?" He braced his forearms on the table and leaned forward. Even though the words were harsh, his tone wasn't. "I can freeze your plate and shatter it too, if you prefer that."

Kolfinna rolled her eyes. "Anyway, what did you want from me?"

"Many things, but the most prevalent one is *answers.*" She could smell the sweet vanilla scent of him. His gaze roved over her face. "First of all, why are you here with the military? And secondly, what have I done to make you avoid me at all costs?"

Nothing, really. Except string her along and confuse her.

She couldn't have any attachments for when she left this place, and he was the stickiest attachment she had, but she couldn't tell him that.

"Nothing."

"Is it because of the trial? I'm really sorry about that. I ..." Blár sighed and rolled a dried cherry between his fingers. "I'm sorry."

Kolfinna hated to see him look so distraught. As much as she wanted to keep it to herself, she found herself needing to open up to him. The heavy weight on her shoulders groaned in agreement.

Kolfinna rubbed her wrist where the rune was etched into her skin. "It's more than just the trial, Blár. I needed you and ..." She sighed and showed him her wrist. "Do you know what this is?"

Blár stared at the gold rune on her wrist and then met her eyes. "A rune?"

"Yes. A rune." She picked up her spoon and stirred her porridge again. "Sijur offered me a way out of the trial. He'd save me and I'd work under him. Except, he didn't just accept my word. He bound me to him. With rune magic." She raised her wrist. "And now I'm stuck here and I can't leave, even if I want to."

Blár blinked at her, horror slowly seeping onto his face. "*What?*"

"Yes, and it gets worse." She ate a mouthful of the sweet meal and chewed to keep from snapping out the words. "I'm bound to his will. Anything he wants, I have to give to him." Her voice dropped to a whisper. "Or else."

"Or else?"

She shrugged, taking another bite. "I'm not sure, but I get this intense pain whenever I disobey him. I think ... I might even die if I disobey. Of course, I'm not sure since I haven't tried it—"

Blár slammed his fist on the table, and the plates rattled. "*What?!*"

"Shh." Kolfinna glanced around the room warily, but there weren't enough people around them to be eavesdropping. "You can't talk too loud about it."

"And why not? Will he attack you for it?"

"Well, no ... But ..." She didn't like the idea of finding out what Sijur would do if she was prattling about their little contract.

The water in the glass in front of Blár started to form ice crystals. "Sijur bound you with rune magic? Is he ... a fae?"

"No, he had someone do it to me."

"There's another fae here?"

"Yes, but ... I can't say who." She didn't know why she was protecting Joran, but it felt wrong to tell Blár about his secret. As much as she didn't like Joran, she couldn't betray her own kind by sharing a secret like that.

Blár tapped his fingers against the sticky tabletop, a myriad of emotions flashing over his face, particularly anger and horror. The temperature around him swayed from chilly winter to a cool breeze. Like he was struggling to temper the rage freezing beneath the surface.

Finally, he swore under his breath and gave her a glacial stare. "And you're bound to him *forever*?"

"No ... Just fifteen years."

"*Fifteen years*?" His eyes nearly popped at that. "What in the actual hell? Kolfinna, you bound yourself to that snake for fifteen years?"

"I didn't have a choice," Kolfinna snapped. She stuffed her mouth with a spoonful of thick porridge and swallowed, but when she looked up, Blár was still staring at her like she was insane. "It was either die by the Royal Guards or"—she raised her wrist—"this."

"Do you have a way out of this? There has to be something—"

"I'm working on it." She released a long breath and took a bite of her food again; it was sweet with the honey, and it helped ease her buzzing nerves. "I'm planning on leaving this place and ... I figured it's easier to just cut off ties with everyone. So yes, I have been avoiding you. I know it's not good to just cut ties, but I can't get too involved with you or anyone else. I'm only here to follow directions, act like a good soldier, and when Sijur doesn't expect me to, escape."

Blár watched her carefully. She couldn't tell if he was worried for her, angry at Sijur, or furious at her—or maybe a mixture of all three. "But this goes against everything you've been working for."

She cringed. She had told herself in the Royal Guards that she was going to find a place for herself in society. That she didn't want to run away anymore, but that was exactly what she was doing now. "I know," Kolfinna said. "But I can't just give up and be a slave to Sijur now, can I?"

"No, but there are other options."

"Other options?"

"Only Sijur knows about your contract with each other, right? You can break the bond or whatever he has over you, and then transfer to another unit. You don't have to run away. No one but Sijur will know what you did."

"But he's the son of the commander-in-chief. Don't you think he'll find a way to get back at me for going against our deal? I don't think he'll take too kindly to that." She winced as she thought of Olia. "He's definitely not averse to taking violent measures if he needs to. I'd rather not be targeted by him."

"It's not your first time being targeted by someone powerful." He probably meant for it to be a lighthearted comment, but it only made her flinch.

"Yeah, and I'm still recovering from Hilda. I'd rather not repeat that."

"Kolfinna ..." Blár raked a hand through his hair and then frowned at the wet droplets that were now tiny icicles. He brushed them out of his hair distractedly and the frozen drops sputtered over the tabletop. "That bastard took advantage of you."

"I didn't have a choice."

"I know, *I know*." He shook his head in disbelief. "I'm just ... aggravated that he did that."

"While you were gone," she added.

He grimaced. "I ... I didn't realize that would happen."

"You knew I was going to be on trial. Come on, what did you think was going to happen?" Kolfinna let out a mirthless laugh.

"You knew I had to face the king and the Royal Guards for something that was out of my control. And you knew that you were my only ally! Fenris couldn't save me because he has to act as the captain, and even though he's *kind of* my ally, he's not really! So I had no one there for me who could actually help me. Meanwhile you ..." She let out a shaky, angry breath. "You were too *busy*."

Blár lowered his head, his hands bunching together on the table beside his plate. "Look, it wasn't like that—"

"Really, it wasn't?" Kolfinna pursed her lips together. "Then what was it like? Because all I know is that I had to face everything on my own. The only person who offered me help was Sijur, and even though I didn't like the terms he gave me, I didn't have a choice! I couldn't even consult with you about it because you weren't there! You left town!"

Guilt passed over Blár's face, but it was overtaken by rage just as quickly. He looked away. "It wasn't like that, Kolfinna. I already apologized too."

"Then what was it like?" Her words came out in a harsh whisper.

"I ..."

"Yes?"

"I did it for you."

She pulled back, her eyebrows knitting together. "For me? How does leaving help me?"

He opened his mouth to say something, but then a wooden tray slammed down on the table. Kolfinna jumped and swiveled her attention to Gunnar, who wore a toothy grin and seemed unaware of their heated conversation.

"Hello, hello! Morning to you both." He plopped down beside Kolfinna and waved a hand to the fruits, nuts, and smoked meat on his tray. "I was able to nab some of the good stuff before the rest of the pack devoured them." He winked and stole a slice of grilled chicken off the tray, stuffed it in his mouth, and then plucked a handful of cherries off Blár's plate.

Through his food, he laughed at Blár's frown.

"Asshole," Blár said. "Don't just take my food."

"I came with offerings." Gunnar waved to the tray and frowned, his jaw working out slowly.

"At least remove the pits before you swallow." Blár raised an eyebrow while Gunnar struggled to pick out the pits from his mouthful. "And besides, they were serving this up front. We could've easily gotten it."

"But you *didn't.*" Gunnar spat out the pits and plunked them onto the table in front of him. He gave Kolfinna a friendly smile and gestured to the tray. "Come on, have some."

"I think I'm okay." She eyed his pile of cherry pits with a frown. "Are you just going to leave those there?" Before he could answer, she pulled out a handkerchief from her pocket and handed it to him. "Here."

Gunnar took it with a grin. "Why, thank you. Anyhow"—he looked between the two of them—"why the glum mood?"

"Nothing, really." Kolfinna pursed her lips and met Blár's eyes again. What had he meant by saying he left town for her?

"Did you guys hear about what happened yesterday?" Gunnar gathered the cherry pits and folded them within the handkerchief. "We're going on a very unexpected mission. All of us."

Kolfinna gave him a look. "All of us? Why? What happened?"

Was it a magic beast attack?

Blár's expression stilled. "I heard about that."

"About what?" Kolfinna looked between the two men. "What did you guys hear?"

"Four soldiers were found yesterday," Gunnar said, his voice suddenly taking on a serious note. He nibbled on a hunk of white, cratered cheese. "Dead soldiers, mind you. And they had these"—he motioned to his body—"these giant pits in them. Like something blasted holes through their bodies. Like they were"—he raised the cheese and poked one of the dents in it—"like, well, I guess you get the picture."

"Are we going to investigate?" Kolfinna asked.

"We sure will." Gunnar chowed down on the cheese and grabbed a handful of nuts. He spoke while chewing. "We'll be going out pretty soon. There might be some new kind of magic beast that's cropping up in the area. One that can blast magic or whatever."

Kolfinna ate her porridge in silence after that. Her appetite slowly left her as she imagined the corpses of the soldiers. What creature was capable of doing that?

When Kolfinna raised her head, she noticed Blár's eyes on her wrist, at the edge of the crescent moon rune that was partially covered by the cuff of her sleeve. She didn't meet his gaze and turned back to her food. Her heart raced from their conversation, and she couldn't stop replaying it in her mind.

13

Kolfinna was on high alert when their party—Blár, Gunnar, Eluf, Herja, Inkeri, and Ivar—left Fort Løveslot soon after breakfast. The only thing she could think about was what had killed the soldiers. What creature was out there that could cause giant holes in the body? She thought back to the Nuckelavee and how horrifying of a creature it was to face. If this creature also had properties of being able to render them magicless, they'd be in trouble.

She had no idea what to expect, which made the whole prospect even more terrifying.

When they reached the area where the bodies had been found, they explored the surroundings by foot, keeping a watchful eye on the trees and the ground. Usually, Eluf had told them, magic beasts liked to dwell in their territories and had their own hunting grounds. Chances were high that this creature was still nearby.

Inkeri shivered as a powerful gust of wind ripped through her hair. "What do you we know about this thing, other than that it killed four soldiers?"

"They had gaping wounds in their flesh," Eluf said, turning in a slow circle to peer among the many trees. "The wounds were slightly burnt."

"Hm. Strange," Herja said. "Fire isn't accurate enough to burn a hole."

"Exactly. Whatever we're dealing with, it's using strange magic."

Kolfinna swallowed. "But there are no reports of this happening before, correct?"

"Correct," Ivar said.

A part of her wanted to be fearless and not worry about whatever was out there because their entire party was powerful, but the bigger part of her couldn't stop her anxiety from gnawing at her subconscious. She was too careful of a woman to fall back onto arrogance.

Kolfinna walked over fallen branches. The harshness of winter was ebbing away, so there wasn't any snow on the ground, but the breeze was still chilly. Or maybe that was Blár's effect. She wasn't entirely sure.

Closing her eyes, she felt for the mana around the area. She had been feeling a powerful surge of mana ever since they started traveling, but she couldn't pinpoint it anywhere, which might've explained the nauseating anxiety in her stomach. The whole forest was drenched in powerful mana.

"Is something wrong?" Inkeri placed a hand on Kolfinna's bicep gently.

"I'm just trying to feel the mana in the air."

"You can do that?" Ivar asked incredulously from his position in the vanguard.

Gunnar grinned. "Dang. You fae sure have a lot of tricks up your sleeves."

Herja's eyebrows rose, curiosity flashing over her bright blue eyes. "I thought you guys could only do runes and stone stuff?"

"Nature too," Blár chimed in.

"Ooh, I forgot about that one," Gunnar said. "So is your magic　"

All at once, Kolfinna heard movement from the ground,

rushing in on them from every direction. And then there was a flurry of movement up in the sky. Zeroing in on them.

She snapped her attention to the ground and then up in the air. There was nothing—

In seconds, skeletal bird-like creatures materialized in the air, their wings made of sharp bones and their talons crusted with dried blood. Fire blazed in the pits of their empty eye sockets. Hundreds of them surrounded their party. But that wasn't all—thick, fat snakes with purple skin slithered toward them all.

Ice erupted from the ground, freezing the snakes, at the same time that fire and water shot up at the sky of magical birds coming at them. But in the next second, even more creatures filled the sky.

Kolfinna spread her mana into the ground. She didn't have time to think about the ambush. Her gaze flitted to the multiplying snakes and then at the sky.

Since she could do long-distance attacks, she'd probably be better at attacking the skeletal birds. Gunnar and Eluf could handle the snakes. There were more birds than snakes, anyway—

"Kolfinna! Get down!" Blár was running toward her, ice-blue eyes wide. Kolfinna followed his gaze in that split second and her hands froze in the air. A woman holding a silver staff with inky shadows dripping off the metal tip sprinted toward her. She was dressed in black leather and black, scaly armor. Her skin was the color of midnight with sapphire undertones.

Kolfinna couldn't react. Couldn't move.

The woman's eyes were blood red. Her braided hair was pure white. And her ears were pointed.

An elf.

Kolfinna broke from her stunned reverie and drew her mana into the rocks imbedded in the earth, but Blár was faster. His ice shot from his hand toward the woman. Quick as lightning, the woman snapped her wrist and a blast of golden-white light lasered from her hand. It struck Blár's ice and shattered it. Hundreds of shards of ice glittered in the air.

Time froze. Kolfinna sucked in a breath. Blár wore the same shocked expression.

If she could break his ice, that could only mean her magic was equal to his or stronger.

Everyone seemed to be thinking it at the same time.

"I'll take her on, you guys—" Blár didn't have time to finish his sentence because the woman was on him in seconds. Shadows wisped around her staff and she struck Blár with it across the chest. Kolfinna recognized those shadows. She expected the shadows to burst out like flames and eat him alive, but they did no such thing. He only jumped back, seemingly uninjured. His ice grew at the elf's feet and captured her in place for a split second—enough time for him to throw ice daggers at her from a dozen different directions. A black shadow fell over her body like a cloak and the ice daggers sank inside, but in seconds the shadow disappeared and the woman was in front of Blár, unharmed, and about to strike him again. They exchanged blows, light and shadows crashing into blue-white ice.

Everyone else fell into battle as well. Herja lurched back as snakes hissed at her feet, her fire blasting from the ground up to the sky of skeletal birds. Ivar sliced through birds and snakes alike, his water whizzing around him like a barrier. Inkeri was taking down the magic birds with thick currents of air that cut at their wings. Gunnar and Eluf both kicked and stomped on the snakes, careful not to get bitten.

Kolfinna also fell into the rhythm of battle; she shot rocks up at the bony birds. At the snakes burrowing through the ground. She also tried to keep an eye on Blár, but it was hard to do so when the magic beasts relentlessly rained down on her. She could barely focus on what was in front of her.

Even as she chucked stones at the creatures, she couldn't hold back the unease and fear from washing over her. That woman—that elf—was able to rival Blár. That alone drenched her bones with a wary kind of fear. The type of fear that consumed every fiber of her being.

The crash and crack of Blár's ice sent her heart spiking every other second. The adrenaline rushed through her veins. He couldn't lose. He was the strongest person she had ever met. But that woman was also strong. Even though Kolfinna couldn't pause and watch the fight, she could see from her peripheral that the warrior woman wasn't breaking a sweat over fighting Blár. They were both even.

Inky shadows tried to get ahold of Blár, but his ice warred against it, winning most of the time, and other times splintering and falling victim to its vicious hunger.

"*Inkeri!*" Ivar's scream ripped Kolfinna's attention away from the elf woman and Blár.

A giant snake was attached to Inkeri's leg, where it had burrowed its fangs deeply into her calf. Inkeri's eyes were wide, her skin pallid, and her mouth open in shock. Kolfinna took a step in her direction, but at the same second, a snake shot forth from its hiding place in a wire of thorns. It wrapped around her foot and jammed its teeth into her ankle. The white-hot pain was instantaneous. Kolfinna screamed and ripped the snapping snake off her leg and chucked it away, where a blast of fire from Herja's flames devoured it.

Ivar had dropped down to his knees and was holding Inkeri. Her body shook violently. Water whipped around him and attacked any birds or snakes that tried to get close. He was saying something to her, but Kolfinna couldn't hear past the blood rushing to her ears and the darkness creeping at the edge of her vision.

A skeletal bird's talons gripped onto Kolfinna's shoulder in her moment of confusion. She waved her hand, but her vision was doubling and she couldn't tell what she was hitting or not. In fact, the ground was inching closer and the trees seemed to be moving toward her. Her foot throbbed and burned. Herja must've burned her, she thought. That was the only explanation.

One second Kolfinna was swaying on her feet, swatting the birds away, and the next she was on the ground. Another snake bit into her shoulder—or was that her arm? Vicious tremors overcame her body.

"*Kolfinna! Get up!*"

The voice sounded panicked and distant, like there was a barrier between her and that voice. But that couldn't be, could it? She had been fighting—

Her mind drew a blank. What had she been doing?

Fire coursed through her arms and legs until she felt like smoke would erupt from her every orifice. Her vision was a blur of colors. She didn't know how long she lay there, but when her eyes adjusted, it seemed like nothing had changed. Herja was fighting with orange flames in her hands, Eluf and Gunnar were kicking and smashing the birds and snakes alike, and Ivar was still cradling Inkeri to his chest while his water sliced through anything that got within a one-foot radius of him.

The temperature of the area was frigidly cold. Her breath came out of her mouth in white streams. It was the only indication that Blár was still fighting. That and the occasional flashes of light that shone in the sky and disappeared. The elf woman's power, Kolfinna concluded.

"Kolfinna! Come on, get up!" Herja cursed and shot fire at a snake that was two feet away from burying into Kolfinna's arm.

Kolfinna blinked and tried pushing herself up to her feet, but her body wouldn't listen. The burning sensation in her limbs slowly receded. Despite that, she couldn't move and her body was convulsing on its own. Her hand, which was sprawled close to her, was turning purple.

Panic unfurled in her core. She tried to feel the pulsing of her mana, tried to pull her stones close to her for protection, but her control kept slipping. She felt like a fallen leaf caught in an unrelenting storm, crashing and thrashing whichever way the wind desired. With no will of her own. No control over her situation.

Tears budded in the corner of her eyes and she squeezed her eyes shut.

"Kolfinna!" That sounded like Gunnar.

When she opened her eyes, he was kneeling in front of her, a horrified expression on his face. He turned to the others, who were still in the midst of their own battles. "She's down! We need to get her and Inkeri out of here!"

"We can't leave Blár!" Eluf crushed a bird's skull in one hand and slammed the corpse into another bird.

"But—" Gunnar looked over his shoulder and gritted his teeth together.

Kolfinna tried to open her mouth to say something, to ask if Blár was all right, but her body still didn't listen. It reminded her too much of when she wielded the *Død Sværd* and had no control over herself. She wasn't sure if it was the venom that was making her sick to her stomach or the memories of the sword.

She closed her eyes again and calmed her breathing. It was only a matter of time before her body healed itself and she would be able to join them all in battle once more. She needed to remain calm and focus on moving her fingers. The slightest twitch of movement would tell her when the venom's grasp on her was loosening.

Time seemed to be moving excruciatingly slow. Ice crackled. Light flared. Fire roared, and water crashed and slammed into trees, monsters, and the ground alike. Kolfinna could hear the ragged breaths of her teammates. Could smell the acidic scent of monster blood, of burning flesh, of sweat and human blood.

She pulled at her mana and latched onto the closest thing to her—a tree. Instead of her mana disappearing from her, it wavered and wobbled but remained in her control. She had never been successful at manipulating a dormant tree before, even though she had tried several times, but for whatever reason, she felt like she had to try again. Right now.

Manipulating nature had always been Kolfinna's strongest ability. Stone magic didn't come close to how gifted she was with nature. But it still surprised her when she grasped onto the tiny thread of dormant life inside the tree and held it in place. Instead of slipping through her fingers, it remained. It was probably due to her training, or maybe because she was hyper focused on it, but when she pulled on the lifeforce of the tree, it gave in to her demands.

It worked.

She could feel the swaying of the branches, how deep the roots were in the ground, the thickness of the trunk. She opened her eyes and willed one of the roots to stretch out and lash at the ever-growing number of snakes. The root unearthed itself like a violet, sharpened whip. Herja and Gunnar yelped in surprise as the root skewered a nearby snake, and then another, and then another.

Kolfinna made the branches of the tree grow longer and lash the birds in the sky. Her fingers twitched and that was all she needed to try and push herself up. Her weakened body lacked the strength to hold her own weight. Willing a pair of roots out from underground, she wrapped them around her body and pulled herself up. Slowly, she rose to her feet, the roots clinging to her arms and legs. Her vision dotted with shadows and she had to blink several times to clear it.

She could already feel the venom fading from her body, but she doubted the same could be said about Inkeri. She could see through the swirling water enough to see her face was as pale as snow and the tears in her pants revealed purple skin.

Kolfinna stumbled forward. Blár and the elf woman were still fighting in her peripheral. The woman slammed her staff onto Blár's ice spear and shattered it. A host of shadows erupted from her hand, but Blár shoved her with a wall of ice and sent her flying through a thicket of trees. Kolfinna shifted her attention to Inkeri, to the skeletal birds picking at everyone's flesh, to the snakes snapping to bury their fangs into them.

Ivar's water didn't attack Kolfinna as she dropped down in front of him and Inkeri. He held her tightly, his blue-green eyes wide and his hands trembling. She had never thought he was capable of wearing such a vulnerable expression.

Kolfinna placed a hand on Inkeri's sweaty forehead. Her eyes were closed and she seemed to have lost consciousness a while ago.

"Is she going to die?" Ivar's voice was barely a whisper. A bird tried to come toward them, but water sliced it in half. And yet, Ivar hadn't taken his eyes off Inkeri. "You're moving around, but why isn't she—"

"I'm different." She didn't need to tell him that she was possibly part elf, or that she had strange healing magic.

"Maybe"—Ivar placed a hand on Inkeri's thigh—"if we cut off her leg, the venom won't spread—"

Bile rose up her throat and she pushed it down. "Let me try healing her."

"Healing?" His hands tightened on Inkeri's shoulders. "Can you save her?"

"Maybe." Kolfinna had only seen rune magic heal one time in her life, and that was when Revna had healed her leg. She had no knowledge of it, but maybe she could figure it out. She had gotten better at runes, after all. Maybe ... Maybe she could do this.

Kolfinna pressed a hand on Inkeri's calf. Her mind drew a blank on what runes to use. Heal? That was too basic and broad. Runes needed to be very specific in order to work properly. Maybe she could tell the runes to get rid of the venom? But then, how would the runes know what the venom was or wasn't? What if it attacked her whole body?

"How long have we been fighting?" Kolfinna asked. "How long since she was bitten?"

Ivar blinked. "Maybe ... twenty minutes?"

"Okay." Kolfinna's mana spread to her fingertips.

Remove any toxins that entered her body these past thirty minutes.

The magic resisted and even after pouring her mana into them, they didn't appear. Kolfinna cursed softly and tried again. She pushed more and more mana into the words, willing them to show up on Inkeri's body, but they didn't.

Again, like with Olia, the runes weren't listening.

Tears of frustration threatened to spill and she swallowed down the failure. "Ivar, can I use your mana?"

Confusion had him knitting his brows together, but he nodded and tentatively stuck his hand out, his eyes asking her if this was what she meant.

Kolfinna grabbed his hand while keeping another hand on Inkeri. All at once, she felt the rush of Ivar's mana. It was warm and large, like a body of lapping water. It stirred gently, like the sea softly lulling its waves back and forth. Kolfinna threaded that mana into her own body, pulling it forward. A thrill rushed over her body at the feel of magic intensifying inside her, but she pushed those thoughts away and focused on the runes.

She poured everything she had into the runes. Ivar gasped, likely at the pull of mana, and Kolfinna pursed her lips together. This had to work. It had to.

Remove any toxins that entered her body these past thirty minutes.

Golden runes shimmered in the air and imprinted on top of Inkeri's pants before seeping through the material. Kolfinna could make out the glow of the runes on her skin through the tears of her clothes. Kolfinna and Ivar watched in amazement as the purple coloring in Inkeri's skin faded into a light purple and then disappeared altogether. Another minute passed and the runes sank deeper into Inkeri, where they vanished.

Ivar looked between Inkeri and Kolfinna. "Is ... Is it done? Is she healed?"

"I don't know." Kolfinna sat back, exhausted. "This is my first time I've healed anyone."

"You just keep surprising me." He hugged Inkeri's body close to his chest and sighed raggedly. Kolfinna could see the relief loosening his tight features.

"If you love her, maybe you shouldn't be so harsh with her," Kolfinna said, turning away from him and shifting her attention to the rest of the battle.

Before she could launch forward and attack, the birds cawed, flapped their wings in unison, and shot up in the sky, away from them. The snakes did the same, suddenly turning and slithering away in every direction. The root cause seemed to be Blár and the elf woman.

The elf woman's staff was stuck inside a hunk of ice a few feet away from her, and the woman herself was on the ground, Blár atop her with an ice spear aimed at her throat. The woman's legs and arms were pinned to the ground with ice and her head was lolled to the side. Blár was breathing heavily. Splashes of bright, scarlet blood covered half of his face. His cloak was missing, the giant gashes along his uniform were painted in blood, and inky black stains covered more than half of his uniform.

Gunnar held his left arm and watched the birds fly away before stumbling toward Blár. "Is she ...?"

"Dead? No." Blár pushed himself off the unconscious elf.

"Is she ... fae?" Eluf held his abdomen and limped over to them. Sticky blood seeped between his pale fingers.

Herja blew out air. "I've never seen that uniform. Black leathers? Is that common for the Tribes of Kriger or maybe the people of Skarlland?"

"No," Blár said. "I don't think so."

Kolfinna swallowed down the nausea climbing her throat. *An elf.* This woman was an elf.

Her thoughts traveled back to Revna's last words to her about the half-elf commander and his army. This woman ... she couldn't be, could she?

"Her ears are pointed," Gunnar said. "And her hair ..."

"Did you see her eyes? They were bloody *red*." Herja pushed her sweaty, red hair out of her own eyes as she said it. "Do fae have red eyes?"

"She's not a fae." Kolfinna stepped forward, but her body nearly gave out and she grabbed a nearby tree to support herself.

"Hey there!" Herja grabbed Kolfinna's arm and helped steady her. "You've got to be careful. You were also bitten by those snakes."

Another roll of nausea swept over her body and roiled in her stomach like steaming seawater. She wanted to vomit.

Blár was staring at Kolfinna intently but not in the way that would normally make her feel like butterflies were trapped in her body. In the type of way that told her he was thinking deeply. The hard set of his mouth told her that much.

"Kolfinna." He stared down at the elf woman and then back at Kolfinna. "Is this woman ... an elf?"

Kolfinna swallowed. The others exchanged glances with one another.

"An elf?" Eluf asked slowly.

"What's that?" Gunnar's voice was quiet.

Blár continued staring at her. He smeared the blood off his face with his forearm. "I remember reading about it in your home when you were showing me those translations you had done. Is this woman an elf?" He waved at the unconscious warrior. "The white hair? The red eyes? The shadows? The light?" When she didn't say anything, he turned to her sharply. "*Well*?"

Kolfinna nodded slowly. "Yes. I believe so."

Blár cursed under his breath.

"What's wrong?" Kolfinna asked.

"Other than the fact that this—this *elf*"—he waved another hand to the woman, his lip curling back—"shot me a few times with that light and it hurt like a b—" A string of curses left his mouth and he placed a hand on his abdomen, bent over for a minute, and shook his head. "Damn it. This makes things so much worse."

"What?" Herja asked, unease creeping in her voice as she picked out pieces of bird bones from her wild hair.

"What's worse?" Ivar came to stand by them with Inkeri nestled in his arms. She was still comatose and pale, and for a moment, Kolfinna wondered if she was truly healed or not.

"It's classified information but ..." Blár exhaled and looked between them and then at Kolfinna. "A strange army attacked the Southern border last month and took at least three territories and fortresses. The southern soldiers have reported that the soldiers in the army have wings, white hair, red eyes, purple eyes, fae magic, and other strange magic. They wear leather and black scales, they fly on magic beasts, and they have healing magic that makes it hard to fight them."

Kolfinna's blood ran cold. A month ago ... That was when she had faced Revna and Ragnarök at the royal palace.

You woke him and his armies. The commander will come for this kingdom, and he will set our queen free—

She wanted to vomit.

"Wait, an army of fae and ... elves?" Gunnar asked in astonishment. "You can't be serious."

"I am. I found out about it two weeks ago. It's only a matter of time before the news spreads. The higher-ups want to keep it under wraps to not cause country-wide terror. Hilda Helgadottir is there, so the situation is somewhat controlled. But"—he gestured to the elf—"if they're able to come all the way here, I'm wondering what their aim is."

"Is it Ragnarök?" Ivar asked.

"I think so."

"We need to get this woman to the fort," Eluf said. "We can question her there."

Kolfinna couldn't speak as everyone began discussing all at once. She stared at the woman on the ground, whose white hair stood out against her dark skin. If this woman was from the half-elf commander's army, then why was she here? Was she looking for her?

If Kolfinna truly did wake the half-elf commander and his army, and if she truly was the heir, then it only made sense that Ragnarök and the half-elf commander was after her, since she was the only person who could awaken the queen.

But there was the chance that the woman had no idea who Kolfinna was and was only investigating near the area, especially since this was somewhat close to the Forest of Great Divide, where the heir had supposedly been sealed away in the cave. Maybe they didn't know about Kolfinna or her strange connection to the heir.

She truly hoped that was the case.

14

It took two days for the venom's effects to wear off completely. In those two days, Kolfinna was bedridden and relieved of any training duties. She wasn't alone, though. Inkeri was with her. It was probably for the best that Kolfinna was stuck in bed because she didn't want to do anything but curl up under her blanket and forget everything.

Her anxiety was a giant hole ripping open wider and wider until all she could see, hear, and smell was black *nothingness*.

The half-elf commander and his army were awake, and if Revna was telling the truth, it was because Kolfinna had awoken the *Død Sværd*. Somehow it was all her fault. *Again*.

Her involvement in the Eventyrslot ruins, waking up Revna, fighting in the palace, wielding the sword—everything seemed to be clicking into place for Ragnarök. And somehow, Kolfinna was at the center of it, unknowingly stringing the events together.

She didn't want to think about the heir situation and what it meant for her. She couldn't be the heir. How could she? She had parents and a sister, and they weren't a part of Ragnarök.

The rune mark on her wrist seemed to be the least of her problems, but it all coalesced until she felt overwhelmed and helpless.

A knock on the door interrupted her thoughts and she sat up straighter. Inkeri poked her head out from the blanket and exchanged a confused look with Kolfinna. Visits had been discouraged these past two days so they had time to recuperate.

"Come in," Kolfinna called out.

Joran poked his golden-haired head in from the doorway, his green eyes flicking from Kolfinna to Inkeri and then to the floor. "H-Hello."

"Joran." Kolfinna couldn't hide the surprise in her voice. Nor the disappointment—she had thought it was Blár. "Come in."

Inkeri pulled the blanket up to her chin. "Good evening."

Joran nodded and rubbed the nape of his neck. He opened the door wider but didn't step any closer. "How are you both?"

"I could be better." Kolfinna shrugged.

"I feel like I almost died," Inkeri said with a hollow laugh.

"Because you almost did," Kolfinna noted.

Joran chuckled but then seemed to think better of it and coughed. "A-Anyway, um, Kolfinna, Lieutenant General Bernsten is calling for you."

"For what?" Kolfinna pushed the blanket off her body. He hadn't bothered her until now. Her heart raced wildly. Had he found out about the heir? About the half-elf commander? Did the elf woman say something?

Joran didn't meet her gaze. "You'll see."

Her stomach twisted. She didn't like the sound of that. "Give me a minute. I'm going to change into my uniform."

He only nodded and stepped out of the room. Kolfinna's heart was pounding loudly in her ears as she stripped out of her sleeping gown and pulled on her gray military uniform. By the time she left her room and followed Joran down the hall, she was ninety percent sure that Sijur must've known she was somehow connected to the heir and the elves.

She gave the fae a side glance. Maybe Joran had noticed too. Maybe they were luring her into a trap. Maybe—

"I was worried when I discovered you were injured," Joran

said quietly. He laced his hands together and stared at the tiled floor as they walked.

"Oh? Um, thanks." Silence filled the awkward space between them. "So ... Do you know why Sijur called for me?"

"Yes." The tension in her chest tightened.

Her mouth was dry when she spoke next. "Joran, what's happening? Why are you not telling me?"

"Because ... You won't be happy."

She couldn't question him further because he paused in front of a door and gave her an unreadable glance. It almost looked like he wanted to grimace, but his expression smoothed away and he pushed the door open.

Inside, the room was fairly normal. Thick rugs were laid out in the center of the room, colorful tapestries with blocky shapes and designs hung over the walls, and there were two plush couches in the center of the room. A coffee table sat in front of the couches, with an array of teas and cookies laid out on it.

Sijur was sitting on the couch, his arm draped over the backrest and his legs propped up on the table. He was nibbling on a cookie while talking to the woman beside him. She was in her mid-to-late thirties, her chestnut locks draping over her shoulders. Her dress was tight and hugged her small waist, and the neckline was scandalously low. Upon seeing them, her red-painted lips curved into a grin.

Kolfinna licked her lips nervously and lowered her head. "Lieutenant General, you wanted to see me?"

"Kolfinna! So good to see you out and about." He lowered his legs off the table and propped his elbows on his knees. "Birgitta, this is Kolfinna, the fae I was telling you about."

Birgitta's smile faltered and Kolfinna could instantly see the discomfort in her body language. Her shoulders had stiffened just slightly, and her gaze flitted around the room "Ah, yes, I remember."

It was a normal reaction to meeting a fae for the first time. That flighty reaction to run away. To fight or maybe even to hide.

Kolfinna spared a glance at Joran to see if he had a reaction to any of this, but he was staring at the floor, so she couldn't glean anything off him. She couldn't smile as she turned to Sijur, the pit in her stomach growing. It was the first time she had seen him since their interaction with Olia.

Sijur rubbed his hands together and nodded down at the food displayed in front of him. "Cookies, anyone?"

"No, thank you," Kolfinna said.

"What about you, Joran?"

Joran shook his head.

"Ah. A shame." He plucked a cookie off the ceramic plate and bit into it. Crumbs fell on his lap, but he made no move to brush them away. "Kolfinna, I read from the reports that you were able to use runes to heal Inkeri. How did you manage that?"

Kolfinna opened her mouth to answer truthfully: that she had used Ivar's mana to overwhelm the runes, since a giant body of mana was needed for such power, but then she could imagine what Sijur would do with that information. If he realized the fae could drain people of their mana and their lifeforce, wouldn't he try to abuse that? Would he make her and Joran test it out on unsuspecting people, in order to grow their strength, and in turn use runes that could enslave people to him? But then she remembered that he had already seen her use Joran's mana—he must have already known that.

Still, she carefully picked her words. "I don't really know. I just used runes to expel the toxins. I didn't think it would work."

"Fascinating." Sijur nodded slowly. "We've been reading about rune magic healing people, but we've never been able to do it, so it truly is fascinating to hear that you were able to. From what Joran has studied, it seems you have to know about the anatomy of the human body to a very specific degree in order to repair tears and not cause further damage to the body. For example, a broken bone will not be healed by simply writing heal on it. You must push the tendons, the flesh, the nerves, and then repair the bone in a way that takes into account what's surrounding it. Since you were able to do it, I'm supposing that simpler procedures or circumstances, such as poison or an upset stomach, or something of that matter where you know what the root cause is, is easier to cure?" He ate the rest of the cookie. "Good job being able to figure it out, Kolfinna."

She could only bob her head.

"I also read that you were able to manipulate nature even though it's winter? How did you manage that?"

Joran lifted his head, his curious gaze cutting over to her.

Kolfinna shifted on her feet as everyone stared at her. Birgitta with thinly veiled confusion, Sijur with intrigue, and Joran with surprise. "I just used it. I've been trying to do it for a few weeks now, but I think I wasn't at a level with my mana manipulation or mana control that I could do it successfully. Even now, I'm not sure if I'll be able to do it again."

"Hm." Sijur rubbed his chin, and bits of cookie crumbs stuck to his clean-shaven jaw before he seemed to notice and brush them away. "That's very interesting. Joran will have to look into that too, won't you, Joran?"

"Yes, sir."

"Um, sir?" Kolfinna cleared her throat and tried to sound as uninvested as possible. "I was wondering, what happened to the woman we captured?"

"The woman *Blár* defeated and captured, you mean?"

Kolfinna hesitated. "Yes."

"The supposed elf." It seemed to her that Sijur was watching for a reaction. "She's here. Imprisoned. That's all you need to know."

"Is it possible that I can meet her?"

He blinked. "Why would you want to meet her?"

To ask her about the half-elf commander. To see if she was a part of Ragnarök. To confirm her suspicions.

"I want to see if she's actually an elf." Kolfinna hoped her smile appeared genuine. "I've only read about them once or twice at the Eventyrslot ruins, and during the fight, we were so busy fighting that I didn't have a chance to see her properly—"

Sijur waved his hand and reached for another cookie. His rings clinked against the ceramic rim of the plate. "There's no need for you to interfere."

Silence filled the room before Sijur spoke again. "Anyhow." He rested his free hand on Birgitta's knee and gave it a pat. "Let's get down business. Do you remember how with Olia, we weren't able to bind her? I've hypothesized it's because she was unwilling to be bound."

Kolfinna's heart sank and she looked between Sijur and Birgitta.

"Well, Birgitta here doesn't have that problem. She's a willing participant. A human too, so we'll see if a willing human is able to be bound or if it's just fae."

Not this again.

She should've expected it, but she had been so preoccupied with the elf woman—who was imprisoned somewhere in this fort —that she hadn't thought that there would be a repeat of the Olia incident. Except this time, with a woman who *wanted* to bind herself. She likely had no idea what she was getting herself into.

She looked at the woman, who was perched on the edge of the couch expectantly. "You're ... a *willing* participant?" Even as she said the words, she heard the doubt in them, and she watched Birgitta's smile fall. "Do you even know what that means? You want to be enslaved—"

"Kolfinna, stop talking," Sijur snapped.

"—to him forever?" As the words came out of her mouth, a wave of pain passed over Kolfinna and she gasped sharply, falling to her knees. She placed a hand on her throat and tried breathing through the throbbing pain that shot up from her rune mark and spread through her chest. She realized bitterly that he had issued an order and she had disobeyed. A few seconds passed and the pain slowly ebbed away.

"You can speak now, but don't try to scare our guest. That's very rude, Kolfinna." Sijur's tone was light and airy, but the razored glare he sent to Kolfinna told another story. He dropped the cookies on the plate with a soft plink, seemingly uninterested in them now.

Kolfinna was dizzy from the pain.

"Let's begin now." Sijur gave Birgitta's knee a final pat before Joran stepped forward. "Ah, actually, Joran, I think Kolfinna should be the one to do this."

Joran paused and then turned to Kolfinna, who stood frozen in place. "Are you sure? I can handle it—"

"Yes, I think it's good for her to practice." Sijur smiled. "Kolfinna? Come now, we don't have all day."

Kolfinna swallowed down her rising panic. She closed the distance between herself and Birgitta. Sitting on the couch, she tentatively took the older woman's hand. Kolfinna's voice came out low, hollow, and bitter. "What should I write?"

Sijur drummed his fingers on the leather armrest. "That she will obey me."

Kolfinna held the woman's hand lightly and closed her eyes. She reached for her mana hesitantly. She wondered if there was a way around the runes. A way to make them not work. If she didn't write the runes or only used a little bit of mana to make sure they failed—

Then she remembered the crippling pain she had been in when she had disobeyed Sijur. If she purposefully failed, she was sure that it would only hurt herself in the end.

But there had to be another way. There had to be something she could do.

"Kolfinna?" Sijur tapped his foot impatiently on the floor. "Is something wrong?"

"No, I'm just trying to focus." She quickly racked her mind for a solution, an alternative, but nothing came to her. Sighing, she reached for her mana and envisioned the runes. *Birgitta will obey Sijur Bernsten.*

Nothing happened.

Kolfinna's brows came together. "It's not working."

"Did you specify a time frame?" Even though Joran was asking Kolfinna, he was staring at Sijur. "You need to add that."

"Ah, yes, I forgot about that." Sijur rubbed his chin thoughtfully. "Let's say ... hm, what about one year?"

Birgitta became rigid but didn't argue.

When no one disputed, Kolfinna wrote the runes again in her mind. Mana sizzled at the surface of her hand. *Birgitta will obey Sijur Bernsten for one year.*

The runes glowed in the air and imprinted on the back of the woman's hand. Birgitta's eyes widened and she held out her hand in fascination. "Is it done?" she asked.

Kolfinna's stomach sank while Sijur jumped to his feet excitedly. "It *worked*. I suppose this means"—he took Birgitta's hand and turned it over to stare at the runes better—"that a willing participant is needed in order to use runes to bind a person. Even a human can be bound with rune magic! I suspected as much when rune magic worked on Inkeri, but I didn't think—" He shook his head and plopped back down on the couch. "Excellent! Truly excellent."

His enthusiasm only chipped away at Kolfinna's guilt and unease. If she didn't hurry up and figure out a way to break the rune binding her to Sijur, then who knew how many people Sijur would force her to bind to his will?

"All right, now, put on another rune." He reached for a teacup and slurped it loudly. When Kolfinna didn't move, he raised a brow. "We're not finished."

She licked her lips. "But ... the runes are set. What more do you want?"

"Write that she cannot hurt me in any way."

Kolfinna placed a hand over Birgitta's forearm this time. She poured her mana into the runes as she envisioned them. *Birgitta cannot hurt Sijur Bernsten in any way.* As she thought them, they materialized over the woman's skin with a bright glow.

"Excellent." Sijur reached for something in his pocket and

yanked out a small knife. He slammed it down on the table and motioned to the woman. "Now, Birgitta, I want you to pick up that knife."

Birgitta hesitated for a split second before picking up the knife. Kolfinna's heart pounded against her ribcage like a loud drum. She could only imagine what Sijur wanted to do with that. She wanted to ask if she could leave so she didn't have to witness anything, but a sick part of her wanted to see this to the end. To see what Sijur wanted here.

"And I want you to stab me."

Kolfinna blinked. This wasn't what she had expected.

"What?" Birgitta said with an uneasy laugh.

"Yes." He held out his hand. "Right here."

Birgitta hesitated and twisted the knife in her hand. "But ... I would be hurting you."

"Yes."

"I ..." She seemed to be at a loss for words. She turned to Kolfinna, but Kolfinna had no advice to offer her, and when she looked over, Joran didn't either. "Are you sure?"

"Hm. You're hesitating even though I gave an order." Sijur lowered his hand and frowned. "That must mean that even though you're disobeying me by not doing it, it's not hurting you. Maybe because the two commands contradict each other?"

Kolfinna was suddenly reminded of her time in the Eventyrslot ruins when Revna was teaching her about runes. Revna had demonstrated to her how runes worked by making her write *hot* and *cold* runes on the spoon. The two runes had neutralized the other. That was likely what was happening here.

"Okay, let's push this even further now." Sijur took the knife from her and placed it on the coffee table beside the plate of cookies. "Kolfinna, write a rune that says she will love me forever."

Kolfinna dug her feet into the floor to keep from swaying. Love him forever? Was it possible to use runes to manipulate someone's emotions? It sounded *wrong*.

"I'm not sure—" she started.

"Do it," he snapped.

Kolfinna took the woman's hand once more. Like before, she pushed her mana into the runes. But unlike last time, nothing happened. No runes materialized over Birgitta's skin. The relief Kolfinna felt was palpable.

"It didn't work."

"Joran, you try it." Sijur motioned for Joran, his voice bordering annoyance. "Maybe Kolfinna used up most of her mana and that's why it's not working."

Kolfinna certainty hadn't used up much mana, but she was more than happy to step aside and let Joran try. She didn't want to manipulate anyone's emotions like that. It made her sick to her stomach.

Joran took Kolfinna's place while Kolfinna stood a few feet away. She thought about backing out of the room altogether, but it was illogical to even think about it. Running away right now wouldn't solve her problems, and who knew what would happen to her if she disobeyed Sijur in that manner? Would she die if she distanced herself too much from him? If he issued her a command and she was too far to even know it?

After a minute, a line formed on Joran's forehead and he shook his head. "It's not working. My guess is that ... you can't manipulate emotions with runes. They're likely too complex."

"Hm." Sijur took hold of the knife and tapped the edge of it on the glass top of the coffee table. "I had hypothesized as much, but it was worth a try to test it out."

Kolfinna wanted to leave. She eyed the exit and then everyone in the room. "So, now that we've tested out the runes, how about we—"

"We're still not done yet." Sijur's smile sent chills down her spine. "I want to see how far the bond will go."

That sounded like trouble.

Birgitta seemed to be thinking the same thing because she laughed nervously. "What do you mean by that?"

"Let's see ... How about you grovel at my feet?"

Birgitta's forehead crinkled. "That's it?"

"Yes, we'll start with that."

Kolfinna watched uncomfortably as the woman got down on all fours by Sijur's feet. Sijur, however, didn't look particularly pleased. It came too easily, his expression seemed to say. He probably didn't need rune magic to make her kiss his feet.

He glanced at Joran and snapped his fingers. "Joran, bring the boy."

Joran's spine became a stiff rod, and Birgitta raised her head. Kolfinna was just as confused as her.

Joran scuttled out of the room, averting his gaze. Birgitta was still curled up by Sijur's feet, seemingly unaware of what was happening. It didn't take long for him to enter the room with a young boy beside him. The boy couldn't have been much older than eight or nine years old. Shaggy blond hair framed his youthful face.

Birgitta's eyes widened and she pulled herself to her feet quickly. Her cheeks reddened with color, though Kolfinna wasn't sure if it was due to anger or embarrassment. "What's the meaning of this? Why did you bring my son here?"

"Momma?" The boy rubbed his arm uncertainly.

"What is he doing here?" she demanded. "I never gave you permission to drag my son into this. I don't work that way, do you hear me? You can buy time with me, but you can't bring my family into this. I think I've had it with this whole strange session." She pushed past Sijur and rushed to her son. She placed her hands on his shoulders. "I'm so sorry, Aksel. Let's go home—"

"No." Sijur smiled wolfishly. "I don't think so."

"I don't care. We're leaving—" A scream ripped through her throat and she fell to her knees, her fingers digging into the runes etched on the back of her hand. Kolfinna inhaled sharply as those same runes she had placed on her were now causing Birgitta excruciating pain. Pain Kolfinna had felt before—and never wanted to feel again.

"You can't disobey me, sweetheart." Sijur sighed. "Come on now, get up."

Tears rolled down the woman's face and she didn't seem to hear him. The boy began to cry too, pulling at his mother's arm. Kolfinna sprang into action, grabbed the woman's arm, and yanked her to her feet. The woman stumbled and fell against her, but that seemed to have stopped some of the pain. The woman gasped and blinked at her through bleary, pain-tinted eyes.

Kolfinna turned to Sijur. "Is this really necessary? You were able to bind her so—"

"I didn't ask for your input, *soldier*." Sijur didn't even look at her and was studying Birgitta intently. Like she was a clipped butterfly pinned for his display. "Birgitta, I have one request for you."

Birgitta held on to Kolfinna's forearm tightly. "Please, let me go. I'm not interested in this stuff anymore. You don't even have to pay me—"

"Tsk, tsk." Sijur clucked his tongue. "Of course I'll pay you, but I need you to do one thing for me—"

"Let my son and me *go*." She gripped onto Kolfinna so tightly that she was sure there would be crescent-like fingermarks all along her forearm, similar to the rune marked on her wrist. "This wasn't a part of our agreement."

Sijur only smiled as he approached them. Birgitta's son grabbed her leg and tugged. His voice was small. "Momma, let's go."

Sijur stopped in front of Birgitta. "Kolfinna, let her go."

Kolfinna hesitated, not keen to let Sijur have his way with this woman and child, but her mark began to burn. She gritted her teeth tightly, torn between helping the family and obeying. The mark continued to burn, as if she was testing its patience, so Kolfinna reluctantly released the woman and took a step back. Shame made her throat constrict tightly. Hopefully, whatever Sijur wanted the woman to do would be a quick task and they would all be on their way.

Sijur held out the small knife he had earlier. The sharp blade gleamed. "I want you to take this knife."

"Why?" Birgitta reached for the blade and took it suspiciously. She turned it over in her hand. Her cheeks were still damp with tears. "Will I be able to leave if I do?"

"Yes."

"Okay—"

"Now I want you to take that knife and kill your son."

Kolfinna inhaled sharply, the words cementing the horror she had been feeling this entire interaction. For a second, Kolfinna wondered if she had imagined the whole thing. Because Sijur didn't look serious as he said it, and even now, he was smiling down at Birgitta as if he had asked her to eat lunch with him. It was so casual. So unnervingly casual.

Birgitta's face slackened and the knife fell from her hand. "You want me to ... *what*?"

"Kill your son." He pointed to the knife. "Now."

"B-But—"

All at once, her expression warped to one of pain and she fell to her knees, an earsplitting scream escaping from her mouth. Kolfinna watched with wide eyes as the woman continued to cry and shout while Sijur stood there unfazed. Her son had backed away, tears running down his cheeks. Panic and confusion marred his youthful face. Joran stood behind the couch, his hands clutching the back of the couch tightly.

Kolfinna snapped out of her horror reverie and grabbed Sijur's arm. "This is madness. Why would you ask her to do that?!"

"Release me."

"Sijur—" Kolfinna gasped as white-hot pain shot through her wrist and she quickly let go of him. She cradled her burning wrist to her chest and breathed through her nostrils. She had almost forgotten she had to obey him. But she couldn't let him do this.

"To you, I'm Lieutenant General Bernsten, Kolfinna. Do not forget that." His gaze was glacial as he peered down at her with dark eyes. He turned to Birgitta, who writhed on the floor in agony. "This is all an experiment, don't you see?"

"An experiment?" Kolfinna's body trembled and her voice rose. "This is madness! This is ... *evil*!"

"Hm. Perhaps. But it's necessary."

Necessary to whom? For him to rise to power?

"Lieutenant General—" she started.

"What's stronger? The rune mark that forces her to obey me, or her will?" Sijur's eyelids lowered as the woman continued to screech. "I wish to see it."

Birgitta clawed at the tiled floor, her fingernails catching at the edges of the tiles. Tears streamed down her face. "Please, make it stop!"

"You can make it stop." Sijur waved to the knife she had dropped, which was only a foot away from her.

Birgitta turned her face away from it. "I would never!"

"I guess we'll wait then." Sijur looked down at her. "I'm very curious to see what will happen. Will you die if you continue to refuse me, or will you succumb to the pain and obey? I guess we will see which is stronger."

Kolfinna's thoughts raced and she realized she had been locking her knees for minutes now. She couldn't let this continue. She closed her eyes to think past the horrible screams, but she couldn't come up with anything. The only logical path her brain kept directing her to was to kill Sijur—because wouldn't everything stop once he was out of the equation? The runes couldn't work if he was dead. And it wasn't like he had added a clause to Kolfinna's rune to make it so she never hurt him, so she could do it, hypothetically. However, it *wasn't* a logical choice at all.

But it was tempting and a part of her mind told her that she was already a murderer, so more blood staining her hands didn't matter.

Kolfinna banished those thoughts. Killing Sijur would only complicate her position.

"There has to be another way," Kolfinna said above the

woman's wailing. Even to her own ears, she sounded desperate and helpless.

Sijur acted like he didn't hear her and instead strolled over to his couch and plopped down on it. He grabbed a cookie, propped his feet up on the coffee table, and leaned into the cushions.

The young boy, Aksel, ran over from his corner, tears and snot running down his face. He fell on his knees beside his mother. He shook her, but she only spasmed more, her screams becoming shriller. "Momma! Momma!" The boy turned to Kolfinna with teary eyes. "Do something! Please! You're supposed to help, aren't you?" He turned his pleas to Joran, who only backed away farther, as if wanting to shrink into the wall. "Please! Help her!"

Kolfinna's chest tightened painfully. She wasn't in the room anymore. She was back in time when Lord Estur had killed Katla and how, later that night, she had cried and cried because she had lost her only family. And right now, if Kolfinna didn't do anything, this little boy would experience the same thing.

The thought alone spurred her into action. She dropped down beside Birgitta and took the woman's hand. Birgitta instantly tried to wrench it away, but Kolfinna held on tighter, so tight that her hand turned white. Mana seeped from Kolfinna's body. The little boy sobbed harder.

You will no longer feel pain.

She poured the mana into the runes. She didn't care what Sijur or Joran thought. She didn't care what would happen to her. She didn't think about any of that.

One thing the Royal Guards had taught her was that it was her duty to protect the people. And there was no way she would let this woman suffer when there was something she could do about it.

"What are you doing?" Sijur demanded from his spot on the couch. He planted his feet on the tiled floor and leaned forward, his expression pinched together.

In her peripheral vision, Joran paled significantly.

Kolfinna poured more of her mana into the woman. Sweat

beaded her forehead. The words didn't appear, but she had to keep pushing until they did.

"Stop, Kolfinna! I order you to *stop!*"

Sijur's angry voice sent a jolt of pain up her wrist. Kolfinna cried out, her focus slipping, but she kept her hand secured on the woman's. Kept her attention on the little boy. She concentrated on him and on the runes. She thought about Katla and her own parents that she didn't remember. She thought about the day she had lost Katla and how her world had turned upside down. She thought about how disappointed Katla would've been in her if she did nothing.

Her wrist was on fire. She doubled over the woman, her control over her mana shifting wildly.

Focus, *focus.*

But it was so hard to focus when it felt like someone was lighting her arm on fire. Like someone was dragging a knife up her arm and slicing ribbons of her flesh off her body like she was a slab of cooking meat. She wanted to scream, wanted to forget about what she was doing, wanted to abandon the woman—

Katla, she thought. *Think of Katla.*

She thought of her sister's vivid green eyes that were always full of kindness. Her laughter that lightened the room. Her smile that radiated—

"Kolfinna!" Joran shoved Kolfinna back with a violent force, sending her sprawling on the floor. Her head cracked against the tiles and she gasped in pain. She blinked back to find Joran's deep jade eyes trained on her, his face hovering a few inches away from her own. His tan skin was crinkled with worry lines and he was nearly pleading with her. "Stop what you're doing! You'll die if you keep this up!"

The pain was already ebbing away now that Kolfinna wasn't disobeying Sijur. She pushed herself into a sitting position, but Joran pinned her shoulders down in place.

"Let me go!" Her shouts mingled with the woman's cries. "I

can't be an accomplice in this! I don't care if the runes hurt me. I can't let you do this to that woman!"

Even as he kept his full weight on her shoulders, he had the decency to look guilty. She tried shoving him off her, but when that didn't work, she brought her knee up to his groin, hard. Joran gasped and instinctively released her. It was all the time she needed to push him off her.

Birgitta's hand clasped around the handle of the knife.

Kolfinna's eyes widened.

No.

Sijur had risen from his seat, an excited gleam in his eyes.

Kolfinna scrambled toward her, her heart racing. If she turned that blade to the boy—

Birgitta pointed the knife to her own throat.

"No!" Kolfinna dove to her. Before the blade could plunge into her neck, Kolfinna shoved the knife into her own hand and yanked it backward. The sharp blade sliced through her hand easily and a pool of thick, bright blood streamed over the floor. Kolfinna gasped in sharp pain, but the adrenaline masked most of it. Birgitta struggled with the knife, trying to wrench it from Kolfinna's hand. They both wrestled each other on the floor. Kolfinna's blood stained everything—the tiles, both of their dresses, the knife, and the expensive center rug.

Kolfinna used both hands to grasp the slippery, bloody blade and the handle. Her blood smeared further over Birgitta's hands, her dress, and the floor. Somehow, she managed to tug it free and toss it across the room. A splash of scarlet followed with that movement.

"No!" Birgitta tried to reach over Kolfinna in the direction of the blade, but Kolfinna pinned her down to the floor.

Rune magic thrummed from her hands with such heat that she wasn't sure if it was the mana or the painful gashes that made everything so clear.

"Accept the runes!" Kolfinna shouted. "It'll stop the pain!"

Underneath her, Birgitta thrashed even harder, almost unseating Kolfinna.

"Kolfinna!" Sijur grabbed her shoulder.

Kolfinna's hands were hot with magic. *You will no longer feel any pain today.*

The runes glowed gold over Birgitta's blood-smeared chest and she suddenly stopped spasming. Kolfinna was ripped away from her in the next second as Sijur sent her flying backward. She rolled on the floor, her shoulder cracking against the tiles.

"Damn it, Kolfinna!" Sijur raked a hand through his hair, wild eyes flicking between Kolfinna and Birgitta, who was gasping like a fish out of water.

"Momma!" Aksel dove toward his mother and hugged her tightly, creating a barrier between her and Sijur.

A storm of emotions passed over Sijur's face, rage being the most notable one. He pinched the bridge of his nose and exhaled slowly. The only noise in the room was Birgitta's panting, Aksel's sobs, and the heavy breath of Sijur's barely controlled anger.

"Kolfinna," Sijur spoke through clenched teeth. "What the hell did you write on her?"

Pain radiated from her hands as Kolfinna pulled herself into a sitting position. "So she won't feel any pain."

Sijur turned to Joran sharply. "Is that true?"

Joran flinched and uncertainly approached Birgitta. He barely glanced at the runes before nodding.

"And why would you do that?" Sijur asked.

"Are you serious?" Kolfinna waved at the mother-son duo. "How can you do that to an innocent woman!"

Sijur flicked his hand dismissively in the air, the words spitting out harshly. "She's a prostitute! Her life has no meaning, no purpose. I paid a handsome sum for it."

"You can't just ... just *buy* people." Kolfinna's hands shook from rage. Blood spotted the floor with every tremble. "She clearly had no idea what she got herself into. And you took advantage of that. You're a soldier. You—no, we—are supposed to protect the people—"

Sijur sighed, long and hard. "Kolfinna, darling." He raked a hand through his hair exasperatedly before his tone became cruel. "You're no longer a Royal Guard, so stop acting like one. You have one job, and that's to listen to *me*. Forget about everything you learned with the guards. Your only job here is to listen to my commands and follow directions. That is what it means to be a soldier. Do you understand?"

No. The word was on the tip of her tongue, but movement in the corner of her eye dragged her attention away. Birgitta was convulsing on the floor, her limbs jerking up and down and slamming against the floor violently. Aksel began to scream and clutched his mother's arms to stop her.

"H-Help!" he screamed.

"What's happening?" Sijur asked.

"I-I don't know!" Kolfinna crawled to Birgitta, her handprints leaving ominous blood stains behind her. She grabbed onto her convulsing figure. Birgitta's eyes were wide and fearful, and she parted her lips to speak. Blood gurgled in her open mouth and the whites of her eyes shifted to a light pink as blood streamed from them.

Birgitta raised a hand and touched Aksel's damp cheek.

"Momma!"

Kolfinna's hold on the woman tightened, her mind whirring and panicking with what she needed to do. There had to be some runes she could make. Maybe something—

All at once, Birgitta stopped moving. Her hand slipped off her son's face and hit the floor with finality. Her eyes were still wide and trained on her son. The life that had shone in them was now gone.

Aksel screamed something incoherent. Kolfinna's breathing hitched. What had gone wrong? She had written the runes perfectly, so why—

It hit her then. Just because Birgitta couldn't feel the pain anymore didn't change that she had been disobeying Sijur's command.

This was the result of going against the rune contract.

Tears stung Kolfinna's eyes and she stared helplessly at Aksel. How long had the entire affair taken? Ten minutes? Fifteen? That was all it had taken to kill Birgitta, and her son had to watch the whole thing.

She wanted to vomit.

She inhaled sharply, suddenly feeling like there wasn't enough air in her lungs. Her head felt light and her breaths became shallow.

Fifteen years.

This would be her fate.

Birgitta's lifeless eyes continued to stare at her son.

Kolfinna released Birgitta and fell backward. Aksel's cries became warbled to her hyper sensitive ears. She could hear her own ragged, quick breaths. Every inhale brought forth a wave of metallic, stinging rust to her nose. She couldn't rip her gaze away from Birgitta's motionless form.

"*—Kolfinna.*"

Sijur touched Kolfinna's shoulder and she jolted back to reality. She shook his hand away. If her actions annoyed him, he didn't show it. There was too much excitement on his face, in the air around him, that her small action couldn't have dampened his mood.

Of course he was excited. He had just learned that disobeying him meant death. He must've felt so powerful in this moment, to drive a woman to death because she refused to kill her son. It made Kolfinna sick to her stomach.

"Do not do that again, Kolfinna," he said. "I'll let it slide this once, but if you do it again ..." He gestured to Birgitta's body. He didn't need to finish his sentence; the threat was already heavy in the air.

Kolfinna's mouth was dry. Joran was practically hugging the

wall, his face pallid. Aksel continued to weep and call for help, but no one paid him any attention.

"What will happen to him?" she whispered.

"Hm?" Sijur was still standing in the middle of the room, his hands on his hips as he stared at Birgitta's limp body.

"The boy."

"Oh. He'll be given the money I promised Birgitta; it's enough to live very comfortably." He shrugged, like it wasn't a big deal. "I'll send him to a reputable orphanage. I'm sure Birgitta would be thrilled to know that."

"Is it enough?" Kolfinna's voice was barely a whisper. She didn't have any strength left. Not after everything.

"Hm? The money? Yes, darling, it's enough."

Darling.

Since when did he start calling her that? Her lips curled back. "Is it enough for her life? You think he'll be happy taking money that was exchanged for his mother's life?"

He looked down at her with mild interest. "Whether you see it or not, Kolfinna, these experiments are necessary to make a better society. All great changes require sacrifices. Birgitta's life would've amounted to nothing. She would have made no difference to society. But now?" He grinned at her corpse. "Now, she has made an advancement in rune knowledge. That is incredibly powerful, don't you think?"

Kolfinna suddenly felt lightheaded again. It might've been due to blood loss, since the gashes on her palms were still bleeding profusely, or it might've been her heightening horror at his words.

Sijur's gaze flicked down to Kolfinna's hands. "You're dismissed. Go get your hands taken care of."

"Is that an order?" She rose to her feet unsteadily.

He considered it and then chuckled. "No."

Kolfinna was more than happy to bolt out of the room.

15

Out in the hallway, Kolfinna couldn't breathe.

She couldn't see where she was going. She couldn't hear past the memory of Birgitta's last breath. She couldn't swim out of the darkness that was consuming her every thought. Her chest was tight. She could imagine herself dying the same way Birgitta had. All it would take would be a few words from Sijur. A command she couldn't obey.

Her shoulder hit a wall and her world veered as she fell to her knees. She pushed herself to her feet, her bloody handprints smearing the wall in ominous streaks. She stumbled to her room once more. The cold seeped down to her bones and she wanted to curl under her blanket and remain there for hours. She didn't want to think past the numbing pain in her chest or the guilt that twisted a dagger to her heart.

She walked and walked until she finally reached her room. When she twisted the doorknob, she was met with resistance. She pounded her fist against the door, her teeth chattering together.

No response.

Damn it.

She didn't have time for this.

Kolfinna pounded on the door, harder this time. More blood

painted the wall and she cursed herself again. Herja must've been in there, she decided because Inkeri was responsible enough to unlock the door immediately, while Herja could've fallen asleep and not cared who came and went or if someone needed something.

Suddenly, the door swung open, but instead of Herja's angry scowl or Inkeri's kind expression, she was met with a broad chest. And farther up, ice-blue eyes that could've chilled any soul.

"Kolfinna?" Blár looked down at her in confusion.

At first, she was confused too. She had gone to her room, but when she glanced around herself at the unfamiliar hallway, she realized she wasn't even on the correct floor. She had never been here before.

The cold.

She had followed that familiar cold up here, to his room.

That realization struck her deep in her chest. She had followed the comfort of the cold up here, and something in her heart squeezed at the realization, at the implications.

No.

Another chill burst from him, dropping the temperature to sub-zero and wrenching her away from her thoughts. Those cold eyes seemed colder, harsher, and almost *uncontrollable* as he peered down at her with glacial fury.

She followed his gaze down to the dried blood smeared on her clothes, up her wrists, and crusted against her stinging hands. She looked like she had stepped out of a bloody battle.

"Who ..." Blár clenched the doorhandle so tightly that ice spread across the metal, snapping and crackling in place. "Who did that to you?"

That unrelenting anger wasn't pointed at her, but she still flinched nonetheless. "I ..." She swallowed. Birgitta was dead, so it didn't matter. And it wasn't like she had tried to kill Kolfinna. She had tried to kill herself. She had rather kill herself than kill her son.

The fire flickering in the sconces in the hallway waned as

another wave of cold rolled out from him. Kolfinna shivered, keeping her eyes to the floor. She should've excused herself and run back to her room where she had intended to go in the first place. She couldn't, though. She wanted to stay here where the wintry chill actually felt comfortable.

Blár touched her shoulder. "Kolfinna?"

The frost-like touch brought her back to reality. Back to the hallway, to the cuts on her hands, the burning in the back of her eyes. To how helpless she felt at this moment and how she wanted to share it with him.

"Can I come inside?" she finally whispered. She hated how broken the words sounded to her own ears.

Blár studied her for a moment before cracking the door wider and motioning her inside wordlessly. The inside was plainer than she thought his room would be. Fur rugs were thrown underneath a four-poster king-sized bed with silk sheets. Thick velvet curtains hung over a giant window overlooking the forest that surrounded the fortress. A stone hearth roared with fire, and every bit of furniture seemed sturdy and made of solid wood.

Kolfinna fell onto the couch in front of the hearth. She closed her eyes and rested her head against the backrest. She heard Blár ease onto the seat beside her. The weight of his stare was heavy even with her eyes closed.

"What happened?" His voice was soft this time. "Who did this to you?"

"She's dead now." The fire snapped and crackled; it drew her attention away from her dark thoughts. "But it wasn't even her fault. She was ..."

Trying to commit suicide.

"Did you ...?" The question hung in the air. She knew exactly what he meant. He had, after all, been chasing her over a year and a half ago for a murder she had committed. It wasn't farfetched to imagine she would kill again.

"No."

"Sijur?"

She didn't miss the sharpness of his tone. "Yes."

She thought of Sijur's excited face, how it had all been an experiment, how little Birgitta's life meant to him. The display had shown her just how much of a demon Sijur was and just how precarious her own situation was.

She could feel Blár watching her. His gaze was heavy and full of questions, questions she didn't want to answer immediately. She was still embarrassed that she had subconsciously gone to him when she was feeling vulnerable and scared. How was it that he had gone from her enemy, to a friend, to … a safe place?

Blár rose from his seat silently and went to a dresser on the side of his room. He rummaged through it and came back to her with a wad of bandages in one hand and a jar of green salve in the other. He nodded to her hands as he sat.

"Let me see."

"It's fine—" she began.

"No. Let me see." He placed the bandages and the jar between them and when she didn't move, he reached for her hand. His skin was frosty to the touch, like pressing against an ice cube. She fell into that touch. Let him probe against the dried blood crusted along the gashes on her palm. The rough calluses of his hands soothed her nerves for some reason.

Blár turned over her hands, inspecting them with a grim expression. His gaze flicked to her. "Did you grab a knife by the blade?"

She nodded mutely.

He sighed. "Kolfinna, what the actual hell were you thinking?"

"You weren't there," Kolfinna said with a grimace as the memory resurfaced. "You don't know what happened."

He frowned. "Fair enough."

He grabbed the pitcher of water that sat on his coffee table and pulled a handkerchief from his pocket. Wetting it, he tentatively brought it to her hand. He slowly worked on cleaning the wound, occasionally dabbing more water on the bloodied handkerchief, which was slowly becoming more and more rust-colored.

Kolfinna watched the way his blue eyes roved over the cuts. It didn't matter if he bandaged her up or not because sooner or later, the wounds would heal by themselves. The only reason it was taking so long, she surmised, was because she had used a good sum of her mana already. Since healing was a type of magic, it had to run on something. And she was almost dried up, so she would likely be healed tomorrow or in a few hours once her mana replenished itself.

"These are pretty deep gashes," Blár said once he had cleaned up all the blood. "You'll need stitches."

"I'll be fine." She reached for the bandages, but Blár held her hands once more.

"You're not."

Exhaustion made the back of her head feel heavy and she slumped deeper into the couch, wanting to slither between the cushions and disappear. "Blár," she said, her voice coming as a fatigued sigh, "can you just bandage me up and forget about it?"

He went still, those icy eyes embodying a frozen lake as he stared at her. The chill of winter brushed over her skin. "Forget about it? Kolfinna, you came into my room covered in blood. That's not something I can easily forget."

Blár unscrewed the jaw of salve and stuck his fingers into the glob-like mixture. "I don't like seeing you all bloodied up. You hear me? After we're done here, I'm going to have a word with that eel-skinned toad." He said a few colorful swear words under his breath, and she could only imagine he was talking about Sijur.

"Eel-skinned toad." Kolfinna rolled over those words in her mouth with a grin. "I like that. No clue what it actually means, but I like it."

"I've got a lot of words to describe Sijur. A slimy snake being one of them." His finger brushed against the rune marked on her wrist.

"It's not that easy," she said with another long sigh. "Remember, I have to obey him, so I'd rather you not talk to him and stir the pot."

"Yeah, I remember, but"—Blár continued slathering the salve on her cuts—"maybe I can knock some sense into that worthless—"

"Blár." She could already feel a headache slowly budding in the back of her head. "I'd rather you not make my situation more complicated than it already is. I know you're just trying to help, but ... I can't have Sijur thinking too negatively about me. Or giving me too much thought, either. My position could be worse, especially since I have to obey him. He could have me locked away somewhere, isolated from everyone but him. He could make me" —she shivered, thinking about the way Sijur had stared at Olia and Birgitta like they meant nothing—"I don't know, do weird things for him. I'd rather keep it this way."

At least the way things were now, she could still interact with people. She could still train, get stronger, go out into the world on new missions. If Sijur thought she was too complicated to handle ... Her freedom might disappear. She hated that he had that power over her, but she had given it to him when she sealed their deal.

Kolfinna didn't have a choice back then, she told herself. The Royal Guards, Hilda, and the king had forced her hand.

Blár spread the salve over her palms gently. "Fine. I won't say anything, but"—his face scrunched together in displeasure, like he had eaten something sour—"it's not really my style to just *take it*."

Kolfinna froze. "Are you saying that I just *take it* from Sijur?"

"No, not just Sijur." He stared at her levelly. "The Royal Guards would do shit, and you just took it from them too. That's not my style. I'd rather bash anyone's face in than let them treat me like shit. Call me uncooperative, but that's how I do it."

She wanted so badly to slap him right then and there, but he still held her hands lightly in his palms. "I don't just—" The words died on her tongue as the realization hit her.

She did just take it.

The Royal Guards had treated her terribly. Edwin, Farthin, Gisela—they were monsters to her, but she had withstood it. She had told herself it was because she didn't have a choice. She was driven to a corner. Her position hadn't been secured yet, so she had to deal with it.

And now she was doing the same thing with Sijur. She kept telling herself she didn't have a choice.

She had told herself that she wouldn't let anyone treat her badly anymore. It was why she had beaten Bjarni on her first day here. It was why she had hammered it in herself that she wasn't here to make friends. But ... it was true that she didn't like confrontation. It made her uncomfortable.

Maybe ... She was being too complacent. Too cowardly.

Once her hands were bandaged up, he dropped the handkerchief, the leftover bandages, and the jar of salve on the coffee table. "So what happened?"

She didn't want to talk about it. Didn't want to keep wrapping her mind around that gruesome scene with Birgitta's lifeless eyes staring at her sobbing son.

"Kolfinna?"

She looked down at her bandaged hands. "I'd rather not relive it."

The fire licked the logs loudly in the hearth. She couldn't meet his gaze.

"Is there anything I can do to help you?"

Kolfinna lifted her head. He was staring at her with an unreadable expression. Unless he had a way to erase runes, he couldn't help her with her biggest problem. But there were a few other tasks she needed to do: sneak into Joran's room and see if he had any books on runes, and sneak into the room Sijur was keeping the elf woman imprisoned.

Could she ask him for help with either of those tasks? She didn't want to reveal that Joran was a fae and she didn't really want to reveal why she was interested in the elf woman. Maybe it was better that she handled it herself?

"Ah. I know that look." Blár leaned back on the couch and grinned. "What can I do?"

"Nothing—"

"No, no, there's definitely *something*."

Kolfinna chewed on her lower lip. She didn't want to involve him. "Do … Do you know where—" She swallowed. Surely it was better to deal with it herself, but she couldn't stop herself. "Do you know where that elf woman is?"

Blár blinked, clearly not expecting that question. "No." He frowned and touched his shoulder where the elf woman had hurt him. "But she's somewhere in the fort. Unless Sijur hauled her off to another location, but that's unlikely, since he deals with everything concerning the west border."

He had gotten injured during his fight with the elf. That in itself was shocking to even think about, and even more shocking that Kolfinna almost forgot about it. "Are you okay? I'm sorry I didn't ask earlier—"

"I'm fine." He waved his hand dismissively. "She banged me up pretty good, though. Blasted me with a few … I don't even know what the hell that was. Light beams? Fiery shadows? Those hurt like a mother—" He grimaced again. "It hurt. Let's just keep it at that. And, to make matters worse, anytime those things hit me, it was hard to focus on my own mana and fight back. I've never seen or experienced anything like it before."

Kolfinna thought back to her own shadowy magic when she had faced against Hilda's crew and then again with that giant goblin, and the way her shadows had overwhelmed her enemies.

She had thought she only had fae magic. Stone magic, nature magic, and rune magic. But now things were complex and she didn't understand any of her powers.

Not anymore, at least.

"So you want to meet this elf woman," Blár said slowly, reeling her back into the conversation. He was leaning against the back of the couch now and his body was angled toward her. "Why?"

"I can't tell you."

A wedge formed between his brows. "Why?"

Because she didn't want to reveal the truth. That she was somehow related to all of this. That she was related to the heir somehow. That Revna had thought she was the heir. That she was potentially part elf. That the best solution to keep Ragnarök down would be to kill her.

"I have my reasons," Kolfinna muttered.

"And those reasons are ...?"

She sighed and balled her hands into fists. They hurt less than they had twenty minutes ago. "Blár, I don't want to tell you. Can't you get the hint?"

"No, I want to know why you're interested in this elf woman. Is it because of what's happening at the southern border? With those fae and elven soldiers?"

She flinched. The half-elf commander's armies. "Sort of."

"You think it's related to Ragnarök?"

"Yes, and I'd like to ask her a few questions regarding it."

"You don't have to involve yourself in it."

"Blár, I have questions for her that maybe only she can answer," Kolfinna said carefully. "I'd like to speak to her. Do you have any idea where she might be kept?"

Blár went quiet and studied her for a minute. Time slowed and she thought he'd never say another word, but then he said, "I'm not sure, but I think Sijur has another facility down below this fort. It's just a hunch, but we've been noticing that he goes down to the lower level and just ... disappears. I'm thinking there's a secret door somewhere, or ... I don't know. Maybe that's where she's kept?"

There was a basement level down below. The one Kolfinna trained in with Joran. Except, there wasn't a secret entrance. It was literally a door—

Unless, Joran used stone magic to unearth the door every time before they trained?

There could potentially be many underground entrances and

exits, then, if Joran was using stone magic to close and open passages and doorways.

She would have to look into that.

"Kolfinna." Blár inched closer to her. She watched as he lifted a white curl and twisted it around his finger gently, his gaze locked on the hair.

Her face warmed and her mind traveled to those moments back on that frozen lake, where he had similarly taken ahold of her hair and kissed it. She had wanted so much more out of that little interaction.

His next words, however, froze her blood. "Why is your hair white?" He said it with mild curiosity, not with harsh judgment or because he was connecting the dots of her potential elf blood, but it still made her mind stutter.

"W-What?"

"Your hair. You never told me why it turned white." He rubbed the white strands between his fingers, ever so gently. Even as her anxiety ramped up, a thrill ran down her spine.

Her heart was still racing. If she was going to tell him everything—about her elf blood, her connection to the heir situation, and all the changes happening to her body—now was the time. Blár was probably the only one she could trust with this information—trust that he wouldn't turn her in. But she couldn't find the words, as if her throat was thick with syrup. "Um, I'm actually not sure."

"Hm." Blár released the curl. "It suits you."

"Does it?" She laughed nervously and tucked the strand behind her ear. "I think it makes me look ... weird. Like I'm getting old or something. It also makes me stand out—"

He pointed to her head. "Is it *just* your hair? Or ...?"

She blinked. He held her gaze.

And then a flush ran over her skin. "B-Blár, what the hell—"

He threw his head back and laughed while she blushed furiously. She smacked his shoulder lightly, the one that had been injured, and he winced, but it didn't stop his laughter.

"A man will always be a man," she muttered, rolling her eyes. "Even a black rank."

He stretched out his legs and winked. "It was a valid question. And besides"—he braced his elbows on his knees and tilted his head to stare at her—"you're smiling. Finally."

"Idiot." She laced her hands together and tried not to stare at Birgitta's blood staining her uniform. The thought of the woman made her smile wilt again. "*Anyway*, I think I'm going to head back to my room. Thanks for ... everything."

Blár jerked a thumb at her outfit. "Do you want me to get you a new uniform before you leave? It might feel weird walking around like that."

Kolfinna shook her head and rested a hand against the stiff, bloodied parts. "I'll be fine. People will think I'm just another fae doing weird fae things, right?"

They were both quiet for a while. Even though Kolfinna said she was going to leave, she didn't. She just sat there, taking in the coolness of his presence, the warmth of the hearth, and the calmness of the room. So unlike the chaos warring in her heart, the anxiety ripping her mental state at the seams.

"You're still treating me a bit distantly."

"Hm?" Kolfinna looked over at him.

Blár had his arm over the backrest of the couch, casually, but his mouth was pursed together. "You're unhappy with me, I think."

Unhappy was an understatement. She was mostly confused. She wanted to avoid him, but she also wanted to be around him. She wanted to ignore the feelings she had for him. She wanted to be something more than friends. She didn't know how to respond to her own emotions.

"You're wrong," she lied. It came out softly—weakly.

"No, I'm not. You're not happy with me still." He canted his head to the side and watched her carefully. "Did I do something wrong? *Again*?"

She wanted to keep quiet and forget about the whole thing.

She wasn't in the mood to be vulnerable with him again, especially so soon. But a log in the hearth fell, the fire licking it up loudly, and the movement spurred her forward. She couldn't stop the words that tumbled out of her, like she had been waiting for this moment to unleash them. "Yes, you keep flirting with me, knowing that this is going nowhere. We're just friends. We're only supposed to be friends and when you talk to me like I'm something more than that, it just makes me feel even more unsure of what we are. Also, you never did tell me why you didn't show up for my trial."

He had gone very still. "Kol—"

"And I know I'm not imagining it. You *are* flirting with me." She clenched her fists together, pain jolting up her fresh wounds. "We danced at the ball. We ran across the frozen lake. You made a joke just minutes ago. I know you don't talk to everyone like that."

Blár suddenly looked unsure. "Does it make you uncomfortable? I'll stop—"

"No, that's the problem. You tell me that we're just friends, but then you flirt with me and it makes me feel like ... like I'm *special* to you. And when I'm just a friend, it *confuses* me." She placed her hands on her lap and resisted the urge to curl them together again. Her body was suddenly so exhausted, and she wanted to flop down on her bed. "I don't mind that you do it, but, Blár, I really need to know—what am I to you?"

He seemed to mull over that. Kolfinna took that moment to bolster her own confidence. She spoke quickly, riding off her momentum, "Because, honestly, I *like* you. I don't know how it'll even work out, but ... but—" Her throat closed up as doubts spread through her chest. She had thought she wasn't the type to ever find someone, and a part of her wasn't sure if any romance would work in her life. She was a fae, and she was a soldier now. And he was ... he was *Blár Vilulf*. Black rank. Wickedly beautiful. Immensely powerful.

And what was she?

Nothing special.

Her insecurities reared their ugly heads and the distance between them seemed to stretch further.

Blár was too quiet. When she spared him a glance, she couldn't read his expression. Ice formed in her chest, tightening a hold on her heart.

She had made a mistake. She shouldn't have said anything.

Of course he wasn't interested in her; he was just harmlessly flirting and she had taken it too seriously. She had jumped to conclusions and now they were both uncomfortable.

She cursed her stupidity.

"Um, n-never mind," Kolfinna said hastily. "I'm not saying that you're interested in me in that manner. I was just explaining my own feelings. I get that you're a black rank and you probably have tons of women who flock around you"—Ivar's words echoed in her mind about how all the ladies were preparing themselves for his arrival, and she flustered further—"so it only makes sense that you would be interested in someone beautiful and interesting and human, so I was only getting these things off my chest—"

He placed a finger beneath her chin and raised her head so she could look straight at him. Straight into the icy depths. Straight into the dark desire she could see unfurling ever so slowly. "You like me?"

"Yes," she whispered.

That desire seemed to intensify. "Do I plague your thoughts?"

Heat pooled in her stomach. "Yes."

"Do you want me?"

"Yes." She felt ridiculous saying all these obvious things, especially since she had no clue what he wanted. She had already laid her feelings bare. It was only fair that he did the same. She coiled her hands over the edge of the couch. "And you? What do you feel?"

His gaze danced between her own stare and her lips. "I feel many things, Kolfinna."

"And what are those feelings? I'm not imagining this, am I?" She waved a hand between them. "Do you flirt with me to pass time or is it more than just that? Because if it isn't, then you need to stop. I don't want to keep feeling like you're stringing me along."

"I feel ..." He raked a hand through his hair, shooting her a grin. "All right, I'll be honest. I think you're gorgeous, and I love your figure."

She almost stopped breathing. "My figure?"

"Yes." He buried his face in his hands and she could see the tips of his ears were reddening. "Of course there's the matter of your personality, right? That's the thing I'm supposed to say. That you're awkward and charming, and I love that, because I do, but damn, if I'm being honest"—Blár removed his hands, and his eyes met her again, deep and ice blue—"you're beautiful. The way you fight, the way you get serious, the way you're just so damned awkward—it's adorable. I love it. I want to keep seeing it. And—" He clamped his mouth shut. "Damn it. I sound like a creep, don't I?"

Chaotic. He was all over the place, and a part of her liked that. Liked the way he was being honest with her, the way he was acting somewhat *shy.*

"The thing is, I've been attracted to you since the Eventyrslot ruins," he said quickly. "But I'm not really sure what to do with *this.*" He flicked a finger between them. "I've never actually felt like this before."

Kolfinna's face flushed with color and she couldn't respond fast enough. She didn't even know what to say. This whole time she had thought he would reject her, that her feelings would be cast aside like they meant nothing. She had been mentally preparing for it, but to hear him say all these things about her made her feel all too warm. All too overwhelmed.

Blár Vilulf *liked* her.

"You're not a creep," she finally managed to say. She couldn't meet his gaze and picked at the stitching on the edge of the couch, her heart hammering in her chest so loudly that he could probably hear it. She had never thought he would feel the same way she did, and now she didn't know what to think or do.

The only noise between them was the crackling of the fire in the hearth. Kolfinna twiddled her bandaged hands together, her fingers grazing the rough gauze. Her chest felt too full in that moment, but there was a niggling thought in the back of her head that wouldn't go away. It was the same thought that made her aware of how itchy her back was—where her scars were. And she wondered briefly what Blár would think if he knew about her elf blood, and all at once, she wasn't so sure anymore.

Would he still feel the same?

Blár rested a hand atop hers, and the coolness of his touch brought her back to reality. He was staring at her curiously. The shadows of the room played across half of his face. "Are you all right? You look pale."

She didn't want to ruin the moment and wanted to relish in these warm feelings, so she cast her thoughts aside and nodded.

Kolfinna leaned her head against his shoulder and laced her fingers through his. She could worry about the elf later. About the heir, the half-elf commander, Sijur, these runes—all of it. At a later time, when she was ready to be burdened with her problems. But right now, she just wanted to hold on to his hand and forget it all.

She closed her eyes and breathed out deeply, the exhaustion suddenly weighing heavily on her. "Let me just rest my head for a bit, okay?"

"Take as long as you need."

The flames continued to eat away at the logs, crackling and snapping, and warring with the coldness of Blár's wintry aura. For the first time in a long, long time, she finally felt at peace.

16

A NIGHTMARE JOLTED KOLFINNA AWAKE AND FOR A moment, she didn't know where she was. She didn't recognize the bed, the walls, the couch—none of it. Until she eased back into the cushions and realized Blár and her were still on the couch, their hands intertwined. Blár's head was lolled back against the backrest of the couch, and he was fast asleep. Kolfinna blinked at him in surprise. How had they both fallen asleep?

A quick glance at the window revealed it was night. Warmth flooded her face as she imagined what Herja and Inkeri would think when they realized she wasn't in bed. How much time had passed?

She silently slipped her hands from Blár's cold ones, and he didn't budge an inch. Rising up to her feet slowly, she tiptoed to his door. Cracking it open an inch, she poked her head out. It was ominously dark, revealing that it was likely the middle of the night.

Kolfinna glanced back at Blár and hesitated. She could leave and go back to her rooms, or she could search for the elf woman right now. It was the perfect time, since it was so late. But wasn't it better to go with Blár? He had seemed on board to help her, but now that she was awake here and contemplating leaving to search for the woman, she wasn't so sure. She didn't want to explain everything to Blár right now, and since he was sleeping, it was probably best not to wake him.

She bobbed her head to herself, her mind made, and quickly slipped out of the room.

AFTER SNEAKING BACK INTO HER ROOM, CHANGING OUT of her blood-stained clothes and into a new uniform, Kolfinna traipsed through the fortress halls like a common thief. If any soldier asked why she was sleuthing down the halls, she could make the excuse that Sijur needed her for something and that she was still on duty. She kept replaying the words in her mind every time she caught a shadow of someone walking in the distance. But the fort was mostly asleep.

Kolfinna went to the lower level of the fort, her footsteps barely making a sound against the stony floor. Every rustle of movement, squeak of a bed, or creaking of a door opening had her on high alert. When she was on the second lowest level of the fort, she rounded the familiar corner that would lead to the doorway to the basement level that she and Joran frequented. But when she reached it, there was nothing there but a wall. Her mouth dropped open in surprise.

She had been positive that there was a door here. She and Joran came here every day, so what—

She didn't have time to think because she could hear two guards talking in the distance. If she opened up a hole in the wall right now, they could definitely hear her and run here. She hesitated for a split second before quickly making her way where she had come from. Her heart was lodged in her throat as they seemed to draw closer.

"—guard this place every night."

"I don't care. It's a waste of our time, don't you think?"

"Would you rather there be anything interesting going on? Think of it this way, this is the easiest job in the whole fort."

She hurried toward the closest door as the soldiers came closer —probably around the bend of the hallway. Ten more seconds and they'd spot her.

"Guarding a random hall that leads nowhere? The only things here are storage units. I'd rather do something interesting. Like going on one of those missions—"

Kolfinna quietly opened one of the doors along the hallway and stepped inside. The door clicked shut behind her, but the soldiers kept talking without missing a beat.

"White ranks don't have that privilege." The footsteps drew closer. "We'd be killed the second a magic beast saw us."

Her eyes adjusted to the small, dark room. Like the soldiers had been saying, this seemed to be a storage unit. Only a crack of light peeked underneath the door, but it was enough for her to make out the boxes lining the room, the dust slowly descending from her quick movement of entering the room, and the rolled-up rugs at one end of the room.

Kolfinna waited for the soldiers' footsteps to drift to the end of the hallway. She leaned against the door and breathed in relief. They didn't notice her.

Her mind traveled back to the doorway that most definitely should have been there. She hadn't made a mistake. She and Joran went to the basement training room every single day without fail. That must've meant that Joran manipulated the stones of the wall to create an opening so she wouldn't notice there were more levels below.

She hadn't noticed it before, but now that she was touching the floor, she could sense with her stone magic that there were at least two levels below this one.

If her hunch was right, the elf was likely located on one of those floors.

Right before the footsteps disappeared, she heard them switch directions and head back toward her. Kolfinna slunk deeper into the room. Were they rounding back here, or had they realized something was amiss?

Her heart pounded in her chest and she waited for the footsteps to stop at her door. But they didn't. The men continued along, their voices drifting away.

Her palms shook and she let out a shaky breath. This was too dangerous of a plan. She should've woken up Blár and made him accompany her. But that thought sent a wave of unease over her. She wasn't sure if she was ready to share her elf blood with him. Not after he had shared his feelings to her.

She dropped to the floor and pressed her hands against the cool stone. She initially wanted to go back to the end of the hallway where the basement door usually was and open it up, but with the guards in the hallway, she doubted she could do it without their notice. That only left her with one option.

With her eyes closed, she felt for the stones below this room. She could make out a larger room below this one. It wasn't the training hall, she realized, because that one was far, far below, with at least twelve feet of stone on all sides of it. Was the training hall the lowest level, and the floor below this one was the floor the elf was kept at?

There was only one way to find out.

She ever so slowly manipulated the stone beneath her hands. The stone melded with her imagination, pulling apart as she raised it higher and higher. Sweat dribbled down her brow as she lifted the stone up. She could've broken a hole and had the pieces fall to the floor below her, but that would create a mess of evidence.

The stone was at least the circumference of her hips. It was heavy, but she was able to lift it in the air. When she finally rested it on the floor beside her, she released a shaky breath. Her training with Joran to levitate stones had come in handy. She wondered what he would think if he realized she had used it in this way.

A distant *thud* made her pause. She tilted her head to the side, trying to listen carefully. It sounded like it was coming from below. Maybe the training room?

She heard it again. Her heart skipped a beat. Was the elf woman doing something? Crashing into the wall in a fit of anger? Breaking down floors and tiles?

Kolfinna poked her head below. It took her several seconds for her eyes to adjust. It seemed to be an office of sorts. The light was dimmer a level below and she couldn't see much, but she squeezed her body through the hole, hung onto the edges, and dropped.

She lithely landed on her feet. The room was almost pitch-black. She carefully stepped around wooden furniture, her hands scouring the space around her. Her fingers danced over velvet and she could make out a backrest—a couch, she realized. She continued through the door and her hip smacked onto a corner. She cringed, her fingers pressing against what seemed like a desk. It took her less than a minute to find a wall and then a door. She wrenched the door open.

Another corridor. This one, unlike the one above her, was completely dark.

As she felt along the walls, she realized this floor was much smaller than the one above. There were only three rooms here. The room she had left was clearly an office. The second room also seemed to be an office. She had felt around the room—couches, tables, and slips of paper, but nothing that seemed like a prison.

The third room, however, she could feel the faint pulse of mana.

Kolfinna stopped at the door, the blood rushing to her ears. This was it. If the elf wasn't in this room, then she had no idea where she could be.

Her hands were sweaty as she twisted the doorknob.

She opened the door to inky darkness and golden runes. Kolfinna stepped through, her gaze flicking over to the glaring runes etched into the floor in a ring. *Magic will not work inside this circle. No one shall leave the circle.*

The only light source was a flickering candle outside the ring of runes. It was all the light Kolfinna needed to make out the cramped room and the woman sitting cross-legged inside the rune circle.

The woman's red eyes were already pinned on Kolfinna, as if she had been waiting for her. She seemed to meld into the shadows, and her brilliant white hair contrasted beautifully with her midnight-like skin. Some chinks of her black scaled armor were missing, courtesy to Blár, but it didn't take away from the vicious image the scaly armor created. It took Kolfinna a split second to realize she had seen scales like that before—on the dreki.

The woman's mouth curved into a grin.

Kolfinna swallowed down the sudden apprehension thickening the air. Now that she was in front of the elf, she couldn't think of anything to say.

"I've been waiting for you," the woman purred. Her voice sounded like smooth velvet—strong and feminine, with a hint of a dialect she had never heard before.

Kolfinna flinched. "Have you now?"

"But of course." The woman rose to her feet slowly. She was at least a head taller than Kolfinna. She peered down at her with gleaming, blood-red eyes.

Even though there was a barrier of runes between them, Kolfinna inadvertently shrank back.

The woman gracefully bowed low, her hand pressing against her chest. "Greetings, Your Highness."

She blinked.

Your Highness?

Her heart hammered. Adrenaline rushed through her veins. "I'm not—" Her throat closed up. She was not ... She was not the heir. She couldn't be. "I'm not royalty."

"You are my commander's daughter." The woman flashed a white-toothed smile. One of her teeth was sharp like a dagger's tip. "I must show my respect."

"No." The word ripped from Kolfinna's mouth sharply.

The woman didn't seem the slightest bit deterred. "My name is Rakel, Your Highness. I came all this way to see if you were here. We've been looking all across this country for you. Just my luck that I found you before the others." She chuckled softly, in amusement, or perhaps something more sinister. "Come now, we must go—"

"No." Kolfinna took another step back. She suddenly became too aware of the fact that she shared the woman's white hair, and that she was likely part elf too. But she couldn't come to terms with it. Couldn't fathom that she was also an elf. "I came here to ask you some questions. Not to go somewhere with you."

Rakel tilted her head to the side, red eyes glowing. "I am more than happy to answer your questions, Your Highness."

"Stop calling me that." It sounded ridiculous out loud. There was no way she could be royalty, but in the back of her mind, she remembered the way the black shadows had melted out of her.

"Your father—"

"My father is dead." She clenched her fists together. The two gashes on her palms had healed hours ago, and the feel of the new scars made her feel even more out of place. "He died when I was four."

Rakel studied her expressionlessly. "Your father is very much alive. The other was not your father."

"I have questions I need answers to. You *will* answer me." Kolfinna didn't know where her confidence came from, but the words came out like fire. Quick and heated. If the woman was intimidated by them, she didn't show it. If anything, she appeared amused. Like watching a child throw a tantrum.

Rakel nodded. "What are your questions?"

"Who are you?"

"Rakel. I have no family name." The woman smiled. "I am one of the four generals under Commander Alfaer."

The half-elf commander. A shiver ran down her spine at the mere mention of his name. Kolfinna recognized it from the journal she had read all those weeks ago.

"Why is the half-elf commander's army awake?" Kolfinna whispered. "He is … from Queen Aesileif's time, is he not?"

"Yes," Rakel said slowly. "The queen is his wife. And you are their daughter."

"That's not possible—"

"When Commander Alfaer set the seal, its condition was that only his daughter Kolfinna could awaken the *Død Sværd*. And thus awaken him and his army." She raised her brows at her. "You woke the blade, did you not?"

All the blood drained from her face. "How do you know my name? How do you even know who I am?"

"It's obvious." Rakel pointed to her. "You look like him and your eyes are pink."

"Pink eyes are normal among the fae."

"No, they're not." Rakel folded her arms over her chest. "Your eyes are pink because you're part elf."

"No—"

"You're a quarter elf. All half-elves and full elves have red eyes. Anyone with less than that usually has pink eyes, unless their elven blood is very strong."

That couldn't be true. Kolfinna had always believed that pink eyes were normal. The fae always had vivid eye colors. Purple. Green. Orange. Yellow. *Pink*—or so she thought.

"How did you know I was here?" she asked.

"I didn't. I was investigating the area the queen left you behind at."

The cave with the rune writing. Where Kolfinna had first discovered what the heir meant. Her blood ran cold. It wasn't too far from here.

Kolfinna swallowed. "I'm not who you think I am. Maybe I'm *related*, but—"

"Someone broke the runes," Rakel interrupted, watching her with half-lidded eyes. "I checked. You were sealed away in a cave with powerful runes. They were supposed to protect you, and when I checked the cave, they were broken. By the residual mana,

I can tell that the seal was broken some sixteen years ago. How old are you now? Eighteen?"

Her heart beat faster.

"It aligns with your age. Your eyes are the same pink as Princess Kolfinna. Your name is the same. You have half-white hair, which aligns with your elven blood. You seem to have healing properties"—she motioned to Kolfinna's body—"seeing as how you're up and about after my snakes poisoned you. You are who I think you are."

Kolfinna's head spun and she suddenly felt weak to her knees. She couldn't be the evil queen's daughter. It just didn't make any sense. Queen Aesileif was legendary, mythical, and there couldn't be a way that she was her daughter. That Kolfinna was the daughter of a terrifying, powerful half-elf commander. Plain old Kolfinna. Who was no one special. Who had no parents. Whose only family member had died a year and a half ago.

And now this woman was saying that she was a long-lost heir?

That couldn't be true. It just couldn't.

"M-My hair wasn't always white," she said, grasping onto the one thing she could deny. "I had black hair before—"

"Did your elven powers recently awaken?" Rakel asked. "Sometimes, for those who have a smaller percentage of elven blood, there needs to be a traumatic event that triggers your magic to awaken. Did something happen to you recently?"

Hilda. The torture room. Her near death experience.

Kolfinna felt dizzy.

"Is your eyesight better than usual? Can you hear things you didn't hear before?"

"It's not possible. How can I be over a thousand years old?" she whispered. The fae queen and the half-elf commander were from a different time period. If what this woman was saying was true, then Kolfinna was ancient. She didn't belong here. All of this sounded like a fairy tale.

"When someone is sealed away, they are perfectly preserved. Haven't you seen it before?"

Her thoughts raced to Revna in the Eventyrslot ruins. To the other fae women who were preserved in their coffins.

Her stomach twisted into a tighter ball.

If Kolfinna was the heir, then that meant ... Commander Alfaer would come after her. He would use her to awaken the queen. Ragnarök would win. There would be a war.

"Are you well? You look pale." There was a hint of concern in Rakel's voice, but there was also that triumphant arrogance. Like she knew she had hit the nail on the head.

Kolfinna stood straighter, but it was hard when those blood-red eyes were boring into her, as if seeing every imperfection. Was she disappointed that Kolfinna didn't meet her expectations? That the daughter of the half-elf commander and the ruthless queen was so ordinary?

Just thinking that made her want to throw up.

The daughter of the half-elf commander.

Her entire life was a lie.

"Your Highness—"

She held up a finger and took a step back. "Don't"—she swallowed down the dryness of her throat—"don't call me that." She wanted to get out of here. If any of the soldiers or the Royal Guards found out that she was the heir, they would kill her. If Ragnarök and the half-elf commander found out where she was, then they would capture her. Either way, she was screwed.

But as long as Rakel was a prisoner here, the half-elf commander would never know that she was here.

Kolfinna needed to find a way to break the rune mark and escape, far away from Ragnarök, the half-elf commander and his armies, and the military. It would only take one slipup for the military to realize who she was. If they started piecing together that she was part elf, it wasn't a farfetched idea that she was somehow related to all of this.

"Princess—"

"I'm not a princess." She blinked away her dizziness. "I'm just Kolfinna."

Rakel chuckled. "You cannot hide from your blood."

That was the last thing Kolfinna heard before she spun around and stormed out of the room. She couldn't think straight, not beyond the cloying fog of confusion and anxiety ebbing her vision and clogging her thoughts.

17

Kolfinna stirred in her bed. She wasn't able to sleep well. Not since she visited Rakel. Her mind was stuck in that room with the circle of runes. Her whole world had been turned upside down—another thing that seemed to be very common every few months. She had suspected that she was related to the heir somehow, but she would've never imagined that she was the actual daughter of the elf-commander.

That she was a *princess*.

None of it felt real.

She worked even harder to break the rune mark. Tried scouring the fort several times for clues. Even sneaking into Joran's room didn't give her anything useful. Other than scraps of paper with doodles and boring books in human languages.

Her mind was completely consumed by the insane thought that she was the long-awaited heir. *How?*

Even if Rakel had shown her a hundred signs and proofs that she was the daughter of the ruthless queen and the powerful half-elf commander, she couldn't believe it. She was too ordinary to be *this* important. Not to mention the notion sounded like a fable.

And then there was the matter of her parents—the parents she had thought were hers—and Katla. If Rakel was telling the truth, why had they awakened her from the cave? Why did they free her? But they were all dead, and she couldn't even ask them what it all meant.

Kolfinna rolled in her bed, those wicked thoughts plaguing her.

Inkeri sat on her bed, embroidering a flower onto a handkerchief. She had been quiet the entire evening, choosing to focus on her embroidery rather than talk.

Kolfinna's attention was drawn to the steady poking and pulling of the embroidery needle into the cloth. She needed a distraction, and the two women in the room were perfect for that. "Hey, Inkeri, I have a question."

"Yes?"

"Do you like Ivar?"

Herja, who had been tossing and turning and trying to fall asleep, perked up at that. "I want to know too."

Inkeri paused and lifted her moon-like eyes at them both. She blinked, clear surprise showing on her face. "What? Like romantically?"

"Yes," Kolfinna said. The thoughts of the half-elf commander, of the ruthless queen, of Ragnarök slipped into a deeper crevice of her mind. She tried smiling, tried focusing on Inkeri's expression and the frivolities of mindless gossip.

"No way," she said with a wave. "He's a jerk."

"Huh, really?" Kolfinna slung her legs over the edge of the bed. "He seems to be in love with you, though," Kolfinna said.

Herja chuckled while Inkeri gave them both a strange look. "No, he's not. Do you see the way he talks to me? He treats me like crap!"

"He's completely in love," Kolfinna pressed, placing her hands on the edge of her mattress as she leaned closer. "He was so worried when you were hurt—"

"Right?! I was thinking that too." Herja sat up and her quilted blanket fell over her lap. "I suspected it for a while—"

"No way." Inkeri crinkled her nose and continued embroidering. "He was only worried because I'm his teammate."

"So you aren't interested in him like that?" Herja asked.

Inkeri hesitated.

Kolfinna's eyes widened. "So you are."

"No," she said sharply. "Not like that."

"Then like what?" Herja asked.

"Do you see the way he treats me?" Inkeri stuck her embroidering needle into the handkerchief she was working on and placed the whole piece on her nightstand beside her lantern. "He always talks down to me and he's *mean*. He knows how much I want to be a purple rank, and he just keeps rubbing it in my face that I'm not at that level yet and that I'm weak." Her voice wobbled before growing harsher. "He's just an asshole all-around. So no, I don't like him like that and if he does"—she brought her trembling lips together—"if he is interested in me, then he's an idiot to think that the way he's treating me would make me reciprocate that."

Herja nodded slowly. "But have you ever thought about sleeping with him?"

Kolfinna gasped, turning to Herja in shock. "Inkeri was just sharing a very vulnerable part of herself with us and you think that's the appropriate question—"

But one look at Inkeri's blushing face clamped her mouth shut. Herja laughed and smacked her pillow. "I *knew* it."

"I-I've never thought about that—" Inkeri covered her suddenly ruddy face with her hands. "Stop looking at me like that!"

Herja leaned forward excitedly. "Do you remember last month when we got back from excavating that collapsed building and there was a mini feast for everyone?" Herja grinned toothily. "I could've sworn I saw you two kiss each other in the hallway. Did it really happen?"

"I want to know too," Kolfinna said, inching closer to the edge of the bed like that would make the answer come out faster.

"Well"—Inkeri smoothed down her nightgown and avoided their gazes—"yes. It did."

Herja covered her mouth. "Holy crap. I thought it was you, but Brenda told me it was probably some other girl because why would *you* be interested in *him*, and vice versa?"

"You *kissed* him?" Kolfinna raised an eyebrow. The way Inkeri and Ivar acted around each other didn't give away that they were romantically involved in any way. But a kiss changed things. "Are you sure you're not interested in him?"

"I don't know!" Inkeri flipped onto her stomach and buried her blushing face in her pillow. "I think it's wrong for me to have any feelings toward him because of the way he treats me, but he's just so ... Charming? Is that even the right word?"

Charming definitely wasn't the word Kolfinna would use to describe him.

"Do I just have a strange type?" Inkeri pushed herself on her elbows and turned her head to them. "Why would I be attracted to a freaking *bully*? Because that's what he does. He's just plain mean to me, so my feelings don't make sense."

"Why don't you just sleep with him once and get all of that out of your system?" Herja asked.

"I can't do that!" Inkeri combed her hair with her fingers. "And besides, that kiss ... I don't even know if it *counts* as a kiss."

"So?" Herja waved an impatient hand. "Are you going to explain or no?"

"Well, he said he wanted to talk to me, and so we went into the hall, and then he ... he kissed me." Inkeri's face was shifting into a deeper shade of scarlet. She twisted a strand of her hair between her fingers. "And, well, he told me he wants to, well, let's just say he said some vulgar things. But here's the thing, he was drunk. *Very* drunk." She blew out air. "He kinda proposed, I think? Said he wants to, um, make me his and stuff—"

"That's not a proposal." Herja laughed. "He wants to *take* you, if you know what I mean."

Kolfinna blinked. "That's what it means?"

"Yes, totally," Herja said with a nod before frowning. As if realizing she was talking to Kolfinna. "If a man says he wants to make you his, I don't think he's thinking the innocent kind of way."

"*Anyway.*" Inkeri cleared her throat. "We kissed a bit and then … he threw up all over me."

Kolfinna couldn't help the laugh that slipped from her mouth; it mingled with Herja's shriek of laughter. Even Inkeri chuckled a bit.

When their laughter subsided, Inkeri spoke again. Her tone took a sharper turn. "But here's the *best* part. He had been so very drunk that the next day, he had *zero* recollection of what happened. I feel so stupid thinking back on it. I even asked him the next day if he wanted to do anything together—and I meant more like, you know, courting each other, eating together, or something—and he looked at me so confusedly and asked me, 'What the hell are you talking about?'" She groaned and fell back onto her pillow with a long sigh. "Do you know how absolutely mortifying that is?"

Kolfinna lifted her brows. She remembered the way Ivar had cradled Inkeri's body when those monstrous snakes had bitten her, the desperation on his face when he'd asked Kolfinna to save her. "Did you try talking to him about it?"

"Not after that, no." Inkeri propped herself back up and blew out the strands of hair covering her face.

"So what you're telling us is that you *are* interested in him." Herja's smile grew even wider.

"No." Inkeri sat straighter and pointed at her. "Absolutely not. I had my moment of weakness, and I have no plans of repeating it."

Kolfinna was fairly certain Ivar was in love with Inkeri, and even though Inkeri was adamant, Kolfinna suspected she felt the same. Inkeri was hurt, that much was clear. Maybe if Kolfinna talked to Ivar, things could clear up between the two of them? But then again, it wasn't her place to interfere.

Inkeri cleared her throat. "Well, what about you two?"

"Hm?" Herja ran a hand through her red locks dumbly.

Kolfinna stared down at her hands.

"Well?" Inkeri pointed an accusing finger at Herja. "I know you're interested in Blár. Have you made any progress?"

Herja flopped down on her bed. "I'd rather not talk about my nonexistent and *messy* love life."

Kolfinna's face warmed and she watched Herja expectantly. She had only seen glimpses of Blár here and there between training sessions, but their minimal interactions had been normal, despite that they apparently felt the same about each other. But seeing Herja now made her all the more aware of her feelings for Blár and how she didn't want the pretty redhead to feel the same.

"So?" Inkeri asked slowly.

Herja shot Kolfinna an unreadable look before shrugging. It looked awkward since she was lying down. "Well, Kolfinna can probably explain better than I can."

Kolfinna blinked back while Inkeri turned her attention to her curiously. "What? I don't know what you mean—"

"He didn't tell you?" Herja frowned at her. "We were talking and I sort of told him I'm interested in him because I'm getting really tired of trailing after him and him not getting the hint, so I was a bit direct. Anyway, long story short, he rejected me." She gave Kolfinna a look. "I'm pretty sure I know why."

A blush crept up Kolfinna's face as the two women turned to her. "W-What?"

"Come on, you can't be *that* dense." Herja raised an eyebrow. "I see the way you look at him. And I think he feels the same."

"Oh, Herja, I am so sorry—" Inkeri started.

"Don't." She raised a hand to stop her. "I'd rather not dwell on it, especially considering the girl I lost to is sitting right there."

Kolfinna flinched, but Herja's tone wasn't sharp or mean. It was void of emotion. Herja was probably too proud to show hurt or weakness in front of her. She reminded Kolfinna of herself and how she would've acted that way too. But Kolfinna never would've shared with Inkeri or Herja if Blár had rejected her. Especially not to the woman he had rejected her for.

Herja pulled herself into a cross-legged position and began braiding her hair. Maybe she needed that distraction, but when she turned to them both, her expression was calm. As if she hadn't admitted anything. "Anyhow, I already have someone else lined up. Potentially. So don't feel bad for me, okay?"

"You have someone else—" Kolfinna couldn't hold back her surprise.

"*Sort of.*" Herja shrugged, her fingers deftly working through her wild, red curls. "Inkeri, do you remember when we were temporarily transferred to the Southern border to help them for a bit when they were low on people? What was that, like four months ago?"

"Yes," Inkeri said with a nod.

"Well, I got involved with another soldier there. Romantical-ly." She now finished the braid, but instead of tying it with a ribbon, she raked her hand through it and undid it. "Or, well, maybe romantically isn't the right word. But anyway, that soldier is now sending me letters. And ... And things are messy, I guess."

Kolfinna tried to wrap her mind around that. "Wait, so you were sleeping with this guy?"

"Yes." Herja shoved her messy hair out of her face. "I mean, Blár's great and all, but it's not like he's the *only* guy I've been pursuing. Especially since Blár and I aren't going anywhere, or weren't going anywhere. And he had transferred out a while ago, so I moved on. And this guy ... Well, he's interested. Now that Blár's rejected me"—she hugged her knees to her chest and shrugged—"there's not much stopping me, right?"

"Except that he's hundreds of miles away?" Inkeri quirked an eyebrow. "Who is he? Do you even like him or are you going to use him to forget about Blár?"

"Ehh, do I need to like him?" Herja flashed a toothy grin while Inkeri chucked a pillow at her. She caught it effortlessly.

"Come on, Inkeri, not everyone is like you and only cares about *feelings*."

"You can't just sleep with this man to get over your feelings for Blár. You'll just feel more and more empty when you do that." Kolfinna could see the concern behind Inkeri's glare. "Give yourself time to get over it—"

"That's why I said things are messy." Herja tossed the pillow back at Inkeri and sat up straighter. She stared at them levelly. "He's asking me to transfer to his unit."

Kolfinna didn't know Herja that well, but she didn't think she would take that offer. She had friends here, after all. But heartbreak could do wild things to people. Maybe she didn't want to see Blár anymore and she would rather transfer than spend her days here, working with him.

Inkeri's face fell, as if she was thinking the same thing. "Are you ... going to do that?"

"No." Herja frowned. "I don't think so. I think I'd rather avoid him."

"Who, Blár?" Kolfinna asked. "Or this new guy?"

"Both, honestly." She rested her hands on her lap. "The more I think about it, the messier things are, you know?"

"It's not really messy, though, is it?" Kolfinna asked slowly. When both of them turned to her, she quickly explained, "I mean, Blár rejected you and that's a clean break, right? And this guy, it's not like you'll see him again anytime soon, so you can just cut off ties with him, tell him you don't want him to send you letters, and then you can start anew? So it's not really messy—"

"It is." Herja gave a sheepish grin. "Because, the guy I'm, uh, involved with is ... Haakon Lykke."

Inkeri inhaled sharply while Kolfinna looked between the two of them in confusion. Was she supposed to know who that was? Judging by Inkeri's shocked expression, she supposed she was.

"*Haakon Lykke*?" Inkeri opened her mouth to say something, closed it shut, and opened it again. "Herja, what were you *thinking*?"

Herja rubbed the nape of her neck. "Hey, hey, I was lonely and he was there, and so ..." She lifted her shoulders. "One thing led to another, and now I think he's obsessed with me."

"How long were you *involved* with him?" Inkeri shifted on her bed until she was facing them.

Kolfinna started to feel like an intruder or an eavesdropper the more the conversation continued. She racked her brain for information on Haakon Lykke but came up with nothing. She had never been extremely interested in important people in the military, the Royal Guards, or the nobility, so unless he was extremely famous—like Blár or Fenris or Hilda—she didn't know him.

Herja tapped her chin thoughtfully. "Uh, two months?"

"You were sleeping with that man for *two months*?" Inkeri's voice rose an octave.

"Who is Haakon Lykke?" Kolfinna looked between the two women.

"A soldier." Herja shrugged.

"A soldier who's *very* dangerous." Inkeri shot Herja a look of disbelief. "He's a lightning elemental. Very powerful. On the verge of becoming a black rank."

Herja didn't look pleased. "There are four people who are said to be close to a black rank, give or take a few years. Haakon Lykke, Ivar Heddle, Lova Voll, and me. Out of those four, Haakon is said to be the closest."

Kolfinna didn't know what to make of this new information. Ivar and Herja were close to becoming black ranks? They were powerful, no doubt, but she didn't realize they were *that* powerful. But then again, Kolfinna had only seen Fenris and Herja use blue flames, and she had never seen a water elemental use water so viciously like Ivar did. So there must have been truth in their ranks.

"And he's also the most dangerous," Inkeri repeated. "Herja, how can you involve yourself with him? He's *crazy* and *sadistic*."

Herja frowned. "I can handle myself fine. I'm also close to a black rank, remember?"

"Close, but not as close as him." Inkeri turned to Kolfinna. "I met Haakon when we were at the Southern border. He's vicious. Terrible guy overall. He's also said to do the military's dirty work from time to time."

"What makes him vicious?" Kolfinna asked. Blár Vilulf had a terrible reputation too, so this guy couldn't be *that* bad, right?

Herja gave another sheepish grin. "He likes to fight. A lot. I think he's killed a few people too ... Like assassination stuff. You know, that sorta thing."

Kolfinna blinked. "*Assassinations?*"

"I thought it was kind of attractive at the time." Herja laughed nervously while Kolfinna and Inkeri pinned her with an *are-you-serious* look. "But now ..."

"Are you still talking to him?" Inkeri asked.

"He sends me letters." Herja fiddled with her pillow and smoothed down the creases along the linen pillowcase. "But I haven't responded to any of them."

"What does he say in the letters?" Kolfinna asked, and she wasn't sure she wanted the answer.

Herja flashed her a mischievous look. "Oh, you know, some private stuff, but mostly he wants me. Obsessively. I've never responded, but ... maybe I should? I mean, isn't the best way to get over a broken heart to go on a new adventure of romance?"

"Absolutely not." Inkeri leaned forward. "You can't be involved with that freak just because you're heartbroken."

They were all silent for a while after that. Kolfinna crossed her legs on the bed and laced her fingers together on her lap. It had been a while since she had gossiped, laughed, and spoken like this. She and Katla used to whisper and giggle during the nights about everything that had transpired that day. She and Eyfura had done something similar during the West Border mission in their tents. She had thought she would never experience that again, but here she was.

Kolfinna cleared her throat and gave Herja what she hoped

was a friendly smile. "So ... What is, um, this Haakon person like? To *you*."

Herja opened her mouth then shut it. "It was complicated. I thought we were both just interested in the physical aspect of things, but ... the fact that he's still writing me letters all these months later tells me otherwise. And, of course, the content of those letters." Herja waved a hand. "Well, whatever. It doesn't matter too much because it's not like I'm going to see him anytime soon."

"You'll *eventually* have to face him." Inkeri gave her a look. "He's the most powerful lightning elemental in the country and you're the second most powerful fire elemental. You both are on the top level, power-wise, in the military, so you probably will have to work together again in the future."

"Yes, and that will be a problem for *future* Herja." She gave a lopsided smile and patted her chest. "This Herja will currently enjoy life and ignore all men." She gestured to Kolfinna. "Enough about me. What's the status of your love life?"

Kolfinna couldn't stop the blush from spreading across her face. "Contrary to what you think, my love life isn't kicking off or anything."

"Really?" She raised an eyebrow.

"Yes, really." Kolfinna felt uncomfortable to be under the limelight, so she motioned to Inkeri. "I was there when you were injured, and Ivar absolutely lost it when you were hurt. If you want my two cents, I think he's interested in you and I think you should pursue it."

Inkeri ran a hand over her face. "Then why won't he *tell* me? Why won't he propose? Or confess his feelings? Or do *something*, other than being an asshole to me all the time."

"Why don't you tell him instead?" Kolfinna said. "Since he seems to be lacking confidence."

Inkeri made a noise of displeasure in the back of her throat. "Me? Tell him? Tell him, what, Kolfinna? No way. Besides, I'd rather my man take the lead."

"I'd rather take the lead," Herja said with a chuckle. "Makes it easier to get what you want. Instead of"—she gestured to Inkeri—"moaning and groaning about how things aren't working out."

Inkeri flicked her wrist in Herja's direction and a gust of air blew her wild curls off her face. Herja chucked her pillow in retaliation, but Inkeri shoved more wind at her, sending the pillow flying straight to her face.

Kolfinna and Inkeri burst into laughter.

"You bitches." Herja grabbed her pillow and chucked it at Kolfinna.

It missed, by a hair's breadth.

"Hey!" Kolfinna sat up indignantly. "I didn't do anything!"

"You laughed. That's a punishable offense."

The rest of the night continued in a similar fashion. With Herja and Inkeri and Kolfinna talking to each other, laughing, and acting like friends. Something Kolfinna hadn't even realized she had missed. It wasn't until they all started drifting off to sleep that Kolfinna's thoughts could travel to Rakel and the haunting words she had told her. But even as those words infiltrated her mind, she was too exhausted to think further about it.

18

KOLFINNA RECEIVED A PACKAGE FROM FENRIS THE fourth night after she met Rakel. It was a thin book with a single note attached to it.

I HOPE THIS IS USEFUL TO YOU. IT WAS THE ONLY ONE I could take. Since I cannot read runes, I tried to find one with a title similar to the runes you wrote out for me. I think this is one of them.
Take care,
Fenris Asulf

SHE HAD ASKED HIM FOR A BOOK OF RUNES AND HAD even written out a few keywords in rune writing that could be useful to her, such as 'rune magic,' 'beginner,' 'rune bonds,' and any other phrases that might help her escape.

Excitement had bubbled in the pit of her stomach when she saw the package, the note, and the embossed title that read *Beginner's Guide to Rune Magic*. But her excitement was short-lived when she spent the whole night reading it, and there was nothing useful. Everything written in it were either things Revna had already taught her or things Kolfinna had picked up on her own.

Kolfinna wanted to bang her head on the floor.

If she didn't find out how to rid herself of the runes—

She didn't want to think about it.

The early morning light filtered through the window atop her bed and she rubbed her grainy, sleep-fatigued eyes. She flipped through the pages one last time, her heart sinking. She already had a plan in mind to get out of here, but it all hinged on *if* she could break the rune. The matter of what to do after that was still unclear: run away as far as she could, or transfer to another unit like Blár suggested? She wasn't sure if going with him was a good choice, since the military would most definitely kill her if they found out how important she was to Ragnarök.

Her eyes skimmed over one of the random pages.

Runes can be broken in two simple ways—

Kolfinna sighed. She had been so excited when she got to this chapter, but it was something Revna had taught her in the Eventyrslot ruins. A very fundamental basics of rune magic.

One, overwriting a rune with another rune to counteract or neutralize the rune. Two, by overpowering the rune with your mana.

It was such a simple concept. Kolfinna had used the latter to break the runes that had kept Revna stuck in the house in the desert dimension in the Eventyrslot ruins. She could still remember how hot it had been that day, with those two suns blazing down her back, and how she had painstakingly broken each rune one by one.

It was one of the basics. She had skimmed past it before, but now she stared at it harder. A thought formed in the back of her mind. What if ...

She tried to calm her breathing as she placed a trembling hand on her wrist atop the golden rune. What could she even use to neutralize the rune? If memory served her right, this rune represented that she would always follow Sijur's will and never disobey him. What could she put to neutralize that?

I will disobey Sijur.

She poured her mana into those runes, but just as the mana touched the rune, she let out a hiss of pain. A white-hot burning sensation tingled her wrist and she squeezed her eyes shut until the pain slowly ebbed away.

Okay, that didn't seem to work.

Maybe it was too close to disobeying him? Was simply making the neutralizing runes going against his will, therefore making it impossible for her to neutralize them?

A headache began throbbing in the back of her eyes.

Maybe it was better to overpower the runes? But that too was going against his will, wasn't it?

Kolfinna tightened her grip on her wrist and poured even more mana into the rune. This time, she focused on breaking it. She imagined a chain of magic wrapping around the rune, squeezing it tightly, and shattering it into pieces. She braced herself for the hot pain that would follow after, but nothing happened.

She kept at it, draining her mana and slamming it into the single, crescent-shaped rune. Sweat formed between her brows, between her shoulder blades and down her itchy spine.

But nothing happened.

She exhaled loudly.

This could take a while.

Kolfinna was so focused on her wrist that it wasn't until a pillow smacked straight into her face that she realized Herja was awake. The pillow plopped down on her lap and Herja laughed, granting her a glare from Kolfinna.

"What the heck," Kolfinna said, snatching the pillow and tossing it back at her.

She caught it with one hand, grinning widely. "Rise and shine, fairy girl."

"What was that for?"

"No reason. Just felt like it." She stretched out her arms and yawned.

Another strange development was that after the night when Kolfinna, Inkeri, and Herja had talked about their relationships and men in general, Herja started treating her more like a friend. It was a jarring turn of events, especially since Herja should've hated Kolfinna more than before. Inkeri had told her that Herja disliked her because she didn't like that Kolfinna meant something to Blár, so it was even more strange that Herja was now acting ...nice?

Maybe after her rejection, she already moved on? Kolfinna couldn't be sure and it wasn't like she could ask her.

Herja plucked a comb that was already fully tangled with her red hair between the wide teeth, and began brushing her hair with it. "Why were your eyes glowing like that? Are you using magic?"

"Something like that." Kolfinna gently closed the book she had been reading and placed it beneath her pillow. The candle she had used to read through the night was almost melted to a stump. She blew out the flickering flame. "When are we going to go on another mission?"

"Not sure." Herja frowned and lowered her comb. "I wonder if the reason we haven't done anything is because of what Blár said the other day. You know, about the weird armies attacking the southern border."

Kolfinna's mouth flattened to a grim line. She turned away so Herja wouldn't notice. "Yeah, I wonder."

"They can't lose." A sudden vulnerable expression passed over Herja's face, quickly replaced by a nonchalant one. But even as she tried to mask her worry, Kolfinna could hear the inflection in her tone. "They have Hilda Helgadottir."

"And Haakon Lykke," Inkeri chimed in from the other side of the room. She pushed the blanket off her body and grinned over at them both. "Don't tell me you're worried, Herja?"

"Of course not." Herja rolled her eyes.

Kolfinna *was* worried.

Because no one, other than Blár, had faced an elf before, and he had a hard time with Rakel. She could only imagine what the other three generals, beside the half-elf commander, were capable of. The mere thought of it sent a wave of nausea to tumble through her body.

Speaking of Blár—

His mana was immense. Couldn't she use his mana to try to break the binding rune?

"Kolfinna, you and Blár mentioned that the woman we faced —that woman with the white hair—was an elf. What does that mean?" Inkeri walked over to the water basin and splashed her face with cold water. She stared at Kolfinna through the mirror's reflection as she patted her face with the water. "I've never heard of an elf before."

Herja continued to brush out her untamable curly hair. "I've heard of them before. In my village where I grew up, we were told stories of elves. They creep up into your homes and eat babies and children." She suddenly frowned, not looking so sure. "Huh, or maybe those stories were talking about fae? I'm not sure."

"Elves are similar to the fae," Kolfinna found herself saying. "They're a race of people like the fae and the humans. They have their own attributes and magical powers. They also can procreate with humans and fae."

"I figured as much." Herja began dressing herself quickly. "I mean, did you see that woman? She looked humanoid. Minus the hair and the eyes, I would've thought she was human."

"Don't forget the ears," Inkeri added.

"Apparently, the fae also had pointed ears," Kolfinna said. Revna had pointed ears as well and had seemed surprised when Kolfinna's weren't pointed.

"I wonder what happened to make them not pointed?" Inkeri said. "Because the fae nowadays don't have them, right?"

"Mixing with humans is probably what changed." Kolfinna shrugged and subconsciously touched her own rounded ears. "After the Last Purge, it's not like the fae had many options with who to have children with."

Shouldn't Kolfinna's ears have also been pointed, since she wasn't "diluted" with human blood?

She didn't know anything anymore, so she shoved that thought aside.

KOLFINNA'S SWORD CLANGED AGAINST ELUF'S BLADE. She circled around the older soldier, her eyes narrowed in concentration to see what he would do next. Inkeri hadn't been able to train with her today, so Eluf took her place instead. Kolfinna appreciated his teaching methods; he would show her where she went wrong and what she could do better after each session, and they would repeat the cycle for another session. It was similar to how Inkeri taught.

Eluf's sword hit hers and the force sent a reverberation up her wrist and rattled her elbow. She gritted her teeth together and parried.

How pathetic, little fairy.

They exchanged blows. Their training swords cracked against each other. Kolfinna stepped back and kept up with her footwork while Eluf pressed forward. Sweat dribbled down the sides of her face.

Is this too difficult for you?

Farthin, Gisela, Edwin, and a multitude of Royal Guards sniggered at her as she darted away from Eluf's wooden blade. Even as she tried to banish their voices, they remained with her, haunting her every step. Her every failure.

She raised her sword higher than her quivering biceps could

handle, and in that split second, Eluf charged her. His training sword sliced down the blade of hers and the tip of his blade caught her wrist. She hissed in pain and automatically dropped her sword. Eluf pointed his sword to her neck.

She bit down a curse, her wrist throbbing painfully.

It will pass, she told herself. But the bitterness of defeat was almost too strong to ignore.

She shook her wrist to ease the pain. "You're fast."

"And you're distracted." Eluf removed the wooden blade from her and stuck it into the sandy ground. "You're also tired. Your movements are becoming sluggish."

She knew that, but she cursed anyway. "I can do better—"

"You can." He nodded, and Kolfinna remembered Blár's words about his wife and baby. "But we should take a break."

"I can still fight."

"I'm sure you can." He stretched out his arms. "But I'm tired, so *I* need a break."

Kolfinna tentatively struck her sword beside his and followed him to the wooden bench at the end of the ring. He sat on one end while she took the other. For a moment, they didn't say anything. She peered up at the afternoon sky; it was grayer than usual, with thick, gloomy clouds filling it. A subtle breeze brushed over her shoulders.

Eluf stared at the soldiers farther down the courtyard sparring with each other. They were white and gray ranked, so they only fought with their swords since they lacked magic.

"Blár seems fond of you," he said.

She blinked back. "Oh?"

"I've known him since he was a child." He glanced over at her, and the dark circles under his eyes seemed darker than usual. More purple. Bruised. "I'm not sure if he's told you, but I was married to his sister."

Kolfinna licked her lips. "Yes. I'm ... so sorry to hear about what happened."

"Thank you." A flash of pain crossed his face and he turned

away. "It consumes me every day that I couldn't protect her or any of Blár's family."

Kolfinna's fingers curved over the edge of the bench, pressing against the wood fibers and the cracks along it. She was terrible at these sorts of things. Talking about tragedies. "I'm sorry."

"It happened seven years ago, but I still remember it like yesterday." Eluf wore a sad, longing expression as he stared off in the distance. "Blár, Gunnar, and I went hunting that day. I wanted to teach them both a few skills. It was stupid of me to even try it, to be honest, because Blár was already so powerful with his magic and he didn't need to learn any of the inconsequential skills I had at catching fish or hunting jackrabbits. I ... wish I hadn't asked him to come. If he had stayed in his home that day, maybe he could've done something. Protected his family. Or maybe ..." He swallowed hard. "I don't know. There are dozens of variations of things I could've done that day, but I'll never know what the right answer is."

Kolfinna's throat constricted and she fought back the rush of memories of Katla's death. How she had imagined different things she could've done to prevent it from happening. How Kolfinna should've been able to control her magic. How she failed to protect her sister.

"Dwelling on the past and what you could've done differently"—she choked the words out through a whisper—"will only haunt you. She wouldn't want this."

"Perhaps, but I can't move on." Eluf's eyes darkened and he grasped the armrest of the bench so tightly that his knuckles turned white. "Not while her murderers are likely still out there."

If Kolfinna hadn't killed Lord Estur, Katla's murderer, would she be plagued with thoughts of vengeance like Eluf was?

"It was the worst day of my life. Returning to that home. I had expected to find Sylvi there with her other siblings. But when we returned, it was ... a scene out of a nightmare." His words were barely a whisper, almost lost in the wind. He grimaced, as if remembering that moment. "Everyone was dead. The entire house reeked of blood. It was splattered over the floors, the windows, and all over the furniture. I found Sylvi—"

Kolfinna hadn't realized she was gripping the bench so tightly until her fingers started to feel numb. She eased her vise-like grasp. "You don't have to tell me all of this."

In fact, they weren't close enough for her to be privy to these memories.

"I need to because you might be able to help." Eluf turned to her, as if he had read her thoughts, and she couldn't look away from the despair, guilt, and anger brewing in the dark depths of his eyes. "Sylvi was already dead when we got there. Blár's mother was missing, and the only one who was alive was Raynee, Blár's youngest sister. She was close to death and it was too late for us to save her. She was only five. Blár held her in his arms and sang her favorite lullaby as she died."

Kolfinna went still. She could imagine it so well in her mind that her eyes stung.

She didn't want to hear any more.

Her stomach turned, but she tried to hold herself together.

"We then tried to cut the baby out of Sylvi's belly." He was whispering now, his words coming out slowly, like he was reliving the moment. "I thought maybe the baby was still alive inside her. But it was too early, so when we did manage to cut him out ... He couldn't—" Tears shone in his eyes and his voice cracked. "He couldn't breathe. I couldn't do anything to save him either."

"I'm so sorry." She couldn't keep the horror out of her voice at the image he was painting. Her throat closed up. This was Blár's family he was talking about. And there were no words she could say that could comfort him, that could make the horrible moment go away.

He placed a hand over his eyes and breathed out shakily. For a few minutes, he remained like that. Kolfinna swallowed down the thickness crawling up her throat. She didn't want to imagine the brutal scene; it reminded her too much of when Katla had been killed. She couldn't stop thinking about Lord Estur holding

Katla's severed head in his hand, about the blood that stained his whole body up to his elbows and against the floors Kolfinna had scrubbed so many times before. And how it smelled—

She squeezed her eyes together. "I'm so sorry you had to go through that."

"The military says it was Ragnarök." Eluf lifted his head. There was a hard set to his mouth as he turned to her slowly. The wind picked up and blew against them gently. "I don't buy it. Neither does Gunnar or Blár. Why would Ragnarök target the Vilulf family? It really doesn't make sense. All three of us have been searching for answers and we haven't found anything substantial."

"And you think I can help you?" Kolfinna asked.

"I think Lieutenant Bernsten knows more than he lets on. The only reason I joined the military under him is because he promised to help me get to the bottom of this mystery, but I think he's just stringing me along. Because, let's say Ragnarok did do it, then I need to know *why*. And if Ragnarök didn't do it, I need to know who did and why the military isn't looking for them."

Kolfinna licked her lips. "Do you think the military is involved?"

"I don't know."

Her mind traveled to the office she had snuck into when she was looking for the elf woman. Was that Sijur's private office? If she were him, she'd hide anything valuable, anything secretive, in that office to keep prying eyes away. If he was hiding something, it had to be there.

"All I'm saying is that if you ever find anything related to the incident, I would appreciate knowing about it." He gave her a weak smile. "Please."

Kolfinna nodded. "Of course, but ... I'm not privy to these sorts of things."

"I see that you go off with Lieutenant General Bernsten rather frequently."

No, she went with *Joran* frequently, but maybe he thought

that when she went to their underground training session, she was going with Sijur? It made sense since nobody knew she trained with Joran, since he didn't want anyone to know he was fae.

Kolfinna found herself bobbing her head. "I'll let you know if I find anything."

19

Kolfinna kept thinking about what Eluf had said. About his wife, about Blár's family. Her heart squeezed painfully as she imagined Blár holding his little sister as she took her dying, last breath. Or Eluf desperately trying to save his child.

She hadn't realized she was staring intently at her roasted potatoes until Inkeri tapped her shoulder lightly.

"Something wrong with the potatoes?" Inkeri asked lightly.

"Ah, no." A blush of embarrassment spread up her neck and to her face. They were both in the cafeteria having lunch. "Sorry, I was lost in thought. You were saying?"

Inkeri poked at her fried fish with her fork. "I was just talking about how strange it is that we haven't gone on any mission since we fought that elf woman."

Herja had previously mentioned that it might have had something to do with the fae and elven armies attacking the south, and Kolfinna was starting to believe that might be the case.

"Maybe we're waiting for … something." Kolfinna sighed and speared a buttery potato with her fork. "I really hope we can start working again."

Inkeri grinned. "Huh, working again? You make it sound like you've been working here for a while."

"I like it better than the Royal Guards," Kolfinna answered truthfully. Minus the stress that came with Sijur, she did enjoy the work here in the military rather than with the Royal Guards. Back in the capital, all she seemed to do was patrol the streets and get verbally badgered by citizens and guards alike.

Inkeri took a bite of her fish and chewed. "I hope we can go on another mission soon. Don't get me wrong, I do enjoy the break between missions, but this is taking a bit too long in my opinion."

Kolfinna's attention drew to a hulking figure in the distance and her nose crinkled as she recognized Bjarni, the tall man she had faced when she had first gotten to the fort. Inkeri followed her gaze and stiffened at the sight of him. He was sitting at a table with a group of other soldiers, eating and laughing casually. She noticed that he was far away from them, and she secretly hoped it was because of their previous fight that he was keeping his distance.

"I haven't seen him around in a while," Inkeri said with a frown.

"Yeah ..." Kolfinna glanced at the other woman. With everything else occupying her mind, she had almost forgotten about the boorish man. "I've always been curious, but ... Why did you let him do that to you?"

Inkeri stared at her plate silently for a few moments.

"Is he threatening you?"

"A little." She sighed and ran a hand over her face. "He asked me out for a date a few months ago and I refused, and he's been bothering me ever since. He's stronger than me, so when I refused him last time ..." She clamped her mouth shut and clenched her fists together. "He hurt me."

Kolfinna wanted to go up to him and beat him again, but she instead placed a hand over Inkeri's. "I'm sorry."

"He just beat me really bad during a spar." She cringed, and Kolfinna felt her hand contract. "I was scared. And then you ... fought him. I never properly thanked you."

"You don't need to thank me." Kolfinna patted her hand. "Just say the word and I'll fight him again."

She chuckled. "Thank you."

It was strange having this comradery in the military; she hadn't expected to find any semblance of it here, when she could barely find it in the Royal Guards.

Inkeri's laughter faded, as did her smile. "It's honestly very frustrating, always being the 'damsel in distress.'"

Kolfinna could tell Inkeri was holding herself back. Like she wanted to spill out as many words as possible but couldn't. "Do you want to talk about it?" she asked quietly.

Inkeri inclined her head slightly, and her eyes shone with unshed tears. "I'm the weakest in the party. The only yellow rank, and I sometimes feel like I'm less than everyone else in our group because my ranking is lower than theirs, and I think they all subconsciously think it too because they're always saving me. Or maybe that's just my incompetence speaking. I was the only one during the mission with that elf who got incapacitated, and both you and Ivar had to rescue me. It's the same every time we go on a mission—I always need to be *saved*. And I even get picked on by other soldiers, like ..." She nodded in Bjarni's direction and then swiped at the tears threatening to spill. "I'm a soldier, a warrior, or at least that's what I'm supposed to be, but I never feel like that. I just feel so ... *useless*."

Kolfinna was terrible at making someone feel better; she was always so incredibly awkward when it came to situations like this. But she did what she would've if Katla was crying; she placed her hand over Inkeri's and gave it a squeeze. "I'm so sorry you feel that way. Being a yellow rank doesn't mean you're weak or useless. To me, you're a powerful warrior. You've taught me so much about being a swordsman and I think you're amazing at what you do."

"I don't know." She sniffled and rubbed her eye. "It's just hard sometimes."

"I get like that too." Kolfinna stared at the table, her mind traveling to the Royal Guards. To the feeling of helplessness. "But you have to stay strong and keep fighting."

Inkeri sighed and blinked away her tears. "I think it's harder when you're paired with people who are freakishly strong. Like Ivar and Herja are close to a black rank, and then Eluf and Gunnar are really strong too, and then you add Blár to the mix—and when you're the weakest? It just crushes you. I know I'm definitely not the weakest in the whole fort and I should be grateful—hell, there are *white* ranks here, so I should be happy that I'm blessed as an Elemental—but ... but ..." She breathed out shakily. "It's just so hard not feeling like a failure when you're with people who are just *extraordinary*."

"You're extraordinary too—"

"I'm not so sure about that."

Kolfinna frowned. "You are. You're a great swordsman, you're great at air magic, and you're an amazing person. You might not be at Ivar's, or Herja's, or Blár's level, but you'll get there eventually."

Kolfinna took a breath to continue—to tell her that she was grateful to have Inkeri around when she felt like she had no one in this fort—but Ivar plopped down on the seat beside Inkeri in that exact moment. His chestnut hair was tousled and slightly damp like he had just bathed; the ends of it curled against the collar of his uniform. And his heterochromatic eyes were set on Inkeri. Kolfinna couldn't read what he was thinking.

Ivar reached over and picked up Inkeri's fork. He then stabbed a potato, ate it, and then went after a piece of her fish. Inkeri swatted his hand and he almost dropped the fork on her plate.

"What are you doing?" she started, rubbing the remaining remnants of tears out of her eyes.

"I came to see what was making you cry." He poked at the fish again with the fork.

Inkeri huffed. "Nothing."

"Nothing?" He gestured to her face with the fork. "Your eyes are red and puffy. Are you telling me that happened from *nothing?*"

"Don't wave a fork at my face." Inkeri reached over for a linen handkerchief and wiped her eyes with it quickly. Her cheeks and nose were red from crying, and her eyes were slightly puffy even though she hadn't shed many tears.

Ivar studied her, and for just a moment, concern washed over his face. Kolfinna looked between the two of them and suddenly felt like she was invading a private moment. Maybe she should leave them two to talk things out? Maybe Ivar could console Inkeri and they could talk about their feelings?

"You look like a stray cat," Ivar said, prodding at the fried fish once more.

Inkeri's eyes narrowed. "What?"

Kolfinna closed her eyes. *This man ...*

"Do you *always* ruin perfectly good opportunities, or just when it involves your love life?" Kolfinna said with an eye roll.

Ivar arched a dark eyebrow. "My love life? I hardly see how—"

"Uh-huh, I'm sure you don't see what I'm talking about." Kolfinna shook her head and noticed the blush spreading over Inkeri's face. Maybe it wasn't Kolfinna's place to say anything, but if she didn't give them both a little nudge, she doubted there would be any progress. "Look, both of you need to talk."

"*Kolfinna.*" Inkeri shot her a mortified look.

"I know, I know, I'm overstepping." She sighed. "But I want to help."

"Help?" Ivar looked confused.

"Ivar, get some confidence and gain some initiative, all right? And, Inkeri? Lighten up sometimes." Kolfinna rose from her seat and picked up her half-eaten plate of food. "I'm not the best person to talk to about romance, but I think you both need to figure out your feelings."

"What are you talking about?" Ivar was still trying to look incredulous, but she could see the redness tingeing his ears, like he had been caught doing something.

"That's for you to figure out." Kolfinna stepped out from the bench and gave them both a hard look. "Good luck."

She really did hope they sorted out their messy feelings for each other.

KOLFINNA FOUND BLÁR IN ONE OF THE INDOOR training rooms. Similar to the underground one she frequented with Joran, it was a large room with tall ceilings and barren walls. The entire room was empty, save for the ice stalactites on the ceilings, the sheets of bluish white that thickened the walls, and the crackle of shiny ice across the floors. Kolfinna almost slipped when she first stepped in. Her breath puffed out in white clouds and she truly felt that winter had nothing on Blár's ice.

Blár stood in the center of the room, surrounded by twenty humanoid ice sculptures. He raised a hand and hundreds of ice needles formed in the air, all of them pointed to the sculptures. He lowered his hand and all the needles shot forward. The sound of ice cracking against ice filled the room and a gust of glittery dust fell in waves around the sculptures.

Kolfinna clapped her hands. "Impressive."

Blár looked over his shoulder at her, his expression unreadable. "It's not impressive. I'm just practicing my mana control. I think I'm getting rusty."

"It's impressive." She smiled at the broken pieces of ice littering the floor. "I can't do that with my stone magic."

And she had been trying too. With Joran. In actually a very similar way to this, but with stones rather than ice. She thought bitterly of her last practice session, and the way her stones hadn't hit the targets.

"You'll get there." Blár lifted a finger and his ice sculptures cracked and crumbled, turning to ice crystals immediately.

Kolfinna watched the destruction. The air was thick with cold and glittering ice fibers. "Are you busy?"

"For you?" Blár flashed a grin. "Yes."

She rolled her eyes. "Too busy for me, huh?"

"Unfortunately so." His tone was light and joking. He crossed the room to where she stood by the open door and picked up a cannister of water off the metal bench against the wall. "Why?"

"Nothing. I was just going to ask for a favor, but since you're busy ..." She shrugged and jammed her thumbs in her pockets. "I guess I'll ask someone else—"

"Come on, I'm just messing with you." Blár took a swig from the cannister. "So what is it?"

Kolfinna closed the door to the training room to keep anyone from hearing and spun around to face him. A shiver ran down her spine from the cold and when she spoke next, streams of white puffed out of her mouth. "Now, let's get to business."

Blár watched with raised brows and nodded his chin toward the now-closed door. "That's rather scandalous."

Kolfinna rolled her eyes again and made her way to the bench, but she couldn't stop the blush from spreading up to her face. "I didn't realize you were a jokester." She eased down onto it but then sprang right up when the cold nearly froze her. "What the—"

He laughed while she patted down her bottom with a hiss. "Careful, this whole place is rather winter-infested."

"Thanks for the heads-up." Kolfinna crossed her arms over her chest and glanced around the chilly room. Ice was everywhere, to the point that she could barely tell that beneath the layers of ice, the walls and floors were gray.

Blár chuckled, and his blue eyes twinkled in a way that made her heart nearly stop.

She tried to smile along, but the twinkle in his eyes made her wonder what he was like as a boy, and then she was bombarded with images of a young Blár holding his dying younger sister in his arms. Crying, with slippery blood running between his fingers, with her tiny little body nestled against him. All at once, her mood dampened and she had to keep herself from flooding with emotions; it wasn't just empathy she felt, but something more. It prodded at her own traumas; she could just as easily imagine herself in that position. Except it was Katla in her arms.

Kolfinna banished those nightmarish memories from her mind. She had a task to focus on. "I'm thinking"—she cleared her throat—"of sneaking into Sijur's office. I'm wondering if you can help me." At his stunned expression, she continued quickly, "Yes, yes, I'm aware it's a bit of a treasonous thing to do, but it's important and you'll have to trust me. Because believe me when I say that Sijur isn't as good of a guy as you think he is—or wait, you probably don't like him at all, right? But anyway—"

"Slow down, slow down." He raised a hand to keep her from blabbering any further and she clamped her mouth shut. "You want to sneak into his office?"

Her voice dropped to a whisper in case anyone was eavesdropping beyond the closed door. "Yes. And I need your help."

"Is this related to *that*?" He pointed to her wrist and she inadvertently brushed a hand over it.

"Yes. He potentially has books that I need." Kolfinna tapped her foot against the thick ice on the floor to keep her nerves in check. She had snuck around the fort before when she was searching for the elf woman, but the prospect of pilfering through Sijur's office and all his important documents made her stomach clench together. "And he might have information about ... you know, what happened to your family seven years ago."

Blár went still, blue eyes widening a fraction of an inch. "Why do you think that?"

"I don't." She paced the slippery floor and thought about Eluf and then all the times Sijur proved to her that he couldn't be trusted. She had no doubt in her mind that Sijur would use any method to string Eluf along into working for him. "He's keeping secrets. I just know it. Call it a hunch, if you will."

She couldn't tell what Blár was thinking because his expression became shuttered. "And what do you need from me?"

"I need you to make sure he's occupied while I go to his office."

"You're planning on going alone?"

"Yes."

"*Alone?*"

Kolfinna's eyebrows pulled together and she stopped her pacing. "*Yes.*"

"Um, no. I'm coming with you." Blár dropped the water cannister on the bench and a loud *clank* sounded throughout the room.

"Why?"

"Because if Sijur is withholding information from me about *my* family, I need to see if for myself. Besides, I know what I'm looking for. It'll also be faster with two people." His mouth curled into a frown. "Not to mention that if you get caught, it'll be easier to make up an excuse with me around."

"If we're caught, Sijur will know we've been snooping around. No excuse will save us." Kolfinna began walking again to ease her jittering nerves. If they were caught, Sijur would likely imprison her. Or who knows what else he would do? Put more runes on her that would make her more bound to his will? "I'm going to his underground office."

Blár's eyebrows arched. "So he does have an underground office?"

"You're the one who told me about it." She gave him a hard look. "Don't act confused now."

"Well, yes, I did say that, but I was only hypothesizing." His frown deepened and he narrowed his eyes. "Wait—how do you know he has an underground office? Did you see it?"

"I may have sleuthed around." She lifted her shoulders like it wasn't a big deal.

"I thought you wanted my help in sneaking around last time?"

"It was sort of spontaneous," she said quickly.

He didn't seem satisfied with that, but he waved a hand. "So when will you sneak in?"

"Tonight."

He rubbed his chin. "Tonight?"

"Blár, are you a freakin' parrot? You keep repeating your words." She fought the urge to roll her eyes again. "Look, I need you to keep Sijur occupied while I go—"

"Hey now, why are you so pissy today?"

"*P-Pissy?*"

"Yes, pissy." Blár plopped down on the metal bench and wiped the sweat from his forehead with his sleeve. "Stop arguing so much and just *calm down.*"

"I can't calm—"

"Yes, you can." He stretched out his arms against the metal backrest. "I'm coming with you, by the way. There's no way I'm letting you do that alone. But I do have a question—why does someone need to keep that asshole occupied? If we go in the middle of the night—"

Kolfinna shook her head. "I think it'll be safer to do it during dinner."

She had planned to do it at night, until Joran had asked her to train with him late at night, since it "fit" into his schedule better. She had declined, of course, but it only made her more wary around him. If he was training by himself in the middle of the night, she might get caught too. And those sounds she had heard when she had first snuck down to see the elf woman, what if those had been from Joran?

"Why?"

"Sijur will be occupied. Also ..." Joran would be occupied for sure. "I think it would be easier that way."

Besides, if she was caught in the hallway in the middle of the night, it was far more suspicious rather than in the daytime, where nobody would think twice.

"All right, I'll be ready."

"Blár—"

"Come on, you didn't come all this way here to ask me to distract Sijur." He gave her a hard look. "You could've asked anyone to do that. Inkeri. Herja. Eluf. Gunnar. Hell, even Ivar."

She screwed her mouth shut. That was partially true; there was a part of her that wanted Blár to come with her, but there was another reason she was here. "Actually, I need something else from you."

"What?"

"Can I borrow your mana? Like last time?" She held up her wrist hesitantly. "I want to try to break this rune, but I don't have enough mana."

"I'm a bit on the low side when it comes to my mana." Blár gestured to the ice surrounding them in the room. "But I probably have enough for your needs."

He held his hand out to her and she took it gratefully. If he noticed that the wounds on her palms had healed, he didn't show it. He stared ahead at the icy walls, and she wondered if he was thinking of his family. Kolfinna squeezed his hand and reached into his mana, trying to be as quick as possible, before he noticed.

Dipping into his expansive mana came quicker to her than it had last time because this time she knew what she was doing. There was none of that tentative tug, like she wasn't sure of how much to take. She pulled at his mana and gathered it into her body, particularly into her hand. His cool mana felt like a breath of snow, of wintry ice, and cool early mornings. It budded on her fingertips, cooling her down to the bones of her fingers.

She placed her cold hand atop the rune on her wrist. She poured as much of their combined mana into it, willing it to crack and shatter like splintered ice.

Kolfinna must've been at it for five minutes before Blár touched her shoulder and broke her from her concentration.

"Hey now, you're going to drain me at this rate."

"Oh—" Mortification rushed over her and she released his hand. "I'm so sorry—"

"No, you're fine." Blár winced and ran a hand over his face. She had used too much of his mana and too quickly too, which probably made him want to drop on the floor and sleep.

Stupid.

To make matters worse, the rune on her wrist was still there, as vibrant as ever.

She cursed to herself and then rubbed his shoulder apologetically. "I'm really sorry about that. I didn't realize I took so much."

"It's not a big deal." He yawned and then stretched his legs out. "I think I'll go take a nap for an hour or two. That'll give us enough time until dinner, yes?"

"Yeah, probably."

"I'll ask Gunnar or Eluf to help me keep that slimy asshole occupied."

"Ew, gross. Those two words don't exactly go together well." Kolfinna laughed, but she really wanted to cry. The rune was on her wrist, golden as ever, and if Blár's mana wasn't enough to break it, she would have to find another way.

20

Kolfinna and Blár walked casually to the lower levels. The soldiers who passed them barely glanced at Kolfinna but gave nods of acknowledgment or greetings to Blár. She could see the awe on their faces when they were around him. It was strange for them to give more attention to the black rank rather than the fae on his side, since she clearly stood out more than he did. It was bizarre that her white hair and her pink eyes seemed to have somehow become normal around this base.

After the fifth soldier that greeted Blár, Kolfinna pulled at his elbow and whispered, "This is a mistake. Everyone will remember that you passed by here."

Blár raised an eyebrow and stared pointedly at her iron-like grip on the crook of his arm. "No one will assume anything. Why would they?"

"Sijur probably has these people keeping an eye out here. You and I stick out too much."

He frowned. There were still three more levels to go down before she would need to create an opening to go deeper under-ground to where the secret office was—an office Kolfinna assumed was Sijur's and held information he didn't want in his normal office. They didn't exactly have much time, either, since dinner wouldn't take more than half an hour at most.

"I don't think we stand out too much—" Blár started.

"We do. Everyone's greeting you." As if on cue, another soldier passed by and bobbed his head to Blár. She thrust a hand in the soldier's direction when he had already passed them. "See?"

Annoyance flitted across his face and he crossed his arms over his broad chest. "It's not my fault people know who I am."

"I'm not saying it's your fault. I'm just saying ..." Kolfinna sighed loudly, resisting the urge to rip a hand through her hair. "I don't know! Maybe this is a mistake."

"Why do you doubt yourself so much? You're always over-thinking." He scowled. "We'll be fine—"

"No, we won't." Her own irritation flared. *Of course* she was overthinking things. She needed to because the alternative was much worse. If she was caught, who knew what Sijur would do to her? She had seen what he was capable of, and she didn't want the same fate as Birgitta or Olia.

There were too many people passing by to go to the dining hall. Too many people who could spot them and later tell Sijur.

"What do you propose, then?" Blár leaned against the wall. "I thought we would sneak around once we got a little lower. Do you want to sneak around now?"

She nodded mutely.

He pushed himself off the wall. "You should've just said that from the start."

She tamped down her annoyance as they carefully peeked around the corner and began to stealthily go down the stairs and across the hallway. They made sure to keep themselves sparse when soldiers were walking by, choosing to go to a different hallway or sneak into a maintenance closet or two. When they finally reached the lowest level, they entered the same storage room Kolfinna had found the first time she had snuck in here.

"I can't see a thing." Blár spread his hands in front of himself and caught the edge of a wooden box stacked atop three similar-looking ones. He ran his hand over the edge of it and his brows drew together. "Is this a box?"

"It is."

"Can you see anything? Like with your fae eyes?"

Kolfinna looked from him to the shadows across the room, to the stacked boxes, rolled up carpets, and piles of uniforms atop wooden crates. The sliver of light beneath the door was enough for her to make out the basic outlines and details of the room. It became even clearer to her that this wasn't normal for "fae eyes," and that she wouldn't have been able to see this well a few months ago.

Elven blood.

The anxiety in her chest tightened.

"We're just going to go down—" Her voice caught in her throat and she quickly tilted her head to the side, to the noise that was approaching down the hall. Her entire body went still.

Click. Click. Click.

It took her a second to realize they were footsteps, and another second to realize that there were two of them—and they were approaching this door.

Kolfinna bolted into action. She snatched Blár's hand and led him to one of the wooden crates at the end of the room. He grunted in surprise, "What—"

"Shh!" Kolfinna yanked him down to the floor until they were hidden behind one of the wooden crates.

Five seconds passed. Blár was crouching uncomfortably beside her, his back pressed against the wall and his knees jammed against the crate. Kolfinna wasn't in a much better position, but at least she wasn't bent up like a pastry roll.

The footsteps grew louder and finally stopped at the door. A shadow warped along the room and the light dimmed. Blár went still beside her and she was sure she had stopped breathing.

The door creaked open and light pooled into the room.

"—don't think he's very interested at all," a feminine voice said with a long sigh. "You know what it's like with men."

"I'm married, so I'm not really sure." Another feminine voice. This one sounded a bit older.

"Oh, come on. There must've been a point that you—"

"Grab those uniforms quickly."

"Ugh."

The two women chatted while rummaging through the room. Blár and Kolfinna sat frozen on the floor. Kolfinna silently prayed they would leave quickly. If they ventured deeper into the room, they would see the two of them crouched down between the wall and a crate. Kolfinna tried to come up with a good excuse she could have ready, but she couldn't think of one.

"Did you get a chance to see that fae girl?"

Kolfinna shot Blár an alarmed look.

"The one who used to be a Royal Guard?"

"Yeah, her."

"What about her?"

"Isn't she ..."

Kolfinna mentally prepared herself for what they would say. A heartless fiend. A monstrosity. Something evil.

"Plainer than you thought? I thought the fae were supposed to be insanely beautiful."

"Huh, I heard that in the stories too. She does look a tad bit plain. Those eyes of hers are a bit creepy, don't you think?"

"I don't know, I think they're kind of pretty. But don't tell anyone that."

Kolfinna blinked in surprise as the women's voices became distant as they approached the door. Seeming to have taken what they needed, they slammed the door shut. Kolfinna could still hear their muffled conversation—now about soldiers who were annoying them—in the hallway.

She sat there for a moment longer, breathing in quietly with the feeling of ... relief? She hadn't expected them to say what they did. Sure, she didn't like the comment about her eyes being creepy, or that she was disappointingly plain, but that one human thought her eyes were pretty. That made something swell in her heart.

Blár was silent beside her for a minute or two after that. It was only then, after the adrenaline rush of running and hiding, that she realized just how close they were. That his thighs were pressing against the sides of her thighs, or that her shoulder was flush against his bicep, or that his every breath tickled the skin on her neck. She was thankful the shadows hid the heat creeping up her cheeks.

"That was close," Blár whispered into her ear. Another shiver ran down the nape of her neck. He was close—too close.

"Yeah ..." She gulped in air; she should get up and out of their hiding place, but her body refused to move. She liked the way he felt against her. She could so easily close her eyes and lean her head against his shoulder and forget about everything—

"So now what?" Blár asked.

Kolfinna crawled out of the hiding spot on her hands and knees. She didn't need to look in the mirror to know that her face was a patchwork of red, blushing skin. She cleared her throat "Right, uh, so now ... I make a hole in the floor."

She could hear Blár shuffle out from his spot behind her. He banged against something and cursed loudly. When she glanced over her shoulder, he was holding his hip and scowling. The corner of a box must've hit him pretty hard.

"You good?" she asked.

"Yeah. Where are you?" He slowly stretched his arms out. "Can you really see in here?"

"I can," she said. "Just stay still, okay? I'll lead you down the hole when I make it. Or better yet, maybe I'll shove you down when I do."

"Very funny."

Kolfinna chuckled to herself and set to work. Like last time, she placed her hands on the floor and began to manipulate the stones. It didn't take her long to create a hole and make a pile of stones beside it. This time, however, she made the hole wider to account for Blár's broad shoulders.

"It's done," she whispered.

"Is it?" He hadn't moved from his spot in the room and glanced over in her direction. "You really can see in here, can't you?"

"I told you—"

"Is that new?"

She hesitated. "Is what new?"

"I don't remember you being able to do that before." Blár searched the darkness for her and took a step closer in her direction, his movements slow. "It would've been helpful in the forest when we were traveling, or when we were fighting those draugrs in the Eventyrslot ruins. But you didn't have that acute of an ability before. So it's new, isn't it?"

He was a bit too sharp for her liking, and a part of her wanted to spill to him that she was actually part elf, and that she was somehow related to this whole mess. But another part of her— that fearful side that was used to hiding—wanted to keep it a secret. Just for a while longer. "Uh, no. And watch where you're going—you might fall—"

"I don't think you'll let me fall." Despite saying that, he stopped walking toward the direction of her voice. "By the way, you're a liar."

"That's not very nice," she muttered, hating the way he saw through her. "Anyway, I made the hole."

"So you're ignoring me now?"

"Blár, we can talk about it some other time—"

"We also haven't talked about your hair—"

"I will shove you down this hole if you don't want to come down with me." Kolfinna jumped to her feet, but he was already closing the distance between them hesitantly, going off her voice alone. "Another step and you're plummeting to your … well, a broken leg at least."

Blár stopped a foot away from the hole and kneeled down. He swept the floor with his hand and stilled when his fingers brushed against the smooth edges of the hole she had created. "See, I told you that you wouldn't have let me fall."

"You put a lot of faith in me—"

She couldn't even finish what she was saying before Blár dangled his legs down the hole and gripped the sides of it as if ready to plunge—and he sure did look ready.

"W-Wait—" Kolfinna placed a hand on his shoulder. She had looked into the hole below and hadn't seen any table they could fall on, or any other piece of furniture that might've hurt, but she still felt uneasy about the idea of him falling down and spraining an ankle since he couldn't see the depth of the plummet or his surroundings. "You'll fall."

"That's the point?"

She could make out the rise of his eyebrows.

Kolfinna bit back a sarcastic reply. "It'll be easier if I go first. I'll be able to see what's down there."

"And then what? You'll catch me when I come down?" He rolled his eyes, though she couldn't be *quite* sure because he had tilted his head down as if to see into the black pit below. "No, I'll go first. I would make an ice spear and gauge the distance, but we don't want to leave behind any hints, right?"

"Right."

"Okay, then—" He jumped without warning.

Kolfinna peered down the hole, her eyes adjusting to the deeper darkness in the office below, but Blár was steady on his feet. He looked around himself slowly, his hands jutting out in case he bumped into anything. Kolfinna released a relieved breath; she shouldn't have been worried about him. He was a black rank after all and had been on many missions—far more than she ever had—and likely knew more about stealth than she did.

Blár raised his head up to her. "You can come down now. It's safe."

By the slight inflection of his voice, the last part was said as a joke.

"Want me to catch you?" Another joke, but with a hint of seriousness.

Kolfinna licked her lips. It was tempting. "No, thanks, I'll just"—she sat on the edge of the hole until her legs were suspended in the air—"come down myself."

She jumped down without a second thought and landed lithely on her feet. Her muscles didn't scream and she didn't stumble, so she could only imagine it was all the training that was finally seeming to pay off.

"Is there a hearth around here? Or a candle?" Blár asked.

It took a few minutes of fumbling to find a stash of candles, a fire steel, and a piece of flint. Kolfinna lit two candles and handed Blár one of them. She spotted a hearth, but lighting that would have left traces of their visit. And considering how Joran was the only other person who could open up an entrance to this place, it would be clear that *she* had visited.

Holding up their flickering lights, they set to work scouring the office. Blár went straight to the desk and began opening drawers and sifting through papers, while Kolfinna rushed to the expanse of bookshelves lining the walls. Her gaze flitted over the worn spines of the books. Most were military histories, strategies, and history books. There was the occasional geography book, but nothing she was looking for. She pulled out books that had nothing written on the spines and flipped through their pages to search for any rune writing, and when she found none, shoved them back in place and repeated the process.

The minutes ticked by. The only noise between them was the rustling of paper.

Kolfinna pulled out a leather-bound book and flicked through it quickly. No runes—

A stray sheet fluttered out of the book and fell to the floor.

She crouched down to pick it up but paused mid-way down as a familiar name stood out on the paper.

Olia.

Kolfinna picked up the paper.

Olia, thief. Rune magic failed three times. On the fourth attempt, when threatened with her life, she said she would accept the runes, but seeing as how the runes didn't work when Joran applied them, I suspect she lied. It didn't work until the fifth time—when she truly decided to accept them. My hypothesis is that the target must be willing to accept the runes for them to work, as was seen in Olia's case.

I was able to test her to her breaking point. She was able to kill on command and even take her life on command. Experiment is deemed successful, despite the many times she refused. Will hope the next will be faster to accept commands.

KOLFINNA'S LEGS FELT WEAK AND AN ASHY TASTE coated her mouth. Her hands trembled as she opened the book once more. Dozens of names were written inside of it. All with a tiny summary of torture, and all of them women.

Thorin, prostitute.

Þórunn, beggar.
Unn, prostitute.
Margrethe, thief.
Astrid, orphan.

UNDERNEATH EACH NAME WAS A SHORT SUMMARY OF
how they eventually accepted the rune mark and what they had
been forced to do for Sijur. Some killed, others tortured themselves so Sijur could see how far the rune mark's influence went,
and others performed certain tasks—like dancing, standing still
for days, or starving themselves—for hours to see if the runes
went beyond the body's exhaustion level. All of them died, and all
were women who likely wouldn't be missed.

Kolfinna turned to the next pages and found even more
names. But the most horrifying section was toward the end, the
more recent entries.

Astra, beggar. Female, eight. Seems to be doing
well with the rune marks. Will keep asking for
simple tasks and see if she's able to do something
beyond her scope of understanding.

Noma, orphan. Female, nine. We gave her the
task of never speaking to anyone except for me. It
seems to be working well, but she spoke once to

*another child, and she felt the pain of the rune.
She didn't misspeak after that.*

*Olaf, orphan. Male, twelve. Understands his
tasks well. His personality is bubbly happy,
cheerful. We will test to see if the rune can alter
his personalities and characteristics. Thus far, there
have been no changes. Will update in a few months.*

SHE DIDN'T WANT TO READ ANY FURTHER, BUT SHE couldn't stop herself. There were three more names written down with their respective ages scrawled beside them. There was no indication that they were killed, but each other these children had a different task set by the runes.

Kolfinna fought the urge to vomit right then and there. He was experimenting on *children.*

And Joran was playing right into it.

She released a shuddering breath. This was so much worse than she had first thought. It wasn't just her life that was caught in this. Sijur would keep experimenting on other people and by the filled pages of this journal, he had already gone through dozens of experimentations. It would only continue, even if she left. So long as he had Joran, he would continue to abuse others. Even children.

But if these children were still alive, were they somewhere in this fort? She had already searched the rooms here when looking for the elf warrior and she hadn't found any, so was Sijur keeping them in a nearby village?

A movement from Blár caught her eye. "I think ... I found something." He held a slip of paper in his hand. His eyes were narrowed to slits and he was holding the paper so tightly that it was crinkled around his fingers.

"Is everything all right?" She shoved the journal back where she had found it and went over to Blár.

He was still staring at the paper. Now that she was up close, she could see that he was pale. "Three Royal Guards took a month-long leave of absence seven years ago. All three of them retired soon after."

"What does that have to do with anything?" she asked slowly, quietly.

"Seven years ago is when the attack happened." He stared at her with unseeing eyes. He was somewhere else, in a memory. "They all were on their leave the same time it happened. All three were from different units. Old men, who served for a long time. Loyal to the crown." He lowered the paper inside the open book he had been looking through. It looked like a record log, with hundreds of names scrawled inside of it, and with a few names circled.

Kolfinna watched him carefully. "Do you think ..."

She couldn't finish the sentence. Was it possible that the Royal Guards might've led an attack on Blár's family? But why would they do anything like that? Blár's family was normal; they hadn't been extremely powerful or well-known. They were simple villagers. Why would the king, or the Royal Guards, want them dead?

"What if this is just a ... coincidence?" Kolfinna asked.

"A coincidence? I don't think so." Blár flipped through the records with a look of disgust. "Sijur has been doing his research. I don't think he was planning on telling me or Eluf anything." He held the paper out to her. "Do you recognize any of these names?"

She scanned the paper and shook her head. "I'm sorry, I don't."

"They must still be alive somewhere. I'll have to ask them

myself." He slammed the records shut and raked a hand through his hair. "If the Royal Guards are involved ..." He cursed loudly. "I just don't understand why they would kill my whole family? Is it because they didn't want the military to take me?" He covered his face with a trembling hand—she wasn't sure if it was a sign of vulnerability or rage.

"Blár ..." Kolfinna hesitantly touched his shoulder.

He flinched at the contact but didn't pull away. His voice wavered when he spoke next. "Why would they kill my family?"

"We still don't know that," she whispered. "But we can find out. You have a lead now. I'll help you."

She didn't know why she said it; she had other things to worry about. Her own safety, escaping Sijur's clutches by breaking the rune mark, figuring out how to elude Ragnarök and this supposed half-elf commander. The old Kolfinna wouldn't have thought twice about leaving him to figure it out on his own. She would've felt bad for him, sure, but she would've left him to his own problems. But she couldn't do that to him. She had to find a way to help him.

Blár nodded and didn't meet her gaze. He unclenched and clenched his fists. The emotions flitting over his face varied from anger to sadness to confusion, and all the ranges that came with those emotions.

"Do you think ... Do you think my mother is still alive?" He barely whispered the words. "Why was she the only one taken away? Why didn't they kill her right then and there with everyone else?"

Kolfinna's heartstrings tugged at the desperation and vulnerability in his voice, on his face, and the slight tremors in his hands. "We can find out once we question them." She didn't want to bring his hopes up high. Truthfully, after all these years, it was likely she was already dead, but she didn't want to tell him that.

"Do you think Fenris knows anything?" Kolfinna asked.

He ran another hand over his face. "Maybe. He became the

captain of the Royal Guards six years ago, so this happened under the previous captain."

"Can we ask him? The previous captain, I mean."

He grimaced. "He died two years ago."

"But these three men ... they're probably still alive, right?"

"I hope so."

Kolfinna stared at the names on the paper. *Braggi Mikkelsen. Gorm Aaberg. Ulrik Helgason.*

She paused at the last one.

"Do you think Ulrik Helgason is related to Hilda Helgadottir?" She pointed at their last name. Ulrik's last name stated son of Helge, while Hilda's said daughter of Helge. It wasn't an uncommon name—Helge—but one thing Kolfinna had learned in the Royal Guards was that it was common for many related nobles to be in the guard together, since their family's influence was what got them there in the first place.

Blár's brows knitted together. "I'm not sure. I don't remember much about her family, but I think she had two brothers. Edwin's father's name is ... Karl, so it's not his father."

Before Kolfinna could brainstorm more, a noise in the upper level caught her attention. Her ears perked up and she canted her head in the direction of the noise—toward the ceiling. It was a banging noise. Not like the previous bang she had heard last time she was here. But more of a ... boom?

"Is something—" Blár started.

A vibration ran along the walls and the ceiling, followed by another distant bang.

Blár's expression morphed from surprise to grimness. He stuffed the paper in his pocket. "What was that?"

"I don't—" The walls shook again and dust fell from the ceiling.

There it was again—another distant booming. An attack, maybe? Or maybe Joran was practicing in the other room?

The walls trembled.

Kolfinna's panicked look met Blár's confused one.

They were in the basement level—nothing should've been able to shake the foundation of the entire fort. Unless ...

Kolfinna ran to the wall and placed a hand over it. She really hoped it wasn't what she thought it was. There was only one thing that could make the entire fort shake like a leaf.

When she pressed her mana into the wall, the presence of another person's mana flared against the workings of the stone, practically shoving her minute amount of mana out from the fibers of the stone. She wrenched her hand back, eyes wide.

There was another fae manipulating the stones. The mana had felt ... cold, so unlike Joran's warm mana, so it couldn't be him. So who?

"What's wrong?" Blár came to stand beside her.

"Someone's manipulating—" Her mind raced to Rakel. She was an elf, yes, but what if she was also part fae?

Kolfinna ran to the office door and pulled it open. She was met with the dark hallway. Blár followed behind her as she ran to the door at the end of the hall. Rakel was probably strong enough to shake the foundation of the fort, if she had been able to fight toe to toe against Blár. If she was trying to escape, then Kolfinna needed to stop her immediately. Rakel knew what Kolfinna was, and if she told the half-elf commander, the entire army would be here.

Kolfinna couldn't let that happen.

She jerked open the door to the room. It took her eyes a split second to adjust to the darkness; the only light was from the bobbing candle in Blár's hand.

It was empty.

The ring of runes on the floor were gone, and there was a single line etched into the dust on the floor written in rune writing.

We will reunite you with your father, Kolfinna Viðarsdóttir.

Viðarsdóttir—daughter of Vidar.

Kolfinna quickly stepped on the dust and disrupted it. Not that Blár could read it, but she didn't want that name staring up at her in that empty room. She spun to face Blár, hoping her expression wasn't as panicked as she felt.

"She's gone. The elf woman was being kept in here, but she's *gone.*"

The room shook again and from above, Kolfinna could make out distant cries and bangs. There must've been a fight going on, and if Rakel was up there ... Blár was *probably* the only one who stood a chance.

"We need to capture her," Kolfinna said, heading back to the office. "We need to stop her."

21

Kolfinna would probably never forget the sound of large, flapping wings—not the kind that belonged to monster birds. It was such a foreign sound—the whoosh of air splitting, the powerful gusts that followed. And she would probably never forget the sight of a pair of wings attached to a man.

That was the first sight Blár and Kolfinna were met with when they emerged from the stairwell and into the main level of the fort. A man with large, feathery wings attached to his back, was flying in the lobby, twin silver blades gleaming with fresh blood in his hands. A dozen soldiers were on the floor, moaning in pain or morbidly still.

Time seemed to stand still.

He was a fae *with wings*.

And he wasn't the only one. There was a gaping hole in one of the walls, leading to the courtyard. Blasts of fire and blue lightning lit up the purpling evening sky. Fae soldiers flew above the courtyard with feathery or gossamer wings. Black leathery armor covered their bodies, and they wore scaly black helmets. Stones crashed against soldiers, clashing against conglomerations of the elements whirring together in blurs of blue and white.

Kolfinna had never seen anything like it before. Yes, the fae

282

had wings, but every fae had their wings cut off at a young age to stave attention from the hunters or the humans. It was so unknown to people about the fae having wings. But Blár didn't let his confusion stop him from stepping forward into battle.

Ice splintered off the floors and rose in spears to jab into the closest flying fae. It dug through one of the wings of the feathery warrior and he went down quickly—but not quick enough. He raised his hand mid-fall, and dozens of stone spears shot out of the floor similar to Blár's, but they pierced through any soldier trying to get close to him.

A hunk of stone hurtled toward Blár and Kolfinna grabbed his shoulder and yanked him back. Blár glanced down at her sharply, blue eyes hardened with battle. He didn't need her help, she realized, and she would only slow him down or disrupt his flow.

"Sorry—" she started.

A wall of ice shot from the floor a foot away from her. She blinked. Three stone spears were frozen in place in the ice shield Blár had erected. The speed of Blár's reaction spurred her out of her sluggish thoughts; she couldn't be stuck on the fact that these warriors had wings. She had to push through. Focus.

"Stay with me—" Blár began, stepping in front of her.

"No, I have to find Rakel." Kolfinna glanced over at the gaping hole in the wall. She could see snakes slithering on the ground, similar to the ones she had seen during Blár's fight with the elf-woman.

"Kolfinna—"

Kolfinna was already pulling away from him. "I'll be fine!"

The flying warriors were jarring to look at, but the only thing fueling her forward was the fear that Rakel would escape—and inevitably draw the half-elf commander here.

Kolfinna ducked away from wayward blasts of fire, lightning, and stones. She leaped over the ridges of the hole until she was out in the courtyard. The ground was pulled and dented and slightly burnt in various areas. Soldiers fought against black-leather-clad warriors. Some had a shock of white hair and blood-red eyes, similar to Rakel, while others were clearly fae with their feathery wings and brightly colored eyes.

A winged warrior swooped down close to her, a sharp sword aimed straight at her head. Kolfinna's mana worked through the ground at her feet in a split second, and a tendril of gnarled roots flicked up above her, catching the edge of the blade. The warrior's orange eyes widened.

Kolfinna dove away from him and ran through the thicket of soldiers and enemies. Her eyes roved over the sea of gray uniforms and black scaly ones.

A blast boomed behind her. Kolfinna turned just in time to find Herja emerging from one of the windows at the upper levels. Blue fire streaked from her hands and lit up the darkening, evening sky.

Kolfinna ducked when a stone spear hurtled her way. It crashed into the fort behind her. Kolfinna turned to find an elf warrior running to her with a sword in one hand. She barely had time to yank her own sword out of its scabbard and meet the elf's blade. Steel bit steel, and the reverberation rattled up to her elbow.

The elf woman narrowed her blood-red eyes. "You are not human," she snarled.

Their swords slammed into one another, again and again. "Neither," Kolfinna said through gritted teeth, "are you!"

The woman pushed her back, strike after strike. Shadows slipped from the woman's hands, blackening the hilt of her sword and leeching onto the silver edge of her blade. Kolfinna lurched backward as those shadows sprang forward. Wisps reached out to her and Kolfinna tried to avoid them, but as she focused on the shadows, the tip of the woman's shadow-drenched sword jabbed straight into Kolfinna's shoulder.

For a moment, the only thing she felt was the painful shredding of her muscles and flesh under the tipped blade, and the grating sensation of something sharp biting into her bone, but then something hot bubbled under the surface of her skin. The elf woman's shadows writhed within her, eating away at her mana and burning her wound.

The shadows rose around her. She could already see her own fate—being eaten alive by these burning, inky shadows. It would happen to her the same way she had killed Hilda's lackeys or even that giant goblin in the caves. She could see herself fighting off the shadows and dying, with black stains left over her body.

Her panic flared. She waved her sword to keep the woman away, but the shadows were multiplying, spreading from that wound and festering into a giant flame across her shoulder.

She screamed and tried rubbing the black away, but it just grew further. Her flesh felt like it was being burned and frozen at the same time. The hot and cold sent waves of pain over her body. Her mana fluctuated in the same way; bits and pieces of it were being torn apart by the hungry shadows.

Kolfinna hadn't even realized she had dropped her sword. Her fingers scratched at the shadows licking up her neck, reaching for her face.

Just as the very edges of her vision turned black, her mana burst uncontrollably from her hands. Something reared inside of her, twisting and thrashing. She didn't even realize what it was until the pain stopped. When she blinked back, the shadows were still there, swarming around her like tendrils of smoke. They snaked around her body like whips and lashed against the elf woman, who jumped back in surprise.

It was Kolfinna's shadows that were fighting. That were protecting her and pushing the woman away.

"You—" the woman started, eyes wide.

Kolfinna couldn't control the shadows as they shot toward the woman silently. They jumped forward, ready to devour her like they had the other times, but the woman raised her hand and a blast of white light split the shadows in half.

The woman's eyes narrowed and she laughed. "You have elven blood, child! And you do not even know how to wield it."

Something slammed into Kolfinna and she crashed backward. She rolled and rolled, her shoulder cracking into something—a stone, maybe?—and her chest felt like it had been ripped open. All of her shadows disappeared around her.

Her vision darkened and she gasped in pain. Her shaking fingers went to her chest. All at once, she felt the absence of her own mana. Her fingers wrapped around a glowing arrow.

Her hands were slick with blood. The arrow was leaching off her mana, she realized as her slippery fingers followed the body of the arrow down to where it was lodged in her right breast. She yanked it out violently, and a burst of stars danced at the edges of her vision. She could feel herself falling into unconsciousness, but she pushed herself into a sitting position to stave off the exhaustion, the shock, and her body's desire to slip into unconsciousness.

Focus.

She would heal, she told herself. She couldn't fall here. She needed to find Rakel.

She could feel her mind slipping further.

Why was she fighting again?

Rakel.

That was right. Rakel. If Rakel escaped ... The half-elf commander would know about her.

Her gaze roamed over the courtyard. At the flying fae facing against air elementals in aerial battles, at the fae warriors using stone magic against the soldiers, at the elf warriors wielding shadows and light. At the soldiers whose lightning boomed and crackled in the sky, at the fire blazing in different shades across the battlefield, at the ice crackling and water slicing through the air, at the crack and splinter of enhancers breaking into walls with the force of their magic, and the whipping of air splitting from air elementals.

It was dizzying to see, and through the thicket, her gaze met with Joran's. His eyes were wide and panicked, and when he saw her, his mouth opened to say something, but Kolfinna couldn't hear a thing beside the crashes and booms and screams of battle. He was a dozen feet away from her, and even in the thick of battle, he wasn't using his powers. He was wielding his sword instead.

Kolfinna tried to stand, but something loomed above her.

A pair of orange eyes met hers.

The winged fae grabbed Kolfinna's bicep and yanked her to her feet. She could barely scream as he tossed her over his shoulder and lurched up into the sky. Her vision blurred and the air slammed into her face quickly. She could still see Joran's shocked expression, could see the soldiers becoming smaller.

Kolfinna could barely protest. The wings of the warrior flapped in the air close to her face, and even though she knew logically that all she had to do was strike the wings, her body stiffened and she couldn't move. They moved so quickly, so powerfully, that if she struck them, she was sure she'd break her hand.

"Let me go!" She punched the warrior's back, but that didn't slow him down. They were rising up even higher now.

She couldn't feel her mana—she was completely drained—and she could barely lift one of her arms. Blood ran down her chest from the arrow wound, and she wasn't sure what was making her dizzier, the blood loss or the altitude?

Down below, Joran raised his hand in her direction.

Yes, Kolfinna thought. *Spear him with the stones. Do something. Save me.*

But then, just as quickly, he lowered his hand and turned away.

Kolfinna's hope shattered.

That was right. He wasn't going to expose himself as a fae. That was more important than Kolfinna's life.

"Let me go," Kolfinna said weakly. The wind tore through her hair and her knees felt weak when she looked down below.

"We have been looking for you," the man rumbled with a dialect she didn't recognize, with a thick accent she couldn't pinpoint either. "Commander Alfaer wants to see you."

The fort became smaller the higher they went and the skirmishes looked like pretty, flashing lights from up here. Kolfinna protested against the man, kicking and screaming and smacking his back, but her punches became weaker and she could barely keep her eyes open.

Right when she thought it was futile, a blast of air crashed into the man and stopped him from going any farther. Inkeri was a few feet away from them, wind swirling beneath her feet and keeping her somewhat upright—although a tad shaky.

"Let her go!" Inkeri screamed.

The man raised his sword to meet Inkeri's. In that exact moment, Kolfinna kneed him in the stomach and wrestled away from him. The man yelped in surprise and Kolfinna wrenched free from his grasp. Except, she didn't have wings. And she wasn't an air elemental.

She saw the flash of panic on the man's face, the same instant she saw Inkeri's mouth open wide.

And then, she plummeted.

Her scream ripped from her throat, and she spun and spun in the air, falling faster and faster. The ground grew closer by the second. The colors blurred around her. The flashes of blue, red, white, and black conglomerated together into a blurring light.

She would die.

Painfully.

In seconds, her head would crash into the ground and she would splatter.

How idiotic, she thought. *How truly idiotic—*

Something collided into her from the side. Her head snapped back violently and she couldn't breathe for a few moments. She blinked slowly, and her dizzying vision began righting itself. Her stomach clenched tightly, and she realized that someone was holding her.

"That was close." A fae woman with blazing purple eyes cursed. Giant, white wings flapped behind the woman.

Kolfinna looked down at the ground, which was only a dozen feet away from her now. Kolfinna didn't think and punched her savior in the face. Her nose crunched beneath Kolfinna's fist and she released her immediately—instinctively.

And Kolfinna flew again, but this time she braced herself for the impact.

She crashed into the ground. Her shoulder cracked and she bit back a scream. A wave of nausea rolled over her, and it took all her willpower to not fall into the dizzying darkness. Above her, she could make out the fae warriors flying. The woman was diving toward Kolfinna again, but ice speared her shoulder and she went careening backward. Kolfinna barely turned her head in time to see Blár and Gunnar running toward her.

"Kolfinna!" Blár dropped down beside her. His gaze roved over her body and she could tell by his stricken expression that she didn't look pretty. His hands trembled over her shoulder and she bit back another scream.

"I'm fine," she hissed through the pain. She clutched the grass beside her and tried to sit up but found she couldn't.

"Are you sure? You ... literally *fell*." He cringed, his hands hovering over the bleeding sections of her uniform. To the blooming deep red on her chest and then to her mangled shoulder. His face was pale, even in the darkness of evening. She wasn't sure if it was because of worry for her that he looked that way, or if it was something else.

Kolfinna tried to laugh. "Come on, I can't look that bad?"

"I wish I could agree." Blár tried to smile, but it came out strained.

Gunnar peered down at her with a grimace and then looked away at the skyline. "They're retreating."

Sure enough, the fae warriors were flying away while the elves were running, their swords dripped through with blood.

Blár tentatively touched the side of Kolfinna's neck, and despite the situation, warmth spread over her face at being so close to him. At him being so gentle with her. "Nothing's broken, is it?"

"I think I might have broken my shoulder," she whispered. "But I don't feel too wounded."

"You're likely in shock." His finger brushed her cheek when he pushed back her hair, and even with a broken body, her body moved in response. His eyes caught hers for a second before he inspected her shoulder. "We need to get you to the physician. Along with ..." He glanced behind himself at the soldiers; some of who were screaming and clutching their ink-stained bodies, others who were unnaturally still. "Many others. Those elves really did a number on us."

"The fae were strong too," Gunnar said. "But ... we were useless against those shadows."

"Or the light," Kolfinna chimed in.

Gunnar frowned. "That too."

Blár scooped Kolfinna in his arms and stood up effortlessly. A whimper escaped from her mouth even as she tried to hide her pain. No matter how much he tried to be gentle, every movement made her shoulder feel like he was snapping it in half.

"What do you think their objective was?" Gunnar asked.

Kolfinna closed her eyes. "I think they came to rescue the elf woman."

Even with her eyes closed, she could feel their eyes on her.

"But then why did they try to take you?" Blár asked.

"I don't know," she lied. She couldn't hold back the tears that prickled her eyes. Through the tears and the pain, she could make out Blár's and Gunnar's confused expressions. "I don't know."

22

THE DAMAGE DONE TO THE FORT BY THE HALF-ELF warriors was worse than Kolfinna could've imagined.

The walls were riddled with holes and partially crumbled in certain sections, many soldiers were injured, and there were clearly more human casualties than the fae or elves. In fact, the fae and elves had been outnumbered, but they still managed to keep their casualties down and accomplish their goal—which was likely to free Rakel.

Kolfinna turned her face away from the corpse of a human soldier who was pinned to the wall with a sword in his chest—and by the looks of the lion-head pommel, it was his own sword, which only made her wonder what kind of battle he endured for the enemy to steal his sword and imbed it into his chest. She didn't stare too long at his pallid, blood-splattered face because she didn't want to recognized him. She did the same with the other causalities, barely giving them more than a glance.

Blár's strong arms tightened around her, and the momentary embrace made her shoulder stiffen in protest. She squeezed her eyes shut; focusing on the pain than on the corpses that lay in wake after the battle was easier.

"Those white-haired bastards are elves, right?" Blár's voice was harsh as he stepped over a blackened, soot-stained chunk of stone that had once belonged to the ceiling.

Kolfinna kept her eyes closed. "Yes."

She wasn't healing. She could tell that much by the way the scrapes on her hands and knees—which usually healed fast—were still present. It confirmed her theory that healing required mana, and now that she was drained, her body wasn't healing itself.

She really hoped she wasn't stuck with these injuries for too long.

"I can't believe they were gutsy enough to attack a fortress," Blár said with a deep frown.

"I can't believe a lot of things," she muttered.

Like the wings.

They were her enemies, but she could sit and marvel at their wings all day. Her back felt even more sensitive as she thought about her own wings that had been clipped from her when she was younger. Too young to remember anything, and yet there was a longing to be in the air like they had.

But then she also remembered how she had plummeted through the sky, and she quickly pushed that thought aside.

Blár kicked down the door to one of the rooms and peeked inside. It was someone's bedroom. Half the wall was missing and broken, with stony shards littering the bed and the floors. The cool night air breezed into the room, made even colder by Blár's presence.

He sauntered inside like it was his own room and carefully placed her on the edge of the bed, then dusted off the remaining pebbles and stony debris off the duvet.

"Thanks," Kolfinna mumbled, glancing at the tattered room. Blood was streaked across one of the walls, indicating that someone had fought in here at some point. "How are the others?"

"I passed by Herja a little earlier and didn't notice any big injuries. Ivar, Inkeri, and Eluf are alive too, if that's what you're asking. A bit shocked and banged up, but otherwise fine."

"That's a relief," she whispered. And it truly was; she hadn't realized how close the little group had gotten to her heart until the prospect of them dying crossed her mind and wrenched her gut.

"I'll get some—"

Blár couldn't finish his sentence because Joran barreled into the room.

Out of breath, he said, "Kolfinna! You're all right."

Kolfinna stiffened. She didn't want to see Joran. In fact, she didn't want anything to do with him. Even looking at his face, at his relieved expression, only filled her with loathing, which she could hardly contain or conceal.

"Joran," she said icily.

Blár blinked and looked between the two of them, while Joran watched her with a conflicted expression.

All she could see was Joran turning his back to her when the fae warrior had whisked her away. She should've been used to the bitter feeling of betrayal—she had experienced it thrice now, once by Revna, another time by Mímir, and most recently by Yrsa—but she still couldn't swallow down the thickness of her throat. Like a clump of ice was stuck in there.

Joran took a hesitant step forward.

"Joran, why are you here?" Kolfinna grasped a handful of the duvet in her clenched fist and glared at him.

"I came to help you." Joran shot a dark look in Blár's direction. "I saw you being taken alone in a bedroom, so I thought to help you."

"Taken alone?" Kolfinna blinked back in surprise and couldn't help the shrill laugh that bubbled in the back of her throat. How dare he act like he *cared* for her well-being. "You're talking like Blár is going to hurt me. He won't."

Blár peered down at Joran with narrowed eyes, and a breeze kicked up from the gaping hole in the room. "Why would you think I would bring her here to hurt her?"

"You tried to kill her once." Joran unclenched and clenched

his fists, like he was itching to punch something—or someone. "I wouldn't put it past you to do it again. Besides, I thought it more appropriate that I come here and tend to her wounds."

The air in the room stilled and Blár's eyes darkened considerably. Like a storm passing over a frozen ocean. Any warmth that was in the room evaporated instantly, and Kolfinna wasn't the only one who noticed. Joran's shoulders stiffened, but he held Blár's glacial gaze.

Blár spoke slowly, his voice smooth yet sharp. "You think you're more appropriate to tend to her wounds? What makes you say that? By the way she's glaring at you, I highly doubt she wants anything to do with your scrawny ass."

"She needs help undressing." Joran's lips wavered. "I—"

"*Undressing?*" Blár took a step forward and the temperature in the room dropped to sub-zero in a split second. "You came in here to help her *undress?*"

Joran's fists trembled, but he raised his wobbly chin up in defiance. "Yes."

Kolfinna wasn't sure what was more shocking, that Joran wasn't stuttering or that Blár was actually speechless. Or the fact that Joran had come here to help *undress* her.

"Joran," Kolfinna finally said, unable to hide her astonishment, "what in the world are you talking about?"

A blush spread over Joran's cheeks—something Blár seemed to notice because his lips curled. Joran cleared his throat and stared at her levelly, pointedly ignoring Blár. "I noticed you're hurt, so I came here to help you. I've seen it all before, so it doesn't matter. Right?"

Blár inhaled sharply while Kolfinna went very still.

Time seemed to freeze. Nobody said anything, nobody moved, and nobody breathed.

That snake. Kolfinna wanted to shout at him, to scream that he was being obscene, or that he would give Blár the wrong idea, but she couldn't move. She could only stare dumbly at him and then at Blár, who had gone rigid as ice.

Blár's voice was low, dangerous. "Who are you?"

"Joran—"

"Listen, *Joran*." He spat his name like it was poison on his tongue. "I don't give a shit who you think you are, but you're not going to help Kolfinna *undress*. I don't give a shit if you saw her buck-ass naked, or if you flashed your two inches at her. Get the hell out of here before I freeze you and chuck you out of here myself."

Kolfinna could see the flash of fear in Joran's eyes; Blár wasn't one to bluff. Joran must've realized that too, but he remained rooted in place. Wide-eyed like a doe in front of a raging wolf. Maybe fear kept him in place. Or maybe stupidity.

Kolfinna rubbed her aching temple with her one good hand. Her shoulder was becoming stiffer by the moment, and the dried, caking blood on her wounds made any movement uncomfortable. "Joran," she said with a wave toward the door. "Please leave. We can talk later."

Blár gave Kolfinna a side-eyed look; he probably didn't like that last part.

But that seemed to perk Joran up—the prospect of talking again. He nodded and backed away quickly, casting a wary glance in Blár's direction. "I'll be back later. Um, I hope you feel better."

After he left, Kolfinna released a breath and sagged on the bed. It was arduous having to stay awake. And with her mana completely tapped out, she was even more exhausted than usual after a battle.

Blár rummaged through one of the nightstands beside her bed; his back was to her. "So," he said, yanking open the bottom drawer. "Who the hell is he? And what was he talking about?"

"He's Joran." Kolfinna stared at the cracks and soot stains lining the ceiling. Whoever's room this was, one of them must've been a fire elemental. "I don't really know why he acted like that. He's normally more ... quiet."

"He felt threatened by me, *that's* why." Blár pulled out a wad of bandages and a jar of thick, dark brown, syrup-like liquid. He popped open the lid, took a whiff at it, and crinkled his nose. "*Shit.*" He gagged and pulled it away from his nose. "I'm guessing this is some sort of medicine."

"What else would it be?"

"The color looks like shit."

Kolfinna leaned back into her pillow. "Nobody would just ... poop in a jar and keep it in their dresser."

Blár gave her a long look while he placed the jar on the nightstand. "You underestimate people. Especially soldiers—*male* soldiers."

Kolfinna laughed again, glad for the joke to relieve some of the tension in the room.

"Maybe this shit belongs to his girlfriend." Blár placed the wad of bandages and whipped out a knife from a hidden pocket inside his boot. "You never know with some of these freaks. Anyway, how are we going to do this? Do you want me to call in a female soldier to help you?"

That was probably the most appropriate of choices. Having a male—and not just any male, but *Blár*—tend to her wounds meant that she would, indeed, have to undress to some degree.

But if the elves and fae came back for her, Blár was the only person who could truly protect her. That was the reasoning she used, but she knew it was deeper than that. There was a part of her that wanted to undress in front of him. Gauge his reaction. See if he actually did like what he saw.

That was probably her vulnerability talking.

Or something else.

"Um." Kolfinna cleared her throat. It didn't really matter whether she got stitched up or not; once here mana replenished itself, she would be healed. Besides, the stitches would only hurt more in the end, when she would need to rip them out of her healed flesh. "Uh. I can do it myself."

Blár looked at her like she was crazy. "Like hell you will. You're injured, Kolfinna. *Badly.*" He gestured toward her shoulder and chest. "I'm actually surprised you're still awake."

"I'm stronger than I look." Her smile was strained. Her wounds throbbed painfully and she could feel the dregs of sleep and exhaustion calling her name, but her mind was racing. Having Rakel flee and seeing the fae and elf warriors only solidified that this was *really* happening. That they were coming for her. That they would find her. That *he* would find her.

Kolfinna still couldn't tell Blár the truth. That she was part elf. That she could heal herself. That she was related to the heir—that she *was* the heir. That she was somehow the daughter of the ruthless queen and the half-elf commander. That she was anything more than just a normal fae. She didn't even know what to make of it herself, and even though a part of her wanted to relieve the weight of her secrets onto Blár, she didn't know how he would react.

Her thoughts were drawn to the hole in the wall, where she could see soldiers helping each other to their feet, or who were tending to their wounds. Everyone was already busy; it wasn't fair to have Blár give her attention when he could help another soldier patch up, especially since her wounds would probably heal in a day or so.

"Go out there," Kolfinna said, nodding to the courtyard. She wanted Blár to stay with her, wanted to continue to feel the coolness of his presence, but duty called for him to help everyone out there. Her feelings clashed with what was right, and even as she wanted to lean into his presence, she tried to hold herself stronger. "They need your help."

"With what?" He sat down on the bed parallel to hers. "Unless there are still some enemies out there, I'm not much help to anyone."

"That's not true—"

"Ah yes, I almost forgot—I can provide words of encouragement," he said with a smirk. "I'm sure that'll be really helpful."

She rolled her eyes. "Blár, you can help bandage someone up. Or if someone is stuck under a building or … I don't know, something like that."

The moonlight reflected off his blue eyes and made them look darker. "Trust me when I say that if they need me, they'll find me." He pointed the tip of his pocketknife at the wound on her shoulder. "Now, if you don't want me to help you out, that's fine, I can call someone who can. But don't tell me to leave with some half-baked excuse that I'm needed elsewhere. I'd rather be here."

Warmth spread across her chest and she was grateful he couldn't see her blush in the darkness. "Well, um, okay." Kolfinna pushed a strand of white hair away from her eyes. She couldn't think straight—she wanted him here, yes, but she was too embarrassed to *actually* undress in front of him. "I want you to stay here, but I would rather patch myself up."

"It'll be painful," he said with a frown. "I can call—"

"I'll be fine. Trust me." She didn't plan on stitching herself up.

Blár didn't look convinced but conceded by placing the knife on the bedside table. "All right then. I'll get you some water to clean the wound."

After Blár found a flask of water for her, she went to work immediately. She cut off her sleeve with Blár's knife, cleaned her wounds with water and a damp cloth, and spread the thick, yarrow-infused concoction on her gaping wounds. Meanwhile, Blár stood at the opening in the wall, his hand lightly pressed on the top edges of the hole while he peered at the courtyard.

"What did he mean when he said he's seen it all before?" His voice was soft, but there was an edge to his tone. "Was he telling the truth?"

Kolfinna paused at wrapping the roll of bandages around her shoulder. "He saw me naked after I took a bath," she answered honestly. A flush of embarrassment washed over her face. She didn't like thinking about that moment. "It was an accident."

"How? The women's bathing room is on a different level than the men's. He couldn't have gotten in there without—"

"It wasn't in the normal baths." She pressed her lips together. "It was in his room."

Blár's shoulders stiffened. "His room?"

"Yes."

"Why ... Why were you in his room?" By the way his hand gripped tighter on the wall, she could tell he was having a hard time not turning his head to pin her with a stare.

Kolfinna placed a wad of bandages to her chest and buttoned her uniform up since that was easier than having to wrap around her chest with one hand. It also gave her time to think as she did that. It bothered him that she had gone into Joran's room. She could tell by his tone and the way his body went rigid at her words. It would probably bother her too knowing that he was in a woman's room, *bathing* or doing who knew what.

Did he think she would jump into Joran's bed? Was he insecure about her feelings toward him?

All she had to do was tell him that Joran was fae, and the only reason she was in there was to try out his rune-magicked bathing room. But for some reason, it felt wrong to tell him. An old habit, most likely; the fae always helped out another fae by keeping their secret.

But why did she need to keep his secret? Joran cared so much about that secret that he was willing to let the fae warrior whisk her away.

"Joran is fae," Kolfinna blurted out before she could think better.

Blár went silent.

"There's nothing between us, by the way," she continued. Her heart picked up in pace at his unmoving body, at the way his fingers were flattened against the ridges of the hole. At how ice clung to his fingertips, spreading out like thin spiderwebs over the cracked wall. "It was an accident, Blár."

Blár sighed. "I believe you. I'm just ... frustrated because that weasel-faced freak saw you in that position and then thought to use that against you. And yes, it worked. I'm angry. At him. At the fact that he saw you naked, and of course at the thought that you were probably very embarrassed when it happened, and him bringing it up probably makes you even more uncomfortable."

Kolfinna distractedly wrapped her arm a tad tighter with the bandages. She was lost for words. She had never had someone angry on her behalf—at least, not like this.

Blár released his iron-like grip from the wall and chuckled. "By the way, are you done yet? Staring at these soldiers isn't very fun."

"Yes, I'm done."

He glanced over his shoulder at her, and even with the darkness of night enveloping behind him, she could make out the tilt of his lips. "And here I thought I'd get to see something more than just your bare arm."

"Keep dreaming." She chuckled and couldn't stop the blush from spreading over to the tips of her ears.

"How's the wound on your chest?" Pebbles bounced off the duvet when Blár dropped down on the bed across from hers. "It looks really nasty. An arrow wound?"

She grimaced as she remembered how that glowing, gold arrow had burrowed itself into her chest and drawn her mana out. "I think it was a rune-marked arrow. It drained my mana out completely."

"You're lucky you're not dead from that." He gave her a strange look as he said that.

Maybe the wound had partially closed before the arrow drew her mana out? That was the only explanation she could think of. But she wasn't going to tell him that. "I don't know," she said with a shrug but then winced. "I must be lucky, then."

Blár stretched out his legs. "So you have no clue why they were after you?"

"None." She thumbed the edge of the bed and eased herself down on it again. The lie rolled off thickly, like it wasn't meant to be there. And she should have trusted him—he had proved himself to be her ally—but her old, deep-seated fear kept her from revealing herself. "Maybe because I'm the only fae here? Who knows."

"Huh."

They were silent for a long time after that. Kolfinna could make out a few muffled cries in the courtyard, the shifting of bodies from one location to the other, the curses under peoples' breaths. She wanted desperately to unhear it all. To shift her mind onto a lighter subject. One that didn't include her potentially precarious fate.

Silence filled the space between them, but it wasn't uncomfortable. It was... calming. And she could feel herself drifting asleep.

"It was terrifying, you know." The bed creaked and she heard him draw closer to her—his boots scuffling against fallen debris, pebbles, and stones. He gingerly sat on the edge of her bed, and the entire mattress dipped with his weight.

"What was?" Kolfinna peeled her eyes open to find him staring down at her with a soft expression.

"Seeing you fall from the sky." He reached forward and brushed a stray curl out of her face. "I thought I was going to lose you too. I'm ..." His fingers were chilly, so close to her ear and cheek. "I'm used to being very powerful, but it seems every time I truly need to be powerful, my magic fails me. Like with my family. Like with that attack from that skinless horse. I can't have it happen with you too." Blár's smile was almost sad, almost pained. "What have you done to me? To have me so terrified of losing you?"

Kolfinna could barely keep her eyes open anymore. "I've bewitched you with my fae charms."

"And I've gladly fallen victim to it."

"Poor you ..."

Despite the adrenaline rush from the unexpected battle and the fear she had for the half-elf commander's army, for the first time in a long, long time, she felt utterly safe. And before she could completely fall into the clutches of sleep, she felt the distinct touch of lips against her forehead.

"Sweet dreams," he murmured, and her hands wanted to move to his face and stay there and never let go, but before she could do so, she fell asleep.

23

The sound of the door swinging open and slamming against the wall woke Kolfinna from her dreamless, deep slumber. Her bleary eyes adjusted to the crackly ceiling, and the first thing she noticed was just how frigid it was in the room—with the hole in the wall, the cool, night air was breezing in uncomfortably. The second thing she noticed was that she had a thick blanket surrounding her and tucked underneath her, and the last thing she noticed was Joran standing by the doorway with a candle in his hand.

Kolfinna jerked upright and then hissed as pain shot through her shoulder and her chest. Joran rushed to her side, the candlelight flickering with his fast movement. "Are you okay?"

He moved to place his hand on her shoulder, but she raised her good hand to keep him at bay, a frown deepening her features. Blár wasn't in the room anymore; had he left her to go to the bathroom, or maybe to assist some of the soldiers outside?

She tentatively touched the thick bandages padding her shirt and cringed when another bolt of pain struck her; if she still wasn't healed, then not much time must've passed.

"What do you want, Joran?" Kolfinna twisted her lips. She didn't mean to sound so harsh, but the pain she was dealing with, the betrayal, and the fact that he woke her up much too early when she should've been recuperating, ticked her off more than she had initially thought.

"I came to see how you're doing."

Kolfinna laughed, and it sounded harsh to her ears. "Funny you say that after what you did."

Joran shrank back, and the candle wobbled in his hand. "What do you mean?"

"Seriously?" Kolfinna bunched her hands over the thick fur blanket. If she didn't grasp something, she was sure she would reach over and wring his neck. He was either pretending like he didn't know what she was talking about, or he really was that dense. "You know *exactly* what I'm talking about," she said through gritted teeth.

"No, I don't." He stared at her levelly, but there was a spark in his eyes that told her he was lying. She had seen him, he had seen her, and he had turned his back on her.

"You didn't even try to help me when that fae grabbed me and flew in the air. I know you saw me."

Joran's lips pursed together and he peered down at her with an expression she didn't like—as if *he* was disappointed in her. "I couldn't do anything in that moment, and you know it too."

You know it too.

In that moment, she saw red.

Her fists clenched together tightly and her nails imbedded into the palms of her hands.

"You betrayed me, Joran. Do you not understand that simple concept? We're supposed to be allies, and instead of helping me when you saw a winged fae had taken me, you did nothing. You could've chucked a stone at his head. Hell, I *know* you have good aim. You could've raised a stone tower and grabbed me with it. You could've created a stone barrier in front of him. You could've tried to grab me with the stones—you could've done anything!"

Joran was already shaking his head before she finished, the

candlelight bobbing and casting shadows over the room. "You know I can't do that."

"You can. You're capable—"

"No, I *can't.*"

"Oh, right, you can't because you don't want anyone to know that you're fae. You'd rather keep your secret than save my life." She wanted to laugh at him right now, laugh at how incredulous he was, how he wanted to act like he cared about her when he wasn't willing to use his powers for her.

"Not that loud," he hissed. He shot a look at the broad hole in the wall and raised his hand subtly, low enough that no one would be able to suspect him. In seconds, the mishmash of stones and pebbles in the room launched at the hole, building upon one another until it was cobbled, but rebuilt. Gaps and fissures from uneven stones stacked together formed between the rocks.

Joran blew out some air. "It's hard to reveal that I'm fae. You should know that."

"Then don't act like we're anything more than just acquaintances," Kolfinna snarled. Now that all the walls were closed in around her, she became increasingly aware that it was just the two of them. The only light source was from the candle in his hand. "Because the way you were acting, what you were insinuating in front of Blár, was infuriating for me. I don't know if you like me —in some twisted sort of way that stems from the fact that we're both fae—but if you truly liked me, you would've saved me from that fae, regardless of what happened afterward, and you wouldn't have used underhanded methods to make it seem like we're more than just acquaintances."

"It's not easy!" Joran's hold on the candle tightened and his fingers indented the yellow wax. "If you weren't forced to be here as a well-known fae, would you keep it a secret or tell everyone? If the Royal Guards had never caught you, would you still announce that you're a fae? Because, forgive me if I'm wrong, you lived your whole life hiding that you're a fae, didn't you?" He took a step closer, and his voice rose now that they were alone. "So why is it wrong that I—and thousands of other fae, mind you—do the same? Why would any fae want to be known as fae? They'd be targets for the Hunter's Association and everyone else who hates fae! You should know that—you went through so much trouble ever since everyone found out who you are. I don't want to do that to myself."

"There you have it," Kolfinna sneered and she fought the urge to spit at him. "You care more about that than you do about me. Which is fine, except when you act like *this*." She gestured to him rudely. "Look at you, acting all worked up on my behalf, like you and I are something, and getting angry that Blár is in the room with me, when you won't do anything to protect me. Or *help* me."

"Do you love him?"

All at once, she didn't want to deal with this conversation anymore. She didn't want to fly into a fit of fury at how infuriating Joran was being, but she also knew that she had to deal with this now.

Kolfinna mustered up the dregs of patience she had left within her and said, "Joran, you and I aren't close enough where I can talk to you about things like that. It's honestly inappropriate for you to even think that I would tell you about my personal life. We are not close. I don't know if I somehow gave you that impression, but we aren't."

"We're in this together." Joran fidgeted with his sleeve and she inadvertently touched the rune on her wrist. He followed her movement and continued quickly, "You're the one who wanted this life, anyway. I don't want to out myself as a fae because this is the life I want. Where I'm protected, where I'm safe. Where no one can hurt me."

"Okay, and good for you? What does that have to do with the fact that you didn't save me when you could have?"

"*You* should've saved yourself."

"You're ridiculous." Kolfinna's fingers tightened around the blanket. She was losing more of her patience by the second. Why was he even here—just to tell that she should've let herself die from that winged fae, and that it wasn't his fault she was captured? "I would've saved myself if I could have! But I couldn't; I was drained of my mana, and I needed help! We're supposed to be comrades. Fellow soldiers."

Joran turned his face away. "I don't want anyone to know that I'm fae."

Kolfinna wanted to bang her head on the wall.

"Yes, you've said that already." She rolled her eyes and waved at the door. "Is that all? Is this why you woke me up when I'm supposed to be resting? To tell me it isn't your fault?"

"No, but I just wanted to let you know—"

"Yes, yes, that you don't want anyone to know you're fae." Her temples began to throb with a budding headache and she stared at the door impatiently, as if Blár would pop in and shoo Joran away. "I don't like how people treat me either, but I really think being open about being a fae is the first step in making people become accustomed to our kind in a positive way. They have to find it normal to see a fae walking around, having jobs, being in the military. I want to make a difference—"

"And that's great—*for you.*" Joran shifted on his feet and the glow from the candlelight made the flecks of orange in his eyes seem more apparent—more fae. "I'm trying to do the same for our people."

"*How?*" Kolfinna laughed bitterly. "By forcing women into a rune bargain with Sijur that will ultimately kill them or make them his slaves for eternity? *That's* how you're helping our race?"

He flinched like she had slapped him. "I-I don't ... I don't have a choice."

"Why do you even have a rune mark or binding with Sijur?" Kolfinna pressed. "I didn't have a choice. I couldn't write down some gibberish—since he can't understand it anyway—because *you* were there to make sure the runes were correct. But you? Which fae was hovering over your head making sure you wrote the correct rune to bind you to Sijur forever? How would Sijur even know?"

Joran fidgeted with the cuff of his sleeve for the hundredth time. The candle bobbed in his hand awkwardly. "I'm indebted to Lieutenant Bernsten."

"So you were naïve enough to forfeit your life to him?" She scoffed. "You can be indebted to someone and still have your own free will. Why would you give that up?"

He didn't meet her gaze.

"Joran."

"Look, things are complicated." Joran's voice became smaller, almost like he wanted to disappear. "Lieutenant Bernsten saved my life. My aunt and I were running to the Mistlands from hunters and ... He saved me. I'm indebted to him."

"And your aunt?"

He stared at the floor.

It wasn't unusual for fae to lose loved ones to the hunters. "I'm sorry to hear that."

"I'm indebted to him," Joran whispered again. "He protects me here. Do you really think life would be easier for us if he wasn't around? Didn't you suffer in the Royal Guards?"

Bitterness filled her mouth, and it wasn't entirely because of the memories from the Royal Guards—but the fact that Sijur had taken advantage of her when she was in a precarious situation. "Life would be easier if I wasn't bound to him for fifteen years."

"He saved me, and he saved you too. If he hadn't stepped in, do you really think the guards would've let you live after what you did? What's fifteen years in the face of death?"

"I'm forced to do whatever he wants in those fifteen years!" She threw her hands up and then grimaced as pain shot up her injured shoulder; it was healing, though, bit by bit, because she hadn't been able to move it earlier. "I don't want that kind of life! And to make matters worse, Sijur wants to do terrible things with my powers. I can't let that happen. This isn't what I signed up for."

"He didn't trick you. He told you exactly what he needed from you and what the exchange was."

"That doesn't mean I'm happy with it."

"That's not his problem."

Kolfinna frowned in disgust. "You're actually ... *loyal* to him?"

"Yes—"

"Tell me this, Joran. If you could escape from here, would you?" Kolfinna already had a creeping suspicious of what his answer would be, but she needed to hear it from him.

Joran stared at her levelly. "No. Why would I? I'm protected here. No one can hurt me, and no one can hurt you either, Kolfinna."

"Joran, are you ..." Kolfinna hesitated. "Are you even bound to him?"

Silence.

"Joran?"

Still, he remained silent, his gaze downcast.

"You're not, are you?" The horror in her voice didn't even begin to cover how she felt inside. His image began to spoil and rot in front of her eyes. She could see Birgitta, and Olia, and all the other people who had been bound to Sijur. And she thought of the children's names she had found in that journal. "You did all those terrible things because of your loyalty? Not because you're bound to him?"

"You wouldn't understand." Anger flashed in his eyes and he stepped closer to her. "He saved me. I have to do the things he wants. And if you were smart, you would too."

Her stomach turned at the sight of his anger. She tried to pull at her mana, but she barely felt any wisps within her. "You disgust me."

"Don't talk to me like that—"

"You're disgusting!" Kolfinna's hands curled to fists and she hated that she had no mana left, nothing to protect herself from him if he decided to get nasty with her. "I can't believe you're listening to him and you're not even bound to him! You can leave if you want to, but you're just—just mentally bound to him because you feel indebted. And—And, what about the children? Did you know about *that*?"

He staggered back like she had punched him in the gut. Finally, some sort of guilt and horror showed on his face. "How do you know about that?"

"So you do know about that?" She hid her trembling hands beneath the plush blanket. "Don't you have any morals?! He's using children to be his slaves!"

Joran took a step forward, his figure looming over hers. "I do feel bad"—his voice hitched—"but I don't care too much about humans! They've taken everything from me, so why does it matter if a few of them die? How many fae children have died because of humans? What's a few here and there got to do with our survival? You don't seem to realize that I'm helping our kind by learning about our magic. Do you know how much history and knowledge I've learned? I did what I had to!"

"Are you serious right now?" Kolfinna wanted to leap forward and shove him out the room, but with how depleted her mana was, she didn't think she'd win in a fight. She wondered again where Blár had gone. "You're okay with a few humans dying for Sijur? For that lunatic? He's a monster, and you're delusional to ignore it all!"

"What have they done for us?" He slapped his chest. "We're fae, Kolfinna! We're not supposed to care about humans!"

"Then why do you follow a *human*?!"

"Because he saved me! He's *different*!"

"He's *not* different! He's just using you for your power. Don't you see that?!"

"Of course I know he wants my power! But he protects me, and I listen to him. That's our deal, Kolfinna, and if you were smart, you would do the same. Because we're in this together forever. So I suggest you—"

"In this *forever*?" She barked a laugh and then pinned him

with a nasty glare. "I'm leaving the instant I can, Joran. Do you really think I'll stay here after the bargain is over?"

His eyes grew into saucers and he clamped his mouth shut. For a second, a rush of victory flooded her, but then something else reigned over it. He was ... hiding something? It was a hunch, but the way he averted his gaze all of a sudden told her that he said something he shouldn't have.

"Joran." Kolfinna hesitated, and his words replayed in her mind. *In this together forever.* "Joran, what do you mean by *forever*?"

Joran turned his face away. "Nothing—"

"Joran."

He didn't answer.

Kolfinna reached for his arm—something to grab onto—but he backed away from her, his face pale even in the dim lighting. "Joran, look at me! What do you mean by forever? I thought this mark was only for fifteen years?"

"It is." He swallowed but couldn't look her in the eyes.

"*But?*"

"You and I will be together forever." His green eyes flicked to hers. "Sijur intends to bind us together through an ancient fae ceremony. We'll grow stronger together."

All the color drained from her face and she dropped her hands on her lap. She knew about that ceremony, had read about it before.

"The *Bryllup* ceremony?" She wanted to vomit.

"You know it?"

It was a marriage ceremony the fae did to share their power together. The drawback was that they would be bound for eternity, even if they split up. Not to mention that they would never be able to do it again with another person.

"I can't ..." She swallowed the dryness in her throat. She couldn't imagine a life like that—bound to Sijur and then bound to Joran for eternity. "I can't marry you."

"Why not? We're both fae—"

"So what? So what if we're fae?" Kolfinna suddenly became lightheaded. Marriage, to Joran? She didn't want that, but Sijur wanted them to become more powerful so they could bind more people to him. People who didn't want to be bound to him. "I can't marry you."

"Why not?" There was a hardness in his tone. "Is it because of Blár Vilulf?"

"No." Her voice became shrill and she gave him a wild look. "Because I don't love you!"

"You could learn to." He grabbed her arm and his fingers dug into her biceps. "You don't love him, do you? *Do you?*"

She couldn't think properly. Did she love Blár? All she knew was that the thought of marrying Blár was far more pleasant than marring Joran. "Let me go."

"Kolfinna, we're both fae," Joran murmured, his pleading eyes searching her face for something. "We'd be good together."

"Joran, stop." She yanked her arm away from him. She felt lightheaded, like all the blood had rushed to her head. Like she was swimming in an ocean of anxiety. "I don't want to marry you."

"You don't have a choice." Joran watched her sadly. "I think you could come to love me. Eventually."

"Joran, *stop*." Her head spun and she had to close her eyes to stop the room from spinning too. He was right—if Sijur ordered her to marry Joran, she wouldn't have a choice in the matter.

"We'll be powerful together," he whispered. "You're a strong fae, and so am I. It only makes sense."

"No. I won't be bound to you like that."

Forever.

She wanted to throw up.

"We'll be good together," Joran repeated and then nodded quickly as if he was sure of it. "You deserve to be with a fae, not a human. You know that's the way it's supposed to be. For our race's survival and for us to remain strong."

Kolfinna scooted on the edge of the bed, her gaze flicking over to the doorway and then to the wall he had repaired. Her only exit was through that door. "Joran, please leave. You're making me uncomfortable."

He opened his mouth to protest but seemed to think better of it.

"All right, Kolfinna. But I want you to know that I'm not your enemy."

She didn't say anything even after he left the room.

24

Twenty people had died, and over a hundred were injured.

The deaths on the enemy's side were abysmal—*three*.

Kolfinna had thought it was a lie when Sijur announced it that morning. He was still standing there, atop a small dais of broken stones and splintered wood. The entire base was in front of him. The crush of soldiers, the smell of sweat and blood, and the anger and fear on everyone's faces were almost too stimulating for Kolfinna. Her head throbbed painfully with the sights, smells, and noises.

Sijur cast a sweeping glance over his army. "Many of you are probably shocked. Confused. Who were those white-haired, red-eyed beings? They didn't appear to be fae? And what about the fae? Why did they have wings? You all must have these questions, and I'm sure, with those uncertainties, there is *fear*."

Sijur paused in his speech and let those words sink in. The soldiers shifted on their feet, but all eyes were still on him. Waiting with bated breath.

Kolfinna had to hand it to Sijur—he spoke with so much authority, like he belonged in this position, in front of hundreds of soldiers. Her previous captain, Edwin, didn't have this effect when he spoke to his unit of the Royal Guards. He had always seemed to be trying too hard, but Sijur fit the role perfectly. She wondered if it was because he was the son of the commander-in-chief.

His voice boomed over the tattered courtyard. "Those creatures you fought are known as elves. They are similar to the fae, in that they are a magical race, but they have different abilities than the fae, as you encountered. We are still looking into the matter with these elves, but they are our enemy. The fae that had wings are also our enemy. We believe this attack came from Ragnarök. An army of fae and elves has emerged in the south and has been attacking our fortresses there. The southern wall has been breached, and we are battling with that army as I speak."

He paused and looked at the soldiers, who watched him with unease.

"We have kept this information under wraps this past month while we contained the situation, but last night was a clear act of war, and we cannot ignore it any longer. These fae and elves will not take our country, not as long as we are alive and fighting for it. We will not allow anyone to take our country from us!"

A cheer rang through the ranks, and Kolfinna could feel the nearby glares sent her way. She stared straight ahead as anxiety curled up in her belly. This rallying speech only intensified the already-present hatred these people had for the fae—and now for the elves.

Sijur raised a hand and the crowd quieted. "We will march to the south and take our territories back from these Ragnarök scum. We will not sit and twiddle our thumbs as these fae folk invade *our* lands!"

Another round of cheers. Another round of dirty looks casted her way.

"Prepare yourselves for battle! We march tomorrow." Sijur stepped down and everyone began talking amongst themselves.

Kolfinna turned around to leave, only to be met with a

looming figure. Bjarni peered down at her with eyes narrowed to slits and a cruel twist on his lips.

"Fae scum," he bit out. "You shouldn't be here. Everywhere you go, you invite death and battle. Are you truly on our side?"

Kolfinna was taken aback. But she didn't have time to wallow in shock; the soldiers around her had all turned to face her. Most were scowling at her, as if she had been the one to fight them last night. They appeared blind to her own wounds—which had partially healed by morning but were still sore and throbbing.

"I'm a soldier now." Her voice sounded small even to her. She tried to straighten her aching shoulders to face them. "I've always been on the side of Rosain."

The soldier beside him snorted. "Your people are not on our side. You should run back to Ragnarök, where you belong."

"She's probably a spy," Bjarni sneered.

"I wouldn't have broken my arm if it wasn't for your people."

"Same here."

Kolfinna swallowed as more and more people glared at her. She hated being the center of attention, and maybe it was foolish to think that she—fae, white-haired and pink-eyed—was able to *not* be in the spotlight.

But she had decided not to let anyone push her around, not since the Royal Guards, so she steeled herself. She put on the nastiest expression she could muster—a mix between Blár's icy glare and Magni's arrogant looking-down-on-someone stare.

"Maybe"—Kolfinna cracked a knuckle for emphasis and injected as much venom in her tone as she could—"if you'd fought better, you wouldn't have to resort to blaming me for your injuries. Now get the hell out of my way before I shove some stones up your ass."

Bjarni bristled. "You—"

She used their surprise to her advantage and slipped past one of them. He reached out to grab her, but Kolfinna shoved past him, purposefully elbowing his injured arm. He cried out in pain while she continued to quickly weave through the thicket of people.

Kolfinna kept pushing through the crowd when a hand firmly grasped her uninjured shoulder. She whirled around, ready to punch whoever it was, but stopped when she met Ivar's blue-green gaze. An amused smirk curled his lips. He raised an eyebrow at her raised fist.

"Are you planning on punching me? Or shoving some stones up my ass?"

Her cheeks heated up with color. "You heard?"

"I sure did." He released her shoulder with a laugh. "I was planning on stepping in and being the savior, but you didn't need my help. I should've known better, especially since you *did* knock a stone across Bjarni's ugly face the first day here."

A ghost of a smile formed on Kolfinna's face; it had been satisfying to do that. "Did you need something from me?"

"Not really." He jerked a thumb toward the fort. "But Lieutenant Bernsten is calling for you in his office."

Her smile faded and dread took the place of her mild amusement. Did he need her to bind someone else? Or was he going to force her to join with Joran in the *Bryllup* ceremony?

"Thanks for letting me know." Kolfinna gave him what she hoped was a sincere smile.

Ivar watched her carefully and his gaze shifted to her white hair. A curious look passed over his face, but if he was suspicious, he didn't say it. "Sure thing."

NO JORAN WAITING ON THE COUCH WITH A BOOK IN Sijur's office. No emaciated woman ready to be unwillingly bound to Sijur. No one but Sijur behind his desk with a mountain of papers covering every inch of the table. He motioned for her to take a seat when she entered.

"How are you feeling?" Sijur pointed to her injured shoulder. "Not too sore, I hope?"

"I'm fine." Kolfinna sank into the velvet cushioned seat across from his office desk. Her shoulder and chest wound had mostly healed; they were still a bit sore and the scab on her chest was still present, but when she had picked on the itchy skin earlier this morning, she had noticed the pink scar beneath it.

She tried to keep herself from glancing at the spot where Birgitta had died on the floor. In the silence, she could still hear Aksel, Birgitta's son, screaming for his mom.

Sijur folded his hands atop a crinkled piece of paper. "I do apologize for the words I spoke during my speech. You know I didn't mean it entirely, yes? I had to say some things to raise the morale, give everyone something to focus on, and to gather everyone toward a singular threat."

That threat being the fae race.

Kolfinna drummed her fingers on her thighs. "So you don't care if you throw us in the lions' den, huh?"

"Come on, Kolfinna, don't be so cruel." He leaned back in his seat, his white teeth gleaming. "During war, it's necessary to rally everyone together. The fae *did* attack us last night."

"But not all—"

"Yes, yes. Not all fae are bad." He waved a dismissive hand. "When this mess is over, trust me when I say that I will be guaranteeing that you and your people will be safe. Those who mean no harm will always be safe under me."

Like Olia? Like Birgitta? Like all those women in his journal he had experimented on? Like all those children who he was still experimenting on?

Kolfinna's fingers dug into her knees to keep herself from reaching over the table and slapping him across the face. "What did you need from me, sir?"

"Hilda sent me a letter." He plucked a paper from his desk

and held it up for her to see the black stamp at the end of the letter.

Kolfinna's breath caught in her throat.

Hilda, who had tortured her in the cabin.

Hilda, who had ordered her to die.

And Hilda, who had likely seen the black-stained corpses of her people.

"She wants me to hand you over to her at the southern border. That's where she's stationed, by the way. She says that she believes you are a threat, and as the leader of the Hunter's Association, she demands I hand you over. You are"—he flipped the paper over so he could read it—"in her exact words, 'a traitorous creature who knows more than she's letting on' and who 'must be interrogated or eliminated.'"

She must've realized Kolfinna was part-elf, or part-*something*. "And?" Kolfinna asked quietly. "What are you going to do?"

"I'm not handing over one of my best soldiers." Sijur winked at her and tossed the letter back in the pile. "Quite frankly, I think Hilda is delusional and spiteful. She hates that you're anything more than a groveling, quivering mess. She wishes all fae died, and I'm sure this unexpected war with the fae is only bolstering her ideals." He shrugged. "The fae have so much history, culture, power—it would be a waste to eradicate all that. I will not be handing you over to her. Ever."

Maybe if he wasn't a self-serving monster, she would've believed he was doing this because he cared about her.

She wasn't delusional like Joran, who believed in this safety Sijur offered. It was only so long as she was useful that Sijur would keep her around.

Sijur smoothed down his oil-slicked hair. "Which is why I called you here. I understand that going to the south to fight these fae and elves will put you in potential danger against Hilda and her little band of hunters. They won't attack you brazenly like they did in the capital, but being there will put you at an increased risk of an attack. Not to mention it's war." He laced his fingers together and leaned forward. "I'm giving you the option to stay behind here. The majority of my troops will leave, but I still need people to man this border. You can stay here and avoid Hilda, or you can join the battle. It's up to you. Whatever you're most comfortable with."

Kolfinna hated Hilda. She wanted nothing to do with that woman, and even the thought of seeing her again made her stomach twist into a ball of fear. She still remembered the feel of the whips, the knives, and the sharp objects she had used to pinch, cut, and slice through Kolfinna's flesh.

Her skin rose with goose bumps and her lungs felt vacant of all air.

She wouldn't have to deal with Sijur and the rune mark if she stayed behind.

But that also meant leaving everyone as they went to battle—Inkeri, Ivar, Herja, Gunnar, Eluf, and most of all, Blár. She was also very sure that staying behind would mean just waiting for the half-elf commander's army to return for her.

As much as Kolfinna wanted to fall back on old habits and run away, she couldn't. She didn't want to leave Blár or anyone else. She didn't want to face the half-elf's people by herself. She didn't want to sit back and do nothing to erase the mark binding her to Sijur.

"I'll go," she whispered.

Sijur smiled, a hint of surprise on his face. "Are you sure?"

She nodded, her resolve growing sharper and stronger. She met his gaze levelly. "I'll go to war with you."

25

THEY SET OUT TO THE SOUTHERN BORDER IN THE morning, just like Sijur had said they would. Kolfinna's nerves were shot through the roof, but she moved forward, one step at a time, refusing to look at the looming threats all around her—Hilda, the hunters, Rakel, the half-elf, Ragnarök, Sijur, and the list went on and on.

Putting on the heavy chainmail and metal armor with Rosain's lion and rose insignia reinforced that she was going to *war*.

Her only solace was that she was traveling with Blár, Inkeri, Ivar, and the rest of their group. She didn't want to be alone with the other members of the army, who very clearly didn't want her there.

By the end of the fourth day when the party set up camp, Kolfinna was too worn out from riding her horse that she didn't even think about anything but sleep. She yanked her metal helmet off her head and placed it by her feet like the others were doing.

The flames of the campfire rose, fell, and swayed in tune with the blustering wind. Kolfinna tightened her cloak over her body, the fur lining brushing against her cheeks and tickling her nose. Night canopied their camp. They would be on their way again tomorrow and according to Eluf, they would reach Fort Aggersborg in a day—maybe two if they took any more breaks.

Little pockets of soldiers were scattered in the open fields of dead grass and barren trees. Ivar sat across from the fire, taking an occasional swig from his canister. There was a slightly reddish hue across his cheeks and nose, which could only mean he was drinking. Herja was chatting with Gunnar while he sharpened his dagger against another dagger. Blár and Eluf stared silently at the fire, and Inkeri was stitching up a tear on one of her shirts.

Kolfinna carefully braided her hair, unbraided it, and braided it again. It was a nice distraction for what was to come. She had never been on a true battlefield before, so she could only imagine how chaotic it would be.

"Ivar, did you—" Inkeri's words faltered on her lips. Her nose crinkled. "Wait, are you *drinking*?"

Ivar smirked and brought the rim of the canister to his lips. "And if I am?"

"Ivar, we're going to go into battle soon! How can you just ... *drink*?"

"Easy." He raised the canister, gave it a shake, and then took a swig. "Like this."

"You're such a moron," she hissed. "So irresponsible—"

"Oh, shut up," he said with a scowl. "You're not my mother."

Kolfinna had to agree with Inkeri on this one. "Wouldn't it be bad if we get attacked while you're drunk?"

"I'm not drinking much." He lowered his drink, his blue-green eyes appearing orange in the firelight. "I just need enough to calm my nerves."

So even he got nervous during battle. It was reassuring.

Inkeri and Ivar both continued to bicker and Kolfinna watched with mild curiosity. Now that she knew they both liked each other—maybe even *loved* each other—it was strange seeing their interactions. Especially since neither of them seemed to know about the other's feelings, or they simply didn't want to acknowledge them.

Kolfinna picked up a rock by her feet and twisted it in her hand distractedly. Carefully, she began chipping away at it with her magic. Piece by piece, it slowly transformed from a clunky, faceted rock to a very crude flower. The petals were deformed and shaped strangely, and the stem was a tad too thin, but it was better than when she had first tried to make anything with her stone magic.

"What's that supposed to be?" She hadn't noticed that Blár was watching.

"A flower." She held out the rock for him. "Here."

"A flower?" He took the carved rock and turned it over in his hands. "Not to be an asshole, but this is a shitty flower."

Kolfinna frowned, her face flushing with embarrassment. She didn't think it looked *that* bad. "I'm practicing my mana manipulation."

"Huh. It's a good thing you're a soldier and not an artist." Blár raised the rock toward the fire, twisting it around until more light caught against the rough edges. "Eluf, look at this—"

"Okay, that's enough." Kolfinna lurched forward to snatch it from his hand, but he only raised it higher so she couldn't. She jumped to her feet at the same time he did, but whereas he was grinning in amusement, her face was pinched together sourly. "Give it back. I didn't think you'd be so mean about—"

"Hey, I said I wasn't *trying* to be an asshole—"

"But you *are*." She held her hand out. "Give it back now."

"You gave me this shitty flower, so it's mine." He lifted one shoulder, and the wind decided at that moment to brush against his hair gently, tousling it against the smirk on his wickedly beautiful face.

Kolfinna didn't let that moment distract her for too long. "I let you *see* it, not *keep* it."

Blár threw his head back and laughed. When he looked down at her, his teeth gleamed white against moonlight. There was a softness in his eyes that melted at something in her chest. "Here's a little thing about me, sweet-cheeks. If something is mine, then it's mine. You'll have to fight me tooth and nail if you want to get this ugly-ass rock from me."

She could see what he was doing: calming her nerves.

It was working, except she wasn't exactly calm. She was a tad annoyed. But maybe that worked too.

"Call it ugly *one more time*," she warned. Her mana pulsed beneath her feet to the roots buried in the earth.

"This deformed, lumpy, hideous thing is offensive to flowers —" he began and Gunnar snorted in the background.

Kolfinna flicked her wrist. One of the roots of a dormant tree slithered out and wrapped around Blár's ankle. It caught him off guard and yanked him to the ground. The flower skittered a few feet away from him as he fell backward. He blinked up at the sky, while Kolfinna burst into laughter.

"That's *dirty*." He rubbed the back of his head with a glare. "I thought you couldn't manipulate plants during the winter?"

"I learned how to do it recently." She shrugged. Ever since she had miraculously used the tree branches and roots during the fight with Rakel, it was like something had clicked into place and she was able to manipulate dormant nature now. It didn't come as easily to her as it did in the summer, spring, or autumn, but she was able to use it well enough.

Eluf chuckled softly from his place near the fire. His dark eyes looked more intense with the fire burning in front of him and he nodded at Kolfinna. "That could be useful. Anytime Blár annoys us, we should have you trip him."

Gunnar snickered. "Yeah, that'd be funny to see."

Blár scowled at the two brothers and continued to dust off his pants. "I wouldn't normally fall for that."

"Pun intended?" Herja chirped in.

Blár paused. "Let's say it was intended."

Kolfinna plopped back down on the ground. Everyone was either laughing or chatting with one another. Her heart clenched together tightly at the sight of them. She didn't want any of them to lose their lives. When she was in the Eventyrslot ruins, the majority of the party had died, and while she had felt guilty and sad over that, it was nothing compared to the thought of losing the people here. She had somehow grown close to them, despite her aversion to friendship.

Was that what they were now? Friends?

The mere thought made her throat close up.

Her gaze roamed over to the other soldiers talking to one another, eating dried meat and cheese, being silent in preparation, or just milling about. Some of them would likely die on the battlefield too. The half-elf commander and his men were probably strong. If Blár had trouble with Rakel … she didn't even want to think about how the others would fare against an equal force.

Joran stood out among the other soldiers. He sat alone by a small fire. The wind tousled his gold hair, and his bronze skin looked darker in the night. What if they ran into an emergency during battle and Sijur ordered her to marry Joran through the *Bryllup* ceremony? Another knot of anxiety tied itself in her stomach.

She didn't want to bind herself *forever* to Joran.

She thought back to the unnamed fae soldier's journal she had read months ago and how he had lamented about being forced to marry someone he didn't want to but had done it anyway because of the war.

Kolfinna didn't want to share his fate.

"You're doing that thing again." Blár flicked her forehead lightly with his forefinger. He pulled his hand away right before she could swat at him. "When you're stressed, you do this thing where your eyebrows pull together and you get a little wrinkle between your brows. Like you're angry, except you're not, you're just anxious. Oh, and your mouth pouts a bit too. Like a little frown." His voice was barely a whisper, as if he didn't want the others to hear.

Her face warmed at his observations. "I don't do that."

"You do."

"No—"

"You're always making that angry face." He grinned, like he found it amusing, and perhaps he did. But Kolfinna only felt slightly mortified. Did she really make a face like that?

She could feel even more heat creeping up her cheeks. No one had told her that before, so surely it couldn't be true?

"You've been stressed out more than usual, haven't you?" Blár's smile faded and he turned to look up at the starless sky. His inky hair blended in with it, and she had the urge to run her fingers through his hair at least once tonight.

Kolfinna picked at her nails distractedly. It was true that she was stressed, but that was her whole existence. Before the Eventyrslot ruins, it was all about survival, hiding, escaping. Then during the Royal Guards, when she finally thought she could relax, it was the same spiel about survival, except she also had to please everyone to keep her position. And now? Now it was worse than ever. She was a slave to Sijur's will, she was potentially a target for the military if they found out about her abilities, and she was what Ragnarök was looking for. To say she was stressed was an understatement.

Kolfinna sighed and wrapped her arms around her legs loosely. "You asked me earlier why my hair turned white, right? Well, I'm sure it's because of stress."

It was a stupid joke, definitely not funny enough to laugh about other than a chuckle, but Blár laughed nonetheless. He leaned forward, his voice quiet. "Ah, is that how it works?"

"I'm sure it is." She tucked her chin on her knees. "I think so long as I'm in the military, I'll remain stressed and anxious."

Blár stared at her wrist and a dark look passed over his expression. "I told you involving yourself with the military was bad news."

She hugged her knees to her chest and wanted to lean against him but resisted the urge. From the corner of her vision, she could tell Joran was watching them intently from where he was seated. "I didn't have a choice."

Blár cursed softly and stared off at the sky, a conflicted expression passing over him. The chill that passed between them could've been from him, but she wasn't sure. Not until he spoke. "It's partially my fault," he whispered, the coldness spreading further. "I should've ... done more."

"This isn't your fault, Blár."

"I could've gotten you out of this mess." He stared at her levelly and she wanted nothing more than to touch the sides of his face and reassure him that it wasn't his fault. That her being a fae meant that she would always face trouble like this. "Do you remember how I abruptly left before your trial?"

"How could I forget?" She snorted and stared down at her feet. The betrayal she had felt still stung, but she didn't want to linger on that feeling.

"Sijur made a bargain with me." Blár's soft mouth curled into a scowl and another wave of winter emitted from him. "If I rejoined his unit for a few months and I did a mission for him up north, he'd let you off the hook from the Royal Guards and the whole trial. He sent me off before your trial on a random mission. Now I realize why. He tricked me." His hands curled into fists, and ice cracked with the motion as little flecks of broken ice fell to the ground. He unflexed his hands and shook off the remnants of his power. "You were supposed to be free from all of this."

She recalled the expression on his face when he had seen her at the fort. *What are you doing here?*

"You ... made a deal with Sijur?" Her mind tried to wrap around that, but she failed. Blár had wanted to help her, and yet Sijur had done what he was great at doing—manipulating people into doing what he wanted. Her fury surged. "He tricked you so that—"

So that both she and Blár would join him.

Sijur's ultimate plan was to have Kolfinna, she realized. If Blár had remained in the capital, maybe he would've figured out a way to save her. Maybe someone else would've helped her. But he needed Blár out of the picture, and he needed him to think he had done his job in saving Kolfinna. All so Sijur could make her desperate enough to bargain with him—fifteen years as his slave.

"Why didn't you tell me?" Her words were almost lost as a blustering wind blew over them.

"Because—" He raked a hand through his hair and exhaled loudly, almost exasperatedly. "Because I felt embarrassed that he was able to trick me and you were here too, when you should've been in the capital wearing that stupid red-and-white uniform." He waved at the camp around them—at the soldiers clustered together, at the tents erected in the fields. "You definitely weren't supposed to be here, with all these people, shoveling your way through monster shit and Sijur's bullshit."

She shivered, but she wasn't sure it was from the cold. "And if Sijur hadn't offered you the deal, what would you have done?" Sijur must've realized there was something Blár could do to save her if he was willing to send him away from the capital—and away from her.

Blár pursed his lips together. "I did have a last resort plan."

She waited for him to continue. He picked at something under his nail and she couldn't read his expression.

"I ..." He sighed and gave her a hesitant smile. "I would've married you."

Out of everything she expected to hear, that wasn't it. Heat spread over her face instantaneously, and for a moment, everyone else around them seemed to disappear. "What?"

"Being a black rank offers many privileges that other people don't have. One of them is that our family is protected. If I had married you, the Royal Guards wouldn't be able to touch you." He said the words quickly, as if he was embarrassed to be telling her this, and yet something within her felt all too hot hearing those words.

Kolfinna cleared her throat and dragged a finger through the dirt distractedly. Her blazing cheeks felt even hotter against the cool air, and she suddenly found it hard to breathe. A bubble of a laugh almost broke through as she murmured, "That sounds wholly unfair."

Blár looked up quickly. "What part? Marrying me?"

"No, not that." She smiled, focused on one lock of his hair, dark beside his eyes. She averted her gaze to poke at the dirt again. "The fact that black ranks get a pass like that—it's unfair."

"It's useful."

She laughed softly to hide the warmth spreading over her chest. He would've married her to protect her; that was all there was to it, but it still made her feel all warm and fuzzy inside. *Blár Vilulf* would've married her to save her. Just thinking it was absurd.

What would it be like to be married to him? She wanted to imagine a life with him, but it was hapless to do that in the middle of a war.

"We'll be reaching Fort Aggersborg soon." Blár's words dispelled her dreamy thoughts. He gave her a telling look. "Are you ready for that?"

She knew what he meant without him having to spell it out for her. Hilda would be at Fort Aggersborg, and then Kolfinna would be forced to confront the woman who had tortured her and tried to kill her. It wasn't beyond the realm of reason that she would try it again or would try to pin another crime on her. And if Hilda was there, that also meant a wing of the Hunter's Association would be there too.

When Kolfinna had agreed to come here with Sijur, she always knew there was a high possibility that she would see Hilda again, but now that the time was drawing closer, her chest grew tight with apprehension.

"I'll be fine," she managed to say. "If Hilda tries anything ..."

Kolfinna's mouth dried up. If Hilda tried something, Kolfinna would be helpless to do anything. She would have to rely on Blár or Sijur to bring her out of the situation—which was infuriating in itself, having to rely on others.

"She won't." Blár pushed an errant strand of her white hair

behind her ear, and the small motion sent a blaze of heat where his finger dragged over her skin.

She blinked through her emotions and cleared her throat. "You seem to have confidence in her."

"No, I always have confidence in myself, not others." His smile vanished, replaced by a grim look—an expression she had seen countless time before he went into battle. "I'll protect you."

"Sure." Kolfinna didn't meet his gaze. She was unfamiliar to these feelings scorching inside her, and all the more unfamiliar with the protectiveness he was offering. "Thanks."

"You don't sound happy about it."

"I don't like the idea of seeing her again, no." She wrapped her hands tighter around herself and stared into the roaring flames. "I don't really know what will happen once we get there, so it makes me nervous to think that she might try something, but at the same time ... I'm also nervous about the elves and the fae attacking." She tightened the cloak over her body. "But I'm a soldier now, so I have to fight."

Blár watched her carefully. "I'd rather you stayed back, you know."

"Why?"

"So that you would be safe."

She was never really safe wherever she went, but she didn't tell him that. From the corner of her eye, she noticed Ivar stand up from his spot across the fire. He staggered on his feet and laughed at something Gunnar said before ambling over to Kolfinna and Blár.

"Sorry to interrupt," Ivar said with a mischievous grin that didn't look apologetic at all. His words were slightly slurred, and his face appeared ruddier against the orange campfire. "I've got something to ask you, Kolfinna."

She blinked up at him. "What is it?"

"Can we talk alone?" He jerked a thumb to an emptier part of the field.

Blár arched an eyebrow. "What do you have to talk to her about?"

"That's between me and her, Nosy-Prick."

Blár scowled. "You—"

"All right." Kolfinna rose to her feet before the two of them could exchange insults with one another. It was all in jest, she was sure, but she didn't want to rile up either, especially when they were on the cusp of battle.

Ivar and her walked away from their party and she could feel Blár's eyes on her the whole time. Ivar's cheerful, careless mask fell away the farther they went. It wasn't until they were well out of earshot from the party that he spoke.

"Something's been bothering me for a while now." He turned to face her. They had stopped near a tiny stream of water in the middle of the field, away from most of the soldiers. Suddenly, he didn't appear too drunk, and his words were steady. "Back in the caves during the first mission you had with us, you fought that green-skin and were completely covered in that black ink. You chalked it up to fae magic, and I kinda bought it because I didn't know what else to think, but now ..." He stared at her levelly, his blue-green gaze conveying his grimness. "Now I'm thinking you have something to do with those elves. They've got the same type of power as you."

All the color drained from her face in seconds. Whatever light-hearted mood she had melted away and her feet felt stuck in the ground, the stars wheeling over her slowly.

"Are you connected to them?" Ivar asked, his voice tight. "Are you a spy?"

"No!" Kolfinna blurted out, wide-eyed. "I'm not a ... a *spy*."

He wouldn't believe her—a part of her realized. It was the same thing with the Royal Guards. Nobody really believed her. He would tell Sijur or Hilda or somebody higher ranked and then she'd be put on trial again, but this time nobody would be able to save her. Or maybe because they were in a time of war, she'd be executed without a trial.

She could already see it happening—the soldiers storming around her, Sijur's disappointed look at her wasted potential, and Blár's fury at being unable to help her. She suddenly felt dizzy, the back of her head feeling like it weighed more than the stars dancing at the corner of her vision. She wanted to lean forward and puke as nausea rolled over her.

Ivar raked a hand through his chestnut waves and exhaled loudly. His gaze flicked over to their party, to where Inkeri was giggling at something Herja was saying to her. "So you're not one of them, right?"

"W-What?"

He turned to her sharply. "You're not one of those soldiers, right? The elves and the fae soldiers."

"I'm not a part of Ragnarök."

"Are you going to be a danger to any of us?"

"No!" She spoke so loudly she caught Blár half turn away from the fire.

Ivar nodded. "What about your powers?"

"I can't really explain it," she said quickly, her heart hammering so loud she could feel the rush in her ears. "I seem to be blood-related to something elf-like, but I'm not sure. I really don't know anything about my parentage, if I'm being honest. They died when I was too young, and all of this is confusing for me too—"

"All right." Ivar sighed loudly and placed a hand on her shoulder. "I believe you."

Had she heard him right?

She stared up at him. "You believe me?"

"I do." Ivar removed his hand from her. "But I think you should explain to the rest of the party eventually. You can trust us, you know?"

Although Kolfinna wanted to trust him and the others, she couldn't. Because it wasn't just a matter of trust. These powers that she had, and what they were linked to, were sinister enough for anyone to turn on her.

"Anyway," Ivar said when she was quiet for too long. "We should head back."

"O-Okay."

"No need to look so spooked. I won't tell anyone." He patted her shoulder once more and gave her a grin. "You're one of us now, fae girl."

2 6

As they approached Aggersborg, the southern fort, Kolfinna's ears perked to the sound of lightning cracking in the air. She tilted her head to the side, her ears picking up on more sounds: the splitting of wind, the violent swish of water, the splintering of ice, and the roaring of fire. All of it distinct enough for her to pick it out.

For a second, her breath caught in her throat as she tried to listen more intently. Then she heard even more noise: grunts, screams, from the distance.

The realization hit her a second later: a battle.

And they were headed straight toward it.

How much longer until they were in the thick of it?

"Eluf!" She spurred her horse forward, breaking formation. Inkeri called out to her, but Kolfinna was already gone. She galloped to the front of their small formation, where Eluf twisted around in his seat with a confused look.

"What is it?" he asked when she reached him.

"I need to get a message to Sijur," she said quickly, gaze flicking up to the sets of soldiers beyond their group. "I can hear a battle happening in the distance and I'm pretty sure we're walking straight into it."

Eluf's expression fell and he nodded. His horse shot forward before she could give an excuse as to why she was able to hear so well.

"Kolfinna!" Gunnar pulled up beside her on his horse. His gaze was set to where Eluf had ridden on ahead. "What's happening?"

"A battle." Adrenaline rushed through her veins and she breathed out shakily. "Where's Blár?"

"Up front, where he's needed." He smiled reassuringly upon seeing her expression. "He'll be fine. Don't worry about him."

She could only nod. The reins slipped from her trembling hands and she fumbled with the leather material for a few seconds, her heart hammering in her chest. This would be her first battle in a war. Would she find the half-elf there? What about Hilda?

"You'll be—" Gunnar closed his mouth. He probably wanted to say something encouraging, but war was always chaotic and unexpected. There was no telling if she would truly be okay. So instead, he said, "Believe in your powers. Trust in that."

In minutes, orders rang out that they would be joining in battle soon. Kolfinna's palms dampened and her ribcage felt like it would constrict itself.

It wasn't until ten minutes later that they entered the battle-field, with Fort Aggersborg in the distance.

Kolfinna could make out flying, winged figures in the sky, could see the devastation of the fields in front of the looming fort. Lightning cracked in the sky, followed by the smell of burning material, but the fae were faster and were evading it easily. Bolts of white light and thick, inky shadows waned in and out of the battlefield.

But one of the most confusing things she could make out were giant, stony, earthen creatures marching forward, swiping enormous staffs on the ground and decimating soldiers with each swing. On top of the stone creatures sat winged fae clad in black armor.

A shiver ran down her spine and if she didn't know any better, it almost felt like she had stepped into a nightmare. She had never thought to use stone magic in such a way. To make it a vehicle for destruction.

She could hear the sharp inhales from the people beside her. It was a terrifying sight to see—these horrendous giants. And even from the distance, she could make out the bloodied corpses littered on the ground by their feet.

"Onward!" Sijur shouted from somewhere ahead, and a hundred other battle cries joined him.

Kolfinna's horse raced forward. She unsheathed her sword swiftly, her horse's hooves clopping on the ground and joining the unison of rushing horses and shouting soldiers.

In minutes, she was in the thick of battle. The first warrior she met was an elf man with blazing red eyes and a mane of white hair. Her sword cut into his shoulder, and his blood-colored eyes turned to her. He didn't even flinch, even as his blood danced over her blade, even as she yanked it back with a spray of blood.

And why should he? She could see the other wounds on his body from the battle were already healing themselves. It wasn't enough to take him down. No—she would likely have to pierce his heart or behead him.

A blast of white light shot from his hand and obliterated her horse's head in seconds. Kolfinna's world spun as she was flung off her horse. She raised her arms to lessen the damage of the fall, but she still crashed onto the ground violently. She rolled and rolled and collided with a group of soldiers. She didn't even know whose side they were on until she met the purple-colored eyes of a soldier through his black helmet.

His sword came down to meet her.

Kolfinna raised her own hand in time. A dozen deeply nested roots sprang from beneath her and struck the soldier in the chest with their sharpened tips. He faltered backward, his hands going to the dents in his armor.

She was already moving to the next soldier. Her vines

whipped around her protectively. The other fae lurched back in surprise and she heard a few shouts and grunts when they were slapped across the face, or when the roots tore through their skin.

Kolfinna had improved her sword skills, but this was where she truly shined—when using her nature abilities.

Strike after strike, she continued to hit the elf and fae soldiers alike.

Streaks of fire and lightning sparked in her peripheral vision.

Waves of chilly air pervaded the battle, signaling to her that Blár was fighting. It calmed her nerves to know that he was out there, in this heavy battle. That he was well and alive, judging by the coldness of his powers. No matter how desperate the situation looked, so long as he was there, they stood a chance.

Kolfinna fell into a steady rhythm of battle; strike, strike, dodge. She barreled through soldier after soldier. Even as swords cut her or she was knocked down to her feet, she jumped back up and continued her assault. Her small scrapes healed almost immediately.

The elves were trickier to fight—they healed just like her. But she wasn't trying to kill everyone she met. She was just trying to survive. Trying to make it past another soldier and then another.

Every time she faced a male elf, her mind stuttered at a singular thought: was this the half-elf commander?

But every time, the elf male wasn't as terrifying or overpoweringly strong like the nightmarish man she had read about. *Not this one*, she kept telling herself.

And she truly hoped she didn't see him at all.

"Kolfinna!" A flare of blue fire caught Kolfinna's attention and Herja yanked her hand out of the chest cavity of a dead, burning fae warrior. Her bright blue eyes landed on Kolfinna, and the relief there was immense.

Strange. Herja was never *this* happy to see her.

"What is it?" Kolfinna shouted as she sent an elf soldier staggering back with a torrent of gnarled vines that tore at his helmet.

"There are sections of the battlefield that are marked with

runes! The soldiers in those areas can't use magic. We need you to break them!" Her words came out in a single breath as she shot balls of fire from her palms. "I can lead the way!"

Kolfinna whipped her sword out of a soldier's leg and whirled around. "Let's go!"

Herja wove through the skirmish, her fire creating a path. A winged warrior swept down low, sword aimed at Herja, but Kolfinna chucked a stone at his face in seconds. He plummeted down, and a wave of Herja's hand sent a blaze of violet fire to consume his body. His screams joined the others around him.

"Hilda Helgadottir is injured and unable to fight!" Herja said above the cries of battle. She ducked from a stray arrow. "The only black rank we have left is Blár!"

Even though that should've relieved her—that Hilda was probably taken away to a physician tent—it filled her with trepidation. As much as she hated the woman, she was a powerful black rank. Judging by the battlefield, they needed all the help they could get.

They fended off soldiers as they wove through the battlefield. In Kolfinna's peripheral, the giant stone creatures were still causing damage. She counted five of them. It had likely taken *a lot* of mana to make that many stones move like that.

"Are you okay?" Herja shouted at her. "You're bleeding heavily!"

"I'm fine!" Kolfinna replied. It was her blood, but most of her injuries had already healed. And she barely felt the ones that didn't. She had too much adrenaline rushing through her veins to care about minor cuts and bruises.

The battlefield slowly morphed into something different the more they continued their way. Instead of the booms and blasts of magic, the clanging of steel against steel filled the spaces between sweaty, bloodied bodies as they fought. The flashes of magic weren't apparent here, and instead, all the humans fought with weapons.

This must've been the area where the rune magic was keeping them from using their abilities.

Kolfinna instantly searched the ground for glowing runes. Blood splatters colored the yellowed, crunchy grass. The twisted, trampled corpses on the ground further hid whatever runes could've been etched on the ground. Kolfinna's stomach twisted. She tried not to focus on the faces. Tried not to linger on what expression they wore right before death.

As she tried to move a dead soldier's arm to see what was underneath, someone tackled her and her vision blurred. She slammed onto the ground at the same time that her roots wildly attacked the man. The man screamed as the sharp ends pierced his flesh through the gaps of his armor. He yanked his sword back, and Kolfinna blinked back at the red blood drenched on the gleaming blade. He wrangled with her roots, but she pushed him back farther, away from her.

She placed a hand on her abdomen and when she pulled it back, sticky, hot blood slipped from between her fingers.

"Kolfinna!" Herja wrestled with an elf warrior, shadows and light pouring out from his body in rapid succession, battling with Herja's bluish-violet flames.

Kolfinna lifted a bloodied hand and a wave of roots and vines captured the elf's wrists and yanked him backward. It gave Herja enough time to touch his throat and send a ripple of fire down his body.

Turning away from the gruesome scene, Kolfinna pulled herself to her feet. Her vision swayed for a moment, but she could already feel her mana draining away from her as it healed the wound slowly. She blinked rapidly to clear her vision.

Fae flew overhead, knocking back arrows and shooting them at unsuspecting humans. Air elementals fought airborne battles, elves fought with shadows and lights emitting from their hands, and human soldiers tried holding them back.

But it was clear that the humans had a disadvantage. These warriors were too efficient and knew how to use their magic effortlessly. Meanwhile, the human soldiers didn't even seem to know how to fight against the different types of magic in the battle.

Rune magic. Shadow magic. Light magic. Winged fae. Stone magic.

It was all too foreign. Too daunting.

Kolfinna had to rip her gaze away from the fights and focus on what she could do—find the runes.

"Are you okay?!" Herja sent another barrage of attacks at a nearby fae soldier. Her bright hair whipped around her sweaty, blood-streaked face like waves of fire.

"It was just a scratch!" Kolfinna lied as she scanned the ground for any hints of gold runes.

"It looked like—" Herja couldn't continue holding a conversation because she was on another soldier immediately, bursts of fire combusting from her hands.

After searching for a few minutes and dodging attacks from fae and elves, Kolfinna was able to find the runes. Herja kept close to her, keeping the others at bay while Kolfinna dropped to her knees in front of the golden inscriptions.

No human can use their magic within this ring.

The runes stretched out and repeated themselves on the ground in what she suspected was a large circle, and everyone within that ring was unable to use them.

Herja must've been outside the ring, which explained why she was still able to use her magic. The others outside the ring might not have realized whether they were going in or out of it, whether they had access to it or not, and they were all fighting with their swords and weapons at this point. It was probably easier than realizing they weren't able to use their magic because they stepped inside the rune magicked area.

Kolfinna touched the runes and injected her own mana into it. She imagined a giant chain wrapping around the runes and squeezing until they snapped.

The runes crumbled to gold dust right before her eyes.

"Herja—" Kolfinna lifted her head at the same time an elf warrior swung his sword at her.

She barely constructed a stone wall when the sword sliced into her shoulder, just narrowly missing her neck. White hot pain exploded through her body. Without thinking, she thrust a stone at the man's chest and hurtled him backward. He didn't have time to dodge when the sharpened tip of her tree root jabbed straight into his throat. Blood pooled over the wound, dribbling down the brown root.

She could hardly breathe for a few seconds. Her hands shook as her fingers skimmed over the broken skin and the tears in her chainmail.

A shiver ran down her spine.

She had been *this* close to losing her head.

Kolfinna staggered to her feet. All around her, people started using magic. Clashes of fire and water and stone erupted everywhere.

At the same time, coldness brewed in the distance. Slowly, it spread throughout the battlefield. Kolfinna barely had time to lurch back as ice shot through the ground, spreading farther and farther in waves. The earthen creatures suddenly stopped moving, their legs encapsulated in ice.

Shrieks filled the air one by one.

Blár.

Had he been trapped in the rune ring, unable to use his magic?

It seemed that way because the tide of the battle swiftly changed.

Kolfinna fought through the thicket of soldiers, her vines ripping against black, scaly armor. She didn't think, she just moved toward the core of the wintry chill. If the other fae and elves realized what was happening, they might try to lock Blár in a magicless ring and kill him. She needed to be by his side. Not only for this battle to succeed, but because she didn't want to imagine him *gone.*

A fae soldier barreled into her and she narrowly missed losing an arm from his sharp blade. She shoved a wall of vines between them and pushed him into the fiery blade of a human soldier. The more she stumbled forward, the colder it became. She followed that intense wintry coldness, pushing through the ranks until she finally found Blár.

He fought so effortlessly. His body moved quickly, freezing everything that came close to him. Blood smeared one side of his face, but it only made him look all the more terrifying. Ice spears formed in his hand and he shot them out in quick sequences. More and more ice rose from the ground, peaking in seconds and spearing the flying fae by the dozens. He looked like a monster out there. A living, breathing, winter king.

Kolfinna kept an eye on him as she pushed back the enemies closest to her.

Half an hour must've passed by before a horn blared in the distance.

Suddenly, the fae and elves began fleeing.

Blár raised a hand and walls of ice began to form around the battlefield. Kolfinna watched in stunned amazement as twenty-foot ice walls were erected from the ground up. They spread faster, caging in the soldiers and stopping them from escaping. The fae flew up in the air, and Blár let them escape, but the wingless fae and the elves weren't as lucky.

Kolfinna turned back to Blár. His breaths were white with cold, but his eyes were alive and vibrant, wild from battle.

This was a black rank in action.

27

"Blár!" As Kolfinna rushed to Blár's side, her foot slipped across the ice and she almost fell face first onto the icy earth.

Blár's hand shot out quickly and caught her before she could fall. The cold, tundra-like expression on his face, hardened with battle and the grimness of war, melted at the sight of her. It was like a thin sheet of ice splintering away to reveal what lay beneath —pure relief. He pulled her closer to him until her face smacked against his chest. His cold breath tickled the nape of her neck.

"You're safe," he breathed, and despite the cold he exuded, warmth spread over her body. They were in the middle of a battle-field, with corpses around them, with ice and fire and charred bits of grass and stones surrounding them in chaos, death, and destruction. And yet he warmed her down to her toes.

She closed her eyes and fell into the embrace. She rubbed his trembling arms to bring some warmth into him and breathed through the foggy coldness that surrounded him. If he used up too much of his ice powers too quickly, he grew too cold. She had learned that a few weeks ago when he had erected a giant barrier between the Mistlands and the western border.

"I lost track of you." Blár gently pulled her back so he could peer down at her. His blue eyes appeared so much darker against the backdrop of war. The blood on his face had already dried to a dark maroon color. "Do you know how terrifying that is?"

Normally, she wouldn't worry about him in the midst of battle, where he was most in his element. Because he was Blár Vilulf, the strongest person she knew, the powerful black rank. But here, in this battle, where runes could snatch his magic away, a deep-seated fear nestled in her core.

Without magic, even Blár didn't stand a chance against a fae, or elf, or human.

Kolfinna tried wiping the dried blood off his cheek with her thumb. "I'm sorry. I didn't realize you were looking for me." She became all too aware that nearby soldiers were glancing over at them curiously. She cleared her throat and dropped her hand. "Um, well, maybe we should see if everyone else is okay? And, of course, we probably need to report to Sijur and see what we need to do next."

"Just give me a moment." Blár brought his forehead down until it was touching hers. His gaze pierced her straight through her soul. He closed his eyes, breathing in deeply. "I just ... need a minute."

Kolfinna blushed at the contact. "You're being unusually touchy."

His voice was muffled against her neck. "I'm drained. I don't know what one of them did, but they touched me and stole my mana. Remember how during the Eventyrslot ruins Revna stole a lot of Eyfura's mana and her ... life, I guess?"

Kolfinna stiffened and grabbed ahold of his face with both hands. "They did that to you?" She couldn't hide the alarm in her voice. It only made sense that these fae, who belonged to Queen Aesileif's army, would resort to such wicked tactics. The fae had the ability to draw and manipulate life—that was what nature manipulation was—but they also had a darker ability, the ability to drain mana and life force from a living being. "How much did they take?"

"Not much," he said with a frown. "But a few of them did that with every attack. Normally, I wouldn't ever let anyone get that close to me, especially not an enemy, but at some point, I wasn't able to use my magic. I don't know. Maybe a rune or something caused that?"

"There was a ring of runes in one area of the field." Kolfinna lowered her hands.

Blár grimaced. "I hate that they can do that. I'm guessing you broke them?"

She nodded.

Blár appraised her wounds with a furrowed brow and touched her shoulder lightly. "You look pretty beat up."

The wound near her neck had already closed up, but her abdomen was still sore and stiff with blood.

"I'm fine." She moved his hand away gently and glanced at the other soldiers. She had to make sure Inkeri, Herja, Eluf, and the rest of their group was okay and alive. Also, maybe there was something she could help with? She had healed Inkeri's snakebite a few weeks ago, so maybe her abilities were needed again? "Anyway, let's go check on everyone else. We might have won this battle, but I highly doubt this is the last of it."

"Agreed." Blár's mouth screwed shut and his expression turned grim once more. "I'm going to round up the rest of the enemies. You go get checked up, all right?"

"Don't boss me around," she said jokily, pulling away from him. "You need to get patched up too."

He chuckled and nodded to the left. "The physician tent is that way. I'll get checked out when I'm done. Meet me there, okay?"

KOLFINNA WOVE THROUGH THE CROWDS OF SOLDIERS for the fifth time that past hour. Now that the battle was over, the other soldiers were taking their comrades to the physician tents and tending to them, rounding up the enemies, dragging corpses to one side of the field, and taking account of the damage and seeing who was still alive. Kolfinna had been looking for Inkeri and Herja the whole time.

Her gaze landed on Ivar, who was hunched over a fallen soldier. He rested a hand on the soldier's face and gently closed the man's lifeless eyes. When Kolfinna approached, he looked up at her with a weary expression.

His face was spotted with blood, and there was an ugly gash across his cheek up to his ear, which was a bloody, mangled mess.

She gasped at the sight of it. "Ivar, your *ear*."

He cringed and rose to his feet. "I can still hear out of it."

"You should—"

"Get checked out? Maybe later." Ivar turned his head toward the field of soldiers, both dead and alive. He pursed his lips together. "So many are dead. We didn't stand a chance once we couldn't use our magic."

Kolfinna stared at the right side of the field, where the bodies of her comrades were being lined up as they were talking. It was hard not to notice the devastation the fae and the elves had wrought on them. Many of the soldiers had been crushed with stone magic, clobbered to bits by the earthen creatures, or killed with arrows from the sky. Not to mention the blasts of shadow and light the elves possessed.

"We're not equipped to fight fae," Kolfinna found herself saying. "I don't know how to stop the elf magic, and I'm sure most of everyone hasn't ever faced a full-fledged fae before."

Ivar nodded grimly. "Honestly, I think it would be smart to start training with you. We've faced fae before since we're at the southern border, but most of them weren't that great at using their magic. Not like these soldiers, at least. And most of everyone has never faced anything like it before. If it wasn't for Blár ..."

There was something that was still bothering her about the battle. The fae troops had been winning, and even though Blár's presence changed the tides of war, the retreat had been too quick. These soldiers didn't seem like the type to run at the first sign of danger. So why?

"Have you seen Inkeri or Herja?" Kolfinna asked.

Ivar bobbed his head slowly and pointed to one of the erected tents. "Inkeri is in the physician's tent helping the wounded."

Relief pooled in her chest. "I must've missed her when I went back there."

Truthfully, she had been avoiding the physician's tent since Hilda was supposedly in one of them, so she hadn't looked very hard in the first place.

"She's been going in and out and getting other soldiers in there." Ivar rubbed the side of his face that wasn't wounded, and suddenly appeared exhausted. He gestured to a cluster of soldiers to one side. "Herja went over there to talk to Haakon Lykke."

Kolfinna tried not to show her surprise. Haakon Lykke, the man Herja had slept with at some point. From what it seemed like, Herja had been torn on whether she wanted to see him or avoid him.

Ivar must've read her expression because he said, "Don't worry, it's not like he'll do anything to her. Pretty sure Herja can burn him off the face of this land if she wanted to. And besides, the man's clearly head over heels for her."

"Really?" Kolfinna tilted her head to the side. "She doesn't seem to reciprocate, though."

"Herja has commitment issues." He shrugged.

"Maybe I should check up on her to make sure she's okay."

"Sure, but if you plan on talking to him, that won't work."

"What do you mean?"

Ivar tapped his ears. "Haakon's deaf, so even if he notices you talking, he'll just ignore you."

That seemed like an important tidbit of information that would've been useful to know. But Kolfinna didn't plan on conversing with the man anyway; she just wanted to make sure Herja was okay and he wasn't bothering her, so she headed in the direction Ivar had pointed to.

Finding them didn't take too long. Herja stood out like a sore thumb with her blazing red hair, and the man beside her had his own type of presence that seemed to demand the attention of anyone nearby. Haakon Lykke was taller that Kolfinna had expected—taller than Herja, who was already pretty tall. Black locks of hair fell over his forehead and brushed his shoulders messily, and he had vibrant green eyes that were even more apparent with his thick lashes. With a full mouth, angular jaw, and expressive eyebrows, Haakon was a hell of a lot handsomer than Herja made him out to be.

Herja stood in front of him with her arms crossed over her armored chest. Her long, red locks swayed with the wind over her shoulders. She was talking to Haakon, who appeared expressionless, and kept glancing away from her, as if losing interest.

"—you at least try to *listen*?" Herja tapped his chest to get his attention and he turned back to her. She moved her hands quickly to form signs. "Well, I don't mean actually listen, but I'm trying to talk to you, you piece of—"

Again, Haakon turned away, his gaze roaming over the bodies and the fort.

Herja shook her head and dropped her hands. "You know what, forget this—"

Kolfinna approached them tentatively. "Herja?"

Herja turned to her, and Haakon followed that movement a second later, his vibrant-green eyes landing on Kolfinna. Relief washed over Herja's face. "You're alive!"

"So are you." Even though they had gotten off on the wrong foot, Kolfinna was surprised at how relieved she was to see the red-haired woman. It wasn't like they were buddy-buddies all of a sudden, but maybe in a few months they could be. "I'm assuming this is Haakon?"

Herja waved an angry hand in his direction, her expression sour. "It is."

Haakon stared at Kolfinna's half-white hair and then at her eyes. A flash of confusion flickered over his face, but it was quickly masked by indifference.

"Is everything okay?" Kolfinna asked, looking between Herja and the tall man.

"Yes." Herja scowled at Haakon and then snatched Kolfinna's hands. "How are you? You look bloodied up. Did you get a chance to see the physicians?"

"Err, yes," Kolfinna lied. She couldn't tell her that most of her wounds were partially healed and that going to the physician would only stir up suspicions. "And you?" Herja didn't appear too injured. There were splatters of blood on her pants and crusted on her armor, but she otherwise appeared healthy and unharmed. "Any broken bones? We lost track of each other during the battle, so I was worried about you."

Herja blinked in surprise before a grin stretched up her lips. "I'm not that easy to kill."

"And ..." Kolfinna noticed that Haakon was staring off in the distance again, so she took that moment to quickly add, "What's going on with you and him? And he can't ... hear us, can he?"

"Long story, but he's an asshole," Herja whispered. "But I'm okay, if that's what you mean. And to answer your question—no, he can't hear us, but he can read our lips, so you might want to be careful about that if you want to keep something from him. But seeing as he refuses to look at me, I don't think that'll be a problem." Annoyance leaked in her tone and she glanced at him again. "He's ignoring me, which is sort of what I wanted, but it pisses me off regardless. I'll be fine, though."

"Okay then." Kolfinna pointed at the physician's tent. "I think I'll be helping Inkeri with the wounded, so I'll catch you later, okay?"

Now that everyone she cared about was safe, she could relax

and think of what to do next. The half-elf commander wasn't in this battle, and now that she had seen first-hand how powerful his army was, it was about time she tried to come up with a strategy on how to fight them more effectively. Or *something* helpful.

28

"Kolfinna."

She had just been about to enter the physician's tent when Joran appeared from behind her. His dark gold hair was messy and stained with dirt and grime. He didn't even try smiling when she saw her. Kolfinna gave him a guarded look.

"What is it?" She glanced back at the flap of the tent and then at the soldiers outside the tent. Blár still wasn't here yet, which could only mean that he was helping the others or got caught up with something else.

"The lieutenant wants to see us."

A shiver rippled down her skin and her spine straightened. "Why?"

"Why do you think?" He waved at her to follow him.

Was this the moment he was going to force her to bind with Joran?

Her feet dragged and she looked over her shoulder for an escape route, for something to do. Would running now cause the rune mark to activate and thus hurt her since it was going against Sijur's will? Or did he have to be in front of her and issue a command orally for it to happen? She wasn't sure if it was worth testing it out.

When they reached a black tent, Joran pushed open the flap and gestured for Kolfinna to enter. She made her way through tentatively.

Sijur stood in the center of the tent in front of seven bound prisoners. Two of them were elves, with white hair and blood-red eyes, and the other five were fae with colorful eyes and wings. All of them had been stripped of their armor. The chains around their wrists and ankles glowed with runes.

Kolfinna's heart caught in her throat as the prisoners glanced over at her. She noticed that all of them had pointed ears.

"Kolfinna." Sijur clapped his hands together at her entrance.

A few of the prisoners flinched.

"As you can see, we have a few prisoners of war here." He spread a hand to the men and women, who were now staring at Kolfinna silently.

Kolfinna shifted on her feet. Their gazes bored into hers. Did they recognize her name?

"I'd like for you and Joran to bind them to me." He smiled pleasantly, as if he was asking for tea or a cookie. When his beady black eyes swiveled to Kolfinna, the corners of his mouth rose and a small chuckle escaped from him. "*Come on,* Kolfinna. You cannot act surprised every single time I call you to rune-mark someone." Another chuckle. "We've got a long time together, I'm afraid. It's about time you start realizing your role in my army and your responsibilities as a fae."

One of the prisoners, a man in his mid-forties with salt-and-pepper hair and blazing orange eyes, tipped his head back to laugh. His orange and white ombré wings, which were tied to his back with a rusted chain that went around his chest, vibrated with the motion.

Sijur's smile faded.

"What"—he stepped forward—"is so funny?"

"You three." The fae jerked his chin at Sijur and then at Kolfinna and Joran. He had a thick accent, similar to Rakel's. "Speak of rune-mark? You mean tether, I presume?"

"Tether?" Sijur glanced at Joran momentarily. "Is that what you call it?"

"Yes. Tether." The fae male turned to the other prisoners. "This man hopes to *tether* us."

The man burst into a fit of laughter once more, and the other prisoners joined in, though not as robustly as he did.

"A human *tethering* us?" The man's face became red from laughter. "Fools! All of them."

The prisoner next to him glared at Sijur. "Foolish being. You forget your place."

"Foolish, foolish indeed," the orange-eyed man said with another laugh. "To think a human would do such a thing!"

Sijur's face purpled. "You laugh now, but you *will* be bound to me."

That made the fae laugh even harder, his body shaking against the restraints.

Kolfinna exchanged bewildered looks with Joran.

"Kolfinna." Sijur snapped his fingers and pointed at the man. "Bind him. *Now.*"

When she didn't automatically respond, he turned to her sharply, his lips curled back. "*Kolfinna.*"

She crossed the distance between the prisoner and tentatively kneeled down beside him. He lifted his head to look at her, and something flashed over his eyes before all emotion other than cruel amusement shuttered out.

She didn't want to do this—to rune-mark, or tether, this man, but he was the enemy. It shouldn't have been a hard decision to make, and yet she faltered nonetheless.

Sijur cleared his throat and she placed a hand against the prisoner's calloused, chained one.

The man tensed beneath her touch. Her mana swirled within her, pushing against his skin. But before she could even think of what rune to write down, her mana began draining out of her, like someone was pulling a leash within her and violently yanking tendrils of her being. She gasped and yanked her hand back, stumbling over her legs.

"Kolfinna!" Joran dropped down beside her and touched her shoulder. "What happened? Are you okay?"

"Didn't your *father* teach you," the man said with a chuckle, "not to touch a fae?"

Kolfinna couldn't rip her gaze from the man. *Her father.* This man definitely knew who she was.

"Kolfinna!" Joran looked between the fae male and her, his eyes wide. "What did he do?"

"I'm fine," she snapped, brushing his hands away. "He just ... stole some of my mana. Surprised me, that's all."

She stood before him and tried again. This time she didn't touch him and kept her hand hovering over his. That was right— she didn't *need* to touch whatever she wanted to write runes on, so long as she was close enough for her mana to reach him.

Bind this fae to Sijur Bernsten's will.

Even as she was thinking it, she knew it was futile. There was no way the binding would work without this man's consent. That seemed to be the general consensus with these runes. The other party had to be a willing participant.

Like she anticipated, nothing happened.

"It didn't work," Kolfinna said to Sijur.

The man smirked. "Of course it didn't, little lady."

"The man needs to agree to it." Joran licked his lips. "They all do."

"We can make them agree to it." Sijur unsheathed his sword and pointed it at the orange-eyed fae. "Bind yourself to me."

The man spat on Sijur's feet. "*Never.*"

Sijur stabbed him right in the shoulder. So quickly that it wasn't until the hot specks of blood spotted Kolfinna's face that she registered it. The man didn't even gasp, didn't even *flinch.* The only indication that he was pained was from the tensing of his body.

Kolfinna stepped back, while Sijur stepped forward, a smile

lifting his lips as he dug the blade deeper. The pointed tip emerged from the man's back and grazed the arch of his wing. "Submit to me," Sijur said through clenched teeth, "or we will be at this for a long, *long* time."

The man narrowed his eyes to slits. "I will never submit to a human."

Sijur yanked the sword back and a stream of thick blood dripped from the blade, still connected to the man's gash before splotching onto the ground in puddles. Sijur twisted the blade in his hand and jabbed it into the man's thigh. Kolfinna gasped, while the man gritted his teeth together.

Sijur drew closer. "Submit."

"Never."

Again, Sijur withdrew his blade and stabbed the man again. This time on the other thigh. "Submit to me."

"We can do this all day, and my answer will remain the same—*never*."

The other fae and elves watched with tight expressions.

Sijur kept the sword imbedded in the man's thigh and held his hand out to Joran. "Your dagger, Joran."

Joran fumbled as he removed a dagger with its sheath from his waist. He handed it to Sijur, who yanked the gleaming silver blade from its sheath and tossed the scabbard away like it was garbage. He had his eyes on the man the entire time. Flipping the blade in his hand, he pointed it to the fae.

"We will do this all day and night," he whispered as he kneeled down until he was eye level with the prisoner. He placed the flat side of the dagger against the man's cheek. "I will flay you into ribbons—and I will enjoy it, every second of it."

Kolfinna stumbled back until she hit the wall of the tent when Sijur began carving into the man's cheek. Her stomach rolled and she desperately wished she were elsewhere. Blood pooled on the ground and her stomach continued to churn and churn. She tried looking away, but everywhere she looked, there was something haunting her—the fae faces of the other prisoners, the elves who looked nothing like her but at the same time, were more alike her than the humans.

The man squirmed on the ground as Sijur shoved him down, the dagger's edge slashing into his face violently. Kolfinna squeezed her eyes shut. She wasn't cut out for this kind of stuff. Battles against monsters? Not difficult—at least, not morally. Battles against fae, elves, and humans? Difficult, but she could manage. But this? Pure torture against a man who couldn't do anything to retaliate? It made her want to vomit.

"Lieutenant, don't you think that's enough?" Kolfinna choked out.

Sijur, who was huddled over the man's limp body, glanced over his shoulder at her. A spray of blood coated his face in specks and splotches. When he grinned, a shiver ran down her spine. "What, can't handle a little bit of bloodshed, Kolfinna? That won't do. No, that won't do *at all*."

He slowly rose to his feet. Red smears covered his hands and stained the cuffs of his uniform. She wished she hadn't spoken because he crossed the distance between them and held the dagger out to her, hilt side facing her.

Kolfinna couldn't move.

"Take it," Sijur said, eyes alight with wicked contentment. "Take it and cross that boundary you oh-so-desperately wish to ignore."

"Please." She tried to back away, but her legs were too leaden to move. The strong smell of iron pervaded through her hazy thoughts. "I can't—"

"You *can*." His sticky, warm hands found hers, and he pried her fingers open and nested the handle of the dagger in hers. "You are more than capable of being what you are, Kolfinna. We are all monsters, you and me and Joran, and everyone here in this base."

Kolfinna looked away from the crazed gleam in his eyes and searched the prisoners' hardened faces. None of them looked terrified, but she noticed the tensing of their shoulders in anticipation. She couldn't bear to look at the bloody, pulpy mess of the fae male Sijur had left.

Sijur pressed her fingers closed around the hilt. "You can do it."

"I'm not—" She swallowed down the bile clawing up her throat. Tears pricked her vision. "I'm not a monster."

"You are."

She wanted someone to save her, to take her away from this horrible, horrible place. But no one was coming for her. She would have to do this.

"Is that ... an order?"

Sijur's lips curved. "Do you want it to be? Would that make your conscience feel better? Knowing that you had *no choice* but to do it?"

It would.

He chuckled softly and placed a delicate hand on her cheek. She could feel the warm blood from his fingers streaking her face. "No, I will not order you to do it, but you will do it. Take this dagger and cut that man to pieces, Kolfinna. Slowly. First, his fingers, then his toes, and then ... Well, I'll let you decide which body part to take next. I recommend flaying the skin after that, but I'll let you choose your method of violence."

He pushed her forward and she tripped forward like a drunkard, unable to hold her balance. She fell to her knees in front of the fae male, her knees soaking in blood. He was still alive, his chest moving slowly, and those orange eyes were trained on her. Despite all the red that bathed him so brutally, those eyes were alight with fire.

Kolfinna's breath rose and fell. Her hands shook, the tip of the dagger swaying in quick movements. She didn't want to do any of this.

What could she do? Cut the man and call it a day? Torture him because she had no choice?

"Kolfinna." Sijur's voice came from behind her—close, too close.

Kolfinna looked at the other prisoners. They stared at her emotionlessly. She couldn't get a read on them.

"Please," she whispered to the man. "Just submit yourself to him."

The man closed his eyes. "Never. Not even for you."

She tightened her grip on the hilt. "Please! I don't want to do this!"

The seconds ticked by and she inched the blade closer to him. She couldn't do this. She couldn't.

"Lieutenant—" she began, but Sijur cut her off.

"*Do it.*"

"But—" She choked down a sob. "I can't."

"You can. Now cut him to pieces. His fingers first."

Kolfinna brought the tip of the dagger to the man's calloused, bound hands, but the blade wavered and she couldn't bring herself to cut him. To chop him to pieces like Sijur wanted her to.

If she refused, what would Sijur do? Force her to do it through the rune mark? Punish her? Hurt her?

She would rather take that than this.

"I won't," she whispered, turning to Sijur. "I'm not going to torture—"

Kolfinna turned to Joran, as if he could help, but he pointedly stared at his feet and turned his face the other way. As if telling her not to ask him anything.

"You will. And if you don't, I will make you do the same to all of these prisoners." Sijur waved at the others, and there wasn't a hint of empathy in his dark, dark eyes. Only wickedness. "And then you'll have more on your conscience than a single man."

"But why?" Tears burned the back of her eyes and her vision blurred. "Why are you making me do this?"

"Simple. I need to break down those vulnerabilities of yours." He stared at her levelly, and a shiver ran down her spine. "You would be so much stronger, so much better if you let go of these gray-toned moralities you hold onto. You are a monster. Accept it and kill that *humanity* of yours. You are a *fae*."

Kolfinna breathed out shakily. "I refuse."

"Then all of these prisoners will suffer the same fate. By your hands." Sijur smiled at her. It was jarring to see such a pleasant expression on his face, drenched in blood. "You have what it takes, sweetheart. And you need to bring it out to the surface. If you need me to ease your conscience, I can make you do it through the runes, but eventually, you'll do it without. Now, do you need me to order you to do it?"

Yes, please.

She wanted to say those words aloud, but they were stuck in her throat. They refused to escape. Her gaze drifted back to the man, and she could feel something within her withering away. The other prisoners watched her too—red eyes, blazing blue eyes, purple eyes, but mostly fae eyes.

Kill that humanity of yours.

She couldn't do that. She couldn't throw away her heart and become a monster.

The blade fell from her hand. "I can't do it."

"Kolfinna, you *need* to do it," Sijur gritted out through clenched teeth. "Or else—"

"I refuse!" She turned to him sharply, all too aware that all the fae and elves were watching her intently. She clambered to her feet, her hands trembling and her body feeling light. "I refuse to torture someone because you want to turn him into a slave! I may be a fae, but I'm not a heartless monster like you! I could never—"

"You—" Sijur's lips curled and he took a domineering step forward.

The flap of the curtain furled open and a man barreled inside. Everyone snapped their attention at him. A soldier in a gray uniform underneath his chainmail. *A human.*

He breathed out heavily, panicked eyes roving over the room before settling on Sijur. His hands trembled, and sweat poured down the sides of his face. "I-I- The—"

"What is it?" Sijur snapped when the man continued to stutter. He waved a hand at the prisoners. "We are busy—"

"Reinforcements!" the man sputtered. "The reinforcements have arrived!"

"The what?" Sijur's eyebrows came together. "Why—"

Reinforcements? But Sijur's army was the reinforcements—

"No, no, you misunderstand—" the man began.

One of the prisoners began to laugh, and then the others followed.

Kolfinna looked around the room, and Sijur did the same. The messenger seemed to shrink away from them, his face growing pallid.

"Our general has finally arrived," one of the women said, sharp teeth gleaming as she grinned ferally at Sijur. "You will all die."

The half-elf had finally arrived.

29

Kolfinna was more than happy to flee from Sijur's tent. But what she didn't expect to find outside the tent of prisoners was a sky full of winged fae and drekis. There must have been tens of thousands of soldiers, completely dwarfing Sijur's army and the leftover soldiers from Hilda's unit.

What drew her attention the most was the central figure of the army, and she could tell that he was the general just from how the air seemed different around him. Power clung to his very being. He was straight from a nightmare. Covered entirely in black, scaly, leathered armor, the half-elf commander seemed to demand the attention of the entire battlefield. A black helmet covered his face, and giant black wings kept him afloat in the air. And those wings—how terrifying they were. Unlike the feathery wings or gossamer ones the other fae had, his were similar to that of a dreki. Velvet, black, and with a dark, scaly frame.

Shadowy magic lashed out from him, darkening the sky even further.

Kolfinna's whole body froze at his heavy presence. She had never felt such soul-crushing mana in her life. She wanted to fall to her knees and curl up in a ball with how withering and blood-curdlingly *powerful* it was.

With a black sword in one hand dripping with inky shadows and a spear of light shining in his other hand, he was a sight to see.

He shot spears of light onto the ground, where they erupted upon contact. Smoke and sprays of debris littered the battlefield.

Kolfinna couldn't breathe through the thickness of evil mana pervading the air. Her instincts told her to run—fast and far away—but she couldn't move. Couldn't rip her gaze away from the terrifying man.

And she was related to this man?

There was *no way* this was her father.

Absolutely no way.

Fight or flee? Her mind warred with those two options. She didn't have to think for too long because she was suddenly met with a fae warrior who swooped down in front of her, sword aimed at her neck. Kolfinna swatted him away with a thick, brown root from the ground. It shot him backward and into a cluster of other fae soldiers.

She looked over at the crowds of human soldiers suddenly battling the fae—where was Blár? They were supposed to meet close to the physician's tent. Was he still there?

It hardly seemed to matter right now. He would be fine—he was a black rank after all. But fear took a hold of her heart and unease spread over her like a thick, thorny blanket.

All at once, another fae was upon her. Chunks of stone covered his hands and he punched her in the chest. She reeled back, pain exploding over her sternum and ribcage at the sudden force. Just as she hit the ground, a bolt of lightning flashed before her eyes, and the familiar smell of burning flesh stung her nose.

Haakon Lykke stepped in front of her, lightning sizzling at his fingertips. His sharp, green eyes flicked over to hers—assessing if she was okay. She pushed herself to her feet, and he must've thought she was fine because with a nod, he was off to fight another fae.

Now wasn't the time to be thinking about Blár—he would be fine, she told herself—or even how horrifying the half-elf commander was. Now was the time to fight because one distracted thought was all it took for these powerful foes to cut her down.

Kolfinna launched stones at the nearby fae and elves. Blazes of fire and lightning lit up the darkening horizon. Her eyesight adjusted to the dusk quite easily, she realized, but everyone else—the humans at least—struggled to see as the sun began to set further. It would probably take ten or so minutes for the canopy of night to be upon them.

The ground rumbled and, in the distance, giant earthen creatures emerged with a fae on its makeshift rocky, moss-ridden head. It towered above the legions of soldiers and swiped down on the humans with a long stick of strung-together stones.

She didn't know what to focus on: the fae soldiers all around her, the half-elf commander, or the earthen creatures that were causing mayhem on the battlefield.

The latter was probably something she could take care of—something only *she* could do.

Wrenching another mound of rocks from the earth and flinging them at the nearby fae, she cleaved a path toward the earthen stone-magic creations and shot through the ranks of soldiers—fae and elves alike.

The closer she drew to the earth creature, the more brutal the battle scene became. Crushed, bloodied bodies littered the land in a sea of blood, protruding bones, and scarlet-soaked uniforms. The pungency of death, the iron taste of blood, and the permeating smell of smoke and burning flesh were almost too strong to ignore.

Kolfinna jumped over a fallen comrade, ducked beneath a wave of light magic, and dove out of the way of the earthen creature's leg as it stepped forward. The bright side? The creature moved slowly, which was only natural considering a fae was controlling the formation of rocks and it was heavy. The not-so-bright side? One small misstep and she would be another bloodied pulp staining the field.

Weaving her way toward the creature was relatively easy—the human soldiers were trying to get away from it, and even the fae kept their distance. The creature marched onward. The stones and earth strung together grinded loudly against the shouts, roars, and magic explosions.

Adrenaline rushed through her body the same way her mana did. Three feet away, and the ground was rumbling with every step the creature took. The fae atop the creature's head, moving the earth and stone monster, didn't see her. And how could he, when he was twenty feet above her? She was probably just a small blip in his peripheral—his eyes were set on clobbering the bigger masses of humans.

Kolfinna lurched toward the stony leg. Her mana flared and she latched onto the rocky wall of its heel, her magic pulling at small indents of the leg so she could create handles. She clung to the leg as it moved forward, her body feeling weightless. Sweat formed on her palms as the creature slowly kicked at a group of soldiers. The dizzying motion almost threw her off, but she held on tight and began climbing.

She had never done something so reckless, and it was both fear-inducing and exhilarating.

She moved quickly, grasping chunks of stone, moss, and dirt. Her mana pulled at tiny pieces of the stones outside the creature. Not enough for the fae to notice that she was also manipulating the stones—and thus ensure a tug of war game to take total control—but enough that she could scale the creature.

Her hair whipped around her shoulders violently. The wind and the movement of the creature made her fingers slip over the textured rocks.

Don't look down.

She molded her hands and feet over the stone exterior to keep from falling. Pull one foot out, put another foot in, mold the foot into the stones, one hand forward, mold that hand, and repeat. Over and over.

The methodical movements made it easier to forget where she was, what she was doing, what would happen if she fell.

Don't look down.

Halfway up, a pair of wings in her peripheral caught her attention. She barely looked over to find a different winged fae lunging toward her.

She was too high up to use her vines. Too far to use stones.

Fear seized her. She could jump, but—

A giant, blinding bolt of lightning flashed before her eyes. She blinked, and the fae was cascading down, one of his wings burnt down to the frame, and his other wing futilely flapping to keep him somewhat upright.

Kolfinna's gaze skirted down below, where Haakon Lykke was blasting fae and elves.

Another blaze to her left, this time violet-blue, and another fae fell. *Herja*.

And then another wave of violent magic—a slice of pressurized water that cut through another fae getting dangerously close to her. *Ivar*.

They must've realized what she was doing. Relief flooded over her—she could do this.

She set back to work, this time with more ease. Kolfinna jumped onto the bumpy shoulder of the monster and the fae atop the creature's head finally looked down at her. His eyes widened and he raised a hand, but Kolfinna was faster.

The stones that made the head of the creature, around the fae's feet, jutted out at her will. The fae stumbled backward, but his wings flapped to keep him afloat. The two seconds of distraction was all Kolfinna needed.

She was in front of him in a flash, her sword burying itself into his sternum. Through flesh and bone. His wide fae eyes— sapphire blue with threads of vivid emerald—widened further. Kolfinna placed one foot on his chest, held on to the hilt of her blade tightly, and kicked him off her sword.

He fell and lost control of the creature.

All at once, the creature's arms slammed into the ground, and other parts of it began crumbling.

The battle scene swayed below—the flying fae, the shadowy and light elves, and the humans desperately fending them off.

Kolfinna planted her feet on the head and molded her feet to the stones in seconds. She quickly threw her mana over the remaining parts of the stone creature—the head, torso, and legs. Her mana coursed through it in seconds. She threaded a thin strand over the clunks of stone and earth, holding it together. She spread it out to the fallen hunks of stone that had served as its arms and slowly pulled them back up to the torso.

Her mana drained quickly as she reined control of the stone creation. Sweat broke over her forehead. There was a reason there were so few of these stone-creatures here—they took too much mana, and likely the fae that controlled them had an enormous amount of mana.

Kolfinna moved the creature, being careful not to step on any humans. Her target: the other stone creature.

The fae atop the other stone creature must've not realized she had taken control of it because when she raised the leg of her creature, he didn't react—probably thinking that she was going to crush a cluster of soldiers.

Instead, she kicked the other earthen creature in the chest. Stone gnashed against stone, and the other creature fell easily. A cloud of dust and stones filled her vision as giant chunks of the creature toppled on the ground. She narrowed her eyes against the sudden grittiness. The fae swarming the sky flew above the dust clouds.

There was only one more earthen creature left, but it was halfway across the battlefield. Kolfinna's mana was already halfway drained. If she continued, would she completely drain it and thus become vulnerable to fae attacks in the battle?

She hesitated, still bumping on top of the creature, the dust settling around her.

A sudden burst of wintry coldness waved over the battlefield in seconds. Her breath streamed out in white, cloudy puffs. Kolfinna narrowed her eyes at the battlefield, at the blasts of blinding colors. Blár was out there, fighting, but she hadn't felt *this* cold in a long time.

Was he maybe fighting Rakel?

Or the half-elf?

Someone who required him to use his full powers against?

Something slammed into Kolfinna's back and the next thing she knew, she was somersaulting through the sky. The wind violently ripped through her hair and clothes and skin, and her scream blended in with the rest of the battle. Someone had pushed her. Likely a winged fae. If she hadn't been so distracted—

The ground grew closer and closer. Her thoughts were jumbled and disjointed, and there was one thing she was certain of: *death*.

Kolfinna raised her arms, but right before she could crash and splatter onto the ground, something collided with her and she was flung in another direction. Her stomach twisted and her vision blackened at the sudden jerkiness.

It took her a few seconds to realize that *shadows* were holding her.

But they weren't hers.

"There you are," a smooth, familiar voice lilted over the screams and explosions of battle.

Kolfinna struggled to sit up, but the shadows holding her in place like a giant hand didn't relent their grasp. A few feet away from her, Rakel stood with her staff in one hand and a bloodied sword in the other. Her dark skin melded into the darkness of the night, but her white hair and red eyes stood out vividly. Black shadows danced around her and protectively snaked over her arms.

Rakel smiled and waved her staff toward her, and Kolfinna's body jerked forward. The shadows holding her tightened until stars danced in the corners of her vision. Rakel's hand reached forward and took ahold of Kolfinna's jaw. Her fingers dug into her skin, and something flashed in her red eyes.

"I've been looking all over for you," Rakel said with a grin, "*Your Highness.*"

KOLFINNA CONTINUED TO STRUGGLE AGAINST RAKEL'S shadows as the elf woman dragged her across the battlefield and into a quickly erected tent. She shouldn't have been surprised to see a tent at the edge of the battlefield—after all, even the fae and the elves needed a space to place their wounded—but she was. Because even though she was a fae, she regarded this army almost like they were an ethereal, unstoppable force that didn't need to rest or sleep or heal.

Wounded fae and elves lay on blood-stained bedrolls. Broken wings, mangled limbs, and grunts and wails of pain filled the tent. Rakel appeared unfazed by it and continued to pull Kolfinna forward with the shadows that acted like a leash.

Kolfinna tried manipulating the stones in the ground, but she found it hard to focus beyond the injured people all around her. She couldn't, in good conscience, cause collateral damage to them. It was one thing to fight a soldier head-on during the battle and another to attack the injured who were bedridden.

But the enemy had captured her. If she didn't do something fast, then ... then the half-elf would use her to free the fae queen, and then Ragnarök would win. She had to find a way to escape.

"That was impressive out there." Rakel's shadows yanked her through the back end of the tent and into another section of the tent, this time a room. Fire danced on torches and illuminated the room in waves of orange light. But even with the small fires, the cold was all-encompassing. Blár was still fighting out there. "I didn't think you'd be able to pull off something like that. I should've expected as much, considering you're Commander Alfaer's daughter—"

"Let me go," Kolfinna ground out.

"And why would I do that?" Rakel laughed and slid her sword into its scabbard. She curled her fingers in front of Kolfinna, and the shadowy tendrils holding her tightened enough that it was hard to breathe. "You are invaluable, Kolfinna Viðarsdóttir. Why don't you stop this nonsense with siding with the humans and join us? Your father will forgive your transgressions here."

Her father.

Even hearing those words aloud sounded wrong, foreign, and *unnatural.*

That monster out there wasn't her father.

Kolfinna's teeth began chattering together, and the wintry chill seemed to finally settle in her bones. It was downright frigid. Rakel seemed to notice too because she tilted her head to the side and frowned deeply.

"That man," she asked slowly, "who is he?"

Kolfinna stared at her.

"The ice soldier."

Blár.

"He is strong," the elf said with a hint of unease. "But not as strong as Commander Alfaer."

Kolfinna shivered. If Rakel was here, then was Blár fighting the half-elf commander right now? Was that why he was using his powers to the extent that it was *this* cold?

A knot of anxiety twisted in her belly.

"Let me go," Kolfinna whispered.

"You will stay here until this battle is won," Rakel said with a shrug.

Kolfinna had to do something.

She latched onto the rocks beneath the ground and launched them toward Rakel, but the elf woman dodged them and was in front of Kolfinna in seconds, the shadows holding her so tightly that she couldn't breathe. Her control on the rocks slipped and her vision blurred. Rakel touched Kolfinna's shoulder.

"Do not test me," she murmured, and all at once, Kolfinna's mana began to drain.

The edges of her vision darkened as Rakel stole her mana. The shadows were holding her so firmly that she was sure she'd be cleaved in half. Rakel was speaking, but Kolfinna could barely make it out.

The only thing on her mind was that she was captured, and there was nothing she could do about it.

The half-elf would eventually come here, take her away, and force her to free the ruthless, evil queen. And then all hell would break loose over Rosain. The fae would still be seen as monsters, and the humans would be enslaved.

And it would be all her fault.

All because Kolfinna *existed*.

All because Rakel had captured her here, and Kolfinna had failed to escape.

Tears stung her eyes. Ragnarök would win.

Just as her body seemed unable to hold a coherent thought, unable to inhale any more air other than tiny gasps, a thought emerged from the blurriness. *Never yield.*

It was something unexcepted that Katla had told her one morning while they were doing laundry for Lord Estur and his estate. Katla was never one to talk like that, but she had said it.

"Never yield, Kolfinna."

That single thought caused a ripple of mana to course through her in seconds. A burst of shadows ripped out from Kolfinna's hands and chest. They shoved their way through Rakel's shadows and pushed the elf woman backward. Kolfinna gasped in breaths of air and the inky shadows shot at Rakel with the remaining bits of mana she had. The surge of power made her feel like she had a chance—like she could fight against Rakel—but that flicker of hope dimmed when light flashed in Rakel's hand and beams of it cut through the shadows.

Then, before Rakel could completely push the swathes and waves of Kolfinna's shadows, Kolfinna turned on her heel and sprinted out of the tent.

She pushed back the flaps of the backroom and ran. Her heart raced and she didn't dare look over her shoulders at the elf woman. The shadows poured out of her body and lashed out behind her like they had a mind of their own. She jumped over bedrolls with patients in them and bolted out of the tent.

Rakel shouted something behind her, but Kolfinna was already gone.

She shoved her way through the battlefield, the wind yanking her hair, the shadows whipping around her violently.

Kolfinna kept running, through the thicket of soldiers fighting, and it wasn't until she stumbled into a clearing with ice everywhere, that she realized she had been running toward the icy coldness—toward Blár.

Relief pooled over her chest immediately when she caught sight of Blár—his wicked blue eyes, the winter clinging to his tall frame, and his familiar face—but that relief was crushed in seconds.

Because Blár was on his knees, and the half-elf was in front of him, with his wings spread out like an ominous being. And when he tilted his head to the side, Kolfinna met his gaze.

Cold, red, evil eyes stared back at her.

30

Sʜᴇ sᴀᴡ, ᴏᴜᴛ ᴏғ ᴛʜᴇ ᴄᴏʀɴᴇʀ ᴏғ ʜᴇʀ ᴇʏᴇ, Bʟᴀ́ʀ struggling to stand. Blood drenched the front of his uniform, and his skin was bloodlessly pale. His eyes widened at Kolfinna and he raised his hand as if to stop her. "No," he said, "*run*."

The half-elf stared at her, and Kolfinna stared back, unable to move. Unable to do anything.

Rows and rows of goose bumps rose across her flesh like a wildfire. Whatever strength and determination she had felt seconds ago dissolved at the sight of the half-elf commander—at the mere presence of him this close.

All of her senses told her to run. To listen to Blár and leave as fast as she could.

But she was rooted in place, and she could never abandon him.

The half-elf broke eye contact from her and spoke to Blár in a smooth, velvety voice. "It's a shame, really. You were close. I'll give you that, human. You have so much mana that I almost couldn't hold your magic back. *Almost*." He kneeled down until he was at eye level with Blár. "You will make for a great mana slave."

But Blár wasn't focusing on him. He had his attention set on Kolfinna.

"Run!" Blár coughed and fell down on his hands.

Kolfinna's stomach dropped. She couldn't leave without Blár. She didn't want to run away, even as her mind screamed at her to do just that. Running was the logical answer—at this point, the half-elf probably didn't even know who she was. She could somehow make it out—

But she didn't want to leave Blár.

She couldn't.

"Kolfinna!" She turned in time to see Sijur a few feet away, blood staining half of his face. A shadowy wisp of black magic had snaked up his leg and was holding him in. It was probably the only thing keeping him from running—and knowing Sijur, he would've run as soon as he could. "You don't stand a chance—"

Something rippled in the air, and it took Kolfinna a second to realize it was the heavy, cloying mana that exuded from the man. It seemed to flare, and Kolfinna could only watch with mute horror as the half-elf tilted his head to Sijur, then to Blár, and then finally to Kolfinna.

Sijur had called her by her name.

Her stomach clenched tightly.

"You ..." The half-elf spoke to her this time, and there was a calmness to his voice that reminded her of an upcoming storm. It chilled her down to her bones.

He knew.

He slowly straightened, the air around him continuing to shift with dark mana. Kolfinna couldn't see his expression, only those cold, soulless red eyes. For some reason, that made him even more terrifying to behold—the fact that she had no idea what he was thinking or what expression he wore.

Was he gleeful at finally catching her? Was he thrilled at being one step closer to freeing his queen?

"Let them go," Kolfinna said suddenly. Whatever mana she had flared at her fingertips. She couldn't see beyond Blár's injured body lying on the ground. She had never thought she would see him like this. Not since the Nuckelavee attack, and certainly not when facing a foe with his ice magic.

"Come quietly," the half-elf said. "We—"

"Not happening." Her voice was shrill with panic.

"Kolfinna—" Blár was a foot away from the half-elf, but he didn't seem to have the strength to sit up, much less stand. It seemed it was taking all his strength to even speak, to keep himself on his knees. "Please, run."

"No!" she shouted. "I'm not leaving you!"

"Kol—"

Kolfinna wrenched a stone from the ground and shot it at the half-elf. He didn't even flinch and before the stone could slam into him, it stopped midair and floated there. Kolfinna blinked. He had taken control of the stone. *Just like that.*

He didn't look away from her and she watched in horror as the stone crumbled to dust and pebbles.

"Kolfinna." Blár's eyes fluttered closed and he collapsed on the partially frozen ground.

"Blár!" Kolfinna ran toward him, but a wall of shadows surrounded her in seconds. She fought against them, her own shadows spreading out in defense, but the inky smoke captured her in seconds. She struggled against the shadowy grip, the whips of ink waving over her eyes. Finally, they calmed enough for her to see again.

The half-elf sighed. She couldn't make out his face due to the helmet, and only his red eyes were visible as he stared at her. "I do not wish to fight you," he murmured, and she almost didn't hear it from the backdrop of war—with people screaming in pain and the blasts of magic going off. "It is a ... complicated matter. We must speak—you and I."

"Let me go!" Kolfinna cried, the shadows leaching off her remaining mana. Unlike Rakel's merciless grip that had squeezed all the air out of her, his shadows did no such thing. But they were worse than Rakel's because no amount of her own mana, her uncontrollable shadows, or her magic worked. In fact, she couldn't do *anything*.

She struggled against the shadows nonetheless, screaming and grunting and trying to loosen herself. The half-elf only watched.

"Kolfinna." Sijur pushed himself to his feet. "Kill yourself. *Now*."

Her eyes widened. *What?*

Had she heard right? She couldn't have, but then the rune mark on her wrist burned and excruciating pain wracked her body. She threw her head back, pain swelling and shooting up her arm and feeling as though her flesh was burning from the inside out.

Kill herself? Why would he order such a thing?

Tears filled her vision and she fought against the pain, but it was too much.

"Why?" she choked out.

Sijur coughed and fell to his knees. "Sorry ... Nothing personal, Kolfinna ..." He coughed again. The right side of his chainmail was shredded and revealed his uniform, which was slick and darkened with blood. "But it's better to have you dead than to have you on the enemy side. Do forgive me for this. I suppose this is the end for both of us, hm? Or maybe all three of us."

All three of us— because if she didn't listen to Sijur, she would die. And if she *did* listen, then, well, she was dead.

"You tethered her to you?" the half-elf asked. His voice was controlled and unbothered, but there was a hint of hardness there. Like he was displeased. Or maybe she was looking too deep into something that wasn't there. Maybe the pain was making her hear things.

It was so intense that it had her on her hands and knees, writhing on the ground. It took her a moment to realize the half-elf had relinquished his hold on her because she wasn't chained by his shadows. But it didn't matter because she couldn't focus beyond the haze of pain consuming her.

A hand grasped her chin, and all of a sudden, the pain ebbed away and she was staring into cold, merciless, blood-red eyes framed with thick, white lashes. Where his gloved hand touched, her skin was warm and it took her a few seconds to realize that he had used rune magic on her, the same way she had used it on Birgitta.

But that realization also haunted her because she didn't want to befall the same fate as that woman.

The half-elf rose to his feet and waved a finger toward Sijur. Shadows ensnared Sijur and he shouted something incoherent as he was dragged forward a few feet away from Kolfinna. The shadowy magic whipped the air surrounding Sijur even as it held him. The air was heavy with mana, and Kolfinna was practically choking on it this up close. She found it hard to breathe, her gaze flicking from the half-elf to Sijur and then back again.

Kolfinna was completely drained of mana and energy. The hope she had clung onto was quickly disappearing. Blár was unconscious, Sijur's army was falling apart all around them since Blár was defeated, and she was doing to die.

"Human, why have you tethered a fae to you?" The half-elf's voice betrayed mild curiosity, but there was something else there. Something that sounded akin to amusement.

"Just kill me already," Sijur growled.

"You are foolish." The half-elf clucked his tongue. "There is a reason, human, that the fae do not tether those stronger than them, or those that have the fire to fight back. Because although the tether gives you a false sense of loyalty, a slave will never be loyal to its master. The slave, eventually, will take the blade and slit the master's throat, for that will free them. You are foolish to believe tethering a fae to you is beneficial for you. How can you leash a lion when you yourself are a mouse?"

Kolfinna released a ragged breath. "W-What?"

"The way to free yourself"—the half-elf turned to her—"is to kill him."

That was it?

Sijur stiffened. "No."

"Yes." The half-elf chuckled, and there wasn't a hint of kindness in it. "We fae rarely tether anyone to us because there are too many risks involved. And for what? For someone to listen to our every command? Any slave can do that without being tethered. When you have power, they will bend the knee not because of a rune stopping them from disobeying, but because *you* hold the power over them. Because they fear *you*."

"Kolfinna—" Sijur started.

"Kill him," the half-elf said.

Kolfinna couldn't move. She could make out human soldiers fleeing all around her, and her body was close to keeling over. Sijur ordered her not to listen, but still, she couldn't move. She didn't feel any pain, but if she didn't do something, the rune-mark would kill her.

But then she stared down at the rune on her wrist, and she remembered Birgitta, Olia, all the women's names on the journal, and all the children's names written down.

Killing him would free them all. Killing him would free her.

She staggered forward, her hand going to her waist, but her sword was nowhere to be found. She had likely dropped it when she fell off the earthen creature, she realized. Her gaze fell to the ground, where a broken shard of Blár's ice remained. Sharp and glasslike, she picked it up numbly as she approached Sijur.

Flashes of Birgitta's face, Olia, the names on the journal all came to her.

But still—she hesitated.

Her stomach twisted together into knots and her hand trembled as she positioned the pointed edge of the ice shard against Sijur's neck. His black eyes were wide and wild. His eyelashes had dried blood on them and his lips were stained with dirt. She could smell the fear and sweat rolling off his body.

"My father will come after you if you do this," Sijur whispered, his eyes trained on the ice shard.

"You would die anyway." Kolfinna pressed the ice closer to him. "And you did such terrible things."

"I dirtied my hands to make a better country. To make it better for you and the rest of the fae," Sijur snarled. "Do this, and you will be marking yourself as an enemy to the military and to the whole country!"

"It really doesn't matter anymore," Kolfinna found herself saying. "You said you wanted me to be a monster, didn't you? Well, this is probably the first step."

"Don't let her kill me!" Sijur shouted at the half-elf commander, his voice growing desperate. "I can be useful to you! You can learn so much about this country's military plans from me! I'm still useful!"

The half-elf seemed to consider this, and that was all the time Kolfinna needed to lunge at the commander. Her ice shard slammed into his chest—or it would have, if the shadows hadn't wrenched it out of her hand.

She kicked the half-elf as hard as she could, but he dodged that too, hit movements fluid. Desperately, she fought back, her remaining mana coursing through her body simultaneously with the rush of adrenaline.

Gnarled roots shot from the ground and slammed into the half-elf, but the little damage they caused seemed to be healed instantly. He was too quick on his feet, even in all that heavy-looking armor.

Kolfinna sent a barrage of roots after him, but right when she thought she had him, the roots froze. The half-elf raised his hand and she realized he had taken control of them.

Out of all her magic, she was most confident with her nature manipulation. But he had her beat there too.

The half-elf lowered his hand, and the roots straightened into sharp-tipped spears, all of them pointed toward the sky. His wings unfurled, making him appear larger and more sinister.

"Do not waste your time fighting me, when you have little time to kill the man," the half-elf said, his red eyes flinty. Suddenly, the roots all aimed toward Blár. They hovered over his body and Kolfinna couldn't breathe.

"No, please, no!" Kolfinna raised her trembling hands, her gaze glued to Blár's unconscious body. "Please, not him."

"Kill the man tethering you, or I will kill this man, whom you seem to," the half-elf said with a curious tilt of his head, "care for so much."

It didn't make sense why he wanted her to kill Sijur when he could've easily done it himself.

Was this another test? Just like how Sijur had tested her an hour earlier? Was this man also doing the same, wanting to see how far she would go?

Kolfinna hesitated while Sijur shouted something incoherent. "If I kill him ... Will you let *him* go?" She nodded toward Blár, who looked unnaturally pale at this point. How much blood had he lost? All she wanted to do was rush over to Blár, tend to his injuries, and take him to the wounded tent and never leave his side.

The half-elf chuckled. It was soft and she almost missed it by how quiet it was, but the slight rumbling of his chest told her he was laughing. At her.

"You seem to misunderstand the situation you are in," he said, red eyes flashing with murderous intent. "All of you are at my mercy. I am not here to make any bargains. You will either do as I say, or I will do things as I wish. The outcome will be the same."

Kolfinna had no choice in the matter?

She dropped down to her knees, as if to surrender. "Please, just don't hurt him."

"Once again, you misunderstand. You are in no position to make requests—"

She snatched a broken fragment of a sword and placed the sharp edge of it to her own neck. It was cold and sharp against her skin. The half-elf froze, his eyes narrowing.

"I know you need me alive," Kolfinna snapped. "So on the contrary, I *do* have options."

"You wouldn't—" he started.

She pressed the blade further against her neck and gasped as fresh blood welled over the metal shard. The half-elf took a step closer, but she raised her other hand to stop him. "Not another step, or I will kill myself."

"Why go so far for these"—he gestured to Blár with disgust—"*humans.*"

"Because I love him." Even in the midst of battle, with the worst enemy she had ever met standing in front of her, she had never been so sure of anything. Kolfinna's blood ran down her hands and she ignored the throbbing pain. "And I know you need me alive for your sick plans of freeing the evil queen."

The half-elf's eyes narrowed further.

"Let Sijur and Blár go, and I'll go with you willingly," Kolfinna said. She hated that she had to keep Sijur alive, but he was the only one who could take Blár out of this situation. "Sijur, you'll have to take Blár out of here."

"Yes, yes, of course!" The relief in Sijur's voice was palpable and he bobbed his head quickly. "I can do that!"

"You act as though I've accepted your terms," the half-elf snapped. "I have not."

"Really? You haven't?" She dug the blade harder to show him she was serious, but not hard enough that she would kill herself.

"Wait."

"Let them go, and I'll go with you."

"You wouldn't—"

"Don't test me!" she shouted. "You don't know what I'm capable of!"

He sighed loudly, but before he could give her an answer, Kolfinna's vision blurred and when she blinked, it grew even hazier. Her chest felt like something had burst. Suddenly, she couldn't hear either, like something had pooled in her ears and created a barrier. She looked up at the half-elf, whose eyes had widened. He was saying something, she thought, but she didn't know what.

She tasted iron in her mouth and her body gave out. She fell to the ground, her energy slipping away. In the edge of her vision, the last thing she saw was the rune mark on her wrist glowing violently, and that was when she remembered that even though the half-elf had taken the pain away, she had still been disobeying Sijur.

So this is death.

31

A DEEP COLDNESS AWOKE HER, LIKE THE EMBRACE OF A wintry death that wouldn't let her slip away.

When Kolfinna blinked, she was surrounded by darkness. There was a single barred window in the cramped, dark, tiny room, and water dripped down the walls in thin rivulets. For a moment, fear seized her and she thought Hilda had gotten to her again, and that she was locked away in another torture room, but then reality slowly sank in and the last moments she remembered came to her.

Her hands flew to her face. She didn't feel any crusted blood. Had someone washed her?

A quick glance at her wrist revealed that the rune mark was gone. A cold sweat dampened her body at the sight of it. Sijur was probably dead. She had wanted so badly to rid herself of it, but now that it was gone ... She realized she had other problems to worry about.

Was that why she was still alive? Because the half-elf had killed Sijur? Or had he ordered Sijur to unbind her? The former seemed to be an easier option.

Kolfinna gingerly sat up. Tears stung her eyes.

They had *lost*.

She had been stripped of her armor and chainmail, and only wore her worn-out gray uniform. The entire front of her shirt was darkened and stiffened with blood and when her weak, trembling fingers undid the last few buttons to inspect her injuries—particularly the abdomen wound—she saw the thickened scar tissue on her chest. Her scar was pale pink—fresh. With how little mana she had during the end of the battle, and with how battered her body had been, how had she healed herself?

She already knew the answer. Of course the half-elf would heal her. Either with rune magic or whatever strange elf magic he had because he needed her alive.

A strangled cough jerked her away from her thoughts. Her heart raced and she swiveled her attention toward the noise—a man on the floor a few feet away from her. She had been so caught up with her own thoughts that she hadn't even noticed him.

His wrists and feet were bound with shadowy, smoke magic. The skin of his wrists was raw and burned by the shadows, and even with all the blood and grime coating him, Kolfinna recognized Blár.

Her relief rushed over her like a flood, and she lurched forward so quickly she fell on her knees. "Blár!"

Blár groaned in pain, his eyes slowly peeling open. She scrambled on her knees in front of him and didn't know where to touch him. His arm was very clearly broken by the way it was twisted, his face was a map of bruises, cuts and blood stains, and the rest of his body didn't look any better.

She couldn't hold back her tears as she brought a shaking hand to his face. She brushed his hair back and choked down a sob. "Oh, Blár."

"Kolfinna?" He blinked up at her, his eyes glassy and unfocused. "Is that you?"

"Yes, yes, it's me." She brushed back his hair and her fingers skimmed over his bruised and broken skin. It was a miracle he was awake, or even *alive*.

Blár coughed, and speckles of blood dotted the floor. Her eyes had adjusted enough to make out these details.

"Where are we?" he whispered.

"I think ... the fortress?" Kolfinna pushed herself to her feet and walked over to the window. Sure enough, she could make out the remnants of the battlefield beyond the barred window. She quickly looked away from the macabre scene—the upturned stones and the bloodied bodies everywhere.

Her whole body began to shake. *They had lost.*

Now it was only a matter of time before—

She didn't want to think about it.

"I'm sorry," Blár said. He was staring up at the ceiling, his expression wracked with guilt, anger, and helplessness. The vulnerability made something in her chest crack, and she wanted to rush over and embrace him tightly. "I couldn't save you."

"Don't say that." Kolfinna sank to the floor beside him, her voice thick with emotion. "There's still hope so long as you're alive."

If there was someone who could change the tides of war, it was Blár.

He was the most powerful person she knew—

And yet the half-elf defeated him.

She cast that thought away and placed a hand on his cheek. "I'm so happy you're alive."

Blár closed his eyes and let out a shuddered breath. "I couldn't beat him. The man with the black helmet and the red eyes. All the wounds I inflicted kept healing, meanwhile my wounds ..." He hissed in pain when he moved his shoulder. That slight movement made his whole body tense up. Being bound like this didn't help. Blár exhaled raggedly. "I don't think he's simply an elf. He had fae powers."

"Yes." Kolfinna grimaced.

"What happened to everyone else?"

"I don't know."

"And Sijur?"

She absentmindedly rubbed her naked wrist; she had somehow gotten used to seeing it so often, that now that it was gone, it almost looked strange. Like a part of her uniform was stripped from her. And it probably was—because now she wasn't a soldier anymore. She was a prisoner.

"Dead," Kolfinna whispered.

Blár tried sitting up and instantly doubled over.

"Don't move too much!" Kolfinna rested a hand on his shoulder to keep him down.

"No, we have to get out of here," he gasped, blinking in the darkness. "Do you think you can open up the wall with your stone magic?"

"I can try." She concentrated on her mana; it rushed to her fingertips in seconds, but when she placed a hand against the cool stone floor, her mana wouldn't leave the pads of her fingers. She tried again, but once more, nothing happened. It was then that she noticed the golden runes on the walls.

Kolfinna cannot use magic. Kolfinna cannot escape.

She cursed softly, her hands curling into fists. If she couldn't use her magic, then did that mean they were stuck here permanently?

"Well?" Blár asked quietly.

"I can't use magic because of the runes, but they don't mention you, so you should still be able to."

He tried shimmying his wrists against the shadows binding him and let out a string of curses. "I can't. I don't know why."

Kolfinna tried touching the shadows, but they seemed to roar to life, growing wilder like flames.

"Maybe ..." She motioned to the shadows. "Those are stopping you?"

"Maybe." He tried moving his hands, but a movement from his broken arm made him curse again and his face darkened in pain. "Damn it. Now what?"

Kolfinna folded her hands together on her lap. She didn't know what to do anymore. Sit tight and be a prisoner for an ancient elf and fae army? And the half-elf had mentioned that he would use Blár as a mana slave. If she couldn't save herself, she at least wanted to save him from that fate because if there was someone who could defeat the half-elf, it was Blár.

He just needed more practice. More experience against elves and fae alike.

Jumping to her feet, she rushed over to the window once more. They were on the second floor, and the drop below was the battlefield. There were a few fae flying about, picking up the bodies of their fallen comrades, and she noted that they ignored the human corpses altogether. Judging by how the darkening sky was slowly ripening, the sun would rise soon.

If they managed to break these bars, they could probably squeeze through and sneak off into the forested area beyond the battlefield. Especially if they slunk along the corpses and if Kolfinna created a camouflage of stones and rocks to protect them.

It was possible.

Kolfinna placed a hand on the runes circling the room. She closed her eyes to better focus. She tried not to listen to the moans and groans of the battlefield, to the flap of fae wings filling the sky, or Blár's ragged breathing.

She imagined she was somewhere tranquil. In a forest, perhaps. With wild flowers around her, with a stream trickling to her right, to birds chirping cheerily in the background. She channeled her mana into the runes and tried breaking them.

Nothing happened.

Kolfinna breathed out deeply and tried again.

Still nothing.

By the fifth time, she stopped altogether and slammed her fist against the golden runes. "Damn it!" she said, tears stinging her eyes. The runes were too strong, and no matter how much mana she flung at them, they refused to break for her.

"Use my mana," Blár whispered weakly. "To break the runes."

Several minutes passed and she tried to use Blár's mana, but even with Blár's expansive mana, which had replenished over the course of the few hours since the battle, the runes refused to yield. She even tried overwriting the runes, but her runes never came to fruition.

"I think we need to break those shadows first." Kolfinna motioned to the shadows holding him hostage. They were barring him from using his magic, after all, but they didn't seem to be leaching too much of his mana like she had initially thought; it was more like a trickle. "But ... I don't know how."

Blár grimaced. "It seems like we're stuck."

Kolfinna racked her brain for something she could do. But what? What could she possibly do in this situation? She couldn't break the runes or overwrite them, so what other option did she have left?

"Blár, when you were fighting the elf commander, was there any time when you were able to break free from his shadows? I remember him mentioning that it was a shame that you didn't have enough mana to hold his magic back?" She remembered how with Rakel, Kolfinna's shadows were able to overpower Rakel's momentarily, and that the elf woman had used light magic to counteract the shadows. Was that what Kolfinna needed to use—light magic? Or did the shadows follow the basic concept of elemental magic? That if the other party's power was stronger, it didn't matter what element it was? If Blár's ice could become stronger than the current shadows, could he overpower them?

Blár stopped struggling to unbind his hands and seemed to think. "In the beginning, when I had more mana, I was able to hold him off with my ice, but as the battle continued, I couldn't. And then, well, I lost." He said the last part with a bitter snarl.

"If you could have a boost of mana, would you be able to break free?"

"I ... Well, these things are already draining me, but I did replenish a decent amount during the night ... But enough to break free? No, not right now."

"How much would you need?"

"Just a bit," he said slowly. "Why?"

"I've never done this before, but let me transfer my mana to you." Joran had done it to her before, so she could certainly do it to him, right?

Kolfinna inched closer to him and touched the side of his face. She didn't want to touch his bound hands because that only made the shadows seem to grow fiercer, as if to sway her away.

For a moment, nothing happened.

"Do you sense my mana?" she asked as she prodded her mana against his skin.

Blár's eyebrows came together. "No."

She tried again, but her mana wasn't able to go beyond her own flesh. She had done this before, with Eyfura in the Eventyrslot ruins, so why couldn't she now?

The shadows around Blár's wrists rose in her peripheral vision, and she bit back a curse. "I think the shadows are stopping me from transferring my mana to you."

Blár sighed loudly. "So we're stuck in a damn loop." Frustration leaked in his voice. "We can't break out of the room because of these shadows. But the way to break the shadows requires mana, but we can't use mana because of the shadows, and we can't leave the room because of the runes."

Kolfinna tried to think of another way, but the only thing she could think of was ... too farfetched of an idea, and there was no guarantee it would work either.

"There ... might be a way," Kolfinna's whispered. The words stumbled out of her mouth clumsily. "Remember when we went to the western border, and I was telling you about that fae ceremony that boosts your magic? It, like, makes you share your magic with someone?"

"The *Bryllup* ceremony?" Blár asked slowly, and then his eyes widened. Time seemed to slow as they both stared at each other. "Do you think that'll be enough? If my mana combines with yours, I'll have enough to break out."

"My mana is replenished completely." She touched her chest,

and sure enough, she had enough mana. "But ... Maybe it's better that we just wait until your mana replenishes completely?"

"That could take over two days." He winced as he tried sitting up.

"Your mana takes that long to replenish?" Her mouth almost dropped open. Her mana usually took a night to replenish, and that was it. Was it just because he had so much that it took that long?

"For it to *completely* replenish, yes." He sagged against the wall of the room and tipped his head back. "I don't think we have enough time for that, and if we want to escape now, then we need to do that ceremony and leave as soon as possible. The sun is about to rise. We can still use the darkness to our advantage and escape. It seems the enemy is too distracted to focus on us right now, and they're probably arrogant enough to believe that we have zero options to leave."

She looked at him carefully, at the way his hair fell across his forehead, at his strong arms bound so tightly behind him, and she remembered the words she had spoken on the battlefield. "But, Blár, if we do the ceremony, that means—"

"That we'll be married?" He laughed and there was a small twinkle in his eyes she almost didn't catch. The corner of his mouth rose into a half-smirk. "I always knew you'd be my woman one day."

A blush spread over her face and she suddenly felt too warm in the room. "You ... what?"

His laughs quickly turned to grunts of pain. "We have to be quick," he said with another grimace. He jerked a chin at the metal door that had no handle. "They're probably planning on turning us into slaves."

"You're right ..." Kolfinna cleared her throat. She didn't have time to dwell on the fact that Blár had always known she would be his, or that she was going to marry *Blár Vilulf*. Her heart raced and she tried to focus beyond her fluttering, giddy thoughts. "Do you want to do it? I don't know if it'll work with a human and a fae, but we have nothing to lose."

The worst that could happen was that it failed, and they'd be stuck here nonetheless. But if it worked … Then they would be free.

Blár's eyes glinted into an icy silvery-blue in the dim lighting. "Yes, let's do it."

Kolfinna quickly slid her hand into his. Her pulse raced and she tried to find the words to speak, tried to remember what was written in the journal of that fae warrior. He was so close to her in this moment, and she wanted to lean even closer, to feel the coolness of his magic. "I, Kolfinna, intend to marry Blár Vilulf, and we intend to bind ourselves and our magic together in the *Bryllup* ceremony."

"I, Blár Vilulf, intend to marry Kolfinna …" Blár's squeezed her hand, the words coming out clumsily, "and bind myself— ourselves—and my—ahem, *our* magic together in the *Bryllup* ceremony."

Nothing happened.

"Well?" Kolfinna asked, giving his hand another squeeze. "Do you, uh, feel something?"

He stared at her blankly. "No."

Her eyebrows came together. Did it fail?

Seconds ticked by, but there was no burst of energy. No crazy mana pulsing between them. Nothing.

"Maybe …" She chewed on her lower lip, gaze darting to the window. They didn't have much time. "Maybe I can try something?"

"What?"

Instead of answering, she brought her face close to his. He inhaled sharply, blue eyes narrowing to search her face, to maybe make out the shadows of her expression. It was probably too dark for him to see her, but she could see everything about him. The bobbing of his throat, the feverish redness over his skin, and the dried blood caking the side of his face.

Her heart pounded in her chest like a beating drum as her lips brushed against his lightly. She gasped at how surprisingly soft his mouth was, how it molded so perfectly to hers, and for a moment, she forgot why she was even doing this. Her hands tentatively went to his shoulders, and she rested a hand against his cheek, breathing in the scent of him.

A surge of raw energy buzzed between their lips and pumped through her veins. She gasped against his mouth as a clash of ice and her own warm mana hummed in her chest, leaking into the beat of her heart and sending electric pulses through every fiber of her being. She pulled back, eyes wide, and he did the same, his own face showing alarm.

Her chest heaved and she fell back on her bottom. She brought a trembling hand to her lips, and a flush warmed her cheeks.

All at once, another surge of mana overcame Blár, and she could feel it. Could feel his mana like it was her own; could feel it rise higher, and higher, until it poured out of his hands. He yanked at his wrists and the shadow magic snapped off like metal cuffs and dissolved into the grimy floor.

He rubbed his wrist and grimaced in pain. "It ... worked?"

They both stared at each other in awe. *It had worked.*

The feeling wore off quickly because Blár suddenly took a hold of her hand and urged her toward the window. Even though her focus should've been on escaping, she couldn't stop thinking about the kiss. Her lips still tingled from it, and she resisted the urge to bring his face down to hers again and kiss him once more.

What is wrong with me?

Blár placed a hand on the bars and in seconds, ice escaped from his fingers and froze the metal. He snapped the bars off and tossed them aside, his gaze flicking between the sky and then the flying fae.

"Will they see us? With their fae eyes?" He nodded toward the winged people.

"No," she said because only elves had extraordinary sight. Unless, some of those fae were like her—part elf.

"Good." He raised his uninjured arm and glass-like ice steps protruded from the walls of the fortress all the way down to the ground.

He pulled himself through the window and landed on the ice panel directly below the window. Straightening, he turned to her and held his blood-stained hand out. "Let's go."

Kolfinna tried to grab his hand, but as if there was an invisible force, her hands didn't go past the window. Her smile faded and she slowly turned to the runes on the wall. They seemed to glow even stronger now, and between their glowing and the sun slowly peeking through the horizon, she didn't know which was brighter.

Blár didn't have time for her to figure out a way to escape. She knew that.

Seconds ticked by and they both stared at each other, neither wanting to face the truth.

Kolfinna tried to smile, tried to show him confidence, but her mouth wobbled. "You have to go," she said. "Without me."

Blár shook his head and reached over the window and grabbed her hand. His touch was ice-cold, like winter itself, and she wanted to lean into it, but she couldn't.

"I'm not leaving without you," he said. "Now let's go—"

"I can't! Blár, the runes won't let me, and I can't break them. You'll have to go without me. We don't have much time," Kolfinna said quickly. Over her shoulder, the door to their room was still sealed shut, but who knew how long it would take before they checked in on them? And with the sun slowly creeping up the horizon, Blár didn't have more than ten minutes. "Please, go!"

His eyebrows came together and he searched her face, as if expecting her to say something else. "I can't." His voice came out hoarse and his hold on her hand tightened. "I can't leave you."

"You'll have to."

"No."

"Blár!" Tears prickled her eyes and she held his hand firmly. She didn't want to let him go, and she certainly didn't want to be alone in this room, alone as a prisoner, but she also didn't want him to suffer any longer. She'd be brave and face this alone. "You have to go, *now*. You're the only one who can stop all of this. I know you can do it."

"Kolfinna—"

Tears slipped down her face. "You have to go now, *please*. You can find a way to get me out later, but for now, you have to go, Blár. You're the only hope we have of stopping them. I know you'll find a way to get me out. I know it—you're Blár Vilulf after all." She swiped at her cheeks while he looked at her with a helpless expression. He was close to the windowsill, as if he wanted to vault himself back into the room. The sun was beginning to rise. "*Blár.*"

"I can't leave you," he whispered. "I can't let you face all of that alone—"

"I'll be fine." She smiled, even as tears ran down her cheeks. "Now go!"

He hesitated, gaze faltering between her and the horizon, and then he leaned over, took a hold of her face, and pressed his mouth against hers. This time, the kiss wasn't for the ceremony or for their power. It was slow, his mouth moving against hers. He smelled like sweet vanilla, and blood, and sweat. Of battle, and hard work, and winter.

Both of her hands went up to his face and she held him tightly. She relished the feeling of their bodies pressed so close. She wanted the moment to last longer. She kissed him back fervently, her heart breaking at the thought of never seeing him again. It felt like the moment could last forever, but it broke too soon. He released her, and she couldn't stop her lower lip from wobbling. But she held her tears in this time.

His expression hardened, as if he was trying to mask everything he was feeling. And he probably was.

"I'll be back for you," he whispered. "I promise."

And like that, he left.

Kolfinna watched as he created an ice splint for his broken arm, scaled down the fortress wall and traversed through the battlefield, wary of the winged fae above. She placed her fingers over her lips and sobbed. She doubted the half-elf would let her out of his sights, not until he used her to free his queen, and especially not after Blár's escape. Kolfinna would likely be a prisoner for a long, long time.

"Goodbye, Blár Vilulf," Kolfinna whispered as she watched his strong frame disappear into the forest. She closed her eyes. Her lips were still cold with the memory of their shared kiss, and she replayed the moment in her mind again. It was only then that she could sink to the floor in relief. Her heart squeezed together painfully and she pressed her head against the cold stone wall.

She would see him again, she promised herself through her tears. There was no way she would let this moment be their last.

To be continued ...

ABOUT THE AUTHOR

Maham Fatemi is an avid reader, writer, and cat lover. When she's not obsessing over her cats, you can find her skimming a new cookbook, reading comics, or drinking an unhealthy number of oat-milk lattes. Maham lives in the Chicagoland area with her husband, son, and five cats. For new releases and signed copies of her books, visit her website at mahamfatemi.com